The BRIDE Found

BOOK #2 IN THE CIVIL WAR BRIDES SERIES

NEW YORK TIMES & USA TODAY BESTSELLING AUTHOR
PIPER DAVENPORT

The Bride Found is a work of fiction. Names, characters, places, and incidents are the products of the author's imagination and are used fictitiously. Any resemblance to actual events, locales, or persons, living or dead, is entirely coincidental.

Cover Art
Jackson Jackson

TRIXIE
PUBLISHING

2017 Piper Davenport
Copyright © 2017 by Trixie Publishing, Inc.
All rights reserved.

ISBN-13: 978-1978324756
ISBN-10: 1978324758

Published in the United States

The BRIDE Found

BOOK #2 IN THE CIVIL WAR BRIDES SERIES

A NOTE FROM PIPER

Hello lovely readers!!!

The Civil War Brides Series was my very first set of babies (the first one, written in 2009), and I'm excited to re-release these stories with the sexy new covers and spicy sex scenes.

It's incredibly fun to go back and visit old friends, and I truly hope you'll fall in love with my sassy brides, and the men who love them, the same way I did. Thanks to those of you who have been with me all these years! If it wasn't for you, I couldn't do what I do, and I love you for giving me this amazing life!

Piper
aka Tracey Jane Jackson

PRAISE

"Tight, absorbing fast paced plotting that keeps you guessing as you hold onto your seat for a ride you don't want to get off! A love story that grabs you by the heart, pulls you in and doesn't let you go long after you turn the last page!" *Claudy Conn – Paranormal Author*

"Sizzling and original!" *Leah Banicki – Historical Author*

"This deserves more than just 5+++ stars, but since it is the highest rating it will let me give, it will have to do. Now I am off to read the next book and probably be very sleep deprived in the morning." *Amazeballs Book Addicts*

DEDICATION

For Mike G.
Who spent his important retirement time reading my stories.

For Ellen Tarver
You rock my world! Thanks for being such a great mentor and friend.

Portland, Oregon
Present Day

*E*MMA WELLINGTON STARED at the television in hopeful silence.

"Theodore Cary unable to take over the Washington State Senate seat, despite his attempts to impeach Senator Robin Wade."

"Yes!" She grinned as the reporter droned on. "You'll never get her, Ted. She's too good, and quite frankly, it's about time we had someone *honest* in politics!"

"Controversy and questions still surround the validity of the Cary camp's impeachment charges."

"Ya think? If Ted Cary's claim is legitimate, then I'm freaking Miss America." Grabbing the remote in disgust, Emma flipped through the channels until she found a romantic comedy and then dropped the remote on the coffee table.

Not that she would watch. The saga of Westley and Princess

Buttercup would be utilized as background noise. Emma had heavier issues on her mind. Well over a year since her sister, Sophie, and brother-in-law, Jamie, disappeared mysteriously, Emma stood in the parlor of their historic 1870s Victorian home and struggled with her current predicament.

Her brother-in-law had no living relatives, so Emma was the sole heir to his assets, but without proof of death, everything had been frozen. Now she was left to pay a mortgage. Small though it might be, thanks to her sister's financial prowess, it was still beyond her pay grade.

The quintessential modern woman and self-confessed technology junkie, Emma always had the latest iPhone, Blackberry, Blueberry, whatever berry was currently hitting the market. But a checkbook and its balancing scared her to death.

She let out a sigh and decided to have Sophie's best friend, Alex, help her when she got home. Alex and her husband Lucas had moved in a few months ago because Emma hated to live alone, and so far, the arrangement was working out perfectly.

She had a session with her dance partner tomorrow and she needed to plan for that, so flipping off the television, she headed into the kitchen to see what she could throw together to eat, then sat down and mapped out her routine.

* * *

Harrisburg, Pennsylvania
October, 1863

Clayton Madden's frustration manifested itself in the death grip he had on the arms of the high-backed leather chair in the house he shared with his brother, Richard. Since the beginning of the war, Harrisburg had become his secondary home, and he didn't get much time to visit. His primary residence was in Washington, D.C., where he worked for Lincoln's War Cabinet. His friend and colleague, Christopher Butler, had given him the leeway to return to Harrisburg to check on Richard, not easy to do when they were preparing for the President's trip to Gettysburg

2

in a month.

However, Richard had promised to deliver horses to Maryland, and Richard had yet to fulfill his commitment. Vincent Butler, Christopher's father, was a prominent farmer and horse breeder for many of the counties in Maryland, and with the shortage on horses due to the war, relied on the ones Richard provided. Clayton had known something must be wrong, but had no idea Richard's drinking had become as bad as it is.

For three days, Clayton had watched Richard drink himself into yet another stupor—a violent one. Richard Madden, wounded severely at Gettysburg, hadn't done well after his stay in the hospital, and although his injuries were healing, he continued to self-medicate with alcohol.

Richard told Clayton the reason he chose whiskey over other available methods of pain relief was to avoid the "Army Disease" of addiction to laudanum or morphine. Trouble was, he didn't seem to realize, or refused to see, his growing addiction to alcohol. Truth be told, his dependency began long before any physical injuries.

A broken heart compounded Richard's need for alcohol. Forced to watch the object of his affection in love with and pregnant by another man left him crushed. Clayton relaxed his hands and settled his forearms on his knees as he leaned forward. "Richard. You need to slow down, your conduct is atrocious."

"You don't know a damn thing about any damn thing, Clayton," Richard snapped.

"I know you're drinking entirely too much. Why don't you drink water for the remainder of the day?"

"Why don't you go to hell?" Richard bellowed as he shook his half-empty glass at Clayton. "Did you see how she treated me last night? Her husband came to her rescue as though I did something wrong." Richard took another swig and stared off into space for several minutes.

Clayton sighed. "Richard."

"The lieutenant has been nothing but trouble since he got here."

3

"She's pregnant, Richard, and you tried to accost her."

"I did not accost her! I *greeted* her."

"With your lips. On her *mouth!*" Clayton ran his hands through his hair.

Richard waved his glass in the air dismissively, mumbling incoherently.

Clayton knew bits and pieces of the Sophie Ford story, Richard's lost love... or new obsession... he couldn't quite discern which. Her arrival to Harrisburg nine months ago had been a strange one, and still unexplained. He'd met her briefly when her life had been threatened, and had also made the acquaintance of her husband, Jamie. Clayton liked the man. He was genuine, had a gift with people, and did his best to be patient with Richard, despite the fact that his brother treated him poorly.

But the issues with Sophie were simply the last straw. Richard had wounds far deeper than anyone had ever been able to reach.

Polar opposites in personality, Clayton and his brother were a combustible combination. Richard could be aggressive and a bully at times, whereas Clayton was the peacemaker. Clayton made his point with words, rather than his fists. Growing up with Richard, however, made him a crafty fighter. He'd had to be... just to survive the frequent brawls with his older brother.

Clayton hadn't realized how badly his brother was doing. The rumors didn't come close to the truth, and he was both shocked and saddened by the sight of Richard's deterioration. "I'm leaving on the four o'clock train. I would like to report to the President that all is well here. Why don't you go upstairs and try to rest?"

"I'm perfectly rested," Richard slurred.

"You need to sober up."

Richard staggered to his feet. "And you need to get the hell out of my office!"

Fists clenched, Clayton stood and walked slowly towards the office door. He knew he had to take a walk or he would end up punching his brother. And no good ever came out of a fight with

4

Richard. Taking a deep breath, he turned towards him. "Richard, be sober before I return, or I'll be forced to take action."

The ring of Richard's humorless laughter followed Clayton as he quietly pulled the office door closed and made his way to the stables to check on the cavalry training. Hearing the forceful voice of Sergeant Lowe directing the horses in several military movements as he approached the arena, Clayton took a deep, steely breath, and tried to shake off his anger towards his brother. A slight breeze carried the briskness of the ensuing winter and the scents of horseflesh, and the soldiers took advantage of the mild weather to get in an extra exercise session.

Clayton's thoughts were diverted when he saw Jamie in deep conversation with his wife. Feeling slightly like a voyeur, yet unable to turn away, Clayton watched as Jamie smiled down at her as though she were the only person on earth. Tall with long, blonde curls that cascaded down the middle of her back, Sophie commanded attention by the men around her. However, she seemed unaware of her effect. Jamie looked up as he approached and Sophie turned, welcoming Clayton with a quick smile.

No wonder Richard is a mess.

"Good afternoon, Clayton." Jamie stretched his hand out in greeting.

"Good afternoon." Clayton removed his hat and turned to Sophie with a slight bow. "Mrs. Ford, lovely to see you again."

"You, too, Mr. Madden."

"How's Richard?" Jamie asked. At Sophie's grimace, he wrapped his arm around her back and pulled her up against him.

Clayton tucked his hat under his arm. "Not doing well today, I'm afraid."

"What time is your train?"

"Four."

Jamie frowned. "Will Richard see you off?"

"I doubt it." Clayton crossed his arms. "I'm hoping he'll pass out soon. I'd hate a scene at the station."

"I'm so sorry. I hadn't realized it'd gotten that bad," Sophie whispered sadly.

Clayton held his hand up. "Please don't apologize, it's his

5

doing."

Sophie leaned heavily against Jamie with a sigh.

"If you need a ride, let me know," Jamie offered.

"That won't be necessary." Clayton grimaced. "Richard was supposed to deliver horses to Maryland. However, in his condition—" He paused with a scowl. "Nevertheless, Andrew Simmonds has offered to deliver them to Vincent Butler, so we'll ride them to the station. I'll disembark at Union Station, and Andrew will continue with them to Camden."

Jamie nodded. "When will you be back?"

"Not for several weeks, I would imagine. I have to report to Christopher Butler and the President, which will require time."

Sophie raised an eyebrow. "Will you let them know about Richard?"

"I will tell Christopher. The President has too much on his mind to be concerned about my brother. I am satisfied with the work in spite of Richard's illness."

"Excellent." Jamie gave a quick nod. "Well, my wife needs to rest, so we'll see you next time you're in town."

Clayton shook Jamie's hand and watched him lean down to whisper something in Sophie's ear as they walked away. A few seconds later, Jamie handed her a handkerchief. Clayton hoped it wasn't something he'd said.

"Clayton!" Andrew approached him, leading a pair of award-winning Morgans.

Andrew had to fight to keep the stallion from sidestepping into the mare, so Clayton rushed to assist. "They're beautiful."

Andrew nodded. "Richard chose well with these two. Once Vincent mates them, their foal will be a nice addition to his stable."

Clayton took the stallion's lead from Andrew and noticed he grabbed his knee briefly before standing again. Andrew Simmonds had been severely injured at Shiloh and was left with a badly damaged knee and scarring on his face. He would joke that the scar finally made him less pretty, but Clayton always felt there was something deeper behind his comedic façade. "I have nothing to take with me, so I'll check on Richard and meet you

6

out front in ten minutes, if that is acceptable."

Andrew nodded. "Yes, fine. My bag's on the back of the mare, so I'm ready to go."

Clayton jogged back to the house and made his way to Richard's office. He pushed the door open to find Richard passed out in his large leather chair. With a curse of disgust, Clayton penned a quick note, put another log on the fire, and met Andrew outside.

* * *

"You'd better catch me." Emma stood with her hands on her hips and narrowed her eyes at her dance partner.

Mark Battaglia rolled his eyes. "Who are you talking to? We've been practicing this routine for weeks… and you've lost a hell of a lot of weight."

"I haven't lost that much."

Mark chuckled and Emma couldn't help but smile. Mark had been her dance partner for three years. They taught together, fought together, and danced outrageously choreographed routines that no human should be able to do… usually dances she choreographed.

He'd had a crush on her since the beginning, and although Emma liked the *idea* of Mark, she didn't really like him enough to do much past flirting… and that she did well enough to keep him around. He was gorgeous enough she supposed… in a dark, mysterious kind of way… not really her type, but other women's for sure. She liked being on his arm. He was protective and attentive, and she knew they had any room's full attention wherever they went. One thing Emma loved was being the center of attention.

He was up for a role as one of Rayne Green's backup dancers. She was a vocal sensation, and along with an incredible voice, she put on a great show, and Emma was determined to help Mark make the group. He'd be perfect. He was all man… and strong. The perfect partner for any woman.

Mark drew her focus back to the present when he pressed play on her iPod. "Come on, Em. Do it."

7

Emma dropped her glasses on top of her bag. "I wish I had my contacts."

Mark smiled. "Don't worry, four-eyes, I've got you," he called over the music.

Emma took a deep breath, skipped into her tumble routine, and found herself lifted high above Mark's head and then thrown into a split on the ground.

Mark let out a holler as he pulled her up and wrapped his arms around her waist. "That was amazing."

Emma wrapped her arms around his neck. "I'm so glad you caught me."

He gave her a gentle squeeze. "I told you I would." He leaned down to kiss her, but Emma waited until the last second and turned away. Mark sighed and leaned a hip against the balance bar. "Are we going to that party?"

Emma grabbed a towel and wrapped it around her neck. "Of course."

Mark grabbed the ends of her towel and pulled her closer. "Are you going to wear your blue dress?"

Emma grinned and ran a finger down his chest. "If you'd like me to." Her "little blue cocktail dress" was low at the neck and high at the thigh. With a pair of Jimmy Choos and platinum hoop earrings, she could hold the attention of every man she met while wearing it.

"Will your contacts be here in time?"

Emma leaned back with a mock scowl. "Are you saying I'm ugly with glasses?"

Mark snorted as he pulled her closer. "Impossible. But sexy librarian isn't really gonna work for the Rayne Green party."

The studio door opened and Emma's best friend Hannah walked inside. "Hey there."

"Hi, Han-Han." Emma stepped back.

"Hi, Mark." Hannah gave him a little wave.

"Hi, Hannah."

Hannah set her bag on the floor. "Emma giving you a hard time?"

Mark gave a half-smile. "No more than usual."

8

Hannah giggled. She used to argue with Emma about how she treated Mark, but in the end, realized Mark was getting something out of the deal as well, so left it alone. It wasn't like Hannah didn't have her own issues with men. She refused to date. She was petite, almost six inches shorter than Emma, with dark glossy hair that framed an oval face. A liberal smattering of freckles covered her nose and cradled hazel eyes that bordered on green. She was gorgeous, talented, and the perfect dance partner... mostly because she was so compact. Everyone wanted her, but she rarely did partner work anymore, unless it was ballet.

"What's up?" Emma slipped her glasses on.

Hannah slid a lock of hair behind her ear. "The school found my application. I got accepted at DePaul."

"That's awesome! I'm so proud of you." Emma gave a little squeal and clapped her hands. "Wow! Chicago."

"I know! I can't wait." Hannah glanced at Mark and then back at Emma. "Did you guys finish the routine?"

Emma shook her head. "No, we were going to do one more run-through. Wanna watch?"

"Yeah, I do." Hannah sat cross-legged on the floor.

Mark hit play and the sound of Emma's favorite song from the Citizens echoed through the space. Emma handed her spectacles to Hannah and lost herself in the routine, barely registering when she had to throw herself into Mark's arms. She did it without thought.

Hannah jumped to her feet and clapped before hugging both of them. "That was amazing, guys. If Rayne doesn't pick you, Mark, she's crazy."

He grinned. "Thanks."

Emma grabbed a towel and wiped her face. "Who wants to grab lunch and shop?"

Mark held his hands up. "No shopping with you, crazy lady. I'll take a rain-check on lunch, though."

Hannah smiled. "Only if there's Orange Julius in there somewhere."

Emma chuckled. "I find it interesting that with all of the

9

yummy things America has to offer, your favorite is Orange Julius."

"I know, eh?"

"I'll stop at home and shower and then meet you there... unless you want to come home with me?"

Hannah shook her head. "I have to swing by my house first anyway. I was on my way there when I saw your car."

"Okay. I'll call you when I'm leaving the house."

"Sounds good." Hannah waved and left the studio.

Mark promised to lock up before leaving, so she hugged him and took off for home. She got home to a message from Alex letting her know the movers would deliver the final boxes in the morning.

Emma had been ecstatic when Lucas and Alexandria Smith moved in less than a month after the idea was first presented. Emma finally felt settled—well, almost. After showering and changing into something a little less comfortable, Emma called Hannah. "Hi, Han-Han, I'm on my way."

"Usual place?"

"Yep. See you in twenty." Emma flipped her phone closed as she shut the front door and locked it. Turning to walk down the steps to her car parked on the street, she noticed a familiar sight. A dark green sedan sat under the shade of a tree just south of the house. A man with dark sunglasses sat behind the wheel and watched her. She didn't miss the raised scarring over his cheek, and she shivered as she hit the unlock button on her sister's Mercedes.

Climbing into the driver's seat, she started the engine and pulled away from the curb. The sedan followed.

"Time to have some fun, dumbass," Emma grumbled.

She pulled up to a light just as it turned green. Moving into the left-hand turn lane, she waited for the light to turn yellow and then burned through it, leaving the green sedan stuck behind a red light. She knew it wouldn't necessarily be that easy, so she took a few back streets to her destination, and didn't see the car again.

Pulling into the parking lot at Jantzen Beach, she met Hannah as planned, and proceeded to drag her around the mall for the next two hours. They purchased a few new dance outfits and Emma bought shoes. Emma *always* bought shoes. Once Hannah had had enough, the girls chose a table in the food court and sat down to eat.

"What's the game plan with school?" Emma asked.

Hannah laid her napkin on her lap. "Well, they're giving me a scholarship, so I'll start with law through them and then concentrate on the forensics side."

"Good for you! When do you have to leave?"

"In a few weeks. Classes start August 13."

"Seriously?" Emma's eyebrow went up in surprise.

"Yes, quick, eh?"

Taking a sip of her drink, Emma sat back with a sigh. "Yes, and kind of a bummer! No dance class."

Hannah shook her head. "No, sorry about that."

"How long until I see you again?"

Hannah popped the lid of her Orange Julius and stirred it with her straw. "Why don't you come and visit for Christmas?"

Emma smiled. "Yes, Christmas might be an option."

"Good." With a grimace, Hannah rose to her feet. "I actually have to go. I have an essay to finish."

Emma hugged Hannah and then visited her nail salon before heading home.

Finding the house empty when she arrived home several hours later, Emma stashed her bags in the foyer, and made her way to the kitchen. After grabbing a quick bite to eat, she decided to put her purchases away before flopping in front of the television with a tub of ice-cream. Messy by nature, she felt this was a great sense of accomplishment on her part.

Walking slowly down the hall, Emma couldn't help but think how perfect her sister's home would be for a horror movie. The approach to the library always creeped her out, and she rubbed her arms as a shiver made its way up her spine. It was where her brother-in-law had disappeared from, and where they found a small puddle of dried blood, determined to be Jamie's after he went missing. The smell of old books and aging leather engulfed her senses before she'd even reached the door, and her mind suddenly flooded with memories.

As she gathered her bags, she noticed the door to the room was slightly ajar, which seemed strange to her. She was certain she'd closed it up tight before she'd left. With a shudder, she pushed open the door, which squeaked in protest. Her intention was to make sure no one was inside, so that she could escape to her bedroom. Instead, she found herself staring into a room entirely different from the library.

No, not a room—*a barn?*

Emma did a quick check behind her and saw the familiar stairs and foyer décor, then turned again, expecting to see the library.

What's going on?

Sudden, excruciating pain shot through her forehead, and as she touched her fingers to her temples, her world went black.

TWO

*E*MMA GROANED AS she came to. Her head throbbed and she felt nauseous. Putting her hand to her forehead, she slowly sat up. A jab in her hip produced a wince, and when she moved slightly, she found the brush she'd just bought.

Great, just freakin' great.

Noticing the fuzzy outline of a few of her purchases scattered around her, she let out a frustrated sigh. Somewhere along the line, she'd lost her glasses. Virtually blind without them, especially in the dark, Emma got on her hands and knees and swept her immediate surroundings.

Confusing her further was the hay on the ground. She looked up and noticed she was in some kind of barn, but not the barn where she and Alex kept their horses. With such inadequate lighting, she spent another ten minutes trying to locate everything. Her glasses were trapped under her purse, but she was relieved to find they were undamaged as she put them on and had a good look around.

Where am I? Whose barn is this and what happened to the library?

The smell of horses and hay flooded her senses, and although darkness engulfed the space, there appeared to be a lantern lit at the front of the building.

Why would they use a lantern with all this straw around?

A shiver distracted her confusion when she suddenly realized she was freezing. Her short-sleeved shirt was entirely inadequate to ward off the cold.

Why am I freezing in the middle of summer?

As goose bumps crawled over her body, her head pounded in protest, so she dug in her purse for her stash of Advil and popped two, hoping it would take the edge off. Pulling out her cell phone, she flipped it open and scowled. No bars. She scrolled down to Hannah's number and typed out a text message, but after hitting send, the phone went blank. She sighed.

I must be in a dead zone.

She consolidated her packages and shoved them into her carpetbag. Surprisingly, everything fit. Pushing herself up off the floor, she brushed the straw from her jeans and scanned her surroundings. A glance to her left revealed an old-fashioned buggy, and to her right, four stalls only half-filled. Before the sound of heavy feet fully registered in her mind, Emma was staring at a young black man holding a bridle.

Emma gasped.

His eyes widened. "Who are you?"

Emma squared her shoulders. "Who are *you*?"

"I'm Jack, missus."

"Oh." She backed up slightly. "Do you know where I am, Jack?"

Jack's eyes widened. "You don't know where you is?"

Emma wrapped her hand around a metal bar on one of the stalls and steadied herself. "No. I'm afraid I don't."

"You's in Mr. Madden's carriage house, ma'am."

'Cause that clears it up so succinctly.

"Um, who is Mr. Madden, and where is his carriage house?"

Jack hung the bridle on a peg. "Mr. Madden is the boss and

14

you's in his carriage house."

"Okay, let's try this again." A shiver shot up her spine, even as she fought the urge to roll her eyes. "Is Mr. Madden here?"

"No, ma'am, he gone to Harrisburg."

Emma pointed to the floor. "And we are still in Portland, yes?"

"No, ma'am. We's in Washington."

How did I get over the bridge without knowing it?

"Well, if you'll just give me the address, I'll call my friend and have her pick me up."

Jack shrugged. "If you's close enough to call her, why she need to pick you up? You could jus' walk."

He must be involved in some kind of a mentally challenged work program. I hope this Mr. Madden doesn't take advantage...

Emma wagged her finger and forced a smile. "You have a point, Jack."

"Yes'm."

She slid her bag onto her shoulder. "Um, if you could point me in the direction of a cab, perhaps I'll find my own way home."

"Yes'm. I can."

Emma let out a sigh of relief. "Oh, thank you."

"I'd gladly point you in the direction of a cab, if'n you's tell me what a cab was."

Emma took a deep breath. "Transportation. I'd like to hire someone to drive me home."

"We's not in a place buggies come, missus. I could walk ya to the main street if'n you want."

"Jack?" A large black woman came rushing into the carriage house and stopped short when she saw Emma. "Jack," she hissed.

"Yes, Mama?"

"What is you doin'?"

"This white lady's lost and she's needin' help to get home."

Emma grimaced and quickly took in the old-fashioned dress and apron. Even with the sun setting, she noted the drabness of the gray fabric. "Sorry. I've caused a bit of confusion, I think. Jack's offered to walk me to where I can catch a cab."

Jack's mother pushed her son out of the structure and squeezed his shoulders. "You's never to be alone with a white woman, Jack, you know that."

"She jus' showed up, mama. I didn't mean to."

Emma inched her way out of the carriage house. "Ma'am, I'm sorry if I got him in trouble. It's all my fault. If you could direct me to a place I could hire a cab, I'll be on my way."

"Missus, if you goes out on the street like that, I'm afraid what might happen."

"Excuse me?"

"You's almost naked."

Emma swallowed. "Look, lady. My patience is wearing thin. I just want to know where I am so that I can go home."

The woman lowered her eyes and backed away. "I's sorry, ma'am."

Guilt filled Emma. "Oh, please, *I'm* sorry. I don't mean to be rude." She rubbed her arms. "I'm just very confused."

"Yes'm. I can see that."

Emma shifted from foot to foot. "Let me start again. My name is Emma Wellington. What's yours?"

"I'm Martha, missus. This here's Jack."

"Yes. Um, I don't know where I am, exactly."

Martha pointed to the carriage house. "You's in Mr. Madden's carriage house."

"Yes, that's what Jack said." Emma forced back the squeal of frustration threatening to come out. "Is Mrs. Madden home?"

"There's no missus, ma'am."

"Okay," Emma said slowly. "Would it be possible to come inside and use the phone?"

"Phone?"

"Yes, the phone. I need to call my friend for assistance."

The clip-clop of hooves interrupted the confusing conversation, and two men rode into the alleyway between the house and carriage house. Emma shrunk back as they approached, the large blond man assessing her with open interest.

16

"Martha?"

Martha grinned up at him and nodded. "Mr. Madden. Mr. Simmonds. Welcome home."

Jack rushed forward to take the reins and held the horses while the men dismounted. Mr. Madden removed his top hat and gloves as he closed the distance between his horse and Emma. "Ma'am?"

Emma cleared her throat and shrunk back. "Hi."

His light blond hair was swept back over a smooth forehead, and full lips smiled between a mustache and soul patch. She couldn't take her eyes off of him. He was gorgeous.

He'd be perfect in one of Sophie's Civil War reenactments.

He glanced at his friend and then back at Emma. "Do you require assistance, ma'am?" he drawled in a thick southern accent.

Shoot! I hate cowboys.

"She done wandered into your carriage house, boss." Jack tied the horses to one of the posts and bobbed his head up and down. "She says she's lost."

His concerned gaze swept her face. "Are you lost, ma'am? May we be of some assistance?"

Emma stood frozen, shivering from both the cold and fear.

Why are they in costume?

"No one will harm you." Clayton held his hand out to her. "You have my word."

I'm sure Ted Bundy used that line a time or two...

Emma swallowed. "And you are?"

"My name is Clayton Madden." He pointed to his friend. "And that is Andrew Simmonds."

* * *

Clayton paid close attention to the young woman as she backed away from his outstretched hand. Stunning. Tall and curvy, her blonde hair was styled strangely and she wore a pair of spectacles that magnified her large blue eyes. The dark pants that seemed to have been painted on showcased long legs, and her tight-fitting, short-sleeved blouse was low cut and flared at the bottom, hiding none of her obvious bounties. Clayton scowled. *She is showing too much.*

Taken back by his possessive thought, Clayton tried to rein his emotions. "Can you tell me your name?"

"Emma. Wellington."

Andrew stepped forward and faced her. "Ma'am? Where did you come from? Is there somewhere we can take you?"

The lamp caught the sheen of tears as she shook her head and backed up again.

Andrew leaned forward and narrowed his eyes. "Ma'am? Can we help?"

"Andrew, don't crowd her." Clayton pulled him back. "Can't you see she's frightened?"

"She might be mad, Clayton."

"I'm not crazy." Emma licked full lips and took a deep breath. "Um, I'm just not sure where I am."

Clayton smiled. "You're in my carriage house."

Irritation crossed her face as a quiet snort escaped between clenched teeth. "I think I should just call a cab and be on my way. If one of you could help me with that, I'd appreciate it. Let the cab company know I need to go to Portland."

Andrew stepped forward. "Portland, ma'am?"

Clayton pulled him back again with a warning glare and then faced her again. "Portland's quite a distance from here. Are you certain you need to go there?"

A tear slid down her cheek and she wiped it away quickly. "Yes. My home is in Portland. I don't know how I got over the bridge without knowing it, but if you could help me, I'll be on my way."

Andrew let out a quiet snort. "There's no bridge to Portland—"

"Andrew," Clayton hissed.

"Who are you people?" Emma whispered. "I need to go home."

"Ma'am," Clayton said gently. "Washington is several miles away from Maine, and without a bridge."

Emma rubbed her forehead. "Maine? No, Oregon. I'm from

Oregon. Just over the river from Washington. We are in Washington, right?"

"Yes, ma'am. Washington D.C."

Emma's head whipped up. "What?"

Clayton watched fear cover her face and her attempt to hide it again. She began to inch away from the group and then bolted.

"Ma'am! Wait!" Clayton went after her, his heart in his throat. If she made it to Main Street, she'd run the risk of running into the crowded traffic. He caught her just as she reached the third row house, grabbed her around her waist, and pulled her up against him.

Emma screamed bloody murder.

"Shh, ma'am, I'm not going to hurt you. I promise," he whispered gently in her ear, momentarily distracted by her incredible scent—peach, apricot, and sandalwood. Emma's whimper brought him back to his senses. "Take a deep breath."

* * *

Emma gasped in an effort to catch her breath. Her side cramped in protest from her frightened run and her feet were killing her.

I shouldn't have worn these damn boots.

"Ma'am?"

I'm losing it. Why am I thinking about boots? I'm in the arms of a possible rapist and I'm thinking about boots? I'm insane.

She took a deep breath.

"Good. That's better. Do you feel better?" He turned her to face him.

He sounds kind, not at all like a rapist. But, didn't they always say that? He was such a quiet man. Nice to my cat. Shit, I'm losing my ever-blessed mind.

She nodded.

"All right," he said gently. "Will you allow me to help you?"

There was something genuine about him, but her mind raced, and logic told her not to believe the kind words and sexy voice. Logic told her to run. She waited until he lowered his arms just enough and bolted again. This time in the opposite direction.

"Wait!" he hollered. "Come back here. I am not going to

harm you."

That's what they all say.

She ran. Bile rose unbidden as she forced her feet forward, and although she was ready to throw up at any second, she pushed herself anyway. She saw his friend rush out into her path so she tried to zig when he zagged.

BAM!

She went down. Emma screamed as she tried to put her hands out to brace her fall, but her bag was heavy and awkward, and she landed on her chin despite her best efforts to catch herself. She dropped her bag and lost her glasses again, so she was now blind and in pain. Through her sobs of frustration, she saw the men jogging toward her.

THREE

CLAYTON HELD A hand out to slow Andrew. He felt a deep sense of protectiveness as he hunkered down beside her, and didn't want Andrew to scare her. "Are you all right?"

"Do I look all right?" she snapped.

"Her feet went right out from under her," Andrew said from his place above her.

Emma glared up at him. "I wouldn't have tripped if you hadn't been chasing me."

Andrew cocked his head to the side. "I was trying to help."

She grunted as she tried to slide away from Clayton. He laid his hand gently on her knee and smiled. "Did you hurt yourself?"

Emma tipped her leg away from his touch and nodded. "I think I twisted my ankle."

"Which ankle?"

"What?"

"Which ankle did you twist?"

"Never mind. It's okay." Emma leaned her body to the side as if to stand.

"I cannot help you if you don't tell me which one hurts," he prodded gently.

Emma whimpered. "My right one."

Peeling off her leather boot, Clayton couldn't help but notice her shapely leg. "Did you hurt anything else?" He attempted to focus on her injury, not her provocative form.

"I landed on my chin and scraped up my hand." Her pathetic tone twisted his heart. "I don't know where my glasses are and I'm blind without them, which means I am never going to find my way out of here, and now I've gone and injured myself, which means I won't be able to walk to safety, which means I'm probably going to die alone, and that just sucks!"

Endeavoring not to laugh at her rambling and strange speech, Clayton placed his hand on her dainty ankle and felt the swelling already in progress.

Andrew bent to pick up her discarded bags. Emma tried to grab for them. "Hey, don't touch those. They're personal."

Clayton handed her the glasses he'd rescued from the ground. "Ma'am, how are we going to assist you without touching your bags? I must get you out of this street, and if you can't walk, then I'll carry you."

"You're not carrying me anywhere, so it's a moot point." She slid her glasses on and waved her hand toward Andrew. "Put them down."

Andrew shook his head and turned toward the townhouse, ignoring her.

"Hey!" Emma snapped.

Clayton slid an arm under her legs and wrapped the other around her waist, lifting her without effort. "You have a nasty sprain and possible break. Let's get you into the house and determine if we need to call a doctor."

"Do I have a choice?"

Clayton shook his head and the slight scent of mint carried when she let out a huff of derision. Her body shook and he

22

frowned at the goose bumps forming on her arms. "You're freezing."

"I wasn't prepared for winter weather," she whispered.

"No, apparently not." He pulled her closer. "Let's get you inside and by the fire."

She didn't object as he carried her into the townhouse.

Martha met them at the front door. "Jack's fixed the fire and gone for ice and Miss Gwen."

"Thank you, Martha." Clayton settled Emma on the chair closest to the warmth. "Please bring blankets and something to eat."

"Yessuh."

Clayton knelt beside Emma. He lifted her foot onto a footstool and pulled her sock off. Her expression spoke volumes as he tried to feel for breaks. "Can you move it?"

Emma wiggled her toes, but when she tried to move her foot in a circle, she whimpered and buried her face into the side of the chair.

Clayton stood and cupped her chin, appraising her face for injuries. "You have a nasty scrape." He lowered his hand. "I don't think your ankle's broken, but it's definitely sprained. I'm sure you're in a great deal of pain, but it will heal."

She nodded.

Martha bustled in with blankets and laid them over Emma before Clayton could direct her. "You's must be freezin', ma'am. We'll get you warm afore you know it."

Clayton drew his eyebrows together in concern. "I don't like the look of your chin, Miss Wellington. Perhaps we should send for the doctor."

Emma pressed against the sore spot and shook her head. "I think it's fine. Probably just a bruise. Like my ankle."

He crossed his arms and paced the room. "I'll wait until tomorrow to send for him. However, if it's not considerably better, I'll not accept an argument." Clayton forced the frown from his face and smiled in an effort to make her more comfortable. "Do you like wine?"

Emma nodded. "Yes."

23

"Would you like some?"

Emma shrugged. "Sure."

"I'll be right back."

* * *

Emma watched Mr. Hottie leave the room and her gaze shifted to Andrew, who stood holding her bag. A flash of anger covered his face. Emma shivered and forced down the panic as he stalked toward her.

"Who are you?" he demanded.

Emma widened her eyes in shock at his tone. "What do you mean? My name is Emma Wellington."

Andrew sat across from her. "I heard you the first time." He dropped her bag at her feet. "What I want to know is who the hell you are."

Emma gasped. "I have no idea what you're talking about!"

Andrew pointed to the bag. "You're not from this time. Who sent you? Are you here to try and kill Sophie again?"

Sophie?

Emma covered her mouth with her fingers. "How do you know my sister?"

"Your sister?" Andrew sneered. "So that's your plan."

Emma's stomach churned. "My plan?"

"You look quite a bit like her, I suppose. I would imagine they assumed you'd be convincing." Andrew rose to his feet and bent over her. "I know what you're up to, madam, and I would suggest you let your superiors know that she is safe and as long as I am aware of your time traveling, you won't get anywhere near her."

Emma squealed. "Time traveling?"

"Not nearly convincing enough—"

"Andrew Simmonds, why does that poor woman look petrified in your presence?"

Emma glanced at the beauty standing in the doorway. Andrew straightened his spine and made his way to the new arrival. He took her hand and kissed her knuckles. "Good evening, Gwendolyn."

24

"What did you say to her?"

"Gwen," he grumbled. "Nothing."

Something secret was exchanged between the two, but before anymore was said, Gwen pushed Andrew out of the way and made her way to Emma. The chill that Emma felt earlier returned with a vengeance as she took in the beauty's appearance. She wore a gown that looked an awful lot like her sister's reenactment day dress. Emma couldn't think.

Hoop skirts? Time travel? No, no, no, no.

"I understand you've been hurt." Gwendolyn stretched her hand out to Emma. "I'm Gwendolyn Butler."

Gwendolyn, an exquisite beauty with what could only be described as a rich chestnut mane of hair that fell—no, cascaded—to the middle of her back, smiled warmly. She was full-figured with dark green eyes, which bordered on emerald, and flawless skin.

Emma took her hand but dropped it quickly when she caught Andrew's glare. "I'm Emma Wellington," she whispered.

"Well, you've landed in just the right place." Gwendolyn sat in the chair opposite hers. "Clayton and I will have you nursed back to health in no time."

Heavy footsteps sounded in the hall and then a deep sigh. "Gwendolyn. Thank God."

Gwen stood with a swish and Emma turned to the sexy sound of Clayton's voice. Clayton gave Gwen a hug and Emma stared back at the fire unprepared for the pang of jealousy that hit her.

Who was she to Mr. Hottie?

"Miss Wellington has suffered a nasty sprain, and since it would be untoward to have her here without a chaperone, I'd hoped you could assist."

Gwen smiled up at him. "I think we should start with moving her to my brother's."

Andrew grabbed her arm and turned her to face him. "No."

Gwen pulled out of his grip. "It's the only way, Andrew."

"We don't know who she is," he hissed. "I don't want you in danger."

"Don't be ridiculous," Gwen whispered furiously. "She's a

25

lady in distress, and I intend to help her. You have no say in the matter."

"Gwen."

Uncomfortable with the conversation taking place in front of her, Emma pushed herself up from the chair. "I think if you people could tell me how to get home, this would all be resolved."

Clayton rushed forward and steadied her. "Please, Miss Wellington. You're safe here."

"And that's supposed to make me feel better?" Emma sat back down and stared up at him. "I don't know you."

Gwen moved Clayton out of the way and sat down in the chair facing Emma. "Miss Wellington, we're here to help. No one will harm you."

Hoop skirts, candles, no cars… just horses.

"I don't know you." She couldn't bring herself to say anything else.

Clayton hunkered down beside her chair. "Miss Wellington, we'll take you to my colleague's home where Gwen can tend to you. She will be able to find you appropriate clothing and you won't have to feel unsafe."

Easy for you to say.

Clayton stood and faced Gwen. "Is your buggy in the back?"

Gwen shook her head. "No, it's on the street."

"All right, I'll carry her to it and then follow on my horse." Clayton turned to Andrew. "Are you ready?"

Andrew narrowed his eyes in Emma's direction before nodding. "I have one thing I need to do first, but I'll meet you at Christopher's."

Clayton tucked the blankets more firmly around Emma and then lifted her into his arms. Looping her arms around his neck, she relaxed into his grip.

He smells good.

He smiled down at her and a shiver went up her spine. He carried her to the small buggy and settled her inside. "Are you comfortable?"

Emma swallowed. "Yes, thank you."

"I'll see you in just a little while."

26

He strode away from the buggy and Emma glanced to the sky, sending up a silent prayer.

Please don't let him be a serial killer.

* * *

"Jamie!"

Jamie turned to greet Topper Wade, who ran toward him as though his life depended on it. "Topper? Are you okay?"

"A wire for you." He stopped in front of him and panted as he handed him an envelope. "From Mr. Simmonds."

Jamie's eyes widened as he took the note. Glancing at the text, Jamie had to read it three times for it to register. He swore and shoved the note into his pocket. "Topper, I need to speak with Christine. Do you know where she is?"

"Yes, sir. She's inside the house."

Jamie laid his hand on Topper's shoulder. "I need your help. Come with me."

Jamie led Topper inside and the butler informed them the ladies were in the parlor. "Thank you, Daniel."

Pushing the door open, Jamie forced a smile and made his way to Sophie. She grinned up at him and stood for a kiss. "Hi, honey. What are you doing here?"

Jamie kissed her quickly and then settled her back on the sofa. "I had a minute, so I thought I'd come and see my girl."

Sophie sighed and sank further into the settee. "I love having you so close."

Jamie caught Christine's eye and mouthed, "*I need to speak with you.*" He turned back to Sophie and sat next to her.

Christine rose to her feet. "Well, I'm going to speak with Mary about something to eat. Are you hungry, Sophie?"

Sophie shook her head and wrinkled her nose.

Jamie frowned. "Are you feeling sick?"

Sophie rolled her eyes. "Always. I'm not really digging this pregnancy thing."

Christine left the room and Jamie willed himself not to jump up and follow. He laid his hand on Sophie's belly. "I'm sorry, sweetheart. It should be over soon."

27

"Jamie, we should get back," Topper said and then smiled at Sophie.

"Right." Jamie leaned over and kissed Sophie. "I'm sorry I can't stay."

She waved her hand dismissively. "No worries, my love. I have my book."

"I've been replaced with a book?"

Sophie giggled. "Yes. Now, go back to work."

He kissed her again and followed Topper from the room. "Topper, go ahead and go back to the arena. I'll be there momentarily."

"Yes, sir."

Jamie sped down the hall and into the library. "Christine?"

"I'm here." Christine slid from behind the door. "What's amiss?"

Jamie pulled the note from his pocket. "Andrew sent this."

Christine read the missive and let out a quiet gasp. "Could it be true?"

Jamie started to pace. "I don't know. But I need to find out. If it *is* Emma, then she's probably scared to death. If it's not, then Andrew's right and Sophie's in danger."

"What can I do?"

He took the note from her outstretched hand. "I need you to watch Sophie like a hawk. I have to go to D.C. and find out what the he—, sorry, what the heck, is going on."

"Yes, I suppose you do." Christine sighed. "She's not going to like it."

"Christine, if I tell her, she'll insist on going, and if I don't let her, she'll follow on her own. I just can't risk her safety. It's better she not know why I'm going. I'll tell her there's a problem with one of the horses and that I'm needed."

"Why don't you tell her the President has requested an audience?"

Jamie dragged his hands down his face. "Are you kidding me? If I said that, she'd threaten death if I didn't let her go. Lincoln's her hero."

Christine smiled sympathetically. "Very good point. I'll act as if I know nothing more than her, but will keep her inside as much as I can."

"Thank you. Topper can help with Samson." Jamie started to walk out the door. "Now I need to get to the train station."

"James, wait. If it *is* Emma, she'll require appropriate clothing."

"I didn't think of that."

Christine nodded. "Why don't I find an outfit of Sophie's and pack it for you?"

Jamie kissed her cheek. "You're a lifesaver. Thank you. I'll swing by in twenty minutes to grab everything."

* * *

During the ride to Christopher's townhouse, Emma's nerves threatened to break through her skin. Her entire body shook, and she forced back tears as they pulled up in front of the red brick structure. Not one car, not one person in normal clothing had been seen as they drove down several streets in order to get to their destination.

She saw the Capitol Building and the White House, though, so she knew she was in D.C. She just didn't know how she got there, or whether or not she was insane. Gwen set the brake and turned to face her. "Miss Wellington, we're here."

Emma swallowed and forced a tight smile.

Gwen took her hand and gave a gentle squeeze. "You're safe here. I promise. My brother is an important man, and no harm will come to you while you are under his roof."

Emma pulled her hand away and nodded quickly. She turned when she felt a light touch on her elbow, and for some unknown reason, burst into tears as soon as she saw Clayton's concerned face gazing up at her. Her glasses fogged up, so she pulled them off and slid them between her breasts.

Clayton reached into the buggy and lifted her into his arms. "Shh, you're all right now. We'll take good care of you," he drawled.

The fear she'd been tamping down erupted in the form of uncontrollable sobs, and she buried her face in his neck as he carried her into the parlor.

Gwen moved two chairs to face each other. "Set her here, Clay."

His arms tightened as she continued to cry and he shook his head slightly. "Let's just give her a minute, Gwen."

"I'll organize some ice."

"Thank you."

* * *

Clayton's heart began an unexpected war with his head as he stood in the middle of the room and held Emma until her shaking subsided. Once the hiccups began, he knew the sobbing was over for now, so he settled her in one of the chairs and lifted her foot onto the other. His heart slammed into his chest at the sight of her swollen eyes and red cheeks. Handing her his handkerchief, he smiled down at her. "Everything will be fine, Miss Wellington."

Emma squeezed her eyes shut and took a deep, shaky breath. Gwen returned a few minutes later with ice wrapped in linen and settled it gently on Emma's ankle. "There. That should help the swelling. Are you hungry? Can I get you something to eat or drink?"

Emma cleared her throat. "No, thank you."

Clayton caught Gwen's eye. "Gwen? A moment, please?" He led her into the hallway and closed the door to the parlor. "What are your plans?"

Gwen frowned. "Plans?"

"Weren't you supposed to return to your parents' tomorrow?"

"I can't very well go now, can I?"

Clayton sighed in relief. "Thank you."

"I'll arrange some appropriate clothing for the lady… imagine walking the streets in what she's wearing." Gwen shuddered.

"I've never seen anything like it either." Clayton's reaction was somewhat different than Gwen's, but he kept his opinion to himself.

"I'm going to retrieve some of Christopher's whiskey for

Miss Wellington." She wagged a finger at him. "Don't you dare tell him."

Clayton chuckled. "I won't tell a soul."

Gwen shuffled off toward Christopher's office and Clayton made his way back into the parlor. Emma sat with her face toward the fire, a blank expression on her face.

"Miss Wellington?"

"Hm?" She blinked and turned her head toward him.

"Gwen is retrieving something that might help with the pain." He sat in the chair opposite hers. "How are you feeling?"

FOUR

*E*MMA WINCED INTERNALLY.

How am I feeling? Well, if you must know, I'm in-jured far too badly to escape. I'm stuck in the Twilight Zone and I have to pee. That's how I'm feeling.

Instead, she muttered, "I'm fine. Thank you."

Clayton shifted his weight, and she thought he might touch her. Instead, he asked, "Is there anything I can get you?"

Emma tucked a stray lock of hair behind her ear. "Do you have my bag?"

Clayton stood and poked his head into the foyer. "Have you seen the lady's bag?" A muffled reply brought Clayton back into the room with a frown. "I'm sorry. Andrew has it with him. He should be here shortly and I'll fetch it for you."

"Mr. Madden?" she whispered.

"Clayton, please."

"Clayton." Emma laid her hand on her chest to calm her heart. "I really need that bag. My whole life is in it."

He clasped his hands behind his back. "Both you and your bag are safe, Miss Wellington. Upon my word, nothing will happen to either."

Emma dragged her lower lip between her teeth and nodded.

The door to the parlor opened and Emma glanced up to see Gwen pause, a decanter in one hand, a glass in the other. Emma's pulse increased. She blushed when Gwen smiled sweetly and handed her the glass half-filled with amber liquid. "This is whiskey. It should help with the pain."

Emma emptied its contents with one deep swallow. The liquid flowed down her throat and she thought she'd never tasted anything so good. And she should know... her desire for the finer things in life, and the need to quell the pain from the loss of her sister, had led her and Hannah on an exploration to find the best single malt they could.

Gwen's eyes widened in surprise. "My word."

Goddammit. Now she thinks I'm a boyfriend stealer and a drunk. Just great.

Clayton sat back on the footstool. "Perhaps one more, Gwen?"

Emma handed the glass back to Gwen. "No, that's good." She cleared her throat. "I feel better already."

"I think Miss Wellington should rest now." Gwen set the glass aside and laid her hand on Clayton's shoulder. "Would you carry her upstairs, please?"

Clayton smiled and stood. "Yes, ma'am." Gathering Emma into his arms again, he followed Gwen up the stairs and down the hall.

Emma gave him a half-smile. "I'm so sorry."

"For what?" he whispered.

"For you having to carry me everywhere. I could probably walk, you know."

"It's nothin'." Clayton grinned. "You don't weigh any more than a bag of cotton seed."

"Is that some kind of a southern expression?"

He smiled. "I suppose it is."

They reached a doorway at the back of the house, and Gwen

33

paused with her hand on the knob. "That's far enough, Clayton Madden. I'll take it from here."

"Are you certain?"

Gwen narrowed her eyes with a curt nod. "Yes, I'm certain."

Clayton gently lowered Emma to the ground and Gwen wrapped her arm around her waist. "Ready, Miss Wellington?"

Emma nodded and Gwen helped her hobble inside. After settling Emma against the bed, Gwen threw the door closed with a pointed smack. "I hope you'll find everything you need here. There's a commode in the corner and fresh water on the dresser. I brought an extra nightgown with me, so I'll collect it for you. I have a day dress that Sarah should be able to alter for you, there's plenty of hem to let down, and we'll work on the rest when you're feeling better."

Emma didn't know who Sarah was, but didn't want to ask. She gripped the duvet and leaned against the mattress. "Thank you... uh... I'm sorry, I don't know what to call you."

Gwen smiled. "Call me Gwen. May I call you Emma?"

"Yes, of course."

"If I leave you here, will you be all right?"

Emma nodded. "Yes. I could use a few minutes alone."

Gwen's eyes widened. "Yes, I imagine you would. I'll be sure to knock."

Emma grimaced. "I appreciate that."

Gwen opened the door, and Emma was surprised to see Clayton poke his head inside. "How do you feel, Miss Wellington?"

Gwen placed her hand on his chest and pushed him backward. "Emma is fine. However, she requires privacy, so please go downstairs and wait for Christopher."

An argument ensued as Gwen closed the door, but Emma was too distracted to care. She hobbled to the commode and lifted the lid. A porcelain bowl sat nestled in the wood and Emma shuddered.

I cannot believe I have to pee in a bowl.

* * *

Clayton paced the floor of his office and retraced the events of the evening. Andrew and Christopher had arrived at Christopher's townhouse just before dinner, but Gwen decided Emma was far too hurt to join them, so Clayton didn't have another opportunity to speak with her. He'd argued, so much so, that Gwen had laughed at his discomfort.

"I knew you'd react this way." Gwen crossed her arms. "This is precisely why she's safer here. You'd compromise her in a second."

"Gwendolyn," Christopher admonished.

Clayton shook his head. "I simply want to make certain she's comfortable."

Gwen snorted. "You couldn't keep your hands off her, Clayton Madden. It's unseemly."

Christopher frowned. "Gwendolyn. Do not use that tone when addressing Clayton."

Clayton didn't miss Andrew's slight movement as he laid a hand gently on Gwen's back. She shook it off and glared at her brother. "I will use any tone necessary to protect that woman upstairs."

"I think you're spending entirely too much time with Charity," Christopher accused.

Charity Short, Gwen's childhood friend, was closer than a sister. She was considered to be a forward thinker, as she was often outspoken and opinionated.

Clayton sighed. "I would never harm Miss Wellington."

Gwen shrugged. "I'm aware of that, Clayton. However, you are also much like my brother when it comes to the treatment of women—"

"What exactly do you mean by that?" Christopher interrupted.

Gwen sighed. "You don't touch them. Ever. Even when you're friends with them."

Clayton raised an eyebrow. "I don't have friends who are of the fairer sex."

35

Christopher groaned. "This is an entirely inappropriate conversation to be having in mixed company."

Gwen rolled her eyes. "Well, the truth of the matter is that Clayton could not seem to keep his hands to himself, so I'm here to make certain she's not compromised. I put laudanum in her tea and now she's sound asleep."

Andrew handed Clayton a glass of whiskey. "Have a drink and relax, Clay. We don't know who that woman is, or who sent her. I've sent some inquiries and all we can do is wait."

Clayton frowned. "Sent inquiries? To whom, exactly?"

"No one in particular. I thought I'd ask a few of my contacts if they recognize her name or description. You'll be able to question her tomorrow."

Clayton stopped pacing.

Why would Andrew care about who she is?

Andrew had been acting out of character since they'd found her, and Clayton hadn't liked the way Emma appeared frightened when Andrew would glance her way. But he also knew that Andrew Simmonds would rather be drawn and quartered than to harm a lady, so Clayton chalked it up to the fact that Emma was simply confused.

Clayton knew he wouldn't get answers tonight. Emma was safely sleeping and he should do the same, or he wouldn't be any use to anyone the next day. He blew out the lamp and slowly made his way to his bedroom.

* * *

"Emma?"

Emma forced herself to open her eyes and focus on the voice. "Emma?"

"Lamie?" She used his nickname as a way to confirm it was actually him.

"It's me, Squirt. You need to wake up now. I'm going to take you to Sophie."

Tears spilled from her closed eyes as sadness washed over her. "Sophie's dead. This is a dream. A horrid dream."

"Andrew, what did they give her?" Jamie hissed.

36

Emma whimpered. "Ow."

"Emma, open your eyes. Try. For me?"

Her head pounded in protest. "I'm so tired."

"Damn it, Andrew. They better not have given her laudanum."

"Don't yell, it hurts," Emma whispered.

Jamie lowered his voice. "Sorry, Em. I really need you to open your eyes for me."

Emma took a deep breath and forced herself to look at him. Her brother-in-law came into focus—and so did Andrew. Emma gasped and tried to push herself away, twisting her ankle again as she put pressure on it. She cried out.

Jamie grasped her arms. "Shh, sorry. I didn't mean to frighten you."

"*You* didn't," she snapped.

"Andrew?" Jamie glanced at Andrew. "Why are you frightened of Andrew?"

Emma shook her head. "What are you doing here?"

Jamie stood and held his hand out to her. "I'm here to take you to Sophie. You need to get up and get dressed so that we can catch the early train."

Emma waved her hands in disbelief. "Um, no, you need to explain to me what the hell is going on. You were dead! Sophie was dead."

Jamie ran his hands through his hair. "I don't have time to explain, but I will. I promise. We need to get out of here before anyone discovers who you are or where you're from."

"Where are my jeans?"

"Okay, right." Jamie coughed. "Well, you can't wear them. I've brought something of Sophie's, and as embarrassing as it might be, I'll need to help you dress."

"Um, *why?*"

"Andrew." Jamie pointed to the door. "Leave us, please."

Andrew gave a curt nod and stepped outside. "Christopher's an early riser, Jamie. Don't forget that."

"Got it."

"Jamie, why are you wearing your wedding uniform?"

Jamie turned back to Emma. He dropped a bag onto the bed and pulled what looked like one of Sophie's old corsets out.

"Oh, *hell*, no!" Emma snapped… now wide-awake.

"Squirt, it's 1863. You have to wear a corset. I have one of Sophie's day dresses for you and I think we can do without the hoops, but you have to wear the corset." Jamie held it up for her. "You get it hooked and I'll tighten the laces for you."

"This is beyond humiliating."

"I know, Emma. I'm sorry. Did they give you laudanum?"

"They tried. I took a couple of sips, but it tasted funny… I poured the rest into the basin."

Jamie chuckled. "Good thinking."

Emma smirked. "I *did* listen to Sophie on occasion, and the fact the tea was cloudy raised a flag."

"Good girl. Okay, get dressed." Jamie turned his back. "Let me know when you're decent."

Emma groaned and backed off the bed, doing her best to baby her ankle. She slid her good foot onto the floor and steadied herself against the mattress in order to get the corset on and hooked. "Okay."

Jamie turned and tightened her laces and then stepped outside so that she could finish dressing. Emma had several moments of nausea from the pain in her ankle and the migraine threatening to attack.

"Jamie," she whispered. "I'm ready."

He pushed open the door and stepped back inside. "What do you have in the way of shoes?"

"Just my brown boots, but there's no way I'll get it on my right foot."

"Put the left one on and we'll carry the other." Jamie guided her to a chair and handed her one of the discarded boots.

"Thanks. Can you find my bag, please?" She slid her boot on and then sat back with a sigh. Jamie handed her the purse and Emma rummaged through it for Advil and her migraine medicine.

"Jamie, the sun's rising," Andrew whispered as he pushed the door open.

Jamie swore. "Em, I'm going to carry you downstairs where we have a carriage waiting. Everything has to go really quickly—and quietly."

Emma nodded and held her hands up. Jamie lifted her while Andrew gathered her belongings. They sneaked down the stairs and out the back door, then through the alleyway and onto the street. Emma couldn't understand why all the subterfuge, but kept her questions to herself, knowing Jamie would answer them as soon as he could.

Jamie settled her into the tiny buggy and Andrew threw her bag in at her feet. Jamie jumped into the driver's seat, saluted Andrew, who stepped back onto the sidewalk, and released the brake. Emma glanced back as Jamie guided them down the street.

* * *

Clayton downed his coffee and dropped the cup with a curse. He'd burnt his mouth in his rush to get out the door. His dreams had been filled with the beautiful Emma Wellington and he'd awoken anxious to see her.

Foregoing another cup of coffee, he grabbed his outerwear and made his way out to the carriage house. Jack led his horse out and tipped his head in greeting. "Mornin', boss."

Clayton grinned "Good morning, Jack."

Jack held the horse's head as Clayton mounted and gave a slight wave as he took off toward Christopher's. He was glad Christopher's townhouse was close to his own. His churning stomach and heart flutter wasn't something he was used to. Rather than riding to the back, he dismounted and tied the horse to the post out the front. He took the stairs two at a time and knocked.

The door was opened by one of Christopher's men, and Clayton spent a few minutes in conversation. He was distracted by an argument coming from the parlor and excused himself.

"Where did she go, Andrew?" Gwen asked.

"Gwendolyn, I cannot tell you."

"Andrew Simmonds, you tell me right now what you've

done with that poor girl!"

Clayton rushed into the room and studied his friend. "Andrew?"

"Goddammit!" Andrew snapped.

Clayton raised an eyebrow. "What's Gwen talking about?"

Gwen crossed her arms. "I woke up this morning and went to collect Emma, but she was gone, along with her belongings."

Clayton frowned. "What do you mean, gone?"

Gwen waved a hand toward Andrew. "Ask him. He won't tell me."

"What have you done with her?" Clayton advanced on him.

Andrew shook his head. "I haven't done anything with her."

"Andrew," Clayton hissed.

He shrugged and gave an apologetic grimace. "She's safe but that's all I can tell you."

Clayton grabbed the front of Andrew's jacket and pushed him against the wall, ignoring Gwen's gasp from behind them. "If you've done anything to harm that woman, Andrew, I will kill you. Our friendship be damned."

Gwen laid her hand on Clayton's arm. "Clayton, please."

Andrew chuckled. "He won't hurt me, Gwen."

Clayton whipped his head back with a glare. "Don't count on that."

Andrew pushed Clayton's hands away and smoothed his jacket. "She's safe. You have my word."

"Tell me where she is so that I can determine that myself."

"I can't tell you," Andrew said. "I've been sworn to secrecy. I'm sorry."

Clayton swore. When Andrew made a promise, he kept it.

"I'll find her myself." Clayton didn't wait for a response as he rushed out of the room and mounted his horse. He arrived at the large war office building and pushed his way through the crowd. If he couldn't use his position to find one beautiful woman, then he was working in the wrong field.

FIVE

$\mathcal{E}$MMA FIDDLED WITH a fraying ribbon on her skirt and glanced over at Jamie, who sat across from her on the train. He'd chosen benches close enough for her to elevate her foot and she sat with her back to the front. In pure Jamie form, his leg bounced up and down in agitation, a movement she'd seen a hundred times, particularly after Sophie got sick.

"Jamie, what's going on?"

"We can't talk here." Jamie leaned forward and smiled. "We've got a couple of hours and then we'll be home."

"Home? Home where, exactly?"

"Harrisburg."

"Pennsylvania?" she squeaked.

He nodded.

"How the hell did you end up in Pennsylvania?"

Jamie dragged his hands down his face. "Emma, just be patient, okay? I know it's not your strong suit, and that you hate surprises, but all will be revealed."

41

She continued to pluck at the ribbon as she leaned her head against the parlor car window. If people in period clothing didn't surround her, she might have fooled herself into thinking she was on a train to Seattle. The terrain whizzing by her wasn't much different.

Jamie had insisted she smooth some foundation over her bruise. In the light of the morning, it had turned a nasty purple color, and he didn't want people staring too closely at her. She still got strange looks from a few of the passengers, but chalked it up to the glasses she refused to take off. If she were being whisked away to some strange fantasyland, she wanted to see it coming.

The whistle blew and the train chugged to a slow crawl as they pulled into Harrisburg Station. Jamie glanced out the window. "Fuck me," he breathed out.

Emma's eyes widened. "What's wrong?"

Jamie groaned. "Your sister."

"What about her?"

"She's here."

"She is?" Emma plastered her face to the window. "Where? I don't see her."

Jamie pointed to a carriage just to the left of the platform. "See that beast of a horse there?"

Emma raised an eyebrow. "The beautiful chestnut Morgan that could only be described as magnificent?"

"You *are* related." Jamie shook his head. "Anyway, that's Samson. Your sister's beloved bane of my existence. If he's here, then she is."

"Oh! There. There she is." Emma waved frantically and jumped up and down in her seat. "She's stunning, Jamie. Look at her!"

Jamie chuckled. "I'm aware of her magnificence."

Sophie turned her head toward the window and held her hand over her forehead to shield her eyes. Emma saw her gasp, even if she couldn't hear it, and then Sophie lifted her skirts as if to run.

Jamie frantically signed something to her through the window, and Emma grimaced when she dropped her skirts and crossed her arms. "Oh, she's pissed now, Jamie."

A beautiful, petite woman squeezed Sophie's elbow and Emma studied her. Strawberry-blonde hair framed a heart shaped-face, and Emma noticed larger-than-life blue eyes. She said something to Sophie, but Sophie continued to glare at the window.

Jamie slammed his hat on his head. "I'm sure it'll get worse before it gets better."

"Why?"

"I left without telling her."

Emma looped an arm around Jamie's neck as he steadied her. "Well, that was dumb."

"What was dumb was telling Christine what I was doing." He sighed as they hobbled down the aisle. "She can't keep anything from your sister."

"*No one* can keep anything from Sophie."

"True." They reached the doorway and Jamie stepped in front of her. "I'll lift you down. Just make sure you have your bag secure." He jumped onto the platform and held his hands up. Emma laid her hands on his shoulders and let him pull her from the small ledge. Jamie wrapped his arm around her waist and raised an eyebrow. "You okay?"

Emma shook her head. "I'm in pain and I gotta pee. What do you think?"

"Nice. Okay, let's face the music."

They'd barely reached the edge of the platform when a flash of fabric came swooping in, wrapping her arms around Emma, and bursting into tears. "Oh, Emma. Where did you come from?"

Emma mirrored her sister's emotions and the two sobbed and hugged, then sobbed and hugged some more.

Jamie wrapped his arm around both of them and squeezed. "We should get back to the house, Ten-Cow. People are starting to stare."

Jamie had given Sophie the nickname when they'd gotten

43

engaged. He said it was based on a fable about a farmer with three daughters and their bride prices. A young man worked for a year to save up enough to give ten cows and other livestock to the father to pay the youngest daughter's price. Jamie said that Sophie was his ten-cow woman.

Sophie pulled away and stomped her foot. "I don't give a flying fuck about people staring. I have my baby sister standing in front of me. And you, husband of mine..." she hissed as she jabbed a finger into his chest, "...are in big ass trouble."

He grabbed her hand and kissed her palm. "I know, baby. But before you kill me, let's get your sister home. She has a badly sprained ankle."

Sophie gasped. "Oh, no, what happened?"

"*Sweetheart*. Home. Now." Jamie lifted Emma into his arms and settled her into the carriage. Sophie muttered under her breath as she climbed up beside her. Jamie turned to the woman who'd spoken to Sophie earlier and tipped his hat. "Hello, Christine. Good to see someone can keep a secret around here."

Christine stood her ground. "She guessed."

"I'll bet."

Christine climbed into the driver's side of the carriage and Jamie glanced up at Sophie. "I'm assuming you'd like me to ride Samson?"

Sophie wrinkled her nose. "Oops, I forgot about him. Yes, please." Jamie grinned and squeezed her leg. Sophie pushed his hand away. "I'm still mad."

"I know, baby." He tipped his hat and mounted Samson.

Christine released the brake and clicked the horse ahead. The buggy jarred forward and Emma grimaced as her ankle whacked the side. Emma didn't notice anything on the drive home. Her focus was on the tiny elves driving mallets to her leg, but she absolutely refused to cry until she was behind closed doors.

She vaguely registered the sound of Christine setting the brake, and then she felt strong arms wrap around her waist. She forced her eyes open and leaned against Jamie with a sigh.

"Just a few more minutes, Em."

Emma slid an arm around his neck. "Where are we?"

"Dr. Wade and his wife, Norine, graciously allow us to live with them. You'll meet them soon, and I know they'll adore you."

Emma's jaw fell open as they approached the large home of the doctor. The scene before her looked like something out of a romance novel, and the brick Federal style manor reminded her of "The Patriot." Seven steps led to a cobblestone porch, housing two large white doors bidding entrance and an iron doorknocker with a lion's head motif. Jamie followed Sophie through the front door and up the stairs.

Christine closed the door behind them. "I'll find Mary and get ice."

"Thanks, Christine," Sophie called as they continued down the hall. She glanced over her shoulder and then forward again. "Betty prepared the yellow room for her."

The threesome made their way into the yellow room and Emma almost laughed out loud. It was totally frilly. Not her style at all, but Sophie's to a T. A large iron bed seemed dwarfed in the spacious room. Someone had started a fire and the room was already warmer than the hallway. Two high-backed chairs faced the hearth, and a small round table was nestled between them. Jamie set Emma down on the bed and her gaze swept the room.

An intricately carved walnut armoire and matching bureau flanked two windows, which were just big enough for a person to climb through. The furniture shone with a deep luster that could only have come from elbow grease and copious amounts of beeswax.

Yellow wallpaper covered every wall, and the daffodils on the china pitcher and bowl matched the color perfectly. An embroidered quilt covered the bed, varying squares of yellow made up the design. "It looks like a daffodil threw up in here," Emma said.

Sophie giggled. "I know what you mean. It's a little over the top, but I still love it."

A knock on the open door brought a tall man, dark blond hair graying at the temples, and a quick smile from a somewhat weathered face. "Christine mentioned there was someone hurt."

45

Jamie waved him in. "Yes. Michael, this is Sophie's sister, Emma."

"It's very nice to meet you." Michael knelt down before her.

"Nice to meet you, too," she murmured as she shifted on the bed.

"Emma wrote that she would visit when the baby came, so we weren't expecting her for some time. I hope it's all right for her to stay."

Michael chuckled. "James, this is your home as well, you may invite whomever you please. Besides, any sister of Sophie's will be loved by the Simmonds women, no doubt about that." He turned back to Emma. "Let's see the extent of the damage."

Michael examined Emma, and Jamie stood next to the fireplace while Sophie paced the room.

"Well, young lady, you appear to have a nasty sprain, but nothing is broken." Michael patted her hand. "I'll get you some ice from the icehouse at the edge of the property and you should keep your foot elevated for the next few days. I'll send Betty in with the supplies."

"Thank you." Emma smiled.

He gathered his medical bag and stood. "Welcome to our home, Miss Wellington."

The doctor left and Jamie stepped outside so that Emma could change. Sophie steadied Emma as she slid from the bed. Once Emma's day dress was removed, Sophie loosened her laces. Sophie started to cry again and pulled out a handkerchief just as a maid walked through the door with extra blankets and ice. Sophie gave a half-smile. "Thank you, Betty."

Betty wrapped Emma's ankle with the ice, elevating her foot with a pillow, and then quietly left the room. Sophie hugged Emma, then hugged her again, before poking her head into the hallway. Jamie stepped inside, closed the door, and pulled a chair close to the bed for Sophie.

Emma's hand shook as she linked her fingers with Sophie's. "What's really going on? The whole story."

"What's the last thing you remember?" Jamie asked.

Emma grimaced. "I went to the library... that freakin' room

46

has always creeped me out. Now I know why."

Sophie squeezed her hand. "What happened then?"

"The room disappeared. Well, the room in front of me did." Emma shook her head in confusion. "I'm not making sense. It was like I was looking through a bubble at something that wasn't the library."

Sophie raised an eyebrow. "Did you see snow?"

Emma's eyes widened. "No, a barn."

"Really?"

Sophie and Jamie exchanged a glance.

"What?" Emma asked.

"I saw snow," Sophie said. "Above my bed. The ceiling disappeared."

"And I saw a field," Jamie said.

Emma raised an eyebrow. "In the library?"

Jamie nodded. "Yes, as you said, it was like the room had disappeared."

"Yeah, exactly." Emma smoothed her hand over one of the patches on the quilt. "Did you cut yourself at some point? We found blood in the library."

Jamie shook his head slowly. "No, I was shot."

Emma's head whipped up. "Excuse me?"

"I was shot."

"Did someone break in? Or a drive by?"

Jamie lifted his shirt and revealed a puckered scar on his ribcage. "I was shot from a Civil War bullet, through the rift in time, or portal, whatever you want to call it."

"Shut up!"

"Weird, huh?" Sophie grimaced.

"Have we really been sent back in time?"

"Yes."

Emma began to shake. Sophie moved to the bed. "Shh, it's okay, baby sister." Sophie pulled her close and rubbed her back.

Emma let the events of the past year and a half wash over her. "We thought you were dead."

"I know, honey. I know." Sophie leaned back. "Where did you end up?"

47

Jamie handed Emma his handkerchief and she took a deep breath and blew her nose. "I ended up in some guy's carriage house." Emma gasped. "Oh, my... a black boy found me... does that mean he was a slave?"

Jamie shook his head. "Clayton doesn't own slaves."

"Clayton? As in, Clayton *Madden*?" Sophie squealed. "I thought you said Andrew found her?"

Emma groaned. "You know *him*?"

"Andrew, yes. Clayton, not so much." Sophie scowled at her husband. "You better start explaining, Jamie."

Jamie held his hands up. "Okay, slow down. Both of you. Let's start at the middle and then we'll go back to the beginning. How did you *guess* what I was doing?"

Sophie slid off the mattress and crossed her arms. "It's not like it was hard. You were all weird yesterday when you stopped in with Topper."

"How was I weird?"

"You were all wound up. And don't think I didn't pick up on Christine suddenly going for food. We'd just eaten."

Jamie rolled his eyes. "Did you accost her right away, or wait until I left?"

"I didn't put the pieces together until after you left. And for your information, Christine wouldn't tell me anything."

"Oh, really?"

"*Really.*" Sophie flailed her hands. "Topper's the one who spilled the beans about the note, and I figured something was up when Christine growled at him." Sophie turned to Emma. "Christine does not growl at anyone for any reason."

Emma nodded. "Noted."

Jamie dragged his hands down his face. "How did you know about the train, Sophie?"

Sophie smirked. "Well, apparently, you've underestimated me, my darling husband, because I took Samson down to the telegraph office and charmed the man behind the counter."

"You, what?" he snapped. "Alone?"

Sophie waved her finger in accusation. "Don't even! I told him that the original message had been slightly marred and

48

asked if he could fill in the blanks for me."

"Meaning, with the right look here, and a little bite of the lip there, he read the entire thing to you, right?"

"Sort of," Sophie mumbled.

"Sophie." Jamie's voice pitched low in warning.

"What? You don't really need to know the rest. All you need to know is that I figured it out."

Jamie stared at her for several seconds and then his eyes widened. "Sophie Jane, what did you wear to get that information?"

"Sophie!" Emma suddenly got an attack of the giggles.

Jamie advanced on his wife. "Sophie, you'd better tell me you did not wear that god damned blue jacket."

Sophie raised her chin, her expression impassive. "I did not wear the blue jacket."

Jamie's shoulders sagged in relief and Sophie turned to face Emma, squeezing her eyes shut and mumbling, "I wore the green."

Emma jumped when Jamie swore. "Are you kidding me, Sophie?"

Sophie spun around. "Well, I had to know what you were up to! Getting information out of Christine is pointless once she's promised not to tell, and Topper's loyalty to you is annoying."

"What kind of a name is Topper?" Emma mumbled, although no one heard her.

Sophie continued to rant, "I'm the one who nursed the child back to freakin' health. Topper should fall at my feet… but, *no*, it's all about you."

"Why do you think I took them into my confidence?" Jamie retorted. "I can't believe you rode into town without an escort."

"And I can't believe you didn't tell me about Andrew's suspicions at the beginning!"

Jamie dropped his hands onto her shoulders. "Sophie, what if it *hadn't* been Emma? What if it really was someone else from the future sent back to hurt you again? He didn't want to take that chance."

"Hello…" Emma waved her hand. "Can someone please fill me in on who this Andrew person is? Other than a total dick?"

49

Sophie gasped. "Dick? No, no, babe, you cannot be talking about Andrew Simmonds."

"Um, if it's the guy with the limp and nasty scar on his face, then yes I can. He totally threatened me in the hottie's office." Emma slapped her hand over her mouth and then mumbled, "I mean, Mr. Madden's office."

Sophie sat back on the bed. "We'll address the hottie comment later, but right now, I want to know what happened with Drew."

Emma filled them in on the scene and Sophie groaned. "Oh, Em. I'm so sorry. You must have been terrified. Andrew and Christine are the only two people who know about our, um, situation. They're related, by the way."

Jamie chuckled. "Sophie, focus."

"Right." Sophie squeezed Emma's hand. "Anyway, someone tried to kill me—"

"What?"

"Long story." Sophie waved her hand dismissively. "Andrew and Jamie were instrumental in finding him. Andrew pulled Clayton Madden in for some help, but told him nothing, and I think he was trying to keep Clayton from getting suspicious."

Jamie poured water into a glass. "Andrew filled me in on what he said to you, Em. He's going to be home in a couple of days, so be prepared for an apology. He feels terrible."

"Seriously. He's a lot like Luke. He probably won't sleep knowing he's offended you." Sophie giggled. "You should absolutely make him suffer, though."

"Sophie Jane!"

Sophie shrugged. "What, Jamie? He's part of the reason she's hurt and the whole reason I was kept out of the loop. So, yes, Em. Make him suffer."

Emma took the glass of water from Jamie and sipped. "I most certainly will."

SIX

A KNOCK AT the door brought servants carrying a large copper tub, followed by more who filled it. Betty poured lavender essence into the water and then set thick towels on the chair closest to the fire. Sophie took a deep breath and promptly threw up into the bowl on the bureau.

Emma let out a quiet squeal. "Are you sick?"

Jamie handed Sophie a washcloth and rubbed her back. "Not sick, *per se*."

Emma tried to shuffle off the bed. "Are you—?"

"Don't move, Em. You'll hurt yourself." Sophie held her hand up. "Yes, I'm pregnant."

Emma clapped her hands and burst into tears. Sophie hugged Emma once her nausea calmed and then shoved Jamie out of the room. She turned the lock in the door and made her way to the bed. Emma gripped her sister's hand as she gingerly climbed to the ground and hobbled to the tub.

"How are we going to do this?" Sophie murmured.

Emma waved to one of the chairs. "Drag that to the tub. I can

51

do everything after that."

Sophie did as she asked and then Emma did a pseudo vault into the tub. Balancing on her good foot, she knelt in the water and then reclined against the side.

Sophie let out a quiet whistle. "Dancing really is useful."

Emma giggled and slid her swollen ankle over the edge. "You should have seen some of the stuff Hannah was doing. She's way more impressive than me."

"How is Hannah?"

"She's great. I have some photos on my iPhone if you want to see. Grab my bag."

Sophie pulled the bag over to the bed and rifled through it. "Ooh, shampoo and conditioner! Nice. Hairspray. Burberry perfume, my favorite. Shower gel and body lotion, excellent. Scrunchies! Is this the new Clay Morningwood novel? Ooh, and D.W. Foxblood?" Sophie held up a couple of paperbacks. "How many have I missed?"

Emma giggled. "I think just those."

"Toothbrushes and toothpaste. *Yes*! Wait, how many did you buy? It would appear your hoarding instinct might have done some good for a change."

Emma rolled her eyes. "Buying multiples of one item does not make one a hoarder. The four-pack was on sale."

Sophie pulled out a bottle of medication she was unfamiliar with. "What's this?"

"They were for Alex. Dr. Higgins told her she could take it during her pregnancy if she was nauseous."

"And they're safe?"

Emma cocked her head and smirked. "Has Dr. Higgins ever steered anyone wrong, Soph?"

Sophie chuckled. "Good point. I'll be stealing them now." Sophie slid them into a pocket and went back to the bag. "Here's your iPhone."

Sophie sat by the fire and scrolled through the photos. Tears slid down her face and Emma's heart twisted for her. Alex was like another sister to Sophie, and Emma knew she missed her. Sophie smiled. "They both look amazing. So does Luke. Jamie will want to see these." She turned it off, wiped her tears away, and stuffed it back into the bag. "We'll show him later."

"Can you explain to me what a Topper is?"

Sophie handed Emma the bottle of shampoo. "*Topper's* real name is Christopher Wade, and he's Michael's nephew. Apparently, his brother, Travis, couldn't say Christopher and the nickname stuck."

"Cute... I think."

"Oh, he is. Actually, he's entirely too cute for his own good." Sophie's eyes wrinkled with mischief. "He looks a lot like a seventeen-year-old Jamie, and could be his little brother. It's a bit uncanny."

Emma rolled her eyes. "You think everyone looks like Jamie."

Sophie wagged a finger at her. "Just wait. You'll see. Oh, and by the way, he's missing his left hand. Don't stare."

Emma frowned. "How did that happen?"

"The war."

Emma sat up in shock. "Didn't you say he's seventeen? How the hell did he get in the war?"

"He lied about his age and paid a high price for it. But he's on a good track now and working with the horses. Jamie adores him and would be lost without him sometimes." Sophie took her seat again by the fire. "He's the only one, other than Jamie, that Samson will let near him, so he's been a Godsend. Of course, he's still a little cretin sometimes when it comes to Michael. Topper likes to push his uncle's buttons... typical teen in any century, I suppose." Sophie smiled. "You cut your hair."

Emma massaged the shampoo into her hair. "Yes. I needed a change."

"Well, I love it."

"Thanks." Unlike Sophie, Emma had been blessed with fine, straight hair. The kind that would dry perfectly, right out of the pool or shower. It never needed to be styled, unless she wanted to fuss with it. For years, she had kept it long, almost as long as Sophie's, but Emma liked to flirt with change and she did—often. Emma submerged and came out of the water with a sigh.

53

"This is heaven."

Sophie studied the fire. "I know what you mean. Although, I do miss a quick shower. It takes so much longer to get ready here."

Once she finished with her hair, Emma focused on her hands and getting the dirt from under her nails. "I don't suppose there's a local salon where I can get a mani-pedi, huh?"

Sophie giggled. "You're on your own there, babe."

"Bummer."

"You have a nasty bruise on your chin!" Sophie exclaimed and rose to her feet. "How did I not notice that before?"

"Jamie suggested I put some makeup on to cover it. It must have worked."

"Are you in pain?"

Emma shrugged. "A little I guess. Really no biggie. Sit down, sis. I'm fine."

Sophie took her seat again. "You told me how you got the sprained ankle, but who gave you the nightgown? I can't imagine Clayton had one just lying around."

"His girlfriend. She's very nice, although, I don't think they have a very good relationship."

"I didn't realize Clayton had a girlfriend..."

"Yeah, she's gorgeous, but he was super attentive to me and I don't think she liked it."

"How attentive?"

"I don't know. Attentive." Emma sighed. "He's so gorgeous, Sophie. And that drawl..."

Sophie raised an eyebrow. "You hate cowboys."

"I know. But he's so... I don't know... yummy." She scooped her hand into the water and let it dribble through her fingers. "Figures. I meet a hot guy and he's taken."

Sophie laughed. "Oh, Emma, I have missed you so much."

"Laugh at my heartbreak. Nice. I can see some things never change."

Sophie covered her mouth with her hand. "So, what's this other woman's name?"

"Gwen."

"Wait." Sophie leaned forward. "Gwendolyn Butler?"

Emma nodded. "Yeah, that sounds right. Her brother's name is Christopher, I think."

Sophie started to giggle uncontrollably. "Oh, Em."

"What?" Emma sat up and immediately regretted the action. "Ow."

"Sorry," Sophie said through her giggles.

"What's so funny?"

"Gwen isn't Clayton's girlfriend."

"She's not?"

Sophie shook her head. "She's Andrew's. Well, not girlfriend in the modern sense. But total love of his life, and Gwen feels the same about him."

"Seriously? Those two were bickering like a couple of old hens." Emma drew her eyebrows together. "She and Clayton, on the other hand, seemed close."

"Oh, I wouldn't doubt it." Sophie rose to her feet and gathered the towels. "Christopher and Clayton are business partners and very close friends. Andrew says that Christopher lords over Gwen, so I would imagine she and Clayton know each other quite well."

"Really?" Emma's heart fluttered. "So, not girlfriend?"

Sophie bit her lower lip. "I might regret this, but no, most definitely not girlfriend. And don't you dare put that thought into Drew's head. He's already a mess by his and Gwen's estrangement, if he thinks Clayton's a threat, I don't know what he'll do."

"Why are they estranged if they're in love?"

"Complicated. I don't even know the whole story." Sophie huffed. "I've tried to get it out of him, but he's tight-lipped. I have a feeling neither of them will ever share."

"So, I could potentially see Clayton Madden again?"

"Not in the near future, sissy. He only visits once or twice a year."

"But he's so close. Just a few hours by train."

"But the trains have been commandeered by the army and

55

are used on official business only." Sophie studied her. "So, unless we go to D.C., I doubt you'll see him for a while."

Emma tugged on a loose string on the washcloth. "Hm."

Sophie loomed over her. "No, *hm,* Emma Justine. You're not here to have some kind of romantic fling."

Emma raised an eyebrow. "Then why *am* I here?"

"You're here because I wished you here."

Emma laughed. "Maybe Mom was right. God really does give you everything you pray for because He's afraid of you."

"You just keep thinking that and we'll be good." Sophie dropped a towel on the chair. "I'm going to get you a nightgown. I'll be right back."

"It's like noon."

"You're going to be in bed for at least two days, so you might as well be comfortable."

Emma groaned. "Fine."

* * *

Clayton swore and threw the stack of papers he held across the desk.

"Bad day?"

Clayton glanced up to see the smirking form of Christopher Butler leaning against his doorjamb. Clayton ignored his question and slumped in his chair. Christopher pushed away from the door and stepped inside the office. He bent down to pick up the discarded sheets and neatly stacked them in front of Clayton. "What's this all about, Clay?"

Clayton stared out the window.

"This isn't still about the girl, is it?" Christopher folded his tall form into a chair across from Clayton's desk. "If she's beautiful enough to get you this riled up, perhaps I should meet her."

Clayton whipped his head around. "You'll leave her alone."

Christopher held his hands up in surrender. "Whoa. I've never seen you like this."

Clayton rose to his feet and started to pace.

"Have you found anything out?"

Clayton shook his head. "She just up and disappeared."

"What did Andrew say?"

"Nothin'." Clayton swore. "It's been three days and the only person who knows anything about her refuses to speak."

"Not that he could now. Andrew left this morning."

"I know." Clayton ran his hands through his hair. "I dropped him at the station."

Christopher chuckled. "Why all the secrecy?"

"I have no idea." Clayton dragged his hands down his face. "I've approached this like any other case... with much less success."

"I suppose you should figure out whose confidence he's holding."

Clayton leaned against the desk and crossed his arms. "Confidence?"

"From all accounts, she doesn't sound like a criminal or someone Andrew would hide without a reason. So, who asked him not to reveal her identity?"

"Yes. Whose confidence." Clayton straightened and began to pace.

"Specifically, whose confidence...in Harrisburg."

"Outside of you and I...there's Gwen, his family... and... the Fords."

Christopher tapped his fingers against the armrest.

"That's it!" Clayton slapped Christopher on the back and laughed. He couldn't believe he hadn't put it together before. "I know where she is. I know exactly where she is."

Christopher stood and motioned toward the door. "I take it you'll need a few days off, then?"

"Yes." Clayton grinned.

"I'll clear it with the President. He's been asking about the cavalry training. I'll tell him I sent you back for a few days."

"I don't know why Gwen accuses you of being void of romance."

"Does she now?" Christopher raised an eyebrow. "Did she tell you that?"

"She'd never reveal that to me." Clayton backed out of his office and waved. "I overheard her telling Charity." Clayton

57

turned and made a run for the front doors, narrowly missing the nib pen Christopher threw at his head.

* * *

Emma's stomach roiled. The sound of retching elicited a physical response and pulled her from sleep. Taking several deep breaths, she forced herself to focus on the sound. "Sophie?"

"Sorry, Em. Did I wake you?"

"No, not at all." Emma sat up on her elbows. "I'm used to the sound of puking in the morning. It's a bit like being awakened by the smell of fresh coffee."

"Sorry." Sophie made her way back to the bed.

"What are you doing in here?"

"I wanted to sneak in and bring you fresh clothes, but it didn't quite go as planned."

"Did you take one of the pills?"

"Not yet." Sophie grimaced. "How's your ankle?"

"Sore. I cannot believe three days have passed and I can still barely put any weight on it. I'm really sick of staring at these walls." Emma flopped back onto the pillows.

"You should read, Em."

"Yeah, right." Emma snorted. "I've read the sum total of six books in my whole life. Other than the two books you just stole from me, I couldn't care less about words on a page."

Sophie tsked. "You're missing out on adventure."

"Oh, please." Emma groaned. "Would you please get my Advil?"

"Sure." Sophie grabbed Emma some water and handed her the pills. "Maybe we could venture outside today. You've only met the immediate family and there's an entire cavalry to introduce you to."

Emma sat up with a grin. "Ooh, men. I *love* men."

Sophie giggled. "Christine will be here for breakfast and she'll probably have her buggy. If she's not busy, we could go for a tour."

Emma swung her legs over the side of the bed. "Seriously?"

"Seriously. I'll clear it with Jamie." Sophie smiled. "Besides,

58

we need to get you measured for your own wardrobe. The Paxton ball is coming up and you'll need a new gown."

"A ball in war time?"

"Little known fact about war time is that there were often parties and balls in an effort to distract from the horrors of war," Sophie explained. "So Stephen decided to throw one this time."

"Well, I never say no to new clothes." Emma rubbed her hands together. "Will there be shoes involved?"

Sophie raised an eyebrow. "Of course. Emma Wellington never goes without new shoes either."

Emma squealed and jumped off the mattress, landing on her good foot.

"Careful, Em."

"I'm fine. Let's just get dressed and go."

Sophie chuckled. "Okay, okay."

* * *

Clayton arrived at the Harrisburg train station just after noon. He'd arrived without baggage—or a horse—so he made his way to the livery. The cavalry had confiscated most of the healthy horses in the nation to use for the war; however, the fact that Richard was such a successful breeder meant the local livery had at least one or two on hand.

He strolled into the cavernous building and came face to face with the proprietor.

"Mr. Madden." William Jenson stretched out his hand in greeting. "Were we expecting you?"

Clayton chuckled and shook his hand. "No, Will. I'm here on an unscheduled visit. No one knows I'm here and I was hopin' you might have a mount that could be spared. I need to get home in a decent amount of time."

Will nodded. "Sure thing, sir. In fact, I was about to head out to your place later today. Your brother was supposed to pick up two from me the day before yesterday. He never showed."

Clayton tamped down his irritation and schooled his expression. "I'll take the horses if you like and then you won't have to make the trip."

"I'd appreciate that." Will made his way to the back of the building. "I'll tack one up and you can lead the other."

Clayton tipped his hat and stepped outside to wait. His brother was growing more and more unreliable, and if Clayton didn't deal with him soon, he'd have to fill the President in on Richard's condition.

Will walked outside with the horses, and Clayton mounted and took off for home. The ride was close to thirty minutes and by the time he pulled up at the arena, he was ready for a fight. He handed the horses off to one of the men and took off toward his house.

Clayton walked inside and heard Richard roar at the housekeeper. The rant was promptly followed by the sound of shattering glass, and the flurry of a woman running out of Richard's office in tears. Clayton stopped her before she could get past him. "Hattie? What has he done?"

"Clayton, what are you doing here?"

"Never mind that right now, dear. What's amiss?"

She pointed to the office. "He's not right in the head."

Hattie Jones raised the Madden children from early childhood. Their father was considerably wealthy in the early 1800s and their mother not the most maternal, so Hattie had been hired to help with the children.

Hattie, a beautiful woman from the backwoods of Virginia, was not yet in her forties, and a big part of the Madden family. Her life had been a tragic series of losses, and Richard and Clayton convinced her to move to Harrisburg with them in an effort to take care of her. Unfortunately, at the rate the elder Madden was going, Clayton may need to take her back to D.C. for her own safety.

"Hattie! Get back here this instant," Richard bellowed down the hall.

She looked up at Clayton with a panicked expression.

"Go on up to your room, Hattie. I'll take care of this," Clayton said and Hattie fled.

Clayton trod down the hall to Richard's office. Richard turned when Clayton stalked through the door and grabbed the desk as he fell against it. Clayton groaned. Richard was drunk and it wasn't even two.

"Where the hell is that woman? I told her to get back here," Richard hollered. "And what the hell are you doin' here?"

"She's not coming back, Richard." Clayton removed his hat. "And I'm here for a few days... just in the nick of time it would seem."

Richard swore, spouting several expletives directed toward Hattie.

"Don't you dare refer to Hattie that way," Clayton warned. "She's been better to us than our own mother. While you sit here feeling sorry for yourself, she takes care of you, including cleaning up your drunken sick."

Richard's snort was followed by the sound of liquid pouring into a glass. "When are you leaving again, little brother? I'm sick of seeing your face."

Clayton crossed his arms. "Now that I've seen you, Richard, I believe I'll have to inform Lincoln of the current state of my highly respected brother. I'll more than likely be forced to stay and clean up the messes that you have created."

"No one asked you to do that." Richard waved his hand dismissively toward Clayton. "You're simply envious of my life and are trying to ruin me."

"You disgust me, Richard!"

The argument escalated to new levels, and Clayton knew it would not end well. Richard came at him swinging, and got one fist to the eye before Clayton could defend himself. Once Clayton got his bearings, he gave his brother several good punches to the jaw, and Richard went down hard. Clayton wasn't sure if Richard passed out from the fight or the booze, but he knew he'd be out for a while.

Clayton waited several minutes before leaving the office and looking for Hattie. He found her in her bedroom, crying on her bed. "Hattie, I would like you to pack a bag."

Hattie grew hysterical. "You're sending me away, Clayton? I didn't provoke him, I promise I didn't."

Clayton grasped her upper arms and squeezed gently.

61

"Hattie! How could you possibly think I'd ever send you away? You're my family. I want to take you to the Wades' for a few days. It's not safe here, and I know they'll give you refuge." Hattie started to shake. Clayton pulled her into his arms and tried his best to comfort her. She was so much like a big sister to him; he hated seeing her so frightened. "Shh. It'll all work out. You'll see. It'll just be for a little while."

"What will happen to Richard?"

"I don't know. I honestly don't know." Clayton sighed. "Just pack a bag and I'll meet you downstairs in ten minutes."

He made his way downstairs and checked to make sure his brother was still out of commission. He let out a disgusted snort at the sight of his brother on the floor. Clayton's eye and hand were killing him, and he'd been home for less than an hour.

Damn his brother!

He made his way to the foyer to help Hattie with her bags, and heard her gasp. "Clayton, your eye! You should get the doctor to look at it."

"I will, Hattie. Although, I think Richard might be worse off." He took a deep breath and led her outside.

The walk next door wasn't long and he delivered Hattie into the welcoming arms of Nona Wade. "Hattie, you can stay for as long as you need. We have plenty of room."

Hattie grimaced. "Thank you, Nona. I just don't know what I'd have done if Clayton hadn't come back."

Clayton removed his hat and gave a slight nod.

"Your eye! Did Richard do that?"

"Yes, ma'am." Clayton grimaced. "He's having a bad day."

Nona nodded. "It's a good thing you're here then, Clayton. Michael's out at the arena if you'd like him to have a look at it."

"Yes, ma'am." He shifted from one foot to the other.

"Is there something else you need, dear?" Nona smiled. "Hattie will be fine if you have business to attend to."

"I was wondering if Mrs. Ford was home."

"No. She and Christine took Emma out for a tour."

Clayton's heart raced and his hands shook slightly as he tried not to grin with joy and vindication. "All right. Thank you, ma'am."

"Why don't you and Richard join us for dinner tonight? We hardly got to spend any time with you on your last visit. You can see Sophie then."

"I'm not certain how well Richard will be feeling, but I'll kindly take you up on the offer."

"Excellent." Nona pulled Hattie toward the stairs. "Six o'clock. Don't be late."

"No way in hell I'll be late for this dinner," he said under his breath as he set his hat on his head and strolled out the front door.

SEVEN

$\mathcal{E}$MMA SAT IN front of the fire while Sophie attempted to pin her hair into some semblance of a nineteenth-century style. "Ow!" Emma grabbed her head. "Ease up there, Attila."

"Sorry," Sophie mumbled with hairpins between her lips. "Your hair is just too soft to do anything with. I get it pinned and it slides out."

Emma waved her hand toward the bed. "I have a couple of hair bands in my bag. Use one of them… and then spray the hell out of it."

Sophie spit out the pins. "Good idea."

"I shouldn't have cut it."

"Why? In case this might happen?"

"Well, you never know."

Sophie chuckled. "Yes, we should warn women in the future about cutting their locks off, *just* in case they get sent back in time and have to fake an old-fashioned hairstyle."

"Why does it matter anyway? Isn't it just the family?"

"Ha! It's never just the family. I heard from Mary—"

"Which one's Mary again?" Emma interrupted.

"The cook." Sophie found the hair bands and made her way back to Emma. "Anyway, Nona told Mary to add three for dinner, so I'm assuming she's invited a couple of Jamie's men to join us."

Emma grinned. "I like Nona. She's good peeps."

Sophie glanced off into space for a second. "Although, no one told Jamie about the dinner invite, which is weird." She shook her head. "Oh well. He's been working so hard lately, it's possible he forgot."

Emma rubbed her hands together. "Who cares? Men in uniform at the dinner table. Works for me."

Sophie gave her hair a gentle tug. "You will act like a modest little mouse tonight. No flirting."

"I don't flirt."

Sophie snorted. "What do you call it then, sissy? The giggling, the witty banter, the little head tilts … all for their benefit."

"That's just conversation."

Sophie sighed. "Well, I'd love to see you find a man who can bring you to your knees and rend you speechless. You have yet to find one who doesn't bore you… and you *play* with them mercilessly."

She stood and let Sophie tighten her corset. "I just like to have a little fun. What's the harm in that?"

"Well, please try not to have fun tonight." Sophie yanked on the laces. "One flirt and you might find yourself married."

Emma giggled. "I'll do my best."

Once Sophie was satisfied with Emma's coif, they finished dressing and Sophie led her to the mirror. Emma gasped. "Sissy, I don't look real."

She chuckled. "I know what you mean. It feels like a costume party that goes on forever."

Emma wore one of Sophie's gowns and it fit her perfectly, other than the length. Sophie had Betty take down the hem, and

65

in the end the very proper housekeeper was satisfied that it covered enough. The v-neck top revealed more than Emma expected and she tried to adjust it for modesty.

Sophie laughed. "Em, I promise, you won't fall out. You'll get used to it."

"But my boobs look huge!" Emma exclaimed.

"Newsflash! Your boobs *are* huge, Em."

Emma grimaced. "I never thought they'd ever look this big."

"It's the corset."

Emma glanced down and then at Sophie. "Are you sure this is kosher?"

"Em, you're showing less than me. You look great." Sophie pulled her into the hallway and closed the door behind them.

Jamie pushed away from the wall and gave them a formal bow. "Ladies. You both look beautiful." He pulled Sophie close and kissed her. "Especially you."

Sophie ran her hands up his chest. "As do you, baby."

He pulled away from Sophie and leaned over to kiss Emma's cheek. "How's your ankle?"

She adjusted her glasses. "Better... I think."

"We'll plop you in a chair and you'll do fine."

Emma wrinkled her nose. "That sounds fun."

"Apparently Nona has invited a few extra guests." Jamie got an evil glint in his eye as he grinned. "So, I plan to keep you away from any eligible soldiers."

Emma groaned. "Sophie already gave me the lecture."

"Let's go." Jamie led them to the landing. "Topper's waiting in the parlor and excited to see you."

"Me, why?" Emma asked.

"I think he fancies himself in love with you."

Emma laughed. "Oh, please. He's talked to me all of twice."

"Yes, but you *talk* to him. Most people don't know what to say and usually end up staring at his injury instead." Jamie looped an arm around her shoulders and steadied her so she could walk down the stairs. "Don't feel too special. He's in love with Sophie, too."

He ushered them downstairs and to the parlor, where Topper

66

waited with several of the other guests.

* * *

Clayton clenched and unclenched his hand before lifting it to knock on the door. He could barely contain his anticipation and had to stop himself from barreling past Daniel when he opened the door. "Good evening, Mr. Madden."

"Good evening, Daniel." Clayton handed the butler his hat and outerwear.

"Everyone is in the parlor. I'll announce you."

Clayton shook his head. "No need, Daniel. I'll announce myself."

"As you wish."

Clayton took a deep breath and squared his shoulders. He strode to the parlor door, paused briefly, and then stepped inside. The breath left his body.

She's beautiful.

Conversation continued around him. No one had noticed his entrance, and then she looked up and her eyes widened in surprise. Her tongue darted out to lick her lower lip, the action causing Clayton's stomach to clench with desire, and he gave her a slow smile. He was rewarded with the blush of her cheeks and the quick rise of her chest.

"Clayton Madden!" Jamie stepped in front of him. "What are you doing back so soon?"

Clayton glanced at him and attempted to look again at Emma, but Jamie blocked his view. Clayton gave him an irritated glare.

Jamie chuckled and held his hand out. "It's really great to see you. I'll bet your brother's happy to have you back. How long are you staying?"

Clayton focused on Jamie, took his hand, and squeezed—hard. "Good evening, Jamie." He grinned at Jamie's discomfort. "I'm back for a little while, and I believe you and I may have a few things to discuss."

"Really?"

Clayton smirked.

67

Jamie pulled his hand out of Clayton's grip and fisted it in his pocket. "Quite a grip you got there."

"Fencing," Clayton said without looking at him.

Emma stood and limped to her sister, who stood with Christine by the French doors. Jamie asked him something, but Clayton was far more interested in the effect he obviously had on Emma Wellington. "Excuse me, Jamie." Clayton walked away in the middle of Jamie's sentence and strode toward Emma. "Ladies."

Emma stepped forward and frowned. "What happened to your eye?"

Damn it! He'd forgotten about his eye.

"It's nothing to concern yourself with." He took her hand and set a gentle kiss on the top. Emma pulled it away and stepped behind her sister. Clayton took Sophie's hand and kissed her knuckles. "Mrs. Ford."

Sophie raised an eyebrow. "Mr. Madden. What a lovely surprise."

Christine closed the gap so that Emma was hidden, and Clayton raised an eyebrow as he lifted her hand to his lips. "Christine."

"I had no idea you were coming back." She grinned and lowered her hand. "How long are you staying?"

"That all depends." He caught Emma's eye between the ladies, and she quickly lowered her head with a blush. Christine let out a quiet snort and Clayton narrowed his eyes. "Were you saying something, Christine?"

Christine covered her lips with her fingers, her eyes dancing with mischief, and shook her head. "No, nothing at all, Clayton. Would you mind retrieving me a glass of sherry?"

Clayton tried to hide his irritation, but he knew she saw it. He also knew she'd made the request knowing full well he wouldn't refuse. "Of course. Would either of you other ladies like something?"

"No, thank you," Sophie said, while Emma simply shook her head.

Clayton gave a slight bow and went off to do Christine's bidding.

* * *

Emma's heart raced as she watched him walk away. She grabbed her sister's hand and forced herself to take deep breaths. "What is he *doing* here?"

Christine giggled. "I think you have an admirer."

Sophie squeezed her hand. "Emma, are you blushing?"

Emma swallowed and felt the heat climbing up her neck. "I need to get out of here. Can we *please* get out of here?"

Sophie shook her head and chuckled. "Not on your life, sissy. Look at you! You're all flabbergasted."

Emma glared at her. "I'm so glad you're enjoying this. What am I supposed to say to him?"

"Seriously?"

Christine drew her eyebrows together. "What's amiss?"

"What's wrong is that my little sister is speechless." Sophie wrapped an arm around Emma's waist. "Have we really just seen the *one* man—across space and time, mind you—that has brought you to your knees?" Sophie tapped her cheek in thought. "Apparently, when I say something out loud, it really does happen, huh? Wow!"

"Sophie," Emma hissed. "Shush."

"Let me see..." Sophie grinned slowly. "I think this might be the man who will make you fall madly in love with him."

"Sophie!"

"Oh, and maybe you two will get married and have lots of babies."

Emma pushed away from Sophie. "You are the evilest creature on earth."

"She is, Emma. I agree." Christine laughed. "Would you like to take a little walk outside before dinner?"

Emma let out a sigh of relief. "Thank you, Christine. I would love to."

Sophie reached out and squeezed her arm. "Your ankle, Em."

69

"I'll hop if I have to, mistress of destruction. I need out of this room."

Christine pushed open one of the French doors. "Why don't we sit on the veranda?"

"Yes, please."

Christine and Sophie steadied Emma on either side and led her out to one of the chairs, settling her foot on another. Christine squeezed her shoulder. "How's that?"

Emma sighed. "Much better. Thank you, *Christine*."

"I thought I saw you three escape." Emma jumped and looked up at Clayton as he stepped outside. He handed Christine her glass of sherry and then faced Emma. "Miss Wellington, I took the liberty of procuring you a glass of red wine. I hope that is acceptable."

A quiet squeak escaped as Emma nodded her head and took the glass from him.

Clayton turned to Sophie. "Mrs. Ford, your husband is looking for you."

Sophie stood. "Is he, now?"

Clayton gave her a challenging grin. "Yes. He's waiting by the refreshment table."

"Thank you." Emma grabbed her sister's skirt, but Sophie pulled out of her grip. "I trust no one is looking for Christine, correct?"

Clayton shook his head. "Not that I'm aware of."

Sophie gave a half-smile. "Good answer."

Emma's stomach battled with the sandwich she'd eaten an hour ago and her lungs fought for air. He was better looking than she'd remembered, and way sexier than any fantasy she could have dreamed up.

"May I join you?" Clayton indicated the chair Sophie had just vacated.

Emma nodded.

"What made you come back so soon, Clayton?" Christine laid her hand on his arm to get his attention. "Is Richard all right?"

He faced Emma. "Richard is not the reason I returned."

70

Emma shifted in her seat and swallowed.

Christine chuckled. "I deduced that, Clay."

He didn't seem to hear her as he leaned forward. "I noticed you're still favoring your ankle, Miss Wellington. Has the pain worsened?"

Emma shook her head.

"I hope you've been resting. I was quite concerned by the swelling."

Goddammit! Why can't I speak?

Emma cleared her throat. "Yes. I'm taking it easy, Mr. Madden. My sister has insisted upon it."

"Clayton, please."

Emma took a deep breath. "Clayton."

"I was wondering if you might like to join me for a buggy ride tomorrow."

Emma glanced at Christine and saw her slight nod of approval. "Yes, Mr.—I mean, Clayton. I'd enjoy that."

Before Clayton could respond, Topper stepped outside. "Dinner is served."

Clayton stood, ready to offer his assistance, but Topper beat him to it. "Emma, may I escort you?"

"Yes, Topper, I'd love that." She pushed up from her chair and held the edge for stability. "You'll need to come closer, bud. You're going to have to be my crutch."

* * *

Clayton glared at Topper, not just because he had the pleasure of escorting Emma into dinner, but also because they seemed close. Logically, he knew Topper was barely seventeen, but he was still a man and obviously someone Emma felt comfortable with. Topper knew it as well, if his triumphant expression was any indication. Clayton would have to watch him.

Clayton's body heated as Emma slipped her hand into the crook of Topper's elbow and leaned against him. As they crossed the threshold, Emma appeared to be having a difficult time balancing, and Topper wrapped his arm around her waist. "Easy, Emma. We'll take it slow."

71

She smiled up at him. "Sorry."

Clayton fisted his hands at his sides. He wanted her to smile at him that way. His irritation grew when he heard Christine's muffled giggle next to him. He sent her a warning glance, but she just raised an eyebrow in challenge.

Emma stumbled and brought Clayton's focus back to her. Topper gripped her harder and grimaced. "You all right?"

She nodded. "Yes. Sorry. I just can't seem to maneuver these skirts and walk at the same time."

Clayton stepped toward her, lifted her in his arms, and strolled toward the dining room.

"What are you doing?" Emma whispered frantically.

"Escorting you to dinner."

"Topper was doing just fine."

He smiled slowly. "I have more practice."

She pushed at his shoulders. "Clayton, this is really silly. I can walk."

"I believe we've had this conversation before."

Emma sighed. "Is that your way of saying the answer's the same?"

Clayton smiled slowly and nodded his head.

"Fine." Emma looped her arm around his neck. "Why do I feel that this is... ah... what's the word? Untoward?"

Clayton chuckled. "You're a lady in distress. I'm assisting."

"Oh, *please*." Emma sniffed. "I have never been considered a lady in distress."

"Em?" Sophie rushed over to her as they entered the dining room. "What happened?"

Emma rolled her eyes. "Nothing."

"Did you hurt your ankle again?"

Emma gave her a pointed stare. "No. Clayton just feels the need to pick me up, apparently."

Sophie hummed in suspicion and then pointed to an empty chair. "Please set her there, Mr. Madden."

Clayton carried her to the seat and gently lowered her into it. "Comfortable?"

Emma nodded. "Yes, thank you."

72

Before he'd straightened his spine, Christine and Topper had flanked Emma, and Topper sent him a victorious grin. Clayton had to hold himself back from lifting the boy from his chair and flinging him out of the room.

"Clayton, I saved you a seat right here." Jamie patted the chair between him and Andrew. Andrew's face was impassive, but Clayton knew him well enough to know that he was enjoying his discomfort.

Once Michael blessed the meal, the group settled into easy conversation. Clayton watched Emma from across the table, frustrated that he couldn't speak with her. She seemed to be enjoying something Topper was telling her, and her laugh caused a physical reaction Clayton was unprepared for.

"I'm surprised it took you this long to figure it out." Andrew grinned and took a bite of potato.

Clayton glared at him. "I'm surprised I've been able to contain my urge to kill you."

Andrew laughed and Clayton bit the inside of his cheek to keep from cursing. Tonight was going to be a long one.

"What happened to your eye?" Andrew asked.

Clayton took a deep breath. "Run-in with Richard."

"He's getting worse, then?"

"Much."

Andrew shook his head. "Something needs to be done."

Jamie leaned in and whispered, "I have a few ideas that we can discuss at a later time."

Clayton glanced over at Emma. She smiled at him and his heart stuttered. He'd need to figure out a way to talk to her alone.

"Clayton?"

Clayton glanced at Andrew. "Hm?"

"Did you hear Jamie?" Andrew sipped his wine.

Clayton sighed. "Yes, Andrew, I heard Jamie."

"I wasn't certain. You seem to be distracted."

"Andrew," he warned in a low growl.

"I was simply ensuring you didn't miss any part of the conversation." Andrew sliced his lamb. "I am here for *you*, Clayton. To assist with whatever it is you need."

Jamie started to laugh and Andrew quickly followed suit. Sophie leaned forward and raised an eyebrow. "What's so funny?"

"I'll fill you in later, sweetheart," Jamie assured her.

Clayton groaned and determined Andrew would find out how much he appreciated the joking when he'd least expect it. His internal plotting made the excruciating dinner somewhat manageable.

EIGHT

$\mathcal{M}$ ICHAEL LAID HIS napkin on the table and rose to his feet. "Shall we retire to the library, gentlemen?"

Nona smiled and addressed the ladies. "We have dessert laid out in the parlor, so please follow me."

Emma pushed back from the table and pivoted in her seat. She took Topper's hand and balanced on her good foot, her ankle now throbbing. Without warning, she once again found herself lifted into Clayton's arms. "Where the heck did you come from?"

His eyebrows drew together in concern. "Are you in much pain?"

"Not at all."

"Emma," he whispered.

"Aren't you supposed to get permission from me before calling me by my first name?"

Clayton sighed. "May I call you Emma?"

"No."

Clayton chuckled. "I'll ask you again, *Emma*. Are you in much pain?"

"A little, I suppose." Emma grinned. "You're going to be trouble, aren't you?"

"Most definitely." Clayton carried her into the parlor and settled her in one of the chairs facing the piano. "Don't get up unless I'm here to assist."

"Have you always been this bossy?"

"Am I?"

Emma couldn't stop her grin. "Go away, Clayton."

He chuckled and left the room.

Sophie brought her a plate filled with varying items of chocolate. "How's your ankle?"

Emma grimaced. "Sore."

Betty quietly came in the room carrying some crushed ice and several towels. "Miss Emma, Mr. Madden asked me to bring this to you. May I assist you?"

Emma sighed with a smile. "Yes, please. Thank you so much." She almost cried at his thoughtfulness.

Sophie patted her shoulder. "I'll run upstairs and get you something for the pain."

Emma took her hand. "No, it's fine, Soph. The ice will be enough."

"Are you sure?"

"Yes. I'll get something else later."

Betty packed her ankle and then left the room. Christine joined them and they delved into a discussion about the upcoming Paxton ball. They didn't delve too deep, as the door to the parlor opened and Daniel cleared his throat. "Mrs. Ford, I'm sorry to interrupt, but we have a situation in the stables."

Sophie sighed and rose to her feet. "Samson, I presume?"

"Yes, ma'am."

Nona stood and addressed the small group. "Why don't we all walk with you, Sophie? Always helps to exercise after a large meal."

Emma grimaced up at Sophie. "Can I stay here?"

"Of course."

76

"I'll stay with you, if you like," Christine offered.

Emma waved her hand dismissively. "No. Please, go for a walk. I'm happy to sit here by the fire."

"Are you certain?"

Emma nodded. "Absolutely."

Sophie squeezed her shoulder. "I won't be long."

Emma shrugged. "Take your time."

* * *

Once the group left the parlor, Emma closed her eyes and tried to relax. She felt a migraine coming on and had a feeling it would be a bad one.

Forget my ankle, I need an icepack for my head.

Hearing the door open, and thinking Sophie had forgotten something, she didn't bother to look up—until someone touched her hair. Her eyes flew open.

"Good evening, pretty girl. I don't think we've been introduced. My name is Richard Madden."

Clayton's brother slurred his words as he staggered toward the chair Sophie had just exited. He tried to sit, but managed to trip and fall instead. He righted himself and then leered at her.

Emma swallowed her fear—tried to, anyway. "Good evening," she squeaked.

"You must be Sophie's sister... Emma, is it?"

Emma nodded.

"You're beautiful." Richard crossed one leg over the other. "I think it's safe to say you're prettier than your sister."

"Thank you." She wiped her palms on her skirt. "I don't think you should be here."

"We're just havin' a conversation, beautiful Emma."

She forced a deep breath. "I would appreciate it if you would leave... or get Daniel."

Before Richard could respond, the parlor door opened, and Clayton stood in the doorway. "Emma?"

Richard laid his hand on Emma's arm. "Now, look who's come to ruin the evenin'?"

Emma pulled away with a grimace. Richard's hands were

77

dirty and the smell of alcohol permeated his breath and clothing.

"Richard." Clayton closed the distance between them. "You need to go home."

Richard staggered to his feet and cackled. "I'm not goin' anywhere! 'Specially when I'm right in the middle of getting to know this beautiful creature." He leaned down and grinned at Emma, his face inches from hers.

Emma wrinkled her nose and swallowed the bile threatening to spill. Before she realized what had happened, Richard was no longer standing in front of her. He was on the floor in a heap. It took a few seconds to register that Clayton was hitting him— over and over.

"Clayton, stop. You'll kill him!" Emma pleaded.

Clayton stood and took a deep breath. He pushed Richard's unconscious form with his boot and then rushed to Emma's side. He knelt beside her and took her hand. "Emma, are you all right? Please tell me he didn't hurt you."

Tears slipped down her face as she shook her head. "He just scared me."

Clayton handed her his handkerchief. "I am so sorry."

Emma was humbled by the concern in his expression. She couldn't stop herself from stroking his cheek, gently tracing the bruise around his eye. "Did he do this?"

Clayton nodded and laid his hand over hers.

"Does it hurt?"

He shook his head.

"What happened?" Jamie demanded from the doorway of the library.

Clayton squeezed his eyes shut briefly and then stood. He nodded toward the form of his brother unmoving on the floor.

Sophie pushed Jamie out of the way and rushed to her sister. "Emma? What happened? Are you okay?" Sophie frantically ran her hands over her sister's extremities, checking for injury.

"I'm fine, sissy."

Jamie advanced on them. "Did Richard hurt you?"

Emma shook her head. "No. Clayton stopped him from doing anything."

"Thank you, Clayton," Jamie said.

"I don't know that I'll have time to talk to Joe." Clayton dragged his hands down his face. "I may just have to drop in tonight."

Jamie stood over Richard and scowled. "You're probably right. I'll come with you."

Sophie raised an eyebrow in question. "Sheriff Joe?"

Clayton nodded. "Jamie thought it might help if we lock Richard up and dry him out."

As Jamie and Clayton discussed the plan for Richard, Emma heard Sophie's sharp intake of breath. "Soph? Are you okay?"

Sophie gripped the back of the chair and began to take quick shallow breaths. She groaned and fell to the floor, wrapping her arms over her stomach.

"Sophie?" Emma squealed in fright.

Jamie's head whipped up. "Soph?" Sophie whimpered in response and he rushed over to her. "Baby? What's wrong?"

Sophie grasped his arm. "I don't know." Tears poured down Sophie's face as she gripped her stomach. "Something's wrong."

"I'll get Michael."

Clayton bent down and lifted his brother over his shoulder. "Jamie, I'll take Richard out to Joe. Stay and take care of Sophie and Emma."

Clayton left the room and Jamie followed to retrieve Michael. Emma could see Jamie's terror as he rushed out the door. They weren't in the modern world anymore. Women died in childbirth all the time in the nineteenth century.

Emma already knew how Jamie dealt with the loss of Sophie the first time. She was pretty sure he couldn't take it again. She heard Jamie giving Michael a rundown on what happened, as the men entered the room.

Sophie was curled up on the floor in a fetal position, sobbing. Jamie ran to her and knelt down beside her. "Tell me where it hurts."

"Everywhere. I'm cramping. They feel like period cramps," she whispered.

Michael knelt beside her and Jamie helped to roll Sophie on

79

her back.

"OW! I can't lie like this, it hurts."

"Sophie, draw your knees up and it will help with the pain. I need to feel your stomach." Michael did a brief examination. "James, I need to do a more thorough exam, you should go."

"Forget it."

"James, it's not appropriate for you to be here for this."

Jamie scowled. "I don't care, Michael, I am not leaving."

Sophie grasped Jamie's hand. "It's fine, Michael. I'd like him to stay."

Emma could see Michael was very uncomfortable with his audience as he examined her. "I don't see any blood, Sophie, which is a good sign. I want you to rest for the next few days and then we'll see how you're feeling before the ball."

Sophie nodded and rolled back onto her side. Jamie knelt beside her. "Sweetheart, I'm going to carry you to the bedroom."

Emma pushed up from the chair. "I'll come, too."

"What about your ankle?"

Michael held out his hand. "I'll assist."

Jamie picked Sophie up and held her for a moment before he took her upstairs to their bedroom. Once Jamie settled Sophie on their bed, he sat down next to her and took her hand. Michael left Emma outside of the bedroom, so she hobbled inside and sat opposite Sophie. Sophie seemed calmer, but still looked a bit green.

Jamie kissed her palm. "Are you okay?"

Sophie nodded as she rubbed her stomach.

Emma reached over to help her gently massage the pain away. "What happened with Samson?"

"He kept trying to bite one of the soldiers." Sophie rolled her eyes. "I was feeling a little off, so I asked Topper to take care of him."

Jamie frowned. "Why didn't you tell me you weren't feeling well?"

"Because I never feel entirely well." She pointed to her belly. "I just chalked it up to the alien slowly sapping my life away."

"Hm, mm." Jamie handed Sophie a glass of water. "Well,

you should sleep."

"Okay." Sophie took a sip and then slid under the covers.

Emma stood and hobbled to the door. "I'm going to get some more ice and then turn in."

Jamie turned. "I'll get it for you."

She waved her hand. "No worries. I can do it. Just stay and take care of Sophie."

"Are you sure?"

"I'm sure." Emma grinned. "She needs you more than I do."

Jamie reluctantly nodded. "Come and get me if you need me, okay?"

"I will, I promise."

Emma left the room and walked downstairs. Well, she hopped. Slowly.

Daniel rushed forward, surprised to see her. "Miss Wellington?"

"Oh, hello, Daniel. Would you please find me some ice?"

"Yes, ma'am."

"Thank you. I'll be in the parlor."

Discovering a book full of gown patterns, Emma settled herself on the large sofa in the parlor and waited for Betty to help her with the ice. Less than an hour later, the butler announced she had a visitor.

"I do?"

"Yes, ma'am." Daniel turned and nearly bumped into Clayton, who apparently hadn't waited to be shown in.

Emma smiled with delight as she watched him fiddle nervously with his hat. He was absolutely adorable and her heart beat double-time.

"Emma, I'm sorry for barging in. I know it's late, but I had to make sure you were all right. I cannot apologize enough for what Richard did. If there was a way to take it back I would."

"Clayton. I'm fine. Please sit down." Emma waved to the chair facing the sofa. "Did you get your brother to the jail?"

Clayton took the seat and nodded. "Yes. I told Joe not to let him out or give him anything to drink. He's not going to be happy, but there isn't an alternative." Clayton ran his hands through his hair. "Emma, I'm so sorry."

Emma sighed. "You have nothing to be sorry about. Really."

Clayton smiled. "How is your ankle?"

"It hurts, but I think I'll live."

Clayton rose to his feet. "I brought something that might help" He stepped out of the room briefly and returned carrying what looked like crutches. "I cut the bottoms off, so I hope they'll be the right height."

Emma pushed to her feet. "Oh, Clayton, this is so thoughtful." She slid the crutches under her arms and tested them out. "They work great."

"That doesn't mean you should be on your feet," Clayton said as he helped her back into her chair. "But they'll at least give you some mobility."

"They are perfect. Thank you. Would you like to stay for a little while?"

"It's late, Emma. I should really take my leave."

Emma frowned. "Oh. I'll walk you out."

"No, please don't." Clayton stood. "Would the afternoon be acceptable for our buggy ride tomorrow? Jamie and I are meeting in the morning."

Emma nodded. "Yes. Are you sure you're still up to it?"

"Most definitely." He grinned as he lifted her hand to his lips. "Why don't I pick you up after lunch? Say, two?"

"That's fine."

He reached out and gently ran his finger down her cheek. "I'll see you tomorrow."

Emma shivered. "Good night."

* * *

The next day, Emma woke up in agony. She could barely open her eyes and the nausea threatened her ability to breathe. She was in the middle of one of the worst migraines she could remember. Hearing a knock at the door, she groaned when Jamie poked his head in. "Em, it's time to wake up."

"I need a bowl."

Jamie grabbed the bowl from under the pitcher and handed it to her. "Migraine?"

"Bad migraine," she grumbled.

"Do you have anything for it in your purse?"

"I have some of my migraine tabs in there somewhere, but I couldn't tell you where."

"I'll find them." Jamie rifled through her bag and found one of the foil packs. He handed it to her with a glass of water.

"Thanks. I think I just need to sleep for a little while, okay?"

"I'll let the staff know not to disturb you."

Emma took the medicine and gingerly lay back onto the pillows. "Can you also let Clayton know I can't go for a ride today?"

"Sure."

"Thanks." She pulled her comforter up and over her head and sank into the mattress.

* * *

Jamie closed the door and went back to his bedroom to find Sophie sitting in the bed, reading a book. "Weren't you on that page when I left?"

Sophie slammed the book shut. "Don't start. I'm bored Jamie. *Bored!* I cannot stand this another minute. Do you hear me? Not another minute."

"Ooh, the melodrama." He kissed her cheek.

"Did you wake Em?"

Jamie shook his head. "She's got a migraine, so she's going back to sleep. It looks like a bad one."

"Oh, no. When do you have to meet Clayton?"

He poured Sophie a glass of water and handed it to her. "He'll be here at nine."

"And how long will you be gone?" Sophie asked, her voice lilting suspiciously.

Jamie chuckled. "Don't even think about it, Ten-Cow. Betty and the rest of the household staff know you're not to get out of bed, and you are most certainly not allowed to go out to the barn." She threw the book at his head, but missed. Jamie bent to pick up the book with a grin. "Ten-Cow, is that a respectful way to treat a literary masterpiece?"

"It's a book on Victorian housekeeping," she said folding her arms and pouting.

Jamie chuckled. "You could probably learn a few things in there. Just make sure it's stuff you can do from bed."

"I can think of a few things," she said, raising her eyebrow.

"I bet you can." He ran a comb through his hair.

"I *am* going to check on Emma at some point."

"That's fine, sweetheart, just make sure you don't stay on your feet for very long."

She saluted him. "I'm not sure I like the lieutenant. Can we go back to the CEO?"

He laughed. "It's not like I didn't direct people as a CEO, honey."

"You just weren't as bossy in the twenty-first century."

He raised an eyebrow. "I didn't have a pregnant wife in the twenty-first century, either."

Sophie waved her hand with a groan. "Touché and all that crap."

Jamie sat on the edge of the bed and kissed her. "I love you."

"I love you, too. Even if you are a pain in the butt."

Jamie laughed and left the room. Clayton was waiting in the foyer when he arrived downstairs. "Good morning, Clay. Have you had breakfast?"

Clayton shook his head. "I haven't."

"Good. Neither have I. Join me?" Jamie didn't wait for an answer as he led Clayton into the dining room. "Emma won't be able to go for a ride today."

Clayton frowned. "Is something amiss?"

"She's got a pretty severe headache, but I think if she is able to rest today, she'll be fine."

Clayton shifted from one foot to the other. "Are you certain?"

Jamie chuckled. "She'll be fine, Clay."

They sat down for breakfast and Jamie organized a tray for Sophie, which he gave to Betty to deliver. Choosing not to linger over the meal, they left and rode out to the jail to take care of the Richard situation, arriving to hear bellowing from the inside.

Clayton groaned. "That sounds like my brother."

"Poor Joe."

They walked in to find Joe sitting with his feet up on the desk and a cup of coffee in his hands. He didn't seem to care at all that Richard was yelling obscenities at him.

"Good morning, Joe," Jamie said.

Joe gave a slight nod as he sipped his coffee. "Good morning, gentlemen."

"You bastards. Clay, get me out of here," Richard bellowed.

Clayton shook his head. "No."

Richard wrapped his hands around the bars and scowled. "What do you mean 'no'?"

"You're not leaving that cell until you are prepared to stop drinking."

"Go to hell, Clayton."

Clayton rolled his eyes. "I've already been there, Richard. You were playing the role of Satan. You're out of control and it has to stop."

Richard growled. "You know nothing, Clayton."

Clayton strolled to the cell and crossed his arms. "Let's just revisit what I do know, shall we? I know that your behavior toward the women we care about is unconscionable. I know that you have not been sober in months. I know that you pissed yourself while you were passed out drunk on your office floor, and I know that if you continue to drink, the President will not put up with this conduct."

Richard shrugged. "I can stop drinking whenever I want to."

"I beg to differ, Richard," Jamie said.

"What the hell are you doing here?"

Jamie glared at him. "I'm here to assist. You accosted my wife and my sister-in-law. I have a personal interest in you getting help. The bottom line is that if you don't, I may end up killing you myself."

Clayton stepped away from the bars. "Minister Cunningham has agreed to meet with you over the next week or so. I suggest

85

you take the help. Otherwise, your job, and your family will be lost to you."

Clayton turned and stomped out of the building. Jamie followed and they mounted their horses and took off back to the arena.

NINE

$\mathcal{A}$S CLAYTON PULLED his horse up in front of the arena, Michael came jogging outside waving a note in the air. "He's gone!"

Clayton dismounted and joined Jamie, who'd tied his horse to one of the rails. Jamie took the note from Michael and began to read, then swore.

"Who's gone?" Clayton asked.

"Topper's disappeared." Michael ran his hands through his hair. "He appears to have run off."

Clayton frowned. "Your nephew?"

Michael nodded. "He was told to stay close."

Jamie glanced up. "Where did you find the note?"

"On the desk in my office. He must have left it for me early this morning." Michael frowned. "That boy has always been trouble. It's no wonder his mother couldn't control him."

"Let's not jump to conclusions, Michael. Topper's changed." Jamie read the letter again. "The wording's strange—stilted, not flowing. And there are symbols here."

Clayton raised an eyebrow. "Are you thinking it might be some kind of code?"

"Possibly." Jamie crossed his arms. "I don't know. If it is, it's well over my pay grade."

Michael took the page from Jamie's hands. "Do you know what it says?"

Clayton held his hand out. "May I see?" Michael handed it to him and Clayton studied the writing. An alarm went off internally. He slipped the paper into an inner pocket and gave the men a curt nod. "I'll take care of this."

Jamie's eyes widened. "What do you mean, you'll take care of this? What does it say?"

Michael groaned. "We have to find my nephew, Clayton. My sister will not be happy to know he's run off again."

"I understand that, Dr. Wade." Clayton motioned to one of the soldiers to join them. "We will." Clayton turned to the young private who'd rushed to approach. "Please take a message to Andrew Simmonds. I need him to meet me here, immediately."

The young man saluted. "Yes, sir. Right away, sir."

Clayton turned back to Michael. "I need Andrew to look over the note. If Topper left it, then the symbols may point to exactly where he is."

"How can Andrew help?" Jamie asked.

"Andrew Simmonds was one of the best decipherers during his time in the field. If anyone can break it, he can."

"Well, when you find him, lock him up for a few days – that should teach him a lesson," Michael said.

Clayton raised an eyebrow. "I'll take that into consideration."

"Dr. Wade!" Hyram Jones, a young boy living with his mother close to three miles away, rode as fast as he could toward them. "Dr. Wade!"

Clayton grasped the reins of the horse as Hyram drew up and dismounted. "Dr. Wade. Come quick. Jed's had an accident."

"All right, son." Michael gestured toward the house. "I'll fetch my bag and follow you home."

Andrew pulled up soon after Michael left, and Clayton led

him back to his home. Jamie followed. "Jamie, Andrew and I can take care of this."

Jamie let out a snort. "Nice try. You'll need to get used to my presence, 'cause I'm not going anywhere."

"Clayton, Jamie's someone we can trust." Andrew gave a wry grin. "And he really won't go anywhere. He has a knack of finding out information, sometimes before anyone else does, and he's persistent."

Jamie shrugged. "That's one way to describe me."

Clayton sighed. "All right. Follow me."

* * *

After an hour of several different code cracking options in Clayton's office, there was one portion of the note they could not decipher. Clayton slapped the pages down on the desk. "I've never seen anything like this before. I thought I'd seen every code ever used." He dragged his hands down his face. "I'll wire Christopher and see if he can assist."

Jamie paced the room. "Is that a good idea? What if someone reads the wire? You never know who'll intercept something and pass it on. It could be dangerous, and I'm not convinced Topper just disappeared for some teenage fun."

Andrew shrugged. "His note indicates nothing different, Jamie. He even says that he'll return soon."

"I'm still not convinced he's disappeared for kicks."

A knock at the office door interrupted their conversation.

"Come in," Clayton called.

The housekeeper pushed open the door. "Sorry to interrupt, Mr. Madden. I have a letter for Mr. Ford."

Jamie reached out and took the envelope. He opened it and then rolled his eyes. "I need to get back to the arena."

Andrew rose to his feet. "Everything all right?"

Jamie sighed. "Yes. You two keep working on this, and we'll talk tonight. Will you join us for dinner?"

Clayton and Andrew nodded, and then Jamie was out the door.

Jamie made a run for the arena and scowled when he caught

sight of yellow skirts awfully familiar to him slip inside the barn. "Sophie Jane!"

She poked her head outside the door and grinned. "Yes, love?"

"You're supposed to be in bed."

"Hm, mm. So I heard. But no one could find you or Michael, so they came to me. Samson's going a little nutty." She gave a little wave and disappeared back into the building.

He followed her inside. "You need to get back to the house."

Sophie rolled her eyes. "I would if I could find Topper. Where is that little cretin?" She whistled for Samson who stood just inside his stall, snorting at the young soldier attempting to put a halter on him. "Samson, settle." She held her hand out and Samson trotted over to her. She gave him a sugar cube and patted his head. "Where's our buddy? Huh? Where is that Topper Wade, horse whisperer?"

"Sophie."

"What?" She slipped the halter over his head and then glanced up at Jamie.

"Topper's not here."

"What do you mean?" she asked distractedly as she led Samson outside.

Jamie took the lead out of her hand. "Ten-Cow, stop." Handing the rope over to one of the soldiers, he pulled her aside.

"Jamie, what's wrong?"

"Topper's missing."

Sophie gasped. "What do you mean, he's missing?"

"Come on back to the house, and I'll fill you in."

* * *

Emma groaned when the sun streaming in through her window and directly across her face waked her. She squeezed her eyes shut, but the spike of light pierced her skull, so she pulled the comforter over her head.

"Sorry," Sophie whispered. "I didn't realize the sun was that low." She closed the drapes, blanketing the room in darkness again.

90

"What are you doing in here?"

Sophie sat on the bed. "You need to eat. You can go right back to sleep, but you need to get something in your stomach and take one of your pills."

"I thought you were confined to bed."

"Oh, I am. But it's been a crazy day." Sophie patted the mattress. "Sit up and I'll tell you all about it while you eat."

* * *

On Sunday, Emma woke considerably more herself. Having been confined to bed for the entire day, she was relieved to find that not only could she see straight, she was also able to put more weight on her ankle. She climbed off the mattress, found the robe her sister gave her, and pulled it on. Grabbing her crutches, she walked across the hall and knocked on Sophie's door.

Sophie opened the door with her finger on her lips. "Jamie's still asleep," she whispered. "Let's go to your room."

Emma raised an eyebrow. "Are you allowed out of bed?"

Sophie nodded as they closed themselves in Emma's room. "Yes, I have the official okay from Michael. Thank God! I couldn't handle it anymore. I think after church I'm going to spend the day with Samson. How's your ankle?"

"It feels better. I don't think I could dance on it, but the swelling is down." Emma leaned against her bed. "The crutches help, too."

Sophie nodded. "That was really nice of Clayton.

Emma felt her neck grow warm as a blush started to form. "I know."

"What about the migraine?"

Emma smiled. "Completely gone."

"Great. Let's get ready for church. Breakfast will probably be on the table shortly."

Once they were dressed, they made their way downstairs and took their seats at the table.

"What are the plans for this afternoon, Nona?" Sophie asked.

"We'll have lunch as usual after services, but nothing else is planned. We have invited Clayton and a few others to join us for

91

dinner."

Sophie leaned across the table for the salt and glanced at Jamie. "Samson needs some exercise. Can you ride him today?"

Jamie nodded. "I'm sure we can work something out."

Emma salted her eggs. "Any word on Topper?"

Jamie shook his head. "None."

Michael waved his hand dismissively. "He'll come back when he's good and ready, and then I'll ship him back to his mother's."

Nona patted his arm. "Let's not be hasty, dear."

Breakfast seemed to be over before Emma finished her meal. She took one last sip of coffee as Jamie stood and started to gather everyone's outerwear. "All right, you two. Let's get ready."

It was getting colder, so the decision was made to use the large carriage. It seated up to six and was enclosed for warmth. Daniel had one of the grooms hitch up the horses and put blankets inside if they needed them.

"Where are your crutches, Em?" Jamie asked.

"I left them behind. My ankle feels really good."

Sophie raised an eyebrow. "Are you sure?"

At Emma's nod, Jamie helped the ladies in, then sat between Sophie and Emma. "I have to admit, I'm looking forward to a day out with my girls. It's been a long time."

Sophie patted his knee. "True. It's going to be glorious."

The carriage pulled to a lull behind several others at the church, waiting for passengers to climb down and join the small crowd milling in the front. Emma took the time to take in the gray brick structure of Paxton Presbyterian Church.

Sophie peered out the carriage window and sighed. "Isn't it adorable?"

Emma grinned. "Yes, very cute. Will you be telling me the history now or later?"

Sophie rolled her eyes. "Later, smarty pants."

Emma shrugged. "Just checking."

"Looks like they're letting us out here." Jamie pushed open the door on Sophie's side and climbed down. Holding his hand out, he lifted Sophie down first, then Emma. Michael assisted Nona, and then the couple went to speak with friends.

Sophie linked her arm with Emma's and they made their way up the walkway to join the other parishioners. Emma turned as someone touched her elbow.

"Good morning." Clayton removed his top hat and bowed over her hand.

Emma beamed up at him, her heart racing.

"Good morning, Mr. Madden," Sophie said.

"Good morning, Clayton. I'm going to steal my wife for a few minutes." Jamie winked at Emma and she nearly kissed him.

She turned back to Clayton. "Do you attend church on a regular basis, or is this a special occasion?"

* * *

Clayton tried to steady his heart as she continued to smile at him. "I have attended church my whole life. However, I formed a very personal experience only in the last few years. The war has solidified many of those beliefs." He stopped himself, surprised that he'd shared that much with her.

Emma's light blue day dress fit her perfectly. Her bonnet, a darker shade of blue, shielded her face slightly, but when she looked up at him, she took his breath away. Her cheeks were flushed red from the cold, and she radiated beauty, leaving him slightly tongue-tied. He cleared his throat. "You're walking easier. How are you feeling?"

"I feel very well, Clayton. Thank you. I heard you had some excitement yesterday."

Just then, the bell rang to let the parishioners know that services would begin shortly. Clayton held his arm out to her. "May I accompany you?"

"I would like that very much." Emma slipped her hand into the crook of his elbow.

They entered the church and made their way to the Wades' pew. Emma sat next to Sophie, and Clayton followed her into the row. Everyone stood for the first hymn and he wondered what her voice might sound like. He'd have to keep wondering.

She didn't make a sound.

Once the congregation was seated, the minister started to speak, but Clayton couldn't concentrate. Emma's thigh was pressed against his, and it distracted him to no end. When he glanced down at her, he grinned at her blush. She quickly turned back to face the pulpit.

The minister indicated where he would read from the Bible, and Clayton noticed Emma didn't have her own. He opened his, and held it out to her. When Emma reached to share, he brushed his fingers over hers. She looked up at him somewhat surprised and he smiled at her. Their hands were hidden beneath the book, and when she linked her pinky with his, Clayton relished the brief and secret touch.

Before he knew it, the service came to an end. He'd never remembered church being so captivating, and was disappointed that the morning was over. Unwilling to separate completely, he laid his hand gently on her back as they filed out of the pew, wishing for somewhere private. The congregation exited the church, and Michael stopped to introduce Emma to the minister. Clayton continued down the steps, but stayed close enough to hear her conversation.

"Welcome to our church, Miss Wellington," the minister said.

Emma shook his hand. "I enjoyed the service very much, sir. Thank you."

Once introductions were made, she filed out with the rest of the small crowd. Clayton waited for her at the bottom of the steps and held his hand out to her. She placed her hand in his and he escorted her to the family carriage.

"Are you going to join us for dinner this evening, Clayton? It will be a smaller group than usual," Nona asked.

"Yes. Thank you, Nona. I believe I will. I must check on Richard first, but I will come by after." Clayton assisted Emma into the carriage, mounted his horse, and took off towards the jail. He wasn't looking forward to the confrontation with his brother today.

* * *

Arriving home, Sophie and Emma went upstairs to change. Emma put on the same threadbare dress she'd worn on the train, and Sophie handed her a pair of breeches to put on under it. Emma held them up. "What are these for?"

"Just in case you want to ride." Sophie pulled on a light-yellow skirt and white blouse and then pulled her hair back and secured it at her neck.

Jamie knocked on the door and Sophie opened it. "Ready?" he asked.

"Yes!" they said in unison.

Emma followed the couple out to the stables. Sophie called for Samson and he whinnied to her as she approached his stall. As the sun rose higher, Emma realized that her surroundings seemed so normal to her. She wasn't missing the sound of her phone or feeling the need to keep in constant contact with anyone. She was spending an afternoon with her sister, playing with their horses… something they'd done together for years before, only, not necessarily in full period costume.

Emma dropped a brush in the tin bucket and peeked into Gentle Ben's stall. "Sophie, I'm going to watch Jamie ride. Are you coming?"

Sophie slid the brush down the horse's neck. "I can't. Samson goes nuts if I'm around and not riding him. He'll try to throw Jamie if I'm out there."

"Do you mind if I go?"

Sophie shook her head. "Not at all. Call me when Samson's ready to be brushed down."

Emma made her way outside and watched Jamie put Samson through his paces in the large paddock. Hearing the sound of hooves behind her, she turned, and her heart raced to see Clayton on a large gray Andalusian. "Good afternoon, Clayton."

"Good afternoon."

His grin made her legs weak and she reached out for a wooden slat on the railing. Jamie walked Samson to the fence and gave Clayton a quick nod. "Any news?"

Clayton leaned over the saddle and shook his head. "No."

"Topper?" Emma stared up at him and frowned. "Was he kidnapped?"

Clayton glanced at Jamie, who answered for him. "It doesn't look like it. He left a note that indicated he was hiding. We're just unsure where."

"Well, why aren't you scouring the countryside looking for him?"

Jamie gave a half-smile. "We're doing everything we can, Em."

"Kinda wish we had GPS, huh?" she said without thought.

"What is GPS?" Clayton asked.

"Ah…"

Jamie coughed and Emma's heart beat frantically.

"Ah… nothing." Emma waved her hands in dismissal. "I just made that up. Sounds silly now that I've said it out loud."

Jamie jumped from Samson's back and led him out of the paddock. "Emma does that sometimes. We love her anyway."

Emma bit her lower lip and sent a grimace of apology his way. "Yes. Thank you, Jamie."

Clayton didn't ask for any further clarification, which Emma was grateful for. He smiled and dismounted, tying his horse to the fence. "Do you ride, Emma?"

She nodded. "I do."

"Would you like to ride out to the lake with me? We still have several hours of light, and we'd make it back in time for dinner."

Jamie closed the gate and removed Samson's bridle. "You could ride Gentle Ben, Emma. I'd be happy to tack him up for you."

Emma let out a quiet squeal when Samson let out a trumpeted whinny and took off toward the barn. "Jamie! What are you doing?"

Jamie nodded toward the barn. "Look." Sophie stood just outside the large doors and Samson ate something from her palm. "He's her trained pet."

Emma wrinkled her nose. "You guys are crazy." She focused

back on Clayton. "Yes, I'd love to go for a ride with you."

Jamie made his way back to the barn and saddled the horse Sophie had been brushing down. Clayton had already mounted, which gave Sophie the chance to show Emma how to hide her breeches under her skirts. No one would be the wiser that she wasn't riding sidesaddle.

Emma followed Clayton away from the property and out to a dirt road that traveled east toward several groves of trees. They'd ridden about two miles when they came across a group of tents, and Emma was suddenly forced back to reality. They were in the middle of a war. A war that Sophie had somewhat romanticized when discussing it, but as Emma raked her eyes over the scene before her, she realized there was nothing romantic about it.

"Who are all those men?" she asked.

Clayton slowed to flank her as they walked their horses past the site. A few of the men waved, and Clayton nodded back. "These are part of your brother-in-law's unit."

Emma drew her eyebrows together. "But shouldn't they be off somewhere fighting? I understood the war was brutal and miserable. These men don't look like they're starving or lacking the basic necessities to live."

Clayton pulled his horse to a stop and stared at her.

Oh, Emma... you are an idiot!

"Um..." Emma frantically craned her head, looking for rescue of some kind.

"Emma."

Emma turned Gentle Ben and dug her heels in gently, guiding him away from Clayton. "This was probably a bad idea. I'll see you back at the barn."

She didn't factor in Clayton's reach. He gently took her horse's rein in his hand, effectively eliminating any escape, and smiled. "Where are you going?"

97

TEN

*E*MMA SHRUGGED AND stared down at her hands.

"I'll allow you your secret, Emma. However, one day you'll tell me everything. I have no doubt in that." He let go of her horse and shifted in his saddle. "Shall we continue our ride?"

With a nod, she gathered her reins and followed him again.

"Harrisburg is the largest training area for soldiers in the North, lucky for us. Although, Gettysburg was a close call."

She raised an eyebrow. "Really? Why?"

"From what we understand, Harrisburg was supposed to be attacked, but Lee called his men to Gettysburg instead. So far, we've been diligent enough in our patrols to ward off anything further."

Emma nodded. "I suppose it's a blessing in disguise having so many men in one place. You can effectively defend your position."

A man-made lake straddled both properties, and they rode the perimeter in silence.

Once they'd dismounted, Clayton led Emma to the edge of the water. "Emma, you ride very well."

Emma grinned. "Thank you."

"How is it that you are able to ride astride?"

Emma blushed. "You weren't supposed to notice that."

"Forgive me." He chuckled.

"Sophie and I have always ridden that way. We don't have brothers and our parents didn't seem to mind." Hearing rushing water, Emma gasped as they came upon a waterfall. "This is exquisite."

Clayton gazed out over the water. "I don't come here often enough, but enjoy it every time."

"How often do you make it home?"

"Twice since the war began. Usually it has only been for a few days. I haven't been home for this long in over a year."

Emma's eyes widened. "How did it go with your brother today?"

Clayton sighed. "Not well."

"I'm sorry." Emma slipped her hand from his arm. "Is there anything I can do?"

Clayton studied her for several seconds, then leaned down and placed his lips gently on hers. After her initial shock wore off, she wove her hands up to clasp them behind his neck, and opened her mouth for him. He wrapped his arms around her and pulled her body closer. He heard her sigh, and reluctantly broke the kiss. "I have wanted to do that since I first saw you in my stable."

Emma raised an eyebrow. "Really?"

Clayton nodded.

"Want my confession?" At his nod, she smiled. "That was the best kiss I've ever had."

"The best you've ever had?" Clayton frowned. "How many kisses have you had before that?"

Emma shrugged. "Not many, and certainly none like that."

"How many is not many, Emma?"

She raised an eyebrow in challenge. "Um, I'm not sure that's any of your business, is it?"

99

"It is if I am to court you."

Emma let out a quiet snort. "Who said I wanted to be courted?"

"I've just kissed you." He went back to rolling the rim of his hat. "I wouldn't have done that had I not intended to court you."

"I don't recall you asking if I would like to be courted."

"I rather figured it was implied." Clayton paused for several minutes before adding, "And I thought you'd be grateful."

"Grateful?" Emma snapped. "You can't be serious."

"I spent three days searching for you," Clayton said.

"I wasn't lost!"

Clayton mumbled something Emma couldn't make out.

"Is it customary that when a man says he's courting a woman, she simply bows at his feet and thanks him profusely for considering her?" She tried to keep her increasing irritation from her voice.

"The lady doesn't typically kiss back. Unless she's—" He abruptly stopped.

"Unless what, Clayton?"

"Never mind."

Emma gasped out loud. "Unless she's a *prostitute*?"

"Emma."

"That's what you were thinking, wasn't it? Oh, my *god*. Do you think I'm easy simply because I kissed you?" She shook a fist at him. "I should slap you here and now."

"Emma, don't be absurd. It was a wrong choice of words."

"You're damn straight it was. I hope you enjoy the rest of your afternoon, Clayton." She turned on her heel and started back toward the horses.

"Emma, stop."

"No. I'm afraid I need to meet with my pimp. He'll be wondering where his money is."

Clayton followed. "Emma!"

"No!" she yelled. "Huggy-Bear was very particular about how much time I could spend with you. You don't pay, you don't get to play. You messed with the wrong ho."

"What is ho?" he asked as he rushed to catch up with her.

100

"It's slang for prostitute," she snapped.

Clayton gently took her arm. "Emma, please stop. I apologize. It was a slip of the tongue, and absolutely not what I think. Will you forgive me?"

She pulled away from his touch and crossed her arms as she faced him. "This really isn't a good start to the courting process, Clayton."

"No, it isn't." He gently laid his hand on her cheek. "May I start over?"

Emma shrugged. "Knock yourself out."

"Miss Wellington, it would be my honor if you would grant me permission to spend time privately with you." He stroked his thumb along her cheek.

She leaned back. "You need to stop touching my face, it's distracting me."

"Is that a fact?"

"Yes. I can't concentrate when you stroke my cheek like that."

"That's quite inconsiderate of me, isn't it?" He kissed her.

She broke the kiss this time. "Clay, you're not playing fair."

"I didn't realize I was playing a game, Emma," he said earnestly.

She rolled her eyes. "What does courting involve, exactly? Is it an exclusive relationship?"

He nodded. "Usually, yes."

"Usually? But, not always?" She pulled her face away from his touch. "So, it could be that you're courting me here and some other woman in Washington?"

"No, Emma. I'm not interested in courting anyone else."

"You just met me, Clayton—"

"What does that have to do with anything?" he interrupted.

"—less than a week ago," she continued without missing a beat. "How can you say that you want to court me exclusively? You don't know me. I understand that we have a certain attraction to one another, but I'm not certain it constitutes an exclusive relationship."

Clayton failed to conceal his shock. "Are you saying you desire someone else?"

She crossed her arms. "If I did?"

"This would be a good time to tell me, Emma."

"Why? It's not like it's any of your business."

Clayton hissed.

"Clayton, explain something to me." Emma tucked her hair behind her ears. "When I say to you that I'm not sure you courting me would be the wisest thing, why do you jump to the conclusion that I must want someone else? Is it so foreign to you to think that perhaps I may not want to be in a relationship, that I would like to be single?"

"Would you like to be single, Emma?"

"Don't turn my words back on me!"

Clayton chuckled. "If spending time with me is not pleasing to you, please tell me, and I'll return you to your sister."

"You're enjoying this, aren't you?" she said, frustrated at her inability to mince words with him.

He smiled down at her and cupped her face. "A little."

"It's not that I want to be single. It's that I don't want to rush into anything."

"So, you don't want to be single?"

"Okay, now you're just being ornery," she said.

Clayton laughed. "Yes, now I'm just being ornery. We'll take it slow. I'd very much like to court you, but if you're not comfortable, I understand."

"I would love to believe in the fairy tale of love at first sight, but I just haven't had much luck with relationships in the past. That doesn't mean I don't want to get to know you better and it doesn't mean there's anyone else. I just think it's too soon to make a decision on exclusivity."

Clayton frowned. "Would you please explain what you mean when you say 'relationships in the past'?"

Emma didn't know how much she could say to him. She already felt like she'd revealed too much, but he was easy to talk to and there was no doubt she was attracted to him. Her heart wanted to jump in, but she'd been down this road before and

102

been hurt too many times, so she forced herself to wait. "Can we let that be a story for another day?"

Clayton smiled. "Another day... soon."

Emma nodded. "Soon."

Clayton frowned up at the sky. "I think it might rain."

"Really? The sky looks so clear."

Clayton pointed past her. "Not in the distance, it doesn't."

Emma wrinkled her nose. "No, it doesn't. Do you think it will snow?"

He shook his head. "It's too early in the season, but rain is a given." He held his hand out to her. "Let's head back to the house."

He assisted Emma into the saddle and then mounted himself.

They just missed the downpour as they pulled their horses into the barn. Clayton handed his horse off to the groom and then helped Emma from the saddle.

His arms tightened on her waist and he gave her a sexy grin before releasing her. Emma waggled a finger at him. "You better watch that charm if you're going to court me. I won't tolerate you looking at anyone else like that."

Clayton raised an eyebrow. "Are you saying you accept?"

"Ooh, I walked right into that one." Emma chuckled.

Clayton pulled her further into the darkness of the stables and kissed her breathless. "Will you do me the honor of allowing me to escort you to the Paxton Ball on Saturday?"

Her heart raced. "I'm not sure, Mr. Madden. What will all of my clients think?" She needed to get her emotions in check and humor was always her best weapon. She thought she heard him growl as he kissed her again. "Yes, Clayton, you may escort me to the ball."

She'd lost this round to his irresistible charm, and he smiled down at her in triumph. "Excellent."

"Don't you dare think you've won, Clayton Madden. I may enjoy your kisses, but that doesn't mean you're going to get around me every time."

"You admit you enjoy my kisses. I think that's a very good start." He took her hand and placed it on his arm. "I'll escort you home, and then I must change for dinner."

Emma paused at the barn doors and shivered. "I think we're going to need to make a run for it."

The rain fell in sheets, the ground potted with puddles as far as she could see, and Emma's heart soared. She loved the rain. She and Sophie both. They would ride for hours, despite protests from Alex.

Clayton frowned. "Perhaps I should rig up the covered buggy."

Emma snorted. "For a little rain? No way! It's beautiful." She grabbed his hand and started to pull him outside. "Come on, chicken. Let's go."

She lifted her skirts and started to run for the house, forgetting about her ankle. Clayton did not. He scooped her up just as she stopped and grabbed her leg.

"You forgot your injury," he accused.

Emma grimaced. "I did. That was really dumb."

"Dumb?"

Emma sighed. "It's an expression my sister and I use... it means, unwise."

He smiled gently and kissed her cheek. "Let's get you home."

When they arrived at the front porch, he set her on her feet, kissed her hand chastely, and then he was gone. She felt slightly dejected at the separation and hated the unfamiliar emotion. Emma made her way up to her room and peeled her wet clothes from her body. She'd left a note with the maid to inform Sophie she was going to lie down for a little while, so she knew she wouldn't be disturbed.

Stretching out on the bed, she put a pillow under her foot, her ankle now throbbing, and surprisingly fell asleep within minutes.

* * *

Emma woke to a dark room, and wondered what time it was. Lighting one of her bedside lamps, she found and took a couple of Advil, and then did her best to dress by herself. The clock on

104

the bureau said five, which meant over an hour until dinner. Problem was, she was hungry now.

Maybe Mary will have pity on me and let me have a snack.

She started her very slow descent down the stairs, but had to stop a few times to catch her breath, a little dizzy from the pain. She heard footsteps in the foyer and then heard her name. She looked up a little too fast and nearly slipped.

"Emma!" Clayton took the stairs two at a time. He reached her quickly and lifted her into his arms. "You overdid it today, didn't you?"

Emma squeezed her eyes shut and nodded.

"Let's get you downstairs." Clayton carried her into the parlor and set her down gently on the sofa. "Where are your crutches?"

"In my room."

"I'll have Betty fetch them." Clayton left the parlor and returned surprisingly quickly, Betty in tow. He set her crutches beside the sofa as the maid gave her a gentle smile and wrapped her ankle with ice she'd brought with her. Clayton grabbed a pillow and gently lifted her foot onto it. "How's that?"

"Better," she said and turned to Betty. "Thank you, Betty."

Betty nodded and then left the room. Emma frowned. "Why'd she leave the door open?"

"Propriety," Clayton said.

"Is she afraid of what will happen if the door is closed?" Emma whispered.

Clayton smiled. "Betty has always been a moral compass in the Wades' home."

"Is she concerned I'll ravish you?"

"The thoughts you put in my mind," Clayton said with a groan.

Emma giggled and relaxed back into the sofa cushions.

"Would you like some tea?"

Emma licked her lips. "I'd prefer whiskey."

Clayton chuckled. "I'll return shortly."

Emma leaned forward and gripped her ankle. The Advil hadn't even dented the pain, and she really just wanted to curl

105

up in a ball and sleep. Clayton returned with wine, and Emma wrinkled her nose. "No whiskey?"

He shook his head as he handed her the glass. "Michael's office is closed."

Emma downed it and then handed the glass back to him.

"Emma, that'll go to your head if you're not careful."

"That's the plan."

Clayton sat next to her on the sofa and took her hand in his. "Is it that bad?"

"Nope, I'm fine." She turned her head away, tears slipping down her face.

"Emma, it's all right to cry, you know."

Emma sniffed. "I'm not crying."

"I'm sorry, my mistake." Clayton squeezed her hand. "Why don't we find something to distract you?" He kissed her—and kept kissing her. Emma didn't want to stop. She shifted her body to pull herself closer to Clayton.

Her ankle twisted and she broke the kiss with a gasp. "Ow, ow, ow!" She squeezed his arms and pushed him away.

"Sorry." He wrapped his arms around her waist and pulled her up into more of an upright position.

Emma smacked the couch in frustration. "I hate this."

"You'll need to take it slow tomorrow." Clayton kissed her palm. "You don't want to miss the ball."

"Well isn't this cozy?" Jamie stood in the doorway.

"Hi, Jamie," Emma said.

Jamie made his way to the sofa and leaned over to kiss her cheek. "Did you overdo today?"

"I think so. The ice is helping, but I think I'll need to stay off it for a day or so."

Jamie nodded and sat across from them. "Yes, good idea."

"Where's Sophie?"

"She's dressing. She'll be down soon."

Daniel announced dinner and Jamie moved towards Emma. Clayton beat him to her. "I'll assist Emma," he said possessively and lifted her into his arms.

Jamie stepped away, and Emma smiled up at Clayton. "What

was the point of bringing me the crutches, if you're going to haul me everywhere?"

"Crutches? I don't see any crutches."

Emma glanced over his shoulder. "Where are they?"

"Somewhere safe." At her raised eyebrow, he whispered, "I wanted an excuse to get you in my arms." Clayton strode into the dining room and seated her at the table, before sitting beside her.

Several minutes later, a tired looking Sophie walked into the dining room. The men stood and Jamie made his way over to her. "Hi, baby. How are you feeling?" Pulling out her chair, he helped her sit.

"I'm fine. Just a little tired."

"Shall I prepare you a plate?" Jamie asked.

Sophie nodded. "Please."

Dinner was subdued and passed quickly. The day seemed to have sapped everyone's energy, and Emma could see her sister hiding several yawns behind her napkin. Once dessert had been cleared away, Clayton decided to bid everyone a goodnight.

Emma insisted on walking him to the door (well, she hobbled...slowly) and waited for Daniel to hand Clayton his outerwear. "Will I see you tomorrow?"

Clayton shrugged into his coat. "I will try."

That's all I get, really?

"Okay." Emma forced a smile.

Clayton glanced around the space quickly then tipped Emma's chin up gently for a kiss. Emma grasped the scarf hanging around his neck and leaned closer.

Then he was gone.

ELEVEN

OVER THE NEXT few days, Emma was ushered to and from the dressmakers. Normally it was something she enjoyed, but she couldn't seem to stop herself from missing Clayton. By Wednesday, she was thrust deep into a feeling she was unfamiliar with—insecurity.

She wasn't an idiot--she knew there was a war on and that Clayton's job was important, but she really thought he'd at least have sent a note or something to let her know he was thinking of her. That is, if he even was thinking of her.

"Em, I'm going out to the barn, would you like to come?" Sophie asked, when they returned home from the dressmakers.

"Sure."

"Did you hear the latest news? Apparently, Richard has been sober for almost a week. He's still in jail, but isn't fighting it anymore," Sophie said.

"Well I guess that's good, right?"

"Yes, I think it's very hopeful."

Emma frowned up at her. "Why do you care?"

"He's a good man when he's sober." Sophie sighed. "I care enough about him to want him to be healthy."

Emma rolled her eyes. "You're weird."

She followed Sophie into the barn and Sophie called for Samson. He whinnied and stuck his head out the stall door. Sitting on the hay bales outside the stall, Emma laid her crutches down and smiled up at her sister.

"I'm going to take him out in the yard for a bit. Are you going to come?" Sophie asked.

"Yes, I just need a minute."

"Okay." Sophie opened the stall and Samson followed her outside.

"Emma?"

Emma jumped from her seat when she heard Clayton's whisper echo in the dark. Her ankle twinged at the sudden movement, and she quickly fell back onto the hay. "Ouch."

He rushed toward her. "Are you still in pain?"

She shook her head. "Not as much, but jumping on it probably isn't the best way to help it heal." Clayton sat next to her and Emma raised an eyebrow. "Where have you been?"

"What do you mean? I've been here."

Emma scowled. "We're going with that?"

He took a deep breath. "It's been a difficult few days."

She pulled a piece of straw out of the hay bale and twirled it between her fingertips. "Do you want to talk about it?"

"I'm not certain that I can."

"Oh," she whispered.

A few strained moments passed.

"Any word on Topper?" she asked.

Clayton shook his head. "None. That's part of where I've been."

"What do you mean?"

He smiled gently. "I've been scouring the countryside."

"Oh."

Clayton lifted her hand to his lips. "What's amiss?"

Emma shrugged. "Nothing, why?"

"You're unusually quiet."

109

Emma pursed her lips. "*Unusually* quiet?"

Clayton smiled and kissed her palm.

"I'm fine." She pulled her hand from his, picked up her crutches, and rose to her feet. "I should get back to the house, though."

Clayton stood as well, confusion written on his face. "I'll walk with you."

Emma held her hand up and smiled. "No, I'm happy to walk back by myself. I'm sure you have more important things to do. I'll see you later."

Her stomach ached as she strode away. She wished she could run, but her pride—and her ankle—wouldn't let her.

"Emma!" She turned to see him jog toward her. "Stop."

She did. If she didn't, he'd ask even more questions she was unprepared to answer.

"Tell me what I've done."

Emma widened her eyes in surprise. "Why would you think you've done anything?"

He cupped her chin. "Perhaps because you're running away from me."

"Emma!" Sophie called.

Emma turned to see her sister waving her back to the barn. She pulled her face away from Clayton's touch and stepped back. "My sister needs me. Excuse me."

Without waiting for a response, she made her way to Sophie.

Sophie raised an eyebrow at her. "What's up?"

Emma shrugged. "What do you mean?"

Sophie squeezed her arm. "Clayton looks like a little lost puppy right now. I'm assuming you had something to do with that?"

Emma scowled as she whispered, "I haven't seen the man in three days. He doesn't call, he doesn't write. Nothing. He wants to be exclusive, but ignores me? I don't think so. Am I supposed to just jump into his arms now that he's decided to grace me with his presence?"

"He does have an important job, Em."

Emma shrugged. "Then he should get back to it, don't ya

110

think?"

Sophie chuckled. "Oh, Em, you have it bad for this guy."

"I don't," Emma insisted. "I just won't be treated this way."

"Doesn't look like you'll have to be. He's leaving."

She squared her shoulders. "Good."

Sophie hummed in suspicion, but rather than commenting, linked her arm with Emma's and they walked back to the house. "Let's have a bath and then dress for dinner."

Emma smiled. "I like how you're thinking."

Sophie led her upstairs while Betty organized the baths for them. As they arrived at Sophie's bedroom door, Jamie pulled it open. Sophie's eyes widened in surprise. "What are you doing here?"

Jamie held a piece of paper up and stepped back to let them inside. "I thought I'd give the note one more try."

Emma glanced at the note. "Hey, why do you have Navajo code?"

Jamie's eyes narrowed. "Excuse me?"

Emma took the letter from him and pointed at the non-deciphered part of the writing. "This line right here. It's Navajo. It's written in the style they used during World War II to get messages across."

"Emma," he whispered. "How do you know what this is?"

She shrugged. "Did you forget *everything* from history class? The Navajos were touted as being the reason we took Iwo Jima. Remember *Windtalkers*?"

"The movie you made us watch?"

Emma snorted. "Oh, please. The amount of times I had to sit and listen," she glanced at her sister, "or watch something relating to this." She waved her hands around the room.

Jamie shook his head. "Don't lump me in with that. You and your sister find something you like, and push yourselves to become experts."

Sophie giggled. "True story."

Emma grinned. "Guilty."

Jamie sighed. "Anyway, I guess I never picked up on *Windtalkers* being a conspiracy type movie."

Emma moved around the room, reading and rereading the note. "But the movie was a conspiracy in itself."

Jamie smirked. "Of course it was."

Emma pushed her glasses further up her nose and glanced up. "It was accused of being inaccurate and stereotypical, not to mention pushing the Navajo into a background role."

Jamie crossed his arms and raised an eyebrow. "Okay, so can you translate this?"

"I can try. Hannah and I did something like this in History class, but that was a while ago." She squinted at the page. "And I got a B."

Jamie dragged his hands down his face. "What did Hannah get?"

"An A, of course," Emma said distractedly as she scanned the letter.

Jamie leaned against the bed. "Of course."

Emma dragged her lower lip between her teeth and narrowed her eyes. "Something about a building for food. Um, a man with... a stripe... no, a scar. A man with a scar on his face."

"Building for food. Like a silo?"

Emma shrugged. "Could be." She pointed to a word. "This could be wheat. I'm not sure, though. I don't speak or read Navajo."

Jamie nodded. "You've certainly got us further than we were yesterday. You're amazing, Em."

"I know." She grinned. "Why do you have this, anyway?"

Sophie sighed. "Topper left it. The bigger question is how he knows code from eighty years in the future."

"No doubt." Emma chewed on her thumbnail. "Do you think he's safe?"

Jamie frowned. "I'd like to think he is. He's a smart kid."

Sophie shrugged. "He's got a rebellious streak and likes to push Michael's buttons, so it wouldn't surprise me if he's doing this just to get a rise out of him."

"What does Clayton think? Will you tell him about the code?"

Jamie shrugged. "I'm going to talk to Andrew in the morning. I might filter the information through him."

Any further discussions were halted when Betty arrived with staff holding buckets of water.

TWELVE

$\mathcal{S}$OPHIE WOKE EMMA early the next morning. "Rise and shine, Em. We're going riding today."

Emma sat up and yawned. "What time is it?"

"Eight o'clock." Sophie opened the wardrobe and gathered her clothes for her.

Emma flopped back onto the pillow. "Can't I just stay in bed a little while longer? Please?"

"Would you like some cheese with that whine?" Sophie giggled. "Isn't Clayton coming for breakfast?"

Emma yawned again. "Nona said he was."

Sophie crossed her arms. "I thought you'd be jumping out of bed with excitement."

"I'm too tired to jump anywhere."

"Did we keep you up too late?" Sophie settled on the edge of her bed. "I know dinner was a party and a half."

Emma snorted. "It was enough to send me to bed for a year."

Sophie smiled sympathetically. "Then why didn't you sleep?"

Emma sat up and wrapped her arms around her knees. "I don't know, Soph. I can't stop thinking about Clayton. All I want to do is spend every waking minute with him. What am I going to do when he has to go back to Washington? The thought makes me sick to my stomach. This just can't be normal, right?"

Sophie laid her hands over Emma's. "What can't be normal, sissy?"

"No one falls in love this quickly. I don't even know this guy, and he's ignoring me for no apparent reason. I hate it!"

"Oh, Emma."

Emma dropped her chin onto her knees. "I just don't want to make a wrong move, you know? I'm afraid that if I'm too honest with him, he'll run, but I hate feeling like I'm not telling him everything. And what about the future stuff? When should I tell him? Obviously, now is not the time, but do I keep it from him forever? This is crazy!"

Sophie gave her sister a hug. "I know it feels that way. You guys'll work it out, and you can talk to Jamie or me anytime. About anything, okay?"

Emma nodded. "Thanks, Sophie, I appreciate it."

"Now, let's get you dressed." Sophie stood.

"Are we riding right away? I'll put my jeans on if we are."

"Yep, jeans and maybe wear the yellow skirt and jacket. It's not as much material, so it'll be easier to maneuver," Sophie suggested. "How's your ankle?"

Emma climbed off the tall bed and stood for a minute. "It feels okay, other than weak. I'm sure it'll be fine for riding."

"Excellent. Just don't overdo."

"I won't," Emma promised.

The girls finished getting dressed and made their way downstairs to the dining room. Christine and Andrew were already there. Emma sat next to Christine and breakfast commenced with lively discussion about the Paxton ball, which was scheduled to take place the next day. There hadn't been a ball since the night Sophie and Jamie were reunited, so everyone was excited for the momentary escape from the war. Thirty minutes passed and still no sign of Clayton. Emma was a little irritated, but tried to shake off the feeling, knowing that his world didn't revolve around her.

The butler entered the room shortly before the meal wrapped up and let Emma know Clayton was in the foyer. She couldn't understand why he didn't just come into the dining room, but she figured it was probably a nineteenth-century thing. She stood and made her way to greet him. "Clayton?"

He turned and smiled down at her. "Good morning, Emma."

Emma frowned. "Are you all right? You look tired."

He removed his hat. "I'm fine."

"Why didn't you come into the dining room?"

He shifted from one foot to the other.

"What?"

Clayton rolled the rim of his hat. "Emma, I can't stay. I need to leave."

"Why? Where are you going? Wait, let's go into the parlor." She led him out of the foyer and into the parlor. "What's wrong?"

He laid his palm on her cheek. "I can't discuss it."

"You're so monosyllabic today. Why won't you just tell me what's going on?"

He took a deep breath. "I was given word that a friend was killed at Bristoe Station."

"Oh, Clayton, I'm sorry. Were you close?"

"Yes." He cleared his throat. "I need to leave now."

"Will you be back in time for the ball?"

Clayton shrugged. "I hope so."

"Well, all right then. Have a safe trip." She turned to walk out of the room.

"Emma." Clayton took her arm and turned her.

"What? If you need to go, you need to go."

"I'll return as soon as I can."

Emma sighed. "I get that you have a really important job and all, but there must be something you can share with me." He leaned down and kissed her. Emma wove her hands around his neck and melted into him. He broke the kiss, but kept her in his arms. "Clayton, you're going to have to open up to me at some point. Kissing isn't going to get you far for long."

Clayton chuckled. "We'll talk when I get back. I promise."

"Have you eaten?" she asked, admittedly trying to stall him.

"No, but I have no time. I need to get on the road."

"Let me grab you something to take with you." She patted his chest. "A few biscuits at least."

Clayton smiled tightly. "All right. I will take a few biscuits."

She rushed to the dining room, grabbed a napkin, and wrapped two warm biscuits in it. Sophie raised an eyebrow, but Emma didn't have time to explain. Clayton was already out on the porch, ready to mount up and leave. She handed him the food.

He kissed her cheek. "Thank you."

"Clayton?"

"Hm?"

"Wherever it is you're rushing off to, please be careful."

"I will." He gave her one last kiss and left.

Emma went back into the dining room and found Sophie and Christine waiting for her. Everyone else had gone on with their day. Sophie patted the chair next to her. "So?"

Emma sighed and took a seat. "All he said was that a friend was killed at something Bristoe?"

Sophie nodded. "Oh, right. It's the sixteenth today. The Battle of Bristoe Station took place on October 14. The Union forces won the battle, but the Confederates destroyed a railroad during their retreat."

Emma frowned. "Bristoe happened a couple of days ago?"

Sophie nodded. "Yes."

"Would it be likely that Clayton would have heard this quickly about the death of a friend?"

Sophie shrugged. "Well, there are telegraphs, and with the railroad, it wouldn't be impossible to get a message through. What are you thinking?"

Emma shook her head. "I don't know. I'm probably just overreacting. Are we going for our ride?"

Sophie stood. "Yes, we are. Christine, will you join us?"

She shook her head. "I can't today. I have to get to the hospital, but I would love to try and ride astride another time."

Sophie nodded. "Sounds good. We'll get you a pair of breeches and take you out next week."

* * *

Clayton knew he had to tell Richard. Timothy and Anthony Johnson had been their closest friends. Almost identical in age, the boys grew up together. Their sisters were close in age, as well, but Rose was sent off to boarding school shortly before the typhoid breakout. Clayton was relieved that she had been spared the disease; despite the fact they lost Lillian. Rose was only ten when Lillian died, and he knew it had been difficult to lose her best friend.

He arrived at the jail and made his way inside. Everyone was accustomed to seeing him now and he was greeted by name. Richard was surprised to see him. "Good morning, Clayton."

"Good morning."

Richard set down the Bible he was reading. "What's amiss?"

"Timmy was killed." Clayton removed his hat. "At Bristoe Station."

"Goddammit!" he snapped as he ran his hands through his hair.

"I'm riding out to meet Anthony now," Clayton said.

Richard's head whipped up. "Excuse me?"

"I got a missive to meet him."

Richard shook his head. "Clay, you can't. Have you forgotten that he fights for the other side? It's too dangerous."

"I have to, Richard. Tim was my closest friend."

"Clayton, you need to think. You'll be riding into enemy territory. You could be captured or killed. You're in with Lincoln's War Cabinet, which makes you a prime target. Try to be smart about this." Richard laid his hand on Clayton's shoulder. "Tony will understand. You know he will."

"I can't just sit here and do nothing. What about Rose? She's barely nineteen and has lost her big brother. She's probably alone and frightened."

"This is Rose Johnson we're talking about. She'll be fine. There has never been a craftier lady in Virginia. You know that. Tony will help her."

Clayton paced the small space. "I just need some time to think right now. I'll return later."

"Don't do anything rash," Richard called as Clayton left the jail.

Clayton mounted his horse and rode. He didn't have a destination in mind. He just rode. He found himself at the waterfall by the lake. Dismounting, he sat on his favorite rock overlooking the water and his mind wandered to years ago—years when life had been simpler.

Caught between little girl and little lady, his ten-year-old sister, Lilly, was her brothers' complete joy. Never without a smile, especially for Richard, she worshiped him. Clayton could understand why--he worshiped Richard as well.

Clayton had been called home from school to attend his mother's funeral. He hadn't been aware that she was sick, and now he would watch her body be lowered into the ground. He arrived home to chaos, his brother unusually stoic and more on edge than he'd ever seen.

They buried his mother, and then less than two weeks later, his father met the same fate. Now, Lillian lay in bed, fever ravaging her tiny body. Clayton had stayed for their father's funeral, and now he and Richard were forced to wait for their sister's. Richard sat vigil at Lillian's bedside as Clayton paced the tiny room.

"Dickie," Lillian rasped.

"I'm here, little bean."

"I am too, love." Clayton sat on the opposite side of her.

Lillian held out two ribbons.

"What's this, sweet?" Clayton asked.

"Please keep them and remember me."

Clayton didn't stop the tears as he nodded and took one from her.

"When you lay me in the box, will you put Lucy in with me?" she asked, referring to the rag doll she was holding. "I don't

want to be by myself."

"Lilly," Richard whispered. "Of course we will. Don't be afraid."

They were well past the hope that she might recover.

"Clay?"

"Yes, love, I'm here." He gently lifted her hand and lay her palm against his cheek.

"Tell Rosie not to cry for me and that she should stay away until this is done. I would hate for her to get sick."

"I will," Clayton whispered.

"I'm really cold."

Richard gathered her into his arms and held her against his chest. "Is this better?"

She never said another word.

Clayton shook himself from his reverie. Once they'd buried their sister, Richard and Clayton sold everything off, freed the slaves that hadn't already purchased their freedom, and made their way to Harrisburg. Away from Virginia, away from the south, away from the memories. In the midst of making their new life, Clayton found God and Richard found rage—and whiskey.

Now, faced with fear for his childhood friends, Clayton pulled out the frayed ribbon that he kept with his pocket watch and spent several minutes in prayer before he heard horses approaching. He turned to see Emma riding toward him. She dismounted quickly and rushed to him. "Clay? Are you all right?"

He watched Jamie and Sophie ride off in the opposite direction and gave Emma a tight smile. "I'm fine."

She frowned. "I thought you were leaving."

"Emma." He wasn't in the mood.

She smirked. "I warned you this morning that you were going to have to talk to me eventually. Now seems as good a time as any."

He pinched the bridge of his nose.

Emma crossed her arms. "Did you get everything done that you needed to?"

"No," he snapped.

"Nice try, Clayton, but snapping at me is not going to make me go away." She walked over to him and stood directly in front of him. "Did something else happen?"

He squeezed his eyes shut. "I went to see Richard."

"Did he say or do something?" She laid her hand on his arm. "Was he drunk again?"

He shook his head. "No. He's sober, which means he's also thinking straight."

Clayton picked up a stone and threw it toward the lake. It made three perfect skips across the water. Emma cocked her head to the side. "Is that why you're not wherever it was you were going this morning?"

"Yes."

She settled her hands on her hips. "Holy shit, Clayton Madden, trying to get information out of you is like getting blood from a stone."

"I can't talk about it."

She let out a quiet snort. "Is it work related?"

He turned his head away.

"I'll take that as a no."

"Damn it, Emma, I don't want to talk about it."

"Well, too bad." She grabbed his hand, pulled him over to a flat rock, and forced him to sit down. "What happened?"

Clayton took a deep breath. He'd never shared anything of a personal nature with a woman. Ever. The only men he'd ever trusted were Christopher and Timothy, and now one of them was dead.

Emma tipped his chin up. "Hi, it's me. Standing here. Not leaving."

Clayton looked up at her in resigned frustration. "I rode out to the jail to let Richard know about Tim."

"Okay. Then what happened?"

"Richard told me not to meet Anthony."

Emma threw her arms up in the air. "Who are Tim and Anthony? Is one of them your friend who died?"

121

Clayton nodded. "Yes."

"I know you're doing this on purpose, Clayton, but I won't be distracted. We can sit here all day and night if you want. I slept really well," she said, although he didn't fully believe her.

"Richard and I grew up with Anthony and Timothy Johnson. We were all around the same age and Timmy was my best friend. He was like another brother."

"In Virginia?"

"Yes. Anthony sent word of Tim's death and I was going out there to meet up with him."

Emma gasped. "Are you insane? Isn't that Confederate country?"

"Yes," he said sheepishly.

"Clayton, you're one of Lincoln's elite. Do you know what they'd do to you if you were captured? I doubt they'd kill you quickly."

He stood and started to pace again. "That's what Richard said."

"I can't believe you'd risk yourself like that!"

Clayton shrugged. "I didn't see it as a risk."

"How did someone so stupid get to your level?" she snapped.

Clayton bristled. "Excuse me?"

She grabbed his arm and punched his chest when he turned toward her. "What the hell gives you the right to do something so *reckless*? There are people who care about you, and you would leave them to mourn you without looking back?"

"Emma," he growled.

"Screw you, Clayton. All this time, I thought maybe we were getting closer. Sorry to have wasted your time." She stomped away.

"Emma, stop. This has nothing to do with you."

She turned back to him, beyond livid. "It has *everything* to do with me. I'm falling in love with you, asshole, but you planned to ride into enemy territory without any thought of your safety?" She realized she'd just revealed entirely more than she wanted to. She blushed crimson. "Never mind. Go home Clayton. I'll see you tomorrow at the ball."

122

"What did you just say?"

She started to run. "Go home, Clayton?"

Clayton caught up to her and gently pulled her into his arms. "Emma."

"I cannot believe you were so willing to get yourself killed."

"That wasn't the plan when I left this morning." He held her close. "Shh, you don't need to cry over me."

"Sorry, I didn't get that memo. I will cease crying immediately," she said sarcastically.

A low rumble emanated from his chest.

"Oh, good, now you're laughing at my pain. Maybe my pimp was right. I should just cut you loose. He keeps asking for his money and you haven't delivered, so—"

He kissed her. This was not the kiss of the courting couple, but the kiss of a man desperately in love with the woman he held in his arms. "What am I going to do with you?" he asked as he broke the kiss.

"Me? I'm not the one trying to get myself killed." She pushed herself away slightly, but he pulled her back into his arms and held her. She dropped her head to his chest. "Clayton, I really am sorry about your friend."

"Thank you." He gave her a gentle squeeze.

"What will you do now?"

Clayton shrugged. "I don't know. Richard's right about the danger, but I feel as though I should do something. I hate sitting around being idle."

She glanced up at him. "What would have happened if you'd received the news in Washington?"

"I'd have been ordered to stay local."

She looped her arms around his neck. "Well, then I order you to stay local."

"For now."

"Fine." She patted his chest. "But you'll tell me next time you plan to do something that stupid."

"Yes, Emma, I'll tell you. Now, where did your sister go?"

"They probably went back to find food." She wove her fingers with his. "Are you hungry? You could join us for lunch."

"I should check in with the men and make sure they're on track. If they are, then lunch would be appreciated."

She led him to the horses. "I'll need some help mounting, please. These skirts are impossible."

THIRTEEN

$\mathscr{C}$LAYTON HELPED EMMA onto her horse and the couple rode back to the arena. Jamie and Sophie were putting Samson back into his stall when they arrived, so Clayton lifted Emma down and then went off to the arena to check in with the men. Emma entered the barn to find a beaming Sophie brushing Samson down. "I take it the ride went well?"

Sophie nodded. "Yes, it was great. We took it easy, and I feel much better. How's Clayton?"

"He's fine. Getting information out of him, though, makes me want to rip my hair out. He is so monosyllabic."

"Think about his job."

Emma grunted. "I'm not talking about trade secrets, Sophie. I'm talking about personal stuff."

"He's a nineteenth-century man, Em." Sophie paused with her brushing and then patted Samson's withers. "Give him time. You'll bring him around."

"Maybe. Thanks for the privacy, by the way. I thought for sure you'd hover."

Sophie laughed. "Oh, believe me, I wanted to. You can thank Jamie for that. He made me leave."

Emma giggled.

"You summoned?" Jamie said from the doorway.

"We were talking about you, not to you," Sophie said.

"Well, Clayton and I will just have lunch without you, then." He turned to make his way back outside.

"Don't move." Sophie stepped out of Samson's stall and closed his door. "Our baby's hungry."

Emma followed and greeted Clayton, who was waiting for them by the arena. She was disappointed lunch was quick, and even more disappointed when Clayton didn't join them for dinner. He did send a note, so she chalked that up to progress.

"Is he not coming, Em?" Sophie asked after she received the note.

"Apparently not." Emma slapped down the note. "He didn't say why, of course."

"You've had a pretty emotional day. It would probably be better if you got a decent night's sleep. Tomorrow's going to blow your mind."

"Really, Soph? Blow my mind? Isn't that a bit melodramatic?"

She laughed. "You'll see."

"I am tired. I guess I'll see you in the morning." Emma headed to bed and tried her best not to obsess over her newfound insecurity.

* * *

Sophie woke Emma at nine o'clock the next morning. "Good morning, sissy. Time to wake up. Breakfast is over, but I brought you a tray."

"I'm not hungry."

"Really?" Sophie walked over to the side of the bed and looked down at her sister. "Em? What's wrong?"

Emma rubbed her eyes. "I didn't sleep well."

Sophie raised an eyebrow. "How come?"

"Because I'm an idiot who can't seem to control my emotions."

Sophie settled her hands on her hips. "Were you upset that Clayton didn't come for dinner?"

"Yes—and no. I mean, I get that maybe something came up, it's just that he's so freakin' vague about everything."

Sophie laughed quietly. "Oh, honey, you've got it bad, don't you?"

"I want to go home." Emma climbed out of bed and made her way to the bureau. "I can't do this anymore, it's too much."

"Emma Justine, you've been here for less than a month. You have more in you than that."

Emma poured water into the porcelain bowl on the dresser and set the pitcher down with a thump. "Please don't give me the whole 'we are Wellingtons and we don't run' speech! When does it stop, Soph? First mom, then dad, then you and Jamie? How much of this shit do I have to take before I'm allowed to say "enough?" I just want a guy who doesn't cause me any grief. An easy one, who doesn't make me feel like I'm losing my mind."

Sophie smiled. "No you don't."

"*Yes,* I do." She splashed water on her face and stared down at the bowl. "Forget it. I'll skip the ball tonight, not give him a reason why, and see how he likes it."

Sophie handed her a towel. "How about we take a ride this morning before we have to get ready?"

"Riding doesn't solve everything, Sophie."

"It does for me."

Emma snorted.

"And shopping does for you." Sophie grinned. "We could stop in at the general store and buy some new ribbon."

Emma took a deep breath. "Fine. Beats sitting around here doing nothing, I guess. I really *wish* I could get lost in a movie right now."

"Oh? Which one?"

"Terminator."

Sophie laughed. "Wow, you're feeling a little violent today,

127

apparently."

The girls dressed and made their way out to the stables. Emma went straight into the barn, while Sophie went to find Jamie to help her with Samson. Emma tacked up Gentle Ben and led him outside to wait for Sophie. Samson snorted and pawed the ground, obviously excited to have Sophie riding him again. Jamie had one of the cavalry horses ready and had a rare hour to spare to accompany them.

Once they were mounted, Emma noticed Jamie had a shotgun strapped to the saddle, along with a pistol strapped to his hip. She gathered her reins and stared at her brother-in-law. "Do you really need all that ammo for a quick trip into town?"

Jamie nodded. "I get that we're somewhat isolated and protected out here, but you two need to remember we're in the middle of a war. I'm not willing to take any chances."

Emma glanced behind her. "Is that why they're coming?"

Two soldiers rode up behind them and tipped their hats as they pulled their horses to a stop. Jamie dug his heels into his horse and moved toward the road. "Exactly. Stay close, please."

Sophie and Emma fell into easy conversation as they made their way to the bustling center of Harrisburg. Soldiers roamed the area, some on guard, others simply milling around. Jamie and the two that had accompanied them didn't leave Sophie and Emma's sides as they visited a few of the shops. It didn't take long for them to find the ribbons they were looking for, and Jamie decided it was time to head back to the house.

"It's only been an hour," Emma argued.

"Long enough to find your ribbons and return to the safety of the Wades'."

"I know you love to shop, Em," Sophie squeezed Emma's hand, "but you've gotten everything you needed. We can come back another day."

Emma sighed. "Okay."

Jamie helped them mount, and then the five started their trek back to the house. On the way to the main road, they passed the railroad station, and awareness sent a shiver up her spine. She glanced toward the large steam train to see Clayton standing on

128

the platform with a woman who was hanging on his arm—literally *hanging*. Emma's heart sank when she saw that she was beautiful and petite, with long dark hair that fell in perfect little ringlets down her back. A bit like Gwen.

"Who's that?" Emma asked Jamie.

He shrugged. "I have no idea."

Emma shattered. Here she was standing in her drabbest dress, with jeans on under it, no less. She hadn't done anything with her hair, and she just looked plain frumpy.

I am such an idiot.

"Emma?" Sophie whispered. "Let's get back to the house."

Jamie flanked Emma. "This is probably innocent. He may not even know her."

Emma snorted. "He must know her, because she's hanging all over him as though she were an ornament and he the Christmas tree. Clay appears to be completely at ease with her." She turned Gentle Ben away from the couple and gathered up her reins. "That's that, then. I should have known." She dug her heels in and took off toward home.

* * *

Jamie waited for close to an hour for Clayton to arrive home with the woman Emma referred to as "the Fluff." As he spoke with one of his men, he noticed Clayton's buggy pull up to his house. Clayton lifted the lady down, and she grasped his biceps and giggled at something he said. As Clayton carried luggage into the house, Jamie made his way to the front door. Clayton set the bags in the foyer just as Jamie stepped inside without permission

"Jamie?" Clayton frowned. "Is anything amiss?"

"I need to speak with you."

The Fluff removed her bonnet and gloves and set them on the side table. Her gaze raked over Jamie, assessing him with interest. Clayton smiled at Jamie and said, "Of course. May I introduce Miss Rose Johnson of Richmond, Virginia? She's a family friend and has surprised me with a visit."

"Oh, Clayton, I hope I'd be considered something more than a family friend." She giggled and spoke with a heavy southern accent.

Clayton raised an eyebrow. "Rose, this is James Ford."

Jamie gave a curt nod. "It's nice to meet you, Miss Johnson."

She held her hand out like royalty and smiled. Deep violet eyes crinkled at the corners as thin lips stretched over even teeth. "The pleasure is all mine, I'm sure."

Jamie shook her hand awkwardly, dropping it as fast as he could. Turning back to Clayton, he said, "The matter is somewhat urgent."

Clayton frowned. "Of course. We can meet in my office. Rose, would you please wait in the parlor? I'll send the housekeeper in with refreshments, and she can show you to your room."

"Thank you, Clayton. Y'are a doll."

Once Rose was settled in the parlor, Clayton led Jamie down to his office.

Jamie followed him inside and slammed the door. Clayton turned in surprise and was taken aback by the look of fury on Jamie's face. "Jamie? What's amiss?"

Jamie whipped off his hat and threw it on one of the chairs. "What the hell are you doing?"

"What are you talking about?" Clayton asked.

"Who is that woman?"

Clayton crossed his arms and raised an eyebrow. "She's a family friend. Her brother was just killed at Bristoe Station."

"Awfully chipper for someone whose *brother* has just died, don't you think?"

Clayton shrugged. "She was being polite. I have gone through two handkerchiefs since I picked her up from the train station. She has been inconsolable."

Jamie paced the small room. "Are you courting her, engaged, or in some other type of personal relationship?"

Clayton scowled. "What? No, of course not."

"Does she know that?"

"I don't like your tone, James." Clayton stood taller, his body rippling with control. "Just exactly what are you implying?"

130

"Have you made an agreement with her of a personal nature?"

"No, I have not. I am courting Emma."

"Does Rose know that you are courting my sister?"

Clayton shook his head. "I intended on telling her about Emma this evening. I would very much like the two of them to be friends."

Jamie snorted. "You're an idiot."

"I won't stand here and be insulted," Clayton snapped and turned to leave.

"Don't move," Jamie ordered.

"Then, say what you need to say and be done."

"Right now, Clayton, I'd like to beat the shit out of you."

"I welcome you to try," Clayton hissed.

Jamie took a deep breath. "Let me start from the beginning."

"Which beginning?"

"What are your intentions toward my sister?"

"I intend to marry her."

"Do you love her?" Jamie asked.

"I don't believe that's any of your business."

"Right now, it *is* my business, and I would suggest you answer the question."

Clayton shook his head. "I won't tell you something I have not told Emma."

"Fair enough. Exactly what does this Rose woman mean to you?" Jamie pressed.

"She was my sister's childhood friend," Clayton explained. "I suppose I see her as a sister. Similar to how you see Emma."

"How does Rose see you?

"The same way. As an older brother."

"Are you blind or just stupid?" Jamie ran his hands through his hair. "That woman wants you for far more than a brother."

"You have no idea what you're talking about. You've just met her." Clayton turned to leave again.

"You either finish this conversation with me now, or you'll never be allowed near Emma again," Jamie threatened.

Clayton turned slowly to face Jamie once again. "You could

certainly try and stop me."

He understood that this was what Jamie was supposed to do, protect Emma, but Clayton was not interested in having another man tell him how to handle her. She was his and no one would ever take her from him.

Jamie took a deep breath. "Look. I don't want to fight with you, Clayton, but you're going to lose Emma if you go down this path."

"What path?" He threw his hands up in the air. "I don't even know what the hell you're talking about."

"The Rose path. That woman is trouble. If you don't see it now, you will eventually, and it may be too late." Jamie picked up his hat. "My advice to you would be to speak with Emma, *before* you introduce her to Rose."

"I will consider your advice."

"Don't just consider it. Take it." Jamie jabbed a finger toward him. "If you hurt Emma, I will hurt you. Are we clear?" Jamie threw open the door of the office and stormed out, leaving Clayton behind to leash his anger.

Clayton stood for a few minutes, deep in thought, before he left his office and made his way to the parlor. He was a jumble of nerves and the surprise visit from Rose had not helped to calm him. He hadn't seen Emma since the day before and he missed her. He realized that Jamie was probably right. He must speak with her before the ball tonight.

"Clayton? Is something amiss?" Rose stood as he entered the room.

"No. Everything is fine, Rose. I need to take care of something urgent. Would you mind terribly if I attended to the matter?"

"Of course not," Rose said, although he could tell she was disappointed.

He noticed she didn't ask any questions or try to get information from him. Emma would have pushed until he told her everything, but Rose had been raised to be the perfect southern lady and not make waves.

He hadn't realized until that moment, how much he'd hate

132

being married to someone like that. Unable to locate Emma at the arena, he headed over to the Wades'. Daniel showed him into the foyer and then went to let Emma know he was there.

Daniel made his way back to the foyer. "I'm sorry, sir. Miss Emma is not receiving this morning."

Clayton frowned. "Is she ill?"

"No, sir, she is in fine health."

"Would you please tell her it's me calling?"

"I did, sir," Daniel answered.

"Is her sister at home?"

"I shall enquire for you, sir." Clayton watched as Daniel made his way back to the library. This time, it didn't take as long for him to return. "I'm sorry, sir. Mrs. Ford is also not receiving this morning."

"What the hell is going on, Daniel?"

Daniel's eyes widened. "I'm sorry, sir?"

Clayton pointed down the hall. "Go back there and tell Emma I want to speak with her now. I'm not leaving here until I do."

"Very good, sir." Clayton saw Daniel smile as he responded.

Daniel went back into the library, but before he could say anything, Clayton barreled through the door. "Daniel, I'll handle it from here if you don't mind."

Sophie stood. "Clayton, now's not a good time for a visit. Perhaps in a day or two, you could return.

Clayton noticed Emma held a handkerchief to her nose. "I'm not going anywhere, Mrs. Ford." He turned to Emma. "Emma, sweet? What has you so upset?"

Emma turned on him. "Don't you 'Emma, sweet' me, you dishonest pig."

Clayton sighed. "What are you talking about?"

"Just go away. I can't deal with you right now," Emma grumbled.

Clayton ran his hands through his hair in frustration. He took a deep breath and addressed Sophie. "Mrs. Ford, will you please give us a moment alone? I promise no harm will come to your sister." He saw Sophie's hesitation. "Sophie, please?" he implored.

Sophie glanced at Emma and then nodded. "All right. You have ten minutes."

Once she left the room, Clayton sat on the hearth in front of Emma's chair. "Emma, please tell me what I did. I'll fix it, I promise."

"You told me that you weren't courting anyone else."

"Sweetheart, I'm not."

"It didn't look that way to me!"

He raised an eyebrow. "Is this about Rose?"

"The exquisitely beautiful woman, with long dark hair and a perfect face, who was hanging all over you this morning? I hadn't noticed. Is her name Rose?" Emma looked away.

Clayton chuckled. "Emma, will you let me explain?"

She shrugged.

He reached out and slid her hair from her forehead. "Rose is Tim's sister. She showed up this morning and I'm still unsure why she's here, but she is my best friend's sister, and I couldn't very well turn her away. There is nothing untoward happening. Upon my word. Emma, please believe me."

She studied him for several tense seconds.

He rose to his feet. "Come here." He helped her stand and then pulled her into his arms. "I have never been interested in her, sweet, and even if I had in the past, once I met you, that all would have changed. I love you. No one will ever take your place in my heart." He held her for a few minutes before leaning down to kiss her.

"I don't want to be swayed by kisses, Clayton." She pushed away from him. "Have you told her about me yet?"

"No, I wanted to tell you about her first."

"She was all over you at the train station." Emma dragged the handkerchief through her fingers.

"I wondered how you found out about her."

Emma scowled. "She was supposed to be a *secret*?"

Clayton shook his head. "No, not at all. Her message came last minute with the details of her arrival, and I had hoped to

134

speak with you before the two of you met, that's all."

"She's obviously in love with you."

"I really don't think she's in love with me." Clayton delivered a patronizing smile. "I've known her since the day she was born. You probably just noticed how comfortable we are with each other."

"If she's the quintessential southern belle, Clay, then she *shouldn't* look so comfortable with you, right?"

Clayton ran his hands through his hair. "Where do you get your ideas from, Emma?"

Emma shrugged. "I don't know," she grumbled.

"Why don't you rest for a few hours?" Clayton paused for several seconds, before smiling. "I'll be here at seven to collect you."

"Alone?"

"Well, no." Clayton frowned. "Rose has indicated she would like to join us."

Emma took a deep breath. "Then perhaps you should just meet me there."

"Emma."

"What, Clayton? You have a guest. You should return to your guest. It's rude of you to spend so much time with me, when she's waiting for you next door." Turning quickly, she strode out of the library.

He chased her into the foyer. "Emma!"

She ignored him and stomped up the stairs.

* * *

Emma was awakened at four o'clock when Betty came in, followed by staff dragging two large copper tubs. Sophie joined Emma and brought bath oils into the room with her. There was an animated energy in the house, as everyone got ready for the ball. Even the servants appeared to enjoy the chaos. Betty left the girls and went to gather fresh towels.

"Are you excited?" Sophie asked.

"Sort of, I guess." Emma raised an eyebrow. "Isn't there a war on?"

135

Sophie sighed. "We forget sometimes, I must admit. We're very lucky to live where we do, because we have the greatest measure of protection."

"What about when we drive to the Paxton Mansion?"

Sophie patted her hand. "Don't worry, Em. There's not much going on in these parts, if I remember correctly, so we'll be safe."

Emma undressed and climbed into the heated water. "It will be nice to have some entertainment for a change."

Sophie smiled. "Gives you a great excuse to dance."

"Different kind of dancing, Sophie. But I think I can manage a waltz, even with my weak ankle." Emma frowned. "Am I allowed to waltz in this century?"

Sophie climbed into the other tub. "Yes, sissy you're allowed to waltz. Are you worried about the Fluff?"

Emma giggled. "Not worried, necessarily. Pissed off, mostly, but I do feel better after my nap."

Sophie reached over her tub set up next to Emma's and took hold of her sister's hand. "Well, you're beautiful, and once we get you in that dress, he won't be able to keep his eyes off you."

The door opened slightly and Christine poked her head in. Emma tried to cover herself with a washcloth.

"Hi! What are you doing here?" Sophie asked.

"I wasn't going to miss the dressing of Emma!" Christine stepped inside and closed the door. "I also wondered if perhaps you might need assistance washing your hair."

"Do we need a forum to take a bath in this century?" Emma asked.

Sophie grimaced. "Sorry, Emma."

Christine turned her back. "I'm happy to come back later."

Emma sighed. "No, it's fine. Just as long as no one else will be dropping by."

Christine grinned. "Just me. I promise."

"Emma has some special shampoo I'd love to use," Sophie whispered.

"What's shampoo?" Christine asked.

"Oh, it's special soap for hair. I'll give you some to try. It's

136

in that bag over there in the corner." Sophie pointed to Emma's carpetbag. "There's also another bottle called conditioner."

Christine gathered everything up and then assisted the girls with the washing and rinsing of their hair. "What's this container made out of?"

"It's called plastic. I don't know when it was invented," Sophie answered.

"Truly? Something historical and you don't know about it?" Christine retorted.

Emma laughed out loud. "We'll put this one in the history books. Sophie Ford does not know when plastic was invented. You miss the Internet, don't you, Soph? Admit it."

The girls collapsed into uncontrollable giggles. Betty came in with fresh towels and Christine quickly hid the bottles. Once Betty left, Emma found the lotion she had previously stowed, and Sophie oohed and aahed as she applied it to her skin.

"It has been entirely too long without lotion. They have oils that kind of work, but nothing as good as this. Here, Christine, try some." Sophie handed her the bottle.

Christine breathed in the cherry vanilla scent and then wiped some on her arm. "How remarkable that it soaks into the skin. I don't feel oily."

Sophie grinned. "I know, right?"

Emma had no idea what she was going to wear tonight. Sophie and Christine had kept it all a big secret. All three girls got their undergarments on first and then assisted each other with the corsets. They decided to get their hair coiffed before they got into their gowns.

"We should do my hair first," Sophie suggested.

"Won't Emma's be easier?" Christine asked.

"Believe it or not, no," Emma interjected. "Sophie's hair has always been easier to style. It's more versatile. Long and gloriously curly. Ah, if only."

Sophie giggled. "And I feel that way about yours. Perfectly straight and soft."

"Very well, Sophie. Take a seat." Christine wove burgundy

ribbon through her curls and pulled her hair up at the sides, leaving her ringlets to cascade down her back.

"What are we going to do with my hair?" Emma asked wistfully.

"Oh, my sweet, sweet sister. You are in the presence of greatness. Christine can do anything. You'll see." Sophie quickly fixed Christine's hair in a simple chignon and put her ribbons over her crown, leaving them cascading down her back.

Christine's gown was deep green velvet and Emma knew the color would be perfect with her strawberry blonde locks.

"Your turn, Em," Sophie said.

Emma sat down at the vanity as Sophie and Christine discussed what they would do with her hair. Sophie suggested they do a partial French braid design on each side of her head, bringing the sides together in a simple chignon, which they would wrap with the ribbon matching her dress and choker. They swept her bangs to the side for a softening effect, even though it wasn't the style of the day.

The girls then pulled out the most exquisite dress Emma had ever seen. It was an ice blue silk just a slight shade lighter than her eyes. Emma gasped. "Sophie, that's incredible."

They helped her with her hoops and then guided the skirt over her head. The top was off the shoulder and came to a V at her waist. It was low cut and fit her perfectly. The bottom of the skirt had been adorned with a dark blue velvet ribbon, in an intricate loop pattern, and the sleeves of the top also had the design. Her slippers were dark blue velvet, which matched the ribbon.

"Come see in the mirror," Christine said.

Emma grimaced and tried to adjust the top so not as much showed. She was fighting a losing battle. "Could there be any more Cleveland?"

"Just wait until you see mine. With the pregnancy, they seem to have grown two sizes in a month."

Christine and Sophie climbed into their gowns. Emma couldn't get over the opulence. Velvet? In wartime? How was that even possible?

"I thought that during the war, you couldn't get the basics, let alone extras." Emma said.

"That's very true for the South. It's much easier in the North," Sophie answered. "This came from France, I believe. Madame has special fabrics shipped in once or twice a year."

There was a knock at the door and Jamie poked his head in when the all clear was given. "Are you girls ready?"

Sophie motioned for him to come in and she let out a low whistle. "Baby, you look incredible."

Jamie was dressed in his full lieutenant uniform and had pulled his long hair back into a simple queue. "Not as incredible as you three. You are exquisite."

"What time is it?" Christine asked.

"It's six-forty. Everyone has gathered in the parlor for a glass of wine before we leave for Dr. Paxton's."

Emma followed everyone down the stairs and into the parlor.

Introductions abounded and Emma was handed a glass of wine. Andrew kissed her hand and Emma gave him a cheeky grin. When he'd apologized to her, she'd played the offended damsel, even though it was virtually impossible to stay angry with the man. He was so much like Luke, with his easy way and genuine spirit, Emma folded within minutes, and they'd become fast friends.

She took a sip of her wine and tried to calm her stomach. Just as she took her second sip, Daniel announced the arrival of Clayton and his guest. The Fluff walked through the door first and looked beautiful in her pink satin and lace. Emma nearly dropped her wine glass, anger surfacing at the fact he'd ignored her request to meet her at the party.

Clayton followed Rose into the room and Emma's breath left her body. Her anger was joined by total, complete, and unadulterated lust. Was it possible for a man to be beautiful? He was so handsome in evening black and his hair was swept back from his face, rivaling that of Orlando Bloom in Pirates of the Caribbean.

Clayton made a beeline for Emma and the crowd seemed to part for him as he walked toward her. He smiled deeply and lifted her hand to his lips. "Good evening, Emma. You look beautiful."

Emma pulled her hand away. "I thought we were going to meet there."

The rustle of skirts interrupted their private conversation, and then, "Clayton, darlin', we should get going."

Emma let out a quiet hiss, and Clayton gave her a secretive smile. "Rose Johnson, may I introduce to you Emma Wellington? Emma, sweetheart, this is Rose. She is Timothy's sister."

"It's nice to meet you, Miss Johnson. I'm sorry for your loss," Emma said graciously.

Rose stared at her strangely, but Emma saw the southern training in her surface after a few tense moments. "Thank you, Miss Wellington."

Clayton introduced Rose to the rest of the family, leaving Andrew for last. "Rose, this is Andrew Simmonds. He will be escorting you this evening."

Emma and Rose gasped. Rose narrowed her eyes, and if looks could kill, Clayton would have been dead ten times over.

Andrew took Rose's hand and his fingers flexed when Rose tried to pull away. "Miss Johnson, it'll be my honor to escort you this evening. May I say, you look lovely? That is a beautiful shade of pink." He glanced over his shoulder at Emma and winked.

Emma smiled. The rest of the family filed out of the parlor, but Clayton held Emma back. "Shouldn't we join them?" Emma asked.

"In a minute."

As soon as the parlor was empty, Clayton pulled Emma into his arms and kissed her senseless. She laid her hands on his chest and grasped the lapels of his jacket, almost in a desperate attempt to keep from fainting. Finally coming to her senses, she broke the kiss. "You weren't supposed to be here."

"I'm not so easily deterred, sweetheart." He kissed her again. "I have wanted to do that since the moment I walked in here and saw you in that exquisite dress."

She smiled up at him, not altogether steady on her feet, still grasping his jacket. "Well, that makes two of us. You look entirely too handsome in formal attire."

Clayton stroked her cheek. "I'm sorry for being insensitive today. I was so surprised by Rose's visit, I wasn't thinking straight."

"Thank you for that." Emma smiled. "I forgive you."

Clayton lowered his gaze. "I wonder if you might need a shawl throughout the evening."

Emma glanced down and then let out a quiet snort. "Is it scandalous?"

Clayton grimaced. "I wish I could say it was. However, you are the height of fashion, and it's simply my own bias."

Emma knitted her eyebrows together. "Your bias?"

Clayton rubbed her back absently. "Yes, I will not be allowed to monopolize you all evening, and I'm not looking forward to your effect on the other men present."

Emma raised an eyebrow. "Ooh, there will be other men present?"

Clayton kissed her and was rewarded with Emma's sigh. "If they begin to turn your head, sweet Emma, find me, and I will remind you who's important."

Emma grinned. "I'll keep that in mind."

"For now, let's enjoy the ball." He gave her a wolfish smile. "I intend to show you off to everyone."

FOURTEEN

CLAYTON TOOK EMMA'S hand and led her out of the parlor. They ran into Jamie as he walked back through the front door. "I'm the search party."

Emma laughed. "We're coming."

Clayton assisted her into the carriage and then climbed in after her. The others had gone on ahead, so it was just the four of them. Clayton sat next to Emma and smiled as he took hold of her hand and lifted it to his lips.

As the carriage moved, Jamie leaned forward. "What happened with Rose?"

Clayton chuckled. "I spoke with Andrew earlier today. He owed me a favor."

Sophie grinned. "Yes, I'm sure it was a huge imposition for him to escort a beautiful woman to a ball."

"And keep her busy for the duration," Clayton whispered.

Emma's head whipped up. "Seriously?"

"Yes, sweet." Clayton kissed her palm again.

Emma's heart soared and she melted against him with a sigh.

* * *

Arriving at the Paxton Mansion faster than originally expected, Sophie and Emma were in awe as they drove up the driveway toward the house. The large brick home loomed atop a large hill, in the exclusive Allison Hill area of Harrisburg. Four white columns formed a welcoming portico, and a porch covered two sides of the home. The home and outbuildings sat on a hundred and forty acres, and had sweeping views of the Susquehanna River and Blue Mountains.

"Have you never been here, Sophie?" Emma asked.

Sophie shook her head. "I've never been invited."

The carriage came to a stop and Clayton jumped out first, followed by Jamie. As Emma gripped Clayton's hand, she took a moment to take in the scene before her. His gentle squeeze brought her focus back to him, and she caught his smile as he lifted her off the step and placed her hand into the crook of his elbow.

"This is amazing, Clay," Emma whispered.

He leaned down with a smile. "Yes, quite."

Emma glanced back at Sophie and then let Clayton lead her up the stairs of the porch and through the front door. The large crowd in the foyer swallowed them, and the guests made their way slowly through the receiving line. Emma saw that Christine and the Wades had arrived just moments before; they were just ahead of her party in the line.

Dr. Stephen Paxton was a surgeon at the hospital based just outside of Harrisburg. He was at the head of the receiving line, and seemed to linger a little longer than etiquette would deem appropriate when Christine reached him. He held her hand perhaps a little too long and stared at her just a little too deeply. "You are beautiful."

Christine blushed. "Thank you, Dr. Paxton."

"Stephen, please."

Emma giggled quietly, especially when one of the ladies behind them cleared her throat, prompting Stephen to break contact

143

with Christine. Emma squeezed her sister's elbow and whispered, "Do I see a love match?"

Sophie raised an eyebrow. "Christine thinks he's just being polite."

Emma grinned. "How long do you think it'll take him to make his move?"

Sophie shrugged. "Who knows? I'm still shocked by how oblivious Christine is to the whole thing, but I have a feeling he won't wait for her to figure it out."

"Ladies," Jamie admonished in a whisper.

Emma was overwhelmed with the sights and sounds of the nineteenth-century ball. Little nuances of light and sound that could so easily be missed. Tonight she didn't want to miss a thing. Aware of Clayton's hand possessively on her back, she leaned into it more than once as they waded through the line.

After they had introduced themselves to their host, Clayton gently took hold of Emma's elbow and led her into the ballroom. Emma gasped—again. Clayton smiled down at her and Sophie took hold of her sister's hand. "Isn't it magnificent?"

"Yes," Emma whispered.

Exquisite fabrics and colors adorned the nineteenth-century ladies, while the men were either in uniform or formal black. Lit sconces lined the walls, along with strategically placed candelabras on the piano and buffet tables. The scent of fresh flowers mingled with the harvest décor, and the room was a mix of opulence and comfort Emma could have never imagined.

"Let's find a table," Clayton suggested and pulled the group through the crush.

Christine's mother took the seat closest to the window and smiled up at them. "I'm going to sit things out tonight, I think."

"Are you certain, Mama?" Christine asked.

"Yes, dear. I'm happy to watch you young people enjoy yourselves."

Sophie sat next to Miriam and patted her hand. "Well, I can't dance worth a lick, Miriam, so I'll sit with you, if that's all right."

Emma chuckled. "That's an understatement, don't you

think?"

"We'll just tell people you're sitting it out because you're pregnant," Jamie whispered.

Sophie grinned. "Thank you."

The musicians started to play "Les Lanciers," and Clayton pulled Emma onto the floor for a Lancers Quadrille. He assumed, of course, that she could dance, because what nineteenth-century woman couldn't?

This was an area Emma excelled in, and even though her expertise was not in these types of dances, she had learned them all at one point in her training, and could fake it if necessary.

Emma saw Rose corner Jamie by the refreshment table, and by the frown on Jamie's face, he didn't seem pleased by whatever it was she was saying. As the song ended, Clayton led Emma from the dance floor and she guided him towards Jamie.

They arrived to see Rose lay her hand on Jamie's arm. "Bless your heart. I would love a glass of champagne.

Jamie pulled away from her and handed her a glass then excused himself. "I promised Mrs. Simmonds a glass of champagne."

Andrew showed up a few seconds later and apologized profusely. "Forgive me, Miss Johnson for my inattention. I was pulled away by an old friend. It won't happen again."

Rose wrinkled her nose and didn't comment.

* * *

Clayton escorted Emma onto the dance floor one more time, and when the song was over, he went to find champagne for them. On his way back from the refreshment room, Rose cornered him. He scowled. He was going to have to have a conversation with Andrew.

"Clayton, darlin'. I didn't think I would ever get you alone."

"You don't have me alone, Rose." He moved to walk away. "I must get back to Emma."

Rose scowled. "Emma, Emma, Emma," she snapped.

Clayton rolled his eyes. "I'll speak with you later, Rose."

She grabbed his arm. "Clayton, wait. I need to speak with

you about Timmy. He gave me a message just before he died."

"And you're telling me now? Here? You've had plenty of time to tell me before tonight. Why now?"

"Clay," she whined.

He turned slowly to face her. "What did he say, Rose?"

"Let's just step in here, and I'll tell you." She pulled him inside one of the side rooms that appeared to be a library of sorts.

Clayton shifted, his senses on alert. "What's the message, Rose?"

He didn't want to be in a private room with this woman. He didn't want to be in a private room with any woman other than Emma.

Rose indicated one of the chairs in the small office. "Sit, Clayton, this might take a little bit of time."

He shook his head. "I'd prefer to stand, thank you."

"You just have to make everything difficult, don't you, Clayton? And to think, we've always seen you as the amiable one." Rose stroked her hand down his chest.

"Rose, do you have something to say, or are you trying to keep me away from Emma?"

Just then, Andrew walked through the door. "Well, there you are, Miss Johnson. I thought I'd lost you."

"Apparently not," Rose hissed slightly under her breath.

"Some soldier you are," Clayton whispered for his ears only.

"Slippery like an eel, this one," Andrew retorted.

Andrew escorted Rose out the door and back into the ballroom. Clayton returned to Emma and pulled her out on the dance floor for a waltz. He wanted any excuse to get her into his arms and hold her close.

Emma frowned up at him. "Is everything all right?"

He pulled her a little closer. "Rose just tried to corner me in the library. She said she needed to pass on a message from Tim, but I think that was a lie."

Emma shuddered. "She's up to something. I don't know what, but there's something not right about her."

"I think she's simply mourning the loss of her brother."

"Watch her." Emma frowned. "I'd hate to have to hurt the

perfect little princess. But, I swear, if she continues to touch you as though she's entitled to, I may just have to."

Clayton chuckled. "So violent, sweet."

She smiled innocently as he continued to lead her around the dance floor.

When the dance was over, Clayton led Emma back to Sophie. He kissed Emma on the cheek, and made his way to the terrace outside to join Jamie, Michael, and Andrew for a cigar.

Sophie squeezed her hand. "You looked so good out there, sis. I'm envious."

"Thanks." Emma took a sip of champagne. "I've decided you are going to learn to dance, Sophie. Christine and I will help you, right, Christine?"

"Absolutely," Christine answered.

Sophie shook her head. "I'm not teachable."

Emma grinned. "*I* haven't taught you yet."

Sophie waved her hand dismissively. "You won't be able to, either. I guarantee it."

"Thanks Men's Wearhouse," Emma retorted.

Sophie giggled and then explained to Christine about advertising taglines. Emma glanced around the room and realized someone was missing. "Where's Rose?"

Christine shrugged. "We don't know. She said she was going to the ladies' sitting room, but hasn't returned."

Emma scowled. "There is something off with that woman."

"Yes, I agree," Sophie said.

Rose magically appeared seconds before the men returned, which sparked even more distrust in Emma. She didn't have much time to dwell on it, though, as Clayton pulled her out for yet another dance.

"Isn't there a rule about dancing with the same woman three times in a row?"

"Is there? I invite anyone to try and enforce it," he said in warning. "How's your ankle?"

Emma narrowed her eyes. "You ask me now, after three dances?"

Clayton grimaced and paused. "You're right. I'm sorry. Is it

147

too much?"

Emma pushed him back into the waltz. "I'm fine. I would have told you if I wasn't."

The dance ended sooner than Emma would have liked, and she reluctantly let Clayton lead her back to the table. Sophie raised an eyebrow as she sat down.

Emma smiled. "What?"

"There are several other men who would like to dance with you."

Emma's eyes widened. "There are?"

Sophie nodded.

"Then why haven't they asked me?"

Sophie giggled. "Every time they get close, Clayton scowls at them and they scurry away."

"Shut up," Emma whispered.

Sophie turned and patted Jamie's knee. "Jamie, watch Clayton. See that soldier? He's been eyeing Emma all night. I think he's going to ask her to dance. Let's see what happens."

The young soldier had almost reached the group, when Clayton made a possessive move toward Emma and gave him a look of warning. The soldier turned on his heel and walked the other way. Jamie chuckled.

"Clayton," Emma admonished.

"Yes, sweet?" he asked innocently.

Emma rolled her eyes. Sophie turned it into a game. Three within ten minutes, and now a fourth approached.

"He doesn't look as young, maybe he'll get through," Jamie said.

"Not a chance," Sophie said.

Jamie grinned. "I bet you a fifteen-minute foot rub, he won't be intimidated."

Sophie shook his hand. "You're on."

Emma scowled at her sister as the soldier approached. Handsome, with dark hair and a very serious mustache, he seemed confident as he caught Emma's eye. Clayton made his move and it didn't even faze him. He stopped before Emma and bowed. "Ma'am, would you honor me with the next dance?"

Emma wasn't sure what to do, so she looked at her sister, and then at Clayton. She could tell that Clayton was not happy, but he couldn't object. He had to let her go. Emma nodded and then stood and followed the man onto the floor.

"Clayton, sit. She'll be fine." Sophie laughed at his obvious discomfort.

Clayton wouldn't sit though. He kept his eyes on her the entire dance, pacing his way around the outer reaches of the dance floor. Emma looked up at her partner and smiled politely as he cleared his throat. "My name is Lieutenant Gregory Payne."

"Nice to meet you, sir." Emma glanced at Clayton and then back at her partner. "My name is Emma Wellington."

"Are you new to the area, Miss Wellington?"

Emma nodded. "Yes."

"Where do you come from, originally?"

"Why?"

"How is it you know Clayton Madden?"

She shivered at his tone. "That seems like an awfully personal question, sir."

"Forgive me."

She felt more and more uncomfortable as the dance went on. He would pull her closer and she would attempt to push him away, but he would keep trying. When the song ended, they were on the opposite side of the ballroom from her family. She curtsied to him and he bowed, then immediately took her elbow, and began to lead her away. "Sir, I should get back to my family."

Gregory paused. "I thought you might want some punch before we returned."

Emma shook her head. "No, thank you. I would like to get back to my party."

"Of course." He gripped her arm and led her the wrong way again.

"Let go of me." Emma couldn't stop the shiver when she tried to pull away from him, but he tightened his grip. "Get your filthy hands off me," she hissed.

Gregory's expression grew cold, and Emma swallowed. He said nothing as he dragged her into a secluded alcove.

149

"What are you doing?" Emma squealed.

"Shut your mouth," he snapped.

"I'll scream."

He yanked her toward him and glared down at her. "You will do nothing of the sort."

"Unhand her," Clayton ordered from behind them.

Emma sighed in relief at the feel of Clayton's hand on her lower back. She leaned into him and tried to tug her arm away from Gregory. He didn't release her right away, and when Clayton inserted his body between the two of them, Emma whimpered when Gregory's hand tightened.

Clayton grasped Gregory's wrist and did something... she didn't know what... but Gregory groaned and his hold was broken.

Clayton reached behind his back and pushed Emma gently away without breaking eye contact with Gregory. "I said unhand her."

Gregory rubbed his wrist and scowled. "We were simply getting punch."

"If you come near her again, I'll kill you." Clayton grabbed the front of his shirt. "Do you hear me?"

The man nodded and then was gone.

"Are you all right?" Clayton asked in concern.

"I think so." Emma struggled to catch her breath. "I told him I wanted to go back to you, but then he pulled me in here. All through the dance he kept asking me all these personal questions and... it made my skin crawl."

Clayton kissed her hand. "You're safe now."

"Any idea what he wanted?"

Clayton shook his head. "There's something strange going on, and I think we should get you home."

Emma nodded. "I'm fine with that. As long as you'll still stay once we get home. I feel as though we haven't gotten to talk all night. Or other things."

Clayton chuckled. "What other things?"

Emma smiled up at him and winked.

Clayton directed Emma back to the group. Rose pursed her

lips as they arrived at the table. "I do declare, Miss Wellington, you are as white as a ghost."

"I'm fine, Miss Johnson. Thank you."

Rose continued to fuss over Emma, and Clayton pulled Jamie aside. Jamie agreed it would be best to return home, so with the promise from Andrew to keep Rose occupied, Jamie and Clayton gathered up the girls' cloaks and gloves and ushered them out to await the carriage.

Emma shifted from foot to foot as they waited for their ride. Clayton wrapped his arm around her and kissed her temple. "Cold, sweetheart?"

"Freezing." He removed his heavy coat and wrapped it around her shoulders. Emma sighed. "Thank you. Much better."

The carriage inched forward and pulled up in front of them just as rain began to fall. Once they were on their way, Emma sank further into Clayton's side.

"Are you all right, Em?" Sophie asked.

"Yes, just tired. Something's off, and I can't quite put my finger on it, but I'm too tired to think right now."

Sophie leaned forward. "Em? Did you drink too much?"

Emma snorted. "Four glasses of champagne is not too much."

Clayton glanced down at her. "Four?"

Emma shrugged. "I couldn't find the whiskey."

Sophie sighed. "Your humor abounds, I see."

Emma smiled. "My ankle was bothering me, and I liked the champagne. I'm not drunk. Just kind of tired."

Jamie frowned. "Still four glasses over several hours shouldn't make you so tired."

Emma shifted slightly. "Maybe it was the fifth that did me in."

"Emma!" Sophie slapped her palm to her forehead.

Emma giggled then hiccupped. "Come to think of it, it was kind of cloudy. I only took one sip... it tasted weird. Kind of like the tea Gwen gave me."

"Laudanum." Clayton filled in the blanks, then lifted Emma's chin. "Who gave you the fifth glass?"

Emma wrinkled her nose. "Isn't that like an opiate?"

Sophie squeezed her knee. "Emma, focus. Who gave you the last glass of champagne?"

Emma yawned and then mumbled, "Rose."

FIFTEEN

C LAYTON SHIFTED HIS weight when Emma sagged beside him. He wrapped his arm around her and settled her against his chest. She sighed and he kissed the crown of her head. She fit perfectly in his arms. The new development didn't sit well with him, but Sophie assured him that despite the fact the laudanum probably made her sleepy, she hadn't taken enough of it to hurt her.

The trip home took close to thirty minutes. By the time the carriage rolled to the front door, Clayton's arm tingled after being stuck in the same position for the duration. Jamie assisted Sophie out of the carriage first and then Clayton tried to wake Emma.

Kissing her cheek, he whispered, "Emma, we're home."

"Hm?" she grumbled sleepily.

"Come on. I'll help you down and then carry you into the house."

Emma smiled behind closed eyes. "Gallantry is alive and well."

Clayton jumped down and faced the door. As Emma leaned out, she stumbled off the carriage step. "Easy, sweetheart." Clayton caught her and lifted her into his arms.

She looped her hands around his neck and promptly fell back to sleep. Holding her closer, he carried her inside. Sophie and Jamie had removed their outerwear, and Sophie swept her hand toward the parlor. "Let's talk for a little while."

Clayton glanced down at Emma and frowned. "I'm not sure we'll get much out of this one."

"Even if she wasn't under the influence, she'd probably still be asleep." Sophie glanced up at Clayton. "Clay, don't worry. Truly, she'll be fine. She loves to sleep in the middle of it all. I swear that girl can sleep anytime, anywhere. I used to be so jealous of her." Sophie sighed. "I have to have optimal conditions in order to snooze."

Clayton followed Sophie into the parlor and sat on one end of the sofa as he kept Emma in his arms. Sophie helped her stretch out with her head on his lap and laid a blanket over her. Emma barely stirred. Clayton stroked her arm as Jamie sat in one of the chairs opposite them. Sophie handed the gentlemen a glass of port and poured some water for herself.

"Clayton, what's happening with Rose? I agree with Emma and Sophie. I think she's up to something," Jamie said.

"I can't imagine what." Jamie and Sophie glanced at each other. Clayton frowned. "What are you not telling me?"

Jamie leaned forward. "Do you think she might be spying?"

Clayton shook his head. "No, absolutely not."

"Clay, you're part of the War Cabinet. I think she's trying to find information," Sophie argued. "Plus, the whole business with Topper."

"Rose doesn't know Topper. No," Clayton snapped. Emma groaned, and Clayton lowered his voice and stroked her arm. "Rose Johnson would never betray our friendship."

Sophie sighed. "Clayton, think. She shows up unannounced two days after her brother is killed. Wouldn't it have taken her longer than that if she was traveling from Virginia? All of a sudden, she's asking all sorts of questions and going through your

154

personal things at home."

"How do you know that?"

Jamie squeezed Sophie's knee and gave her a quick nod. Sophie sighed. "Hattie told me."

"That doesn't mean anything. She'd just arrived; she was probably searching for something that she needed."

"In your bedroom?" Sophie asked.

Clayton shrugged. "She may have gotten turned around. Perhaps she thought she was in the guest room."

Jamie's eyes widened. "Seriously, Clayton?"

Clayton swore, which seemed to shake Emma from her slumber. She sat up with a groan. "What's wrong?" she asked, stumbling over her words.

Clayton took her hand and gave it a gentle squeeze. "I'm sorry, Emma. I didn't mean to wake you."

She yawned. "Did Jamie give you the note?"

"What note?"

Jamie sighed. "The note from Topper. Emma deciphered more of it."

Emma rubbed her eyes and nodded as she focused on Clayton.

He shifted to face her. "You did? How?"

Emma shrugged. "Um, I don't know. Logic, I guess."

"I took the note to Andrew, Clayton. We were going to speak to you about it tomorrow," Jamie said.

"I'm exhausted." Sophie rose to her feet. "I think I'm going to go on up to bed."

Sophie kissed her sister. "Clayton, why don't you stay for a little while? I know you and Emma haven't had much time together."

"I'll go with you." Jamie gave Clayton a quick nod. "Don't ignore what's right in front of you, Clayton."

Sophie grabbed Jamie's hand and the couple left them alone. Emma folded herself further into Clayton's arms. "I could stay like this forever, you know."

He gently cupped her cheek and leaned down to kiss her. Emma wove her hands through his hair as she opened her mouth for him and the kiss became more intense. The blanket slipped lower and her abundant cleavage seemed to beckon Clayton. He ran his fingertips along the neckline of her low-cut dress and she let out a sigh. He broke the kiss a few minutes later and realized how easy it would be to go further.

"Emma, we need to stop," he said as he breathed heavily.

"I know." She shifted slightly in order to sit up more.

"Sorry, sweetheart. If we don't stop now, I'm not sure I'll be able to."

"I know." She let out a frustrated sigh as she sat back onto the sofa.

Several minutes passed before Clayton said anything. "How did you decipher the note, Emma?"

Emma shrugged. "I noticed some of it was written in Navajo."

"How would you know how to read Navajo?"

"I don't. I just know a word or two." Emma narrowed her eyes. "Why do I feel as though I'm being interrogated?"

"I'm simply confused. I don't mean to make you feel like a suspect." Clayton took a deep breath. "I'm sorry."

Emma pulled her legs onto the couch and stretched out on her back with her head in his lap. "Tell me about Tim."

"What would you like to know?"

She reached up and stroked his cheek. "Whatever you'd like to tell me."

Clayton swept her hair from her forehead. "Our parents had small plantations next to each other. We were unique in that we shared the slaves and their quarters."

Emma frowned. "You had slaves?"

"My *parents* had slaves."

"How many slaves did you own?" She tried to keep the disgust out of her voice.

"About a hundred between the two families."

Emma covered her mouth with her hand.

"Sweet, Richard and I freed every one of them before we sold the property. He and I never agreed with the holding of human beings in bondage."

156

Emma nodded, visibly relieved.

"Our families had been there for what seemed like forever. My father was born in the main house and all of us were born there too. Our two families tended to overlap each other with children. Richard was born, then Anthony, then Timothy, then me. They had another brother who died when he was just six, then came our baby sister Lillian, followed two months later by Rose."

"How sad," Emma whispered.

"We were with each other day in and day out, with the natural order of ages falling into place. I think Richard and Anthony butted heads the most out of all of us. They are polar opposites when it comes to politics, trade, women, you name it, and they constantly argued. I was closer to Tim. He was like a brother to me, and we chose the same school to attend and had the same friends. 1853 was the year it all changed. Tim and I arrived home to find that a typhoid breakout had ravaged our plantations, along with a few others in the vicinity. Our parents succumbed quickly to the disease, so did Lillian."

Emma wrapped her hand around his forearm. "What about your friend's family?"

"The Johnson's came through, except for their mother. Rose wasn't home. She'd been sent off to boarding school before this all happened, so she was safe. But we lost everything."

"I'm so sorry."

He forced a smile and shook his head.

"What did you do after that?"

"Richard and I decided to move to Pennsylvania, away from the memories and away from the slavery we so objected to. We freed the slaves, as I said. All that survived, anyway, and sold the plantation. Tim and I kept in touch through the years, but we didn't see each other again for close to five years. I saw the three of them just before Lincoln was elected, but haven't seen any of them since."

"Wow." Emma smiled. "When you tell a story, you tell a story."

He leaned down and gave her a quick kiss. "I should go."

Emma sat up. "I feel like we haven't spent enough time together."

Clayton rose to his feet and held out his hand. "I know. It's been a long and exciting day, but we'll have more time tomorrow."

"How will that happen with Rose here?"

He tweaked her nose. "I will work something out, Emma."

"When do you have to leave?"

Clayton grimaced. "Soon. I received a wire today from Christopher. Now that Richard's doing better, the President will not allow further leave."

Emma's eyes filled with tears.

"I'm sorry. I wasn't going to tell you until tomorrow. I wanted to make tonight unforgettable."

She sighed and followed him into the foyer. "Well, you succeeded," she grumbled.

He slid his coat on and wrapped his scarf around his neck. "I'll say goodnight here, sweet. It's cold outside."

Emma raised her head for one of his unforgettable kisses and then he was gone.

* * *

The distant sound of gunfire brought Emma out of her slumber. Then her door flew open and Sophie's voice cut through the rest of the fog. "Emma, get up."

"What's wrong?" she rubbed her eyes and yawned.

Sophie rushed to her bedside table and lit the lamp. "We're not sure, but we need to get dressed and be ready for anything. Wear your jeans. We might need to make a quick run."

Emma pushed her fatigue away and jumped from the bed. Splashing water on her face helped a bit, and she threw her clothes on as fast as she could. Her heart raced, unused to being jarred awake by guns.

"Emma, are you decent?" Jamie called from the hallway.

"Yes. Come in."

He stepped inside and handed her a pistol.

"Wh-what? Why?"

158

"Point and shoot, Em. You'll only get one chance. Try to remember that it pulls slightly to the right."

Emma's hands trembled as he showed her how it worked. "Am I really going to need this?"

"I hope not. Grab as many blankets as you can and follow me."

Emma slid the gun into the waistband of her jeans and pulled the quilts from her bed.

Sophie bumped into her in the hallway, a bundle of bedding also in her hands. "We're going to prepare the basement just in case we need shelter. There are escape options from there."

"What's going on?" Emma's voice shook and she tried to clear the fear away.

"We don't know. The guns aren't supposed to come this close. It's possible rebels have broken through the Union lines."

"What does that *mean*?"

"I don't know. Just follow Jamie's lead. We'll figure it out together."

Emma grabbed Sophie's arm. "Jamie's a CEO, not a freakin' Green Beret!"

"Shh," Sophie hissed. "I understand you're scared, but remember where you are." Sophie softened her tone. "Follow me, sissy. We'll be fine."

Emma nodded and forced back her tears. She followed Sophie down the stairs and toward the back of the house. The stairway to the basement had two entrances: one outside underneath storm doors, and one in the kitchen. A group of servants headed for the kitchen and the girls followed.

Maneuvering down the dark narrow steps was difficult at best, but with her hands full of blankets, Emma found it especially hairy. She bumped into Sophie as she took the next steps and heard her sister's frightened gasp. "Sorry."

"It's okay. I caught myself."

Emma grimaced. "Do you know where you're going?"

"Sort of."

Emma frowned. "Great."

Mary's voice cut through the grumbles of the staff as Emma

stepped off the last step. "Blankets over here, please."

Mary Jones was the Wade's cook and could only be described as a genius with food. She was tall and thin, and Emma had agreed with Sophie's opinion that she reminded her of a flamingo. She had the countenance of a strict governess and her dark brown hair, peppered with gray, added to the severe persona.

Emma couldn't see in front of her feet, so she had no idea where "over here" was. Before she could ask, her arms were relieved of her burden and she was staring up into the face of Clayton. She let out a breath of relief. "Thank you."

He handed the blankets off to one of the staff and then led her to a somewhat secluded corner of the basement. "I can't stay, sweetheart. I just wanted to make sure you were safe."

She grabbed his hand. "What's going on?"

"We're not entirely certain. If you are instructed to come down here for shelter, do not leave until I collect you."

"But—"

He squeezed her hand. "Emma, promise me."

She nodded. "I promise, but what are you going to do?"

"Clayton!" Jamie called.

Clayton kissed her cheek quickly. "I have to go. Stay with Sophie."

He took off toward the storm door entrance and rushed up the stairs. Emma glanced around the room and located her sister standing at the bottom of the stairs, ushering people to where they needed to be. Emma joined her. "What can I do?"

"Find out from Mary if she's gathered enough food and water for everyone, please."

"Okay." Emma turned and made her way to Mary, who was giving orders to a few of the maids. "Mary?"

"Yes, Miss Wellington."

"Sophie wants to be sure you have all the food and water that you need."

Mary nodded. "We'll be fine for several days."

Emma gasped. "Several days? You don't really think it'll come to that?"

"One can certainly hope not."

Emma's heart raced. "Well, if you need help with anything, please let me know."

"Sally – put those candles over there, not where we can start a fire," Mary snapped and rushed to assist the maid.

"I'll just be over here, then. In the corner. Counting the cobwebs," Emma grumbled and sat down on an upturned crate.

Sophie joined her a few minutes later and held out her hand. "The snow's started, so it's going to get much, much colder. Let's hang out in the parlor. The fire's been stoked, and I'll bet Mary's organized something yummy to eat."

Emma gave a half-smile and stood. "Okay."

Sophie led her up the stairs and into the main hallway. "How are you holding up?"

Emma shrugged. "Fine, I guess. I wish I knew what was going on."

"You never were good with surprises."

Emma snorted. "We're calling this a surprise situation?"

"Maybe not. I know how you feel. The staff have everything under control, so we just get to sit back and be good little girls, which means, don't interfere."

Emma sighed. "Where's Nona?"

"She's probably directing traffic... or planning a party of some kind for when this is over." Sophie took her hand and squeezed. "Everything's going to be fine, Em. It's probably nothing, and the guys will have it all sorted before we know it."

"Jamie's optimism is rubbing off on you."

Sophie sniggered. "Not really. I'm just trying to say something positive out loud. Secretly, I think these men are going to burn the house down."

Emma groaned as they stepped into the parlor. "Let's hope we get out before that happens."

"Sophie?"

Sophie grabbed Emma's hand and squeezed as they both stalled at the sound of Topper's voice from the other side of the room.

"Topper! What are you doing here?" Sophie rushed to the

window.

"Those men are after me." Topper slid from behind a heavy curtain. "I didn't know where else to go."

"Where have you *been*?"

"I hid in the silo at the edge of town."

Emma gasped. "I was right."

"You better not have done this just to make your uncle angry." Sophie grabbed his arm and pulled him away from the window. He started to sit down, but Sophie shook her head. "You're filthy, bud. Nona will kill you if you get dirt on her settee."

Emma smiled sympathetically. "Are you hungry?"

Topper nodded. "Starved."

"I'll fix you a plate."

Sophie squeezed his chin. "Are you hurt?"

"No." Topper leaned away from her hand. "Just hungry."

Sophie crossed her arms. "You could have been killed, Christopher. What were you thinking?" He shrugged and Sophie narrowed her eyes. "You're going to have to start talking now. I'm not going to let you keep a secret that causes all this chaos. When Jamie gets back, you're going to tell him everything."

"It won't make any difference."

"If you're in danger, he can help…" she raised a finger in accusation, "…and if this *was* just a game to irritate your uncle, then that'll be an entirely different conversation." Sophie flopped onto the sofa. "You cannot wish this away."

Emma handed Topper a plate. "Here you go."

Topper smiled. "Thank you, Emma."

A door crashing just outside the parlor brought Sophie to her feet.

"Tear the house up, men! Find him!" a loud voice boomed.

SIXTEEN

$\mathcal{T}$OPPER SWORE AND dropped his plate on the side table. Sophie grabbed his arm. "In here." She led him to an oversized piece of furniture that had two doors at the bottom.

Topper raised an eyebrow. "I'll never fit in that."

"Check the parlor!"

"Get in there," Emma hissed.

Topper forced his body inside the tiny space and Sophie closed the doors. She turned the key in the lock and dropped it into her pocket. Just as she stepped away from Topper's hiding place, the parlor door flew open.

A large man in a Confederate uniform raked his eyes over each one of them slowly.

Sophie let out a squeal and rushed to her sister. "What do you want with us?"

"Tell me where the boy is," the man demanded.

"What boy?" Emma stood taller and tried not to notice the angry scar down the man's face. Or his cohort. She felt sick.

163

His bearded lip stretched across crooked teeth in a sinister sneer. "The boy y'all are hiding."

Sophie squeezed Emma's hand. "There's no one else in here. I don't know what boy you're referring to."

He waved his pistol to the left. "Move away from the window, ladies."

Emma stepped slightly in front of Sophie as they did as he asked.

"Check every inch of this room," the soldier drawled. "Destroy it if you have to."

Seconds passed before one of the men made his way to the cabinet. He jiggled the door and turned to the officer. "The doors are locked, Lieutenant."

The lieutenant waved the gun at Emma. "Open it."

Emma swallowed. "I can't."

He stepped forward. "What do you mean, you can't?"

Emma tried a nonchalant shrug, despite the fear coursing through her veins. "The cabinet is usually locked," she lied. "I don't have a key."

"Well, who does?"

Sophie stepped out from behind Emma. "Only the lady of the house and perhaps one of the maids. But you can't really think he would hide in there... how would he fit?"

He moved to stand in front of the girls. "Well, now, y'all seem quite nervous. Perhaps you're hiding him somewhere else."

"We're nervous because you're waving guns at us," Emma snapped. "You've checked the room. The person you're looking for isn't here."

"Maybe there's valuables in that cabinet." He turned to the soldier who'd discovered it. "Break it open."

"No!" Sophie rushed toward it.

"Turn around slowly with your hands in the air."

Emma's focus went to the parlor door. Clayton and Jamie stood with pistols drawn, Andrew and Richard directly behind them.

Clayton glanced at her and then back at the lieutenant. "I

said, put your hands in the air."

The lieutenant took a deep breath, but before he could react, Clayton had closed the distance and aimed his gun at his heart. "You try to move and you'll be dead before you twitch." The man knew he was outgunned. He dropped his pistol and directed his men to do the same. While Clayton and Jamie kept guns on the men, Richard and Andrew tied their hands and led them out of the house.

Clayton holstered his pistol and pulled Emma into his arms. "Are you all right?"

Tears streamed down her face. "They didn't hurt us."

He stroked her cheek. "Are you certain?"

She nodded and wrapped her arms around his waist. "Yes, I'm fine, Clayton."

Sophie rushed to the cabinet and unlocked it. Topper slid from his hiding place and began to take deep breaths.

"Where the hell did you come from?" Jamie snapped.

"Jamie," Sophie admonished and rubbed Topper's back. "Are you okay?"

Topper nodded. "Yes, I think so. I tried not to make any noise."

"You did great," Sophie assured him.

"I think I might have broken a few of my aunt's plates."

"We'll deal with that later. I would imagine she won't mind." Sophie groaned. "I'm sorry I thought you were playing a game."

Topper shrugged.

Jamie grabbed the nape of his neck. "You have some explaining to do, son."

"Ow, Jamie." Topper tried to move his head away. "I'll tell you everything, I swear."

"One question. Were you in trouble, or were you playing a game?"

"That's two questions," Topper retorted.

"Christopher Aaron Wade," Sophie snapped.

Jamie glared at him.

Topper sighed. "I was in trouble. I thought I could handle it myself."

"We'll discuss it shortly. I need to assist with the prisoners. These were the last of the rebels." Jamie released Topper's neck and gave him a slap on the back of the head.

"Ow!"

"Don't go anywhere." Jamie pulled Sophie close. "I'm sorry we didn't stop them soon enough."

"We're fine," Sophie assured him. "Take care of what you need to and then hurry back."

Jamie nodded but didn't seem willing to let her go.

Emma's legs grew weak and she suddenly couldn't breathe. Clayton's arms tightened around her waist and he guided her onto the sofa. "Emma?"

Deep breaths only seemed to make it worse.

Clayton hunkered down in front of her. "Tell me."

Sophie rushed to Emma. "Em? What's wrong?"

"He..." breath, "he..." breath, "he watched me."

"She's hyperventilating." Sophie sat next to her on the couch and rubbed her back. "*Who* watched you, love?"

Emma bent forward and wrapped her arms around her waist. "He... the man with the scar..."

Clayton scowled. "The man with the scar watched you?"

Emma nodded.

"Where did he watch you?" Clayton demanded.

"Clayton." Emma grimaced. "I need to talk to Jamie and Sophie alone. Can you please give us a minute?"

"Emma," he whispered. "You can tell me."

She pulled her hand away. "I *can't*, Clayton. Please."

He stood slowly, confusion written in the tight features of his face, and left the room. Jamie stood above her and crossed his arms.

Sophie took her hand. "Who was watching you?"

Emma took a shaky breath. "The man... the one with the scar. He watched the house."

Jamie raised an eyebrow. "Emma, that man has never been on this property. If he had, one of us would know."

Emma groaned in frustration. "Not *this* house."

166

Sophie gasped, her lips parting. "You mean…?"

Emma nodded. "Yes. Our house."

Jamie swore and knelt down beside her. "Tell me everything."

Emma twisted her hands in the material of her skirts, trying to focus on something other than passing out. "There has been a car… actually, a couple of cars… that have been watching the house. I thought it was the FBI, because of everything that happened with you, Jamie, but now I'm not so sure." Emma stood and started to pace. "I am such an idiot!"

Sophie rose to her feet. "Why, sissy?"

"I felt *safe*, Sophie. I thought it was the good guys watching me… following me." Emma sank to her knees and tried again to catch her breath.

Emma vaguely registered the sound of the door opening and mumbled voices, before strong arms wrapped around her waist and pulled her close. "Emma."

She burst into tears and clung to Clayton as he carried her to the couch. "Shh, sweet. Tell me." It took several minutes for her to calm, and despite her attempts to push him away he wouldn't release her.

Emma took another deep breath as Clayton settled them on the sofa and wiped her cheeks. "I'm okay. Really. I just had a scare."

He pulled a footstool over to the sofa and sat in front of her. Grasping her hands, he kissed her palms and smiled gently. "Are you certain that's all it is?"

Emma nodded. "Yes." She nodded again. "You have to go. They're waiting for you."

"Emma, I don't want to leave you like this." He handed her his handkerchief.

She pushed to her feet and held her hand out to him. "I'm fine."

"Mr. Madden?" A sergeant stood in the doorway and removed his hat. "We need your assistance, sir."

Clayton slowly stood and took Emma's hand, pulling her close. "We'll return as soon as we can. Will you be all right?"

"Yes, Clayton. These are tears of victory." Emma forced a smile. "Go. I'm fine."

Clayton reluctantly left her and joined the men milling in the foyer.

* * *

Sun streamed into the parlor. The morning greeted them with fresh snow-covered ground that sparkled when the rays of light hit the ground. Clayton and Jamie had returned an hour ago and dragged Topper into the library for a conversation he'd resisted for all of five minutes.

Sophie had promised Jamie she'd go back to bed, but Emma was too pent-up to sleep so she stayed in the warm room and paced. Now she stood, mesmerized by the winter scene outside.

"Emma?"

She twirled around at the sound of Clayton's voice. "Hi."

He closed the distance between them and kissed her. "I thought you were going to try and get some sleep."

She shook her head. "I couldn't sleep."

He lifted her chin and narrowed his eyes. "Are you still frightened?"

"No. Sophie stayed with me while you and Jamie talked with Topper. I feel much better, now." She rubbed her arms and sighed. "Who were those men, Clay?"

He laid his hand against her cheek. "It's a long story."

"Relating to Topper?" Emma leaned her cheek into his palm and took a deep breath.

"Yes."

"Will you please tell me what's going on?"

"It's not a pleasant story."

Emma shrugged. "I don't care. I want to know what happened to him."

Clayton led her to the sofa and pulled her down next to him. "Topper was stationed with a man in New York who took him under his wing. His name was Newton Brown and he apparently abused Topper repeatedly."

Emma frowned. "How?"

Clayton smiled gently. "You don't want to know. Let's just say that Topper was led to believe something that was a lie."

Emma nodded. "Is that how he lost his hand?"

"In a way." Clayton sighed. "There was a small skirmish at Diascund Bridge in June. Newton somehow separated Topper from the rest of the men and isolated him. He led him to where three other men were laying in wait..."

Emma reached for his hand. "Tell me. All of it, please. No matter how horrible."

"The men were hired to kill him—his hand was confirmation it was carried out."

Emma jumped from her seat. "How did Topper get away?"

"He didn't. They left him when they thought he was dead."

Emma frowned. "How did he get to the hospital?"

"He woke up on a cot in the back of the tent but didn't know where he was. He doesn't know how he got there, either. Had your sister not found him, he might not have survived."

Emma swallowed and laid a hand over her mouth. "Who hired the men?"

"It doesn't really matter who anymore, Emma."

"Why doesn't it matter? He should be protected."

Clayton shook his head. "He's not in danger anymore. He's safe."

Emma glanced up. "How do you know?"

Clayton sat across from Emma and took her hand. "Because Jamie and I have taken care of the threat."

Emma raised an eyebrow. "You got the man who hired them, as well as the ones who fulfilled the deed?"

"Yes."

"How?"

He wrapped an arm around her shoulders and pulled her close. "You don't need to know the particulars. Just know that it's done."

"I'm so glad you're here," she whispered.

As he ran his thumb over her lower lip, Emma couldn't stop her tongue from tasting him. He leaned down and slowly kissed her, and Emma came undone.

"I love you, Emma."

She fluttered her eyes open and stared into his. "I love you, too."

A knock at the door broke their intimate moment. Clayton sighed. "I can't stay. I have to send a wire to Christopher. I would very much appreciate it if you would go back to bed… and change into something more appropriate."

Emma had forgotten she was wearing her jeans. "You don't like my manly attire?"

"The problem is that I like them entirely too much—and so will other men."

Emma raised an eyebrow. "What other men?"

He slipped his arms around her waist. "I'm hoping none. However, if you continue to wear this outfit, I'm certain they will notice and then I'll have to kill them."

She slid her hands up his chest. "Such melodrama."

Clayton kissed her and then grabbed her hand. "Upstairs, sweetheart." He pulled her into the foyer. "Try to get some rest and I'll see you at lunch."

"Clayton? Thank you for telling me about Topper. I know that was difficult." Emma climbed the stairs and blew him a kiss before making her way to her room.

* * *

The next ten days were a whirlwind for Emma. Clayton had been given the assignment of investigating whatever was going on with Topper, which kept him close, but still tight-lipped. Her love grew deeper for him—as did her anxiety. He'd have to return to Washington shortly, and her heart broke at the thought of not seeing him again. Emma tried not to dwell on her gloomy thoughts, but they were hard to ignore as the days drew closer.

There was also the issue with Rose. She hovered entirely too often, and Emma was frustrated. Rose played the poor little southern damsel to a *T*, not to mention the fact, she'd become Emma's best friend, and Emma couldn't pinpoint what her angle was. Emma was still convinced she was spying, but no one had been able to catch her in the act.

Saturday morning, Emma joined Sophie in the parlor for breakfast. Nona had declared the day too cold to eat in the drafty dining room, so the fire was set, and a small repast had been provided. Emma wrapped her hands around a hot cup of coffee and sighed just as Clayton walked through the parlor doors. "I hope that means the coffee is good."

"It's hot, so that means it's good." Emma set her cup aside. "Good morning to you, too." Emma frowned when Rose followed him through the door.

Clayton made his way over to her and leaned down to kiss her cheek. "Good morning, sweetheart. Sophie."

Sophie smiled. "Good morning." She nodded to the new arrival. "Rose."

"Good morning, ladies. I do declare it's as cold as big ol' ice cube this morning." She sat on the chair closest to the fire. "I almost told your man to find me a quilt."

Sophie set her paper aside. "I'd be happy to grab you one, Rose."

Rose held her hands out to the fire. "Bless your heart, Sophie. I'd never impose. The fire's just fine."

Emma rolled her eyes as she grabbed her coffee and glanced up at Clayton. "Are you hungry?"

He nodded. "Starving."

"Clayton, darlin', would you fix me a plate, please?" Rose crooned. "You know what I like."

Clayton nodded and did what she asked. Emma wanted to chuck her cup at her. Once Rose was taken care of, he prepared himself a plate and sat next to Emma.

Sophie took a sip of coffee. "What are your plans today?"

"We're going for a ride, probably out to the lake." Clayton answered. "I have a little surprise."

Emma's eyes widened. "You do? What is it?"

"If I told you, it wouldn't be a surprise." Clayton broke off a piece of his muffin and placed it in his mouth.

"I hate surprises," Emma grumbled.

Sophie chuckled. "Go with it, sissy, you might like it."

Emma narrowed her eyes at her sister. "What do you know?"

Sophie took a bite of her eggs and shrugged.

Clayton dropped sugar into his coffee. "A groom is saddling a horse for you as we speak."

"Is this a private party, or may I come?" Rose asked.

Emma raised an eyebrow pointedly toward Clayton.

"I'm sorry, Rose. I promised Emma we'd spend the day together, but Sophie has offered to entertain you."

Rose huffed, but didn't comment further and focused again on her plate. They finished their breakfast and Clayton guided Emma out to the barn and helped her mount the horse he'd chosen for her. As they made their way to what they now referred to as their personal oasis, Clayton had to work to keep up with her. Emma gave a yell as she cleared a large fence and glanced back at Clayton. "Come on, slowpoke."

Clayton groaned as he spurred his horse on. Emma arrived at the lake a few minutes before him, and waited for him to pull up next to her. Clayton gave her a look of reproach and dismounted. "Sometimes you scare me with all the fences."

He reached up to help her dismount. Once she was on the ground, he pulled her close and gave her a lingering kiss.

"Mmm, what was that for?" Emma melted into him.

He gently ran his fingers down her cheek. "I love you."

Emma sighed. "I love you, too."

He kissed her one more time and then gathered the blankets and saddlebags tied to his saddle. They walked hand in hand over to the waterfall and Clayton laid out the thick blankets for her. Emma sat down, arranged her skirts, and watched Clayton unpack the saddlebags.

"What's in there?"

"So many questions today, sweet. Will you ever be satisfied with the simple enjoyment of a surprise?"

She shook her head. "Nope, never. I hate surprises."

Clayton chuckled and pulled out a carafe. "Would you like some hot chocolate?"

Emma shivered. "Yes, please."

He poured her a cup and handed it to her. "I think it might snow."

Emma took a sip and nodded. "Makes sense, it's freezing."

Clayton raised his head to the sky. "This may not have been a good idea."

"What? The cocoa?"

Clayton raised an eyebrow. "Bringing you out here. Perhaps we should head back."

Emma took another sip. "No way. I happen to the like the cold, and I've spent next to no time with you over the last two weeks." She leaned over and kissed his cheek. "I want you all to myself for a little while. Even if I run the risk of turning into an icicle."

Clayton leaned back on his elbow and stared out at the water. He said nothing for several minutes.

"Clay? Are you okay?"

"Of course, why?"

"You're just wound up so tight today."

He reached over and squeezed her hand. "Emma, I love you."

Emma's heart pounded. "I love you too, Clayton."

"I have never had a closer friend than you. I have never had someone I could share everything with. The good and the bad." He sat up on his knees and faced her. "I feel as though I can trust you with anything."

"You can." She stroked his cheek. "Is everything all right?"

Clayton nodded. "I would like you to marry me."

She dropped her hand. "What?"

"Emma." He grasped her hand and cleared his throat. "Will you do me the honor of being my wife?"

Emma stared at him for several seconds.

"Will you please say something?"

"Oh!" She covered her mouth with her fingers. "Sorry. Are you sure? I mean, we haven't known each other for very long. Are you sure?"

"I'm certain." He kissed her. "Do I get an answer, or am I to stay here all day?"

"Sorry. I don't know what to say."

Clayton sighed. "A yes or no would be a very good start."

"Yes! Yes, yes, yes!" She threw herself into his arms, knocking him over and sprawling across his chest. "It will be a privilege to be your wife."

"Let's make it official." He pulled off her glove and slipped a ruby and diamond engagement ring on her finger then kissed her palm.

Emma gasped. "Clayton, this is incredible. How did you know rubies were my favorite?"

"I asked your sister when I went to her and Jamie for permission to marry you."

"You asked for permission?"

"Of course. Without your father close by, it seemed prudent."

Her eyes filled with tears as she pushed away from him and stood.

Clayton followed. "Is everything all right?"

Emma paced. "There's something I have to tell you, but I don't know how."

"You can tell me anything, sweetheart."

She glanced down at her ring and sighed. "Clayton, it's really big, and I think I'd like to have Jamie and Sophie there. Could we put this part of our conversation on hold and talk about it when we get back to the house?"

"Of course we can." He held his hand out to her. "Come here and let me hold you. I'm not going to get to do that for much longer."

"Don't remind me!" She wrapped her arms around his waist. "When do you have to leave?"

"In three days. We've wrapped up everything here, so I have no excuse to stay." He gave her a gentle squeeze. "I won't stay away long. I'll organize everything for your arrival."

"Oh, right. I didn't even think about that." She pulled away and started to pace again.

"Emma?" She didn't answer, just continued to pace and chew on a fingernail. "Sweetheart, everything is going to work out fine. You'll see."

She glanced up at him and burst into tears. "Clayton, I can't leave Sophie."

"You aren't going to leave her."

Tears streamed unchecked down her cheeks. "What do you mean? When we're married, I go where you go."

Reaching inside his jacket, he pulled out a handkerchief. "Yes, but ultimately this will be our home."

"How is that going to work if your responsibilities are in Washington?"

He stroked her cheek. "I'll work it out. The townhouse will be our second home."

Emma wiped her face and blew her nose. "But what about a week from now?"

"I have to go back, but I will return in a month, certainly no longer than six weeks."

She let out a quiet squeal. "One month? You expect me to be all right with you leaving me for an entire month? Or *more*?"

"Sweetheart, a month isn't very long."

"It's a lifetime, Clayton."

He lifted her face to look at him. "I love you, my sweet, silly girl."

"Don't patronize me, Clayton."

"I wouldn't think of it."

She scowled. "I can't live without you for a month."

Clayton slid a stray lock of her hair behind her ear. "I can't take you back with me until we're married. It wouldn't be proper."

"What if Sophie came with us?"

He shook his head. "Jamie is not going to let his pregnant wife travel to Washington without him, and you know he can't leave his post. He would be considered a deserter."

"So I just have to sit here like a good little Civil War fiancée and wait for her man to come home?" Emma started to pace again.

"We'll figure it out. I promise. Come here, let's talk for a little while." He led her back to the blanket and settled her in the middle.

Sitting beside her, he wrapped an arm around her shoulders

and laid down, pulling her close. She rested her cheek on his chest and burst into tears again.

"Shh, sweetheart. Everything will be fine. You'll see."

"No it won't, Clayton. I'm going to lose you."

"Emma. You're not going to lose me." He tipped her chin up. "What's all this about?"

She shrugged. "I don't know. I just don't want you to go. I have this feeling of doom and I can't shake it."

He shifted so that he was lying on his side and looked down at her.

"Nothing is going to happen to us. I promise." He stroked her cheek and leaned down to kiss her.

He hasn't heard the big news. He's going to run for the hills.

SEVENTEEN

CLAYTON AND EMMA left the lake when the snow began to fall. They arrived back at the arena to find that Jamie and Sophie had just returned from a ride themselves.

"Hi, Em." Sophie rushed over to her. "Did you have a nice time?"

"Yes, miss sneak." Emma held up her left hand.

Sophie squealed with excitement and pulled her in for a long hug. "Congratulations! Are you excited?"

"Yes—and scared. But mostly excited. Thank you for wrangling Rose. I owe you one."

Sophie grimaced. "You owe me more than one."

"Deal." Emma grabbed her hand. "I actually need you guys for something if you don't mind."

"Is it what I think it is?" Sophie asked.

"Yes, and as much as I hate to admit it, I'm chicken to do it without you."

Sophie squeezed her hand. "Okay."

Emma turned when she heard a stall door close with a click. Jamie hung the halter he was holding on the hook outside the door and stepped back when Samson shoved his nose into the aisle. "Sophie, I think your pet needs a good-bye."

Sophie dug her hand into one of her deep pockets and pulled out a sugar cube as she made her way to Samson. "I only have one, Sammy." She reached out and he took it from her palm. "Jamie, Em needs us to join her for a conversation."

Jamie raised an eyebrow. "*The* conversation?"

Sophie nodded. "Yep."

"Okay. I have time now. We could meet in the library for privacy and then have lunch afterwards."

Emma took a deep breath and twisted her hands in the fabric of her skirts. Clayton stepped out of the tack room and shoved his hat on his head as he returned to her side. "Sweetheart?"

Emma swallowed and forced a smile. "Jamie has time now. Do you mind if we go back to the house and talk before lunch?"

Clayton drew his eyebrows together. "Not at all."

His large gloved hand covered hers and she gripped it as they followed Jamie and Sophie back to the house. As they stepped through the front door, Emma's body shook as she slid her hand out of Clayton's and removed her gloves

Jamie handed his coat, hat, and gloves to the butler. "Daniel, we'll be in the library. Please make sure no one disturbs us for at least an hour."

Daniel nodded. "Yes, sir."

Emma felt sick as they walked back to the private room. She held her hand over her stomach, silently begging it not to betray her. Sophie gave her a sympathetic smile as she sat next to Jamie on the window seat. Clayton turned one of the chairs to face them and settled his large body on the edge.

Emma paced. "Clayton, there is something I have to tell you, but I need you to listen to everything first and then you can ask questions when I'm finished, all right?"

Clayton nodded.

"Remember the night you found me in your carriage house?"

Clayton nodded again.

178

"Less than thirty minutes before you found me there, I was standing in the library of Jamie and Sophie's home."

"All right," he said slowly.

"Their home happens to be located in Portland, Oregon." She squeezed her eyes shut and then looked at Clayton. So far so good, she thought. "In the year two thousand and seventeen."

Clayton stood, but still didn't say anything.

"One hundred and forty-five years in the future," she added quickly.

He started to pace. Emma moved toward him, but Jamie motioned for her to wait. Clayton paused at the fireplace and then turned and looked at her. He opened his mouth, but then closed it quickly.

"Clayton, please say something," Emma whispered.

He rubbed his forehead. "I don't know what to say, Emma."

"I don't expect you to believe me right away, but I have proof if you'd like to see it."

"Jamie, why don't you go and get the bag," Sophie suggested.

Jamie nodded and left the room.

Emma took a step toward him. "Clayton?"

He raised his hand.

"Give him a minute, honey," Sophie whispered.

Emma sat next to Sophie and grasped her hand. Time stood still and it seemed like they had to wait forever for Jamie, but he finally returned with Emma's carpetbag in hand. He dropped it on the chair next to Sophie. Emma rose to her feet and moved to Clayton's side. "Clayton? Do you believe that I love you?"

He nodded.

"Do you believe I would never lie to you?"

He took an audible breath. "Yes, Emma. I know you would never lie to me."

"Do you think I'm insane?"

He sighed. "No, I don't think you're insane."

"Okay, will you come and have a look at what I have?" She held her hand out for his and led him to the bag.

Sophie rose to her feet. "What shall we start with, Em?"

"iPod."

Sophie handed Emma the iPod Nano and ear buds, and Emma led Clayton to the chair he'd vacated earlier. "Please sit down." Clayton stalled. "Clay, sit. It won't bite."

He sat.

Emma held the ear buds up. "Take these and put them in your ears. See how this has an R on it and the other has an L. Right ear, left ear, okay? Actually... wait, just put one in. That way if it's too loud, it won't freak you out."

"Freak me out?" he asked as he took the right ear bud and put it in his ear.

"It's a term we use. Never mind. I'll explain another time."

He looked at her and slowly put the ear bud in his ear. Emma turned on the iPod and picked Tchaikovsky's Swan Lake, hoping to ease him into modern music.

"I know this song," he yelled.

Emma and Sophie giggled. Clayton took the earphone out and then put it back in. He repeated this motion several times with a look of awe on his face.

Emma turned and smiled wickedly at Sophie. "Should I put on The Citizens?"

Sophie nodded. Emma picked "Low Ceilings, High Tides," her favorite song from the band, and pressed play.

Clayton jumped out of his seat and pulled the earphone out of his ear. "What is that?"

Emma pressed pause. "It's our favorite band."

"It's *noise!*"

"Sorry." Emma smiled as she held her hand out and waited for Clayton to give her back the iPod. "Are you okay?"

"I feel as though this is all a very strange dream."

Emma nodded her agreement. "Would you like to see something else?"

"All right," he said carefully.

She pulled out her wallet and showed him her driver's license and checkbook. He stared at her driver's license photo and glanced up at her.

Emma pulled out her Julia Quinn paperback. "This is the latest book I have from one of my favorite authors. If you open it up, you'll see the copyright."

He opened the front flap. "Why do you have photos of undressed people in your bag?"

Emma giggled. "That is a romance novel and they use models to illustrate the characters in the books."

"Why?"

She shrugged. "I don't know. It's a way to get lost in the story, I suppose. A great-looking man and a beautiful woman very much in love."

He turned the book over a few times and then handed it back to her. Emma dropped the book back in her bag. "Do you believe me?"

He held his hand out to her. "Come here." She slipped her hand into his and he pulled her into his arms. "I believe you, sweetheart. I believe all of it. I just need my mind to slow down."

"Do you really believe us, Clayton?" Jamie asked.

He took a deep breath and nodded. "From the moment I met Emma, I knew there was something different about her, and although it went against *everything* in my military training, I have trusted her from the very beginning." He smiled down at her. "This would explain the bizarre style of dress you were wearing when I found you… and your unusual spectacles."

Emma grinned. "In a hundred years, these'll be all the rage."

Jamie stood and leaned against the wall. "You're taking this very well, Clayton."

Sophie laid her hand on her stomach. "Yes, we won't have men in white coats showing up at the door to take us all away will we?"

Clayton smiled. "I believe you. I admit, I'm stunned, but I also know you wouldn't lie to me."

Jamie pushed away from the wall. "There are two other people who know."

"Who?"

"Andrew and Christine."

"That's good information to have, but I won't discuss anything unless we're alone."

Sophie stood and picked up Emma's bag. "Emma, we'll take the bag and hide it again and leave you two alone for a little while."

"Thanks." They left the library and closed the door. Emma raised her chin to meet Clayton's gaze. "Clayton, are you okay with all of this?"

"I will be." He kissed her palm.

"How can you accept this so easily? It must be blowing your mind right now."

He gave her a strange look.

"Oh—'blow your mind,' means hard to imagine," she clarified.

Clayton laughed. Out loud. A deep, bottom of your belly kind of laugh, and Emma wasn't sure what to think. He pulled her over to the chair and settled her on his lap. Drawing her chin down, he kissed her and her concern dissipated. He broke the kiss and linked his fingers with hers. "I have to admit, this is all strange. Why are you here? Do you know? How did you get here?"

"I don't know the why or the how. All I know is that I had a strange vision as though the room in front of me was rippling, and then a sharp pain in my head and I came to in your carriage house. I don't know if I was unconscious, or if it was all instantaneous."

Clayton rubbed his chin. "Who would know?"

Emma shrugged. "You're asking me as though I have more answers than you do. I don't."

"Does your sister?"

"We could ask her, I suppose."

"Emma, aren't you at all curious? Why aren't you asking a dozen questions, trying to find out?"

Emma dropped her head back with a sigh. "Because I don't know if I care. Because what happens if I find out and then I have to go back and lose you? I'd rather just live in the here and now, and be done with it."

"All right, sweetheart, I'll drop it for now." Clayton gave her his sexy half-smile. "Would you like to tell me about your parents?"

She reflected back on her short life. "My mother died of breast cancer and then my father died less than a year later. The doctors said his was a heart attack, but Sophie and I think he died from grief."

"How old were you?"

"I was fifteen, Sophie was nineteen." Clayton gave her a squeeze and she continued, "I moved in with Sophie and we just kind of figured out how to make it. Of course, if it hadn't been for Alex's family, we might not have done as well."

"Alex?"

"Sophie's best friend."

"Ah," he said.

"And the man... the one with the scar who was after Topper?"

He cocked his head to the side. "Yes."

"He's from the future as well. He was watching me at my house."

Clayton shifted slightly. "What do you mean?"

"After Sophie and Jamie disappeared, the man would follow me and sit outside my house. I thought he was with the police."

Clayton pulled her close. "No wonder you were so frightened."

"Ow, Clay, my hand."

Clayton loosened his grip and frowned. "Sorry."

"I just want to forget about the past... future, whatever... and move on. We survived and here I am ready to marry my dream man."

"I'm your dream man, am I?"

"Most definitely."

A knock at the door forced Emma from his lap, and he stood beside her as Sophie poked her head inside. "Lunch is ready."

Clayton smiled. "Thank you, Sophie."

Lifting Emma's hand, he tucked it into his arm and followed Sophie to the dining room. Michael and Nona were already there, along with Rose and Andrew.

"Clayton, darlin'! Did you have a nice time with your friend?" Rose whined.

"We had a wonderful time, Rose. Thank you for asking." He held Emma's chair and waited for her to sit down before sitting next to her.

"I'll forgive your inattention, Clayton, if I might have you this evening all to myself."

"Rose, as much as I would enjoy spending the evening with you, I have a wedding to plan. I have already promised Emma my undivided attention until I depart for Washington."

Emma could have sworn she heard Rose hiss and raised an eyebrow toward her. Rose smiled, although it didn't reach her eyes, and Emma dismissed her thoughts.

Nona set her glass on the table and smiled. "Clayton, congratulations!"

"I'm assuming Emma is the lucky lady?" Michael teased.

Clayton chuckled. "Yes, sir, or I'm in some serious trouble." He took Emma's hand and gently kissed her fingers.

"This is a reason to celebrate. Have you told your brother?" Nona asked.

"I have told him my intention, but not that I have been accepted."

"We'll host a small dinner to celebrate."

"Here we go," Jamie whispered.

Emma smiled as Sophie reached over and squeezed his hand.

"May I say something?" Emma broke in.

"Of course, dear," Nona said.

"Clayton has to leave in three days and I'm wondering if it would be possible to get married before he leaves."

Sophie raised an eyebrow. "Emma, are you sure?"

"Yes." Emma faced Clayton. "If that is acceptable to you, Clayton."

"I'm sure Minister Cunningham would be happy to perform the ceremony," Michael said.

Clayton nodded. "I'm visiting Richard this afternoon, so will stop in at the minister's home on the way back."

Nona clapped her hands. "That's a wonderful idea."

As the group made plans for their quiet ceremony, Emma sat silently. She was finding it difficult to catch her breath, her nerves on edge. The thought of not being with her sister scared her to no end, but she felt worse when she thought about not being with Clayton. She jumped slightly when she felt Clayton grasp her hand under the table.

Once lunch was finished, Clayton pulled her back into the library. "Emma, are you certain this is what you want?"

Emma squeezed her eyes shut. "Yes. I wouldn't have said it if I didn't mean it."

"And leaving Sophie?"

Emma felt the prick of tears. "Clay, it's worse for me to think about not being with you. Just promise me we'll be back before she has the baby."

"I promise." He kissed her again. "I have to leave you now. Will you be all right?"

Emma nodded and pulled a handkerchief from her sleeve. "Yes, go."

* * *

Sophie and Christine interrupted her pity party and dragged her into the ballroom. Christine sat down at the piano and waved her hand toward the dance floor. "You're going to teach Sophie to dance."

"Easy as pie," Emma retorted.

An hour later, all they'd accomplished were sore stomachs from laughing so much.

"Sophie! Listen, it is *not* that hard." Emma tried to sound stern but it wasn't working.

"So you say, little sister. But how many of your toes do I have to break before you recognize that I will never get it?" Sophie giggled.

"You self-sabotage yourself! You know you do." Emma turned Sophie again and caught sight of Clayton and Jamie leaning against the open doorway. "Hi!"

Clayton made his way over to her and gave her a quick kiss.

"Isn't there a rule about PDA in the nineteenth century?" Emma joked, adding quickly, "Not that I'm complaining."

"What's PDA?"

Sophie and Emma echoed "Public Displays of Affection," and then dissolved into laughter again.

Jamie rolled his eyes. "Clay, we're doomed. We won't be able to say anything to them for at least twenty minutes. They are too far gone. Join me for a drink in the library?"

"Excellent idea," Clayton said.

They left the girls to their dance lesson.

"So, Miss Christine, what's happening with Dr. Stephen Paxton today?" Sophie asked.

"Why do you always say his full name, Sophie?" Christine groaned.

"Because Dr. Stephen Paxton is a *doctor* and so obviously into you, my friend."

Christine missed a key. "What does that mean?"

Emma adjusted Sophie's hips and grinned at Christine. "It means he would like to court you."

Sophie snorted. "Oh, I think Dr. Stephen Paxton would like to do more than court her, Emma. I think Dr. Stephen Paxton wants to kiss her and hug her and call her his own." Sophie delivered her opinion in an annoying singsong voice while she twirled around in a circle.

Christine slapped her hands on the ivory. "He does not! Don't be ridiculous."

Emma tapped her lip with her fingernail. "He did seem to hold your hand a little longer in the receiving line during the ball. Is that allowed?"

"He did not!"

Sophie nodded. "*And* Dr. Stephen Paxton didn't take his eyes off you the whole night! I'm sure he hated that he only got to dance with you once."

Emma grabbed Sophie's hand and placed it on her shoulder. "Yes, and remember the lady who cleared her throat to remind him to stop touching you?"

186

Christine scowled at Sophie. "Maybe I *should* have organized men in white coats to take you away!"

Emma and Sophie dissolved into more giggles.

"Is sarcasm allowed in the nineteenth century?" Emma asked.

"You two are lethal!" Christine couldn't keep up her façade and laughed.

"May I join in on the joke?" came a voice from the doorway.

Christine stepped away from the piano. "Andrew! We weren't expecting you until dinner."

Andrew leaned against the doorframe. "Sister dear, it's almost five-thirty."

"What?" Sophie broke in. "We have been in here for three hours?"

Emma sighed. "And we have achieved *nothing!*"

"You must not be a very good dance teacher, Emma," Christine pointed out.

"I'm a great teacher. There are just people in the world who refuse to learn. Of course, I won't name names. Sophie."

Sophie wrinkled her nose. "Go with that, Em. That way I don't have to have any more lessons."

"Nice try, Skippy." Emma turned back to Andrew. "Where's Rose?"

"She's in the parlor—with Dr. Paxton."

"Andrew!" Christine punched her brother in the arm. "That's not very nice."

He rubbed his bicep. "What was that for? She really is."

"Stephen's here?" Christine sounded nervous all of a sudden.

"Yes. Michael invited him when he made his rounds at the hospital today."

Sophie pointed a finger at him in accusation. "I can't believe you left that poor man alone with the Fluff. We should probably go save him."

Andrew grinned and then turned and left the room.

Christine laid her hands on her hair. "I can't go in there looking like this."

187

Sophie squeezed her shoulder. "Christine, you look beautiful. You look happy."

"You do, Christine," Emma reiterated.

"All right, if you're certain." She rubbed her hands together.

Sophie pulled Christine toward the parlor. Emma followed. As they walked through the foyer, the front door opened and Clayton and Jamie walked through it.

Emma raised an eyebrow at her fiancé. "Where have you been?"

Clayton removed his hat and handed it to Daniel. "We've been making plans."

"Why does that make me nervous?"

"I'll give you all the details after dinner." He took her hand and they followed Jamie into the parlor.

"Dr. Paxton, thank you for joining us for dinner." Christine made her way to Stephen and his face lit up as he lifted her hand to his lips.

"I thought I asked you to call me Stephen," he said gently.

Christine blushed crimson. "Stephen," she whispered.

"Dinner is served," Daniel said from the doorway.

The group moved toward the dining room.

EIGHTEEN

$\mathcal{E}$MMA SHUFFLED BEHIND everyone into the dining room, feeling a bit like the center of a hurricane as the chaos of dinner whirled around her. She hardly ate anything and when dessert came, she pushed it around her plate.

"Emma?"

She glanced up at her sister. "Hm?"

"You have chocolate in front of you, and you're ignoring it."

Emma sighed. "Not hungry, I guess."

"Not hungry? Not possible." Sophie rose to her feet and grabbed Emma's hand. "Excuse us, please."

"Soph?" Jamie inquired.

"I'm just going to borrow Emma for a few minutes. We'll meet you in the parlor."

She pulled Emma down the hall and into the library. Sophie closed the door and faced her sister. "Spill."

Emma burst into tears. Sophie pulled her into her arms and stroked her hair. "Honey, what's going on? Do you not want to get married? You don't have to if you don't want to. If you feel

189

like it's too soon, we can stop it. Emma?"

"I want to marry Clayton," she sobbed. "That's not it."

"Well, what is it that has you so upset?"

"I don't want to leave you."

Sophie handed her a handkerchief. "Oh, sissy, I'll see you soon. The time will fly by, you'll see."

Emma pushed away from Sophie and started to pace. "But I'll be in Washington alone. When Clayton's working, I'll be all by myself, and I won't know how to navigate this century without you."

"Emma, you'll be fine."

"No, I won't be, Sophie! I won't have anyone to talk to. I'll be shut in the townhouse alone without you, without Clayton, without television." She stomped her foot. "There will be no horses, or music or—anything fun."

Sophie chuckled quietly.

"Don't laugh at me! It's not funny."

"I'm not laughing at you, sissy. I'm sorry." Sophie wrapped her arms around Emma and rubbed her back.

Clayton pushed the door open and peeked inside. Concerned to see Emma in Sophie's arms and sobbing, he stalled slightly, but Sophie motioned him in and let him take Emma in his arms. She left the room and closed the door. Clayton lifted Emma's chin and smiled gently. "Sweetheart? What has you so upset? We don't have to get married on Monday, we can wait."

Emma pushed herself out of his arms and paced. "That's *not* why I'm upset! Why does everyone think that?"

Crossing his arms, Clayton leaned against the back of one of the chairs and waited for her to work it out. He stood quietly until he heard the telltale hiccups that signaled the end of her sobbing.

"Emma?" Clayton held his hand out to her.

She stepped closer to him and sighed. "I'm sorry."

"Why are you sorry?"

"Because I'm an unstable female, who can't seem to control her emotions."

He stroked her cheek. "Tell me what has you so upset."

"It's just really hard leaving my sister. That's probably the simple answer."

"Do you want to tell me the complicated one?" He pulled her over to one of the chairs and waited for her to sit. He sat on the hearth facing her.

"My sister died, Clayton—or, at least, we assumed she did."

"Tell me what happened."

"Well, about two years ago. No, wait, let me rephrase. In two thousand and sixteen, she was diagnosed with a failing heart, probably the same thing daddy had. In order for her to survive, she would need a new heart. She disappeared before she could get a transplant. In my mind, she was gone, but apparently, she was somehow sent here."

Clayton gently swept her hair from her eyes, but didn't say anything.

"I just got her back, Clay, and now I'm leaving her again. But I can't live without you. I know that, too, so I just feel a little between a rock and a hard place. You know?"

"I'm looking forward to the conversation on the ability to transplant a heart, but we'll get to that another time," he said. "Let's tackle this problem with Sophie, all right?"

Emma nodded as tears slid down her face again.

"I know you hate surprises..." He sighed. "I had one planned that I'd hoped you wouldn't discover, but for the sake of my silly sweet girl, it looks as though I'll need to tell you."

She sniffed and he paused while she blew her nose. "Tell me."

"The President has approved nothing yet, but Jamie has agreed that if he is given the go-ahead, he and Sophie will come with us to Washington. My townhouse has plenty of room for the four of us, and it will mean you don't have to be without your sister. Richard will be home tomorrow and will take over the training efforts once again."

Emma gasped. "You did all of this for me?"

He sat back and drew his eyebrows together. "All of what?"

"Um, something huge like asking the President for a favor."

"Sweetheart, I would do anything for you."

191

She grasped the lapels of his jacket and pulled him forward for a kiss. He broke the kiss and they sat there for a few minutes with their foreheads together in an attempt to catch their breath. Emma sat back again. "I don't think chemistry will be an issue with us."

"Why would we need to do chemistry?"

Emma bit her lower lip. "Oh, right. It's a term we use to describe whether or not we find each other attractive enough to—you know."

"I know?"

"Have sex," she whispered.

His smile changed and she knew he'd been teasing her. She smacked his knee.

Clayton laughed. "I think we find each other attractive enough. Are you nervous?"

"What? Me? No. I'm a professional, remember?"

He leaned forward. "Emma, are you a virgin?"

"Are you?"

"*Emma*," he said, lowering his voice.

Emma poked his shoulder. "Just because you lower your voice at me and hold out my name a little longer, does not make me afraid of you, or make me suddenly want to confess all my sins to you."

Clayton took a deep breath. "I will be truthful with you, if you will be truthful with me. Is that a fair compromise?"

Emma grimaced. "I have never done anything except kiss. You will be my first." She saw his shoulders relax. "Now, you."

"Are you certain you want to know?"

Emma gasped. "Have there been that many?"

"There have been a few, but none in the last three years. When I chose to get back on track with God, that was one of the areas I chose to get right."

She covered her ears. "Okay, I don't need any other information."

The door opened and Sophie knocked as she walked inside followed by Jamie. "You look much better, Em."

Emma jumped up and ran to her sister. "You are such a sneak

and I love you!"

Clayton grimaced. "I told her."

Jamie laughed. "I applaud your efforts, but I told you there would be no way you could keep that from Emma."

"I will surprise her one day. It might be when we've been married for twenty years, but I *will* do it." Clayton stood and held his hand out to Emma.

Sophie smiled. "Well, I think you should get some rest, Em. We have a busy few days coming up and you'll want to be rested."

"You're probably right." Emma turned to Clayton. "I'll walk you out."

She led him down the hall and into the foyer. Clayton gathered up his outerwear. "Are you feeling better?"

Emma nodded. "Yes, much better. Thank you."

He leaned down and gave her a quick kiss. "I'll see you at breakfast, sweetheart. Sleep well."

Emma closed the door behind him and made her way up the stairs. Entering her room, she found Sophie waiting for her. "Hi."

Sophie smiled and gave her a hug. "Do you have an idea for a dress?"

"No, actually I haven't even thought about a dress." Emma presented her back so that Sophie could unbutton her gown.

"You can wear mine, if you like."

"Seriously? You'd let me wear your dress?"

Sophie untied Emma's corset and loosened the strings. "Of course I would. We're the same size, so we wouldn't even need to alter it."

Emma slid the hooks open in the front. "I *am* almost an inch taller than you."

"You can wear it anyway, smarty pants."

"Wow, Sophie, I love your dress. I would be honored to wear it. Thanks."

"You're welcome. Are you happy?"

"I'm so happy."

Sophie hugged her again. "About freakin' time."

Emma stuck her tongue out at her sister. Sophie giggled and made her way to the door. "We've got a lot to do over the next week. Sleep well, love."

* * *

Clayton made a surprise visit the next morning and whisked Emma into his buggy without any information as to what was going on. They arrived in town to find Sophie and Jamie waiting for them near the haberdasher.

"What are you guys up to?" Emma asked as Clayton lifted her from the buggy.

"You'll see," Sophie said.

It didn't take long for Emma to figure it out and Clayton chuckled when she clapped her hands and let out a little squeal. "Madame's!"

Sophie nodded. "She sent a message that she had a shipment of new fabrics arriving."

Clayton kissed her palm. "An early wedding gift."

Emma grinned. "I love you."

"There is something you should know, Em," Sophie warned.

"What?"

Sophie glanced up at Jamie and then back at her sister. "Madame is the reason we are here… in the past."

Emma gasped. "Seriously?"

Sophie nodded. "Yes."

Emma narrowed her eyes. "Well, then why didn't you tell me?"

"Mostly because we don't know why *you're* here."

"But you know why you're here."

Sophie grimaced. "Yes."

"Why are you here?"

Jamie groaned. "How about we talk about that after you find out why you're here. It's a really long story."

Sophie nodded. "Yes. I thought you could ask her a few questions. She doesn't know we're coming, so she won't have time to hide."

Emma grabbed Clayton's hand and began to pull him across

the street. "Yes, as a matter of fact, I have several questions."

Emma pushed the door open and Madame Desmarais, in the middle of discussing something with one of her assistants, turned at the sound of the bell on the door. Madame's hand flew to her mouth.

"You!" Emma exclaimed. "What the heck are you doing here?"

Jamie had failed to mention that Madame was the grief counselor who had spent so much time with them over the past year.

"Come with me, *sil vous plait*," Madame whispered and escorted the couples into the back room.

"What's going on?" Clayton asked.

Jamie crossed his arms and gave the dressmaker a "gotcha" look. "This is the woman who consoled us when Sophie disappeared."

Emma nodded. "And the woman who visited me after Jamie disappeared. What are you doing here? *How* did you get here?"

"It is *tres* complicated."

"Why don't we start at the beginning? How did we get here?" Emma asked.

Madame took a deep breath, but did not speak for several minutes. "There is a time portal—"

"Duh!" Emma interrupted.

"Emma," Clayton admonished. "Let her explain."

Madame began to pace. "My husband and I ensure that the wrong people don't end up where they don't belong," she explained.

Emma frowned. "Who determines who the right people are?"

"We do."

"Why?"

"Various reasons."

"Like?" Emma pressed.

"Destiny, mostly."

"Why Sophie? Why me?"

"Sophie knows the reason for her and Jamie's travel, I'll allow her to tell you that story." Madame paced. "As for you,

195

Emma. Your life was in danger."

Clayton pulled Emma against him.

"It was?"

"Yes. Cary's men had failed to silence Sophie, and they watched you to see if you knew anything."

"But I don't."

"They don't know that. However, you also needed to be close to your sister." Madame gave a tight smile. "Unless, of course, you don't want to be."

"What does that mean?" Clayton asked. "Can they go home if they choose to?"

Emma gasped. "Can we?"

Madame sighed. "You can go back."

"We can?" Emma asked.

"Yes. You can go back to your old life, but Clayton would not be able to follow. No one is able to go forward in time, unless they were already there. Clayton would have to stay and you would not be allowed to return."

With a curse, Clayton stalked out of the room.

"Clayton!" Emma rushed after him.

He continued to the buggy and jumped in. Emma climbed in after him and closed the door. She was shocked to see tears in his eyes.

"Clay." She cupped his face in her hands. "I'm not going anywhere. Ever."

"I want you to be happy," he whispered.

"I *am* happy."

"But you're subjected to living without your iPod and other things I know nothing about." He kissed her palm. "I'll let you go if it's your wish to return."

"Stop this!" Emma scowled. "Right now, Clay. You're starting to piss me off."

"Emma," he said with a sigh.

"I love you more than life itself. Nothing… look at me! Nothing could ever make me want to leave you."

"What if Sophie chose to go back?"

"As a corpse?"

"Emma!"

Emma wrinkled her nose. "If Sophie was able to go back and live with Jamie alive in the future and she chose to, I would still want to be here."

"You would miss her."

"Of course I would. She's my sister. I love her. But I love you more and if I couldn't be with you, I would die. I can live without her, but I can't live without you."

"Truly?" he asked.

She smacked his knee. "Yes! Now stop being an idiot. I'm not going anywhere, except back inside. I need to spend your money."

Clayton kissed her once more and jumped out of the carriage. Emma followed him back inside. Sophie reached for her hand with a sympathetic smile. Emma turned to Madame. "So, what do we do now?"

"Nothing," Madam stressed. "You cannot discuss this with anyone. Should they find out you're here, there might be danger."

"Okay, people." Emma sighed. "Can we please change the subject? I'd like to spend my fiancé's money."

Clayton raised an eyebrow and then chuckled. He kissed her cheek and led Jamie out of the store so that Emma could be measured.

NINETEEN

$\mathcal{C}$ LAYTON AND EMMA were married on Monday, November 2, 1863. She wore her sister's dress and Jamie walked her down the aisle.

Just before they entered the church, Jamie kissed Emma's cheek. "Don't question the feelings, Squirt. Just let him love you."

Emma raised an eyebrow. "Is that your advice?"

"No, my advice is to keep the fights clean and the sex dirty, but I'm trying to be poetic."

Emma laughed and then heard Christine start to play the wedding march.

The doors opened and Emma took a deep breath. The church was filled with white roses and the love of her life stood next to the minister in evening black. The look he gave her when he saw her took her breath away. She'd never felt that loved.

"Are you ready?" Jamie whispered.

Emma nodded and they began her walk to Clayton. She tried not to look at Sophie who had turned into a watering pot, but she couldn't help it, which in turn, led to her own tears. It seemed to spread to every woman in the church and the ceremony was over faster than expected.

"You may kiss your bride."

Before Emma knew it, she was pulled into Clayton's strong embrace and kissed breathless. A buzz sounded as the congregation began to chuckle, and when Jamie clapped Clayton on the shoulder, Emma realized they had been kissing for what might have been a little too long. She grimaced as she buried her face in her hands.

"Are you finished?" Minister Cunningham joked.

"For now," Clayton said, for her ears only, and then pasted on a brilliant smile.

"Ladies and gentleman, I joyfully present Mr. and Mrs. Clayton Madden."

The congregation stood, and the newlyweds walked down the aisle and out the church doors. The rest of the small group of witnesses followed and threw fresh flower petals at them as they dashed for their coach.

An open carriage decorated with ribbons waited for them to take them back to the Wades' for the reception. Clayton lifted Emma in and sat next to her. As the carriage took off, Clayton pulled Emma closer to him and laid thick blankets over them. He smiled down at her as he kissed her palm. "Hello, Mrs. Madden."

"Hello, Mr. Madden."

"Are you happy?"

"Probably happier than might be legal."

Clayton laughed. "I love you."

"I love you, too." She kissed him. "How long do we need to be at the reception?"

"Is there something you'd rather do?"

"What do you think?"

"Emma Madden, you are a wicked, wicked girl."

"I do try."

When they arrived at the Wades' home, they found that Jamie had beaten them home.

"Sophie's waiting for you upstairs to help you get out of your gown," he said as he hugged her.

"Why can't Clayton do that?" Emma asked wickedly as Clayton lifted her out of the carriage.

Jamie grinned. "Because then you might not actually join the reception."

"Good point."

Clayton led her inside. "Before you go, I have news."

Emma raised her face to his. "Is it good news?"

"Only if you want Jamie and Sophie to join us in a private parlor car to Washington."

Emma squealed in delight and jumped into Clayton's arms. "I love you, I love you, I love you."

He gave her a quick kiss and then pushed her towards the stairs. She ran up them in pure unadulterated excitement, and when she entered her room, she found Sophie waiting to help her change. "You're coming! You're really coming with us!"

Sophie nodded. "Yep. Oh my gosh, Em. I'm going to get to meet Abraham Lincoln."

"I didn't even think about that! This is going to be so awesome."

"I know. Okay, let's get you out of that dress." Sophie turned her around. "Do you have any questions about tonight? Are you nervous about anything?"

"I don't feel nervous, just excited. I trust Clayton."

Once Emma was dressed, the girls made their way downstairs. Everyone else had arrived and Clayton waited at the bottom of the stairs with a glass of champagne for her.

Nona had once again outdone herself. The party was perfect. Very low key, very intimate, and they kept it short and sweet. Once the cake was cut, Clayton informed everyone that he was going to take his bride home. He ushered her out the front door and back into the wedding carriage. The driver took them to Clayton's house and he assisted her down.

"Where's Rose?"

Clayton lifted her into his arms and made his way to the front door. "Both she and Richard are staying at the Wades' until Wednesday. Hattie has gone to stay with a friend of Nona's."

Emma looped her arms around his neck. "Rose isn't coming to D.C. with us is she?"

"No, sweet. She's going to spend some time with Richard."

"Oh, good."

When they reached the front door, Clayton pushed it open and carried her over the threshold. He gently set her down in the foyer and kissed her. "Welcome home, Mrs. Madden."

Emma groaned when he broke the kiss and he chuckled as he led her upstairs to his bedroom. "There's more of that, Emma. Never fear."

Clayton pushed open the door and Emma gasped. Rose petals covered the room and champagne chilled in a bucket of ice, next to chocolate covered strawberries on a table in the corner. The fire had been lit and only half of the sconces had flame, so the room was romantic and warm. "How did you find strawberries? They're out of season."

He smiled. "If I tell you all my secrets, I won't be able to surprise you."

"Clay, this is beautiful. Thank you." She pulled his head down for a kiss.

"Let's get you out of that dress," he whispered and turned her to reach her buttons.

He slipped each of the buttons free and then slid her blouse off her shoulders. Emma pushed her skirt and hoops off her hips and let them fall to the ground.

Emma heard Clayton's sharp intake of breath. "What are you wearing?"

She wore a lavender demi bra and matching underwear. Holding her hands up, she said, "Okay, now don't have a heart attack. This is what we wear in the twenty-first century."

"What do you mean?" Clayton asked.

"These are our undergarments."

He turned her around... and then again. "Where are the rest of them?"

Emma giggled. "This is all there is. No corset, no pantaloons, no petticoats. Just this."

"Always?"

She nodded. "Yes, every day."

"Heavens!"

"Do you like it?"

Clayton rested his hands on her hips. "I think we'll have your dressmaker make you more of whatever it is that is."

Emma laughed. "Okay, baby, you pick the colors and I'll figure out how to get them made."

He cupped her cheek and smiled down at her. "Emma, you are so beautiful. I'm not sure how slow I'll be able to go."

She shrugged. "So, don't go slow."

He pulled his shirt off and it was her turn to gasp. His chest had been chiseled out of stone. Other than a tiny dusting of light blond hair at his sternum, his chest was bare.

"Yummy." She slid her hands up his chest.

He slipped his hands down her hips and cupped her bottom. She gasped when he squeezed gently. He moved up to her bra strap, but stopped. "Sweet, how do I—?"

"I'll show you how later." Reaching behind her, she unhooked her bra.

He pushed the straps from her shoulders and she pulled her body away just enough for it to fall to the floor.

Clayton's eyes grew large, and a low growl erupted from his throat. "Magnificent."

Sliding her hands down his chest and to the waistband of his pants, Emma slipped the buttons and felt the evidence of his arousal as she pushed them from his hips. He picked her up and laid her gently on the bed. As he stretched out beside her, he stroked her cheek and took a moment to look at her. "I love you."

"I love you, too."

He cupped her breasts, drawing one nipple into his mouth, then another, gently blowing on each and then kissing his way down her body. She wove her fingers in his hair as he knelt between her legs smiled up at her, hooking his fingers in her panties, and slipping them past her hips. She lifted so he could remove them completely and his eyes widened.

"What's wrong?" Emma asked.

"Never seen…ah…"

She cocked her head and then realized what he was saying. "Oh, right. Waxing."

"Waxing?"

"We like to keep things clean and tidy in our century. Is it weird for you?"

He shook his head. "It's beautiful."

He ran his tongue the full length of her and Emma mewed, arching into him. His tongue applied pressure and he sucked gently before gripping her thighs and holding her still so he could suck a little harder.

"Clayton," she whimpered.

He slid a finger inside of her, using his thumb to apply pressure to her clitoris again, then slipping another finger inside of her.

"Clayton," she cried, and her body spasmed around his fingers.

He kissed her inner thigh and slid inside of her, slowly at first, letting her body get used to him. Hovering above her, he kissed her gently and she gripped his biceps.

"Are you all right?"

"I'm fine," she said.

He buried his body deeper into hers and she let out a quiet hiss at the sting, but Clayton kissed her deeply and slowed his pace.

Emma raised her hips to encourage him to continue. "More, baby," she begged.

He slid in again and then began to move, faster and faster each time, until they both came undone. As Emma tried to catch her breath, Clayton pulled her close and settled her cheek against his shoulder. "Did I hurt you?" he asked.

"It hurt less than I expected." Emma ran a finger across his chest.

"Are you certain you're well?"

She looked up at him with a giggle. "Better than well, Clayton. That was incredible. I can't wait to do it again."

Clayton chuckled and stroked her back. A knock sounded at the door, and Emma wrinkled her nose. "Who's that?"

"Your bath."

She pushed herself up. "You anticipated everything, didn't you?"

He grinned and slid off the bed. He held his hand out to her and she let him pull her off the mattress. Clayton quickly ushered her into the dressing room where a tub of warm, scented water waited for her. She stepped in and sighed as she slipped further under the water.

"Is it helping?" Clayton grabbed his robe and closed them into the small room.

"Yes, much." She closed her eyes. He knelt down beside the tub and stared at her. Emma smiled without opening her eyes. "Why are you hovering?"

"Am I?"

She chuckled.

"How are you feeling?"

Emma sighed. "I feel great."

"Are you overly tender?"

"I'm fine, Clay." She opened one eye and then closed it again. "I promise."

He stroked her cheek and leaned over to kiss her. Emma felt her face grow warm when he broke the kiss, and Clayton raised an eyebrow. "What's amiss?"

Emma shrugged. "Was I okay? I mean, were you satisfied?"

"Sweetheart, you are remarkable." He kissed her again. "Are you hungry? Or tired?"

Emma shrugged. "I'm a little tired, but I could do that all over again to be honest."

"Not tonight, sweet. You need some time to heal."

"What about if we sleep for a little while and then do that again?"

"We'll see." Clayton stood. "Let's get you out of the tub."

He grabbed a clean towel and held it out to her. Emma grinned. He wrapped the towel around her body and lifted her from the tub. "You are so beautiful."

"How beautiful?" She wove her arms around his neck and pulled the towel from her body.

"Sweetheart, it's too soon for you. Will you trust me?"

She wrinkled her nose. "We'll see."

"You're not playing fair, Emma."

"I know, honey. But you have now made me want something I didn't know I was missing. So I blame you."

Clayton laughed and she reluctantly wrapped the towel back around herself as they moved back into the bedroom.

"They changed the sheets already?" she whispered.

"Yes," he whispered back.

Emma dropped her face into her hands.

"Why are you hiding your face?"

"I don't know. I guess it feels weird that we're allowed to do this now." She shivered. "And that people know that we're doing it."

"Come by the fire, sweetheart."

She joined him in front of the warm flame and sighed. "I'd rather climb back into bed." She dropped her towel again and pushed his robe off his shoulders as she stood on her tiptoes to kiss him. "Now."

"Are you certain, sweet?"

"Clayton, you are my husband and as such, you have certain duties you are expected to perform."

"Is that so?" He cupped her bottom. "Would you please elaborate on what those duties might be?"

She elaborated, quite poignantly, and he concluded his duties fully to her satisfaction. Over and over again.

* * *

Emma and Clayton didn't leave the house until dinnertime on Tuesday. They were scheduled to join everyone at the Wades' for dinner and only just made it on time.

The Simmonds family had joined together in the parlor as a send-off to the newlyweds, along with Jamie and Sophie. As soon as Emma walked into the room, Sophie grabbed her for a hug before anyone else could.

"So, how was it?" Sophie whispered.

"Mind-blowing," Emma whispered back and kissed her

205

cheek.

Before details could be given, dinner was announced and everyone took their seats. With Richard and Rose staying with the Wades' until Wednesday, it was a full table. It was festive and exciting and everyone seemed to talk at once.

Richard had apologized for his earlier behavior, and he and Emma had achieved a tentative friendship. Trust would take a while to build, but both were willing to make the effort. Even Rose behaved. Although Emma caught her occasional dirty look, she chose to ignore it. Once dinner was finished, the men and women separated.

Sophie pulled Emma aside before joining the other ladies in the parlor. "Do you want the carpetbag to go in with the rest of the luggage?"

Emma shook her head. "I think it should come with us, don't you think?"

"Yes, I do. I just wasn't sure if you would want to lug it around," Sophie said.

"Well, I'd rather keep it close." Emma raised an eyebrow. "Could you imagine what would happen if someone found that?"

"No. It's frightening to think about it."

"What time are we leaving tomorrow, by the way? I've been a little distracted."

"I wonder why?" Sophie giggled. "I think early. Maybe seven? We're bringing Samson, so it'll be interesting."

"Sounds like everything is taken care of. Does that mean I can take my husband home and keep him in bed tonight?" Emma whispered.

"Yes, absolutely. I have your bags packed from this side, and Clay put a few of your clothes over at the house, so you should be all set."

"He did? I didn't see anything over there. I'll have to ask him what he did with them."

"Speak of the devil." Sophie smiled.

Clayton made his way down the hall toward them with a huge grin on his face. "Time to go, sweetheart."

Emma raised an eyebrow. "How did you manage that?"

"I have my ways."

Emma looped her arm with his and let him lead her out the front door and down the path that connected the two homes. "Sophie said some of my clothes were delivered to the house. Do you know where they were put?"

"In your bedroom."

Emma glanced up at him. "I know I've been distracted and all, but I didn't see anything in the room."

"No, sweet. They're in the wardrobe in your room."

She stopped walking. "What do you mean, *my* bedroom?"

"The dressing room joins both of our bedrooms. Along with the entrance in the hall, it also has an entrance through my room."

"We have separate bedrooms?"

"Yes."

"Why?"

Clayton frowned. "I suppose it's something I assumed you'd want."

"Um, no," she snapped.

"I'm sorry?"

"Do *you* want separate bedrooms?"

Clayton shrugged. "I have never thought about it. I don't know anyone who doesn't have a separate room from his wife."

She stood in the middle of the pathway with her fists at her sides, trying to decide how far she wanted to push this. "And I don't know anyone who does."

"Is there a point to this?"

"I don't want separate bedrooms." She sighed. "We go to bed, we stay in bed, and we wake up in bed. In the *same* bed, Clay."

Clayton's eyebrows drooped. "Perhaps we should have discussed this sooner."

"Why? Do you want to sleep apart from me?"

"Not in the least, Emma. I thought you might want to." He shrugged. "Perhaps I snore."

"You don't snore, but even if you did, I still wouldn't want to sleep apart from you."

"All right, sweet."

"Good. I'd hate to have to tie you to it." Emma paused. "Oh wait, maybe I wouldn't."

Clayton laughed. "You might wear me out."

She dragged him into the house and up to the bedroom. "Let's start with you helping me get out of this corset contraption."

"It will be my pleasure."

Clayton tugged at the laces, kissing her neck as he loosened. Once Emma was left in just her stockings and shoes, he turned her to face him. "Beautiful."

She slipped the buttons on his vest, pushing it from his shoulders, jacket and all, then went to work on his shirt. "Off."

He pulled the shirt over his head and she tugged at the waistband of his trousers. "I want you naked.

"I want you just the way you are."

"Deal," she said, and waited for him to remove the rest of his clothes.

"Now what, sweetness?"

"Now I get to play." She knelt in front of him and wrapped her mouth around his growing erection.

He slid his hands into her hair, her pins scattering across the wood floor, and his breath left him with a hiss as she drew him deeper into her mouth. She didn't get to play for long, however, when she found herself hauled off the floor and onto the bed.

"Hey!" she complained as she stared up at him from the mattress. "I wasn't done."

Clayton tugged her to the edge of the mattress and, from his standing position, anchored her thighs to his hips and slid inside of her. "I couldn't wait."

"I was enjoying tha—" She gasped as he shifted.

He leaned forward and palmed her breasts as he thrust inside of her. Emma was no longer able to form a coherent sentence, let alone admonish him for not letting her finish. There'd be plenty more chances to enjoy him in the future and, right now, she had an orgasm to enjoy.

TWENTY

OOD MORNING, SWEETHEART. It's time to wake up." Clayton set a breakfast tray on the side table.

"What time is it?"

"Six o'clock."

Emma opened one eye and frowned. "In the morning?"

"Yes, in the morning. We need to leave in about an hour." He chuckled as he made his way to the bed and pulled the covers off her. He sat down and kissed her as he stroked her face gently. "Come and eat. It's going to be a long trip."

"I'd rather do other things." She pulled him close for another kiss. "I want more."

"I'll give you more—later." He eluded her hands and jumped from the mattress.

Emma blew air through her lips. "Slave driver."

Clayton held up a glass of orange juice. "Freshly squeezed."

"Where did you get oranges in winter?"

"From Nona's greenhouse."

She sat up and raised an eyebrow. "Is there freshly squeezed coffee? I need coffee."

Clayton poured her a cup and she climbed from the bed. She slipped her robe over her shoulders and walked over to the chair by the fireplace. She grabbed a muffin then sat in the chair and tucked her feet under her bottom. "Yum. This is good."

Clayton set her coffee on the small table next to her and stole a bite of her pastry. "That *is* good."

"Sneak." Emma pulled her hand away. "Get your own."

"I've already eaten." He started to dress while she sipped her coffee. Clayton disappeared into the dressing room and returned a few minutes later. "Is this what you wanted to wear today?"

Emma shrugged. "I'd rather wear a pair of jeans and a sweater, but since that's not an option, I suppose that'll do."

"When we're at home, you can wear whatever you like." He laid the day dress on the bed. "Inside. In private."

Emma stood and removed her robe. "Really? How about this?" She settled her hands on her hips. "Can I wear this when we're at home? Inside? In private?"

Clayton slid his hands around her waist. "Anytime you'd like to walk around in the nude will be fine with me." She dragged her hands up his chest and pulled his head down for a kiss. Clayton groaned and stepped away. "We have to go."

Emma glanced down and felt satisfied with the evidence of his discomfort straining his trousers. "Just remember what you're giving up for the next three hours."

He ran his hands through his hair as he turned away and took several deep breaths. Emma stepped into her undergarments, presented her back to him for help with the laces on her corset, and then finished with her dress. She wore a comfortable pair of walking boots and Clayton assisted her with a thick cloak and gloves before they stepped into the frigid morning to meet her sister.

Her bonnet matched her cloak and she finished tying it just as they arrived at the Wades' front porch. Sophie stood against the railing and waved as Emma approached. "Good morning."

Clayton touched her back and whispered, "I'm going to assist Jamie with the beast."

"Okay." Emma climbed the steps and hugged her sister. "There really should be a law about getting up this early."

"Yes, there should be. How are you?"

"I'm great, how are you?"

"I feel good. Just tired."

Emma nodded. "Me too. I'm going to sleep on the train."

"Of course you are," Sophie grumbled.

Emma put her arm around her sister. "Don't hate me. Just because I can sleep and you can't."

All of a sudden, the girls heard pounding hooves and a panicked yell. Samson ran towards the house, sans halter or lead, a frantic groom on his heels.

"What the—?" Sophie rushed off the porch and into the path of her horse. "Samson!"

As soon as he heard her voice, he slowed and trotted toward her. He stopped in front of her and nuzzled her shoulder. Sophie held her palm out with a sugar cube settled in the middle. "Samson. You're going to drive some of these very nice men insane. You realize that, right?"

The groom apologized profusely, gasping for air as he tried to explain. She held her hand out and took the bridle from him and put it on Samson. "What happened?"

The groom leaned his hands on his knees and took a deep breath. "He just took off, ma'am. I'm very sorry."

"It's all right. Is the lieutenant bringing his saddle?"

"Yes, ma'am."

Clayton and Jamie arrived a few minutes later with the saddle and Jamie assisted Sophie into the carriage. Clayton had a brief word with the driver and then lifted Emma inside. They arrived at the Harrisburg Train Station in record time, the small building a bustle of activity. Sophie and Jamie loaded Samson into the stall they had reserved for him and then they were escorted to their private parlor car.

Clayton waited for Emma to sit by the window and then sat next to her. She pulled her gloves off and shoved them into her cloak pocket. "How long will the trip be?"

Clayton mirrored her actions and took her hand in his. "About four hours. We'll stop at Camden Station and then on to D.C."

Sophie sat across from Emma and smiled at her new brother-in-law. "Clayton, thanks for letting me bring Samson. I would have missed him terribly."

"You're welcome."

The train started to move and the group fell into a comfortable silence. An hour into their journey, Jamie and Clayton went to stretch their legs and find some food.

"What are you going to do when you meet the President?" Emma whispered. "Will you try and warn him?"

"About Booth?" Sophie asked.

"Yes."

Sophie shrugged. "I don't know. Every movie I've ever seen about time travel always talked about the importance of never messing with history, you know? But, what would our country be like if Lincoln lived, even a few years longer? What if I could tell him that his only surviving adult child is Robert and that the last descendent from his line dies in 1984? It's overwhelming."

"You've apparently thought about this already," Emma observed.

"Since I got here! I dream about it all the time. How bad would it really be if he lived and such? But, then the question of messing with God's plan comes up in my mind and I'm back to the beginning."

The men returned with a small snack, which interrupted the heavy discussion, and as soon as they were done eating, Emma leaned against Clayton and promptly fell asleep.

"It's so not fair!" Sophie whispered frustrated.

Jamie chuckled. "Why don't you put your head on my lap and at least try to sleep? There's plenty of room for you to stretch out."

"In these skirts?"

"Just lie down and try. You're exhausted and it wouldn't hurt, right? Come on. I'll make sure you don't fall off the bench."

She removed her bonnet, laid down, and Jamie wrapped one arm around her waist to keep her secure. She sighed as he stroked her face and he smiled in silent triumph when she finally fell asleep and stayed that way for over an hour.

* * *

Emma yawned and slid her hand around Clayton's waist. "Mm, where are we?"

He kissed her temple. "We're almost to Camden Station."

Emma smiled and nodded. "I should wake up then."

Clayton chuckled. "Probably a good idea."

She forced her eyes open and sat up. Glancing at her sister, she raised an eyebrow at Jamie. "Is she actually asleep?"

Jamie winked. "Yep."

"You've become the Sophie whisperer."

Jamie stifled a laugh as he brought a finger to his lips. "Shh, she needs to sleep."

"Too late." Sophie pushed herself off Jamie's lap and sat up. "I woke up the moment you started moving your mouth."

Emma grimaced. "Sorry."

The hiss of the steam indicated they'd arrived in Maryland.

Sophie fixed her hair and set her bonnet back on her head. "Do I have time to check on Samson?"

Clayton nodded. "Yes. We'll be leaving again in about thirty minutes."

Jamie stood and took Sophie's hand. As they left the parlor car, Emma turned to Clayton. "We're alone."

Clayton raised an eyebrow. "Yes, we are."

"In a private parlor car."

"Yes. In a private parlor car," he repeated.

"And, we probably have at least fifteen minutes."

"Yes, we probably do." Clayton pulled her into his arms and began to kiss her.

A bang on the door elicited a very unladylike curse from Emma.

"Tickets!" came a voice on the other side of the door.

"Tickets?" Emma frowned and pushed away from him. "We have a private car, why would he be asking for tickets?"

Clayton set her next to the window before he opened the door.

"You opened that door entirely too quickly," a low voice admonished.

Clayton chuckled. "Samuel Powell, what are you doing on this train?"

"I'm returning from a quick visit home." A tall blond man shook Clayton's outstretched hand and then stepped over the threshold. "I ran into Jamie when I was boarding."

"Join us, then. We have plenty of room." Clayton held his hand out to Emma. "May I introduce my wife? Emma, this is Sam Powell."

Emma rose to her feet and reached out her hand. "It's nice to meet you, Mr. Powell."

Light blue eyes crinkled with warmth as he smiled and raised her hand to his lips. "Sam, please."

Clayton pulled Emma's hand away from Sam's mouth with a low growl. "Mr. Powell will suffice, Sam."

Emma raised an eyebrow and squeezed Clayton's hand. "Thank you, Sam. You must call me Emma."

Sam laughed and clapped Clayton's shoulder. "You did well, I see. I'm sorry I missed your wedding."

Emma took her seat again and Clayton sat next to her. Sam sat across from them just as Jamie and Sophie returned and took their seats. Clayton took advantage of the distraction, kissing Emma's fingers and leaning over to whisper, "We'll be home soon, sweet. I'll make sure you are no longer frustrated."

"You better."

Sophie removed her gloves and bonnet and tried her best to tame the locks of hair that had escaped her pins.

"How's Samson?" Emma asked.

"He's not happy." Sophie rubbed her forehead. "He doesn't like the moving stall and he's snorting up a storm, apparently. So far, though, he hasn't kicked anything, and I was able to calm him down a bit. We don't have much longer, so I think he'll

214

survive."

Emma ran her finger across Clayton's palm. "What's the plan once we get to the station?"

Clayton tried to close his hand, but Emma grinned and continued to entice him. "A carriage will be waiting to take us to the townhouse. I have arranged for an additional horse also, in case we want to ride."

Sophie grimaced. "I think I should ride Samson."

Jamie patted her knee. "If the weather stays mild, you and I can ride. If you're okay with riding in the carriage, Clayton."

Clayton nodded. "Yes, that's fine with me."

* * *

The train pulled into Union Station and Clayton led the group out onto the platform. Sam said his farewells as Jamie and Sophie went to retrieve Samson, and the bags were loaded onto the awaiting carriage. Emma's heart raced a little as Sophie led Samson over to them. He snorted and shook his head, sidestepping as she tried to bring him under control. Emma couldn't remember seeing a bigger horse, and he certainly wasn't happy.

"Knock it off, Samson. You're off the train now." Sophie slipped her hand into the pocket of her skirts and handed him a sugar cube. She pulled him over to a tree stump she could use to mount him and Jamie stood at his head holding the reins while she climbed into the saddle.

"I'm not sure this is such a good idea, Ten-Cow."

Sophie patted Samson's neck and gathered the reins in her hands. "He'll calm down. He just wants to go."

Jamie checked her stirrups and girth and then mounted the horse Clayton had provided.

Clayton assisted Emma into the carriage and then turned to Jamie. "Are you ready?"

He nodded and Clayton climbed in the carriage with Emma. The carriage rocked forward and Emma relaxed into the back of the seat. Clayton sat across from her and lifted her feet onto his lap. Gently removing her boots, he started to massage her feet.

Emma sighed in bliss. "How long until we get home?"

215

He loved that she was already referring to his home as hers. "Probably thirty minutes. Why?"

Emma smiled, pulled her feet out of his hands, and stood. He reached up and grasped her waist. "What are you doing? You'll fall."

She moved over to him, lifted her skirts, and straddled his hips. "Let's see if the rocking from the carriage adds to the pleasure."

He put his hands on her hips and began to kiss her. "Are we considering this research?"

"Yes, that's good, baby, it's research. We really shouldn't rush it. We need to make sure our data is absolutely correct. We must be thorough."

Clayton slid his hand between her legs and let out a surprised chuckle. "You naughty minx, you have nothing on under your skirts."

"I'm nothing if not prepared."

He raised an eyebrow in question. "You had clothes on when we left the house."

"Did I?"

Clayton's eyes widened as he opened her blouse. "I appreciate your dedication to the job, sweetheart"

"Mmmm, yes. I'm dedicated."

He tugged her chemise down to expose her breasts and kissed one, then the other. "Hold the straps, sweetheart."

Emma grabbed the straps on either side of the carriage and anchored herself while Clayton unbuttoned his breeches and guided himself inside of her.

His hands slid up her thighs, past the top of her stockings and cupped her bottom. Squeezing gently, he pressed his cock deeper into her and Emma dropped her head back.

Clayton sat up slightly, drawing a nipple into his mouth and biting down gently as Emma rode him, her movements matching those of the carriage.

"Get there, Clayton," she demanded and he kissed her as her walls contracted around him. She let go of one of the straps and gripped his chin. "You didn't get there."

216

He chuckled. "I plan to, Emma. But we have time, and I'm enjoying myself."

She leaned down and kissed him. "I want you to bite me some more."

He nodded to the window. "Straps."

She grinned and grabbed the strap again, sighing as Clayton ran a tongue over her pulse before drawing a nipple into his mouth and biting down again…this time a little harder.

Emma dropped her head back again. "Ohmigod, yes."

Keeping her nipple in his mouth, he gripped her hips and slammed into her while she kept herself steady. He had full range of motion, but with her hands occupied, she wasn't able to touch him. This drove her crazy. Crazy hot.

He pressed a palm against her mound and she ground her clit against it with a whimper of need.

"Climb off, sweet."

"What? Why?"

He grinned. "Trust me."

She stood as much as she could in the small space and Clayton guided her onto the bench across from him. "Brace your feet, Emma."

She stretched her legs across the small aisle and while he knelt in front of her and pushed her skirts higher, tugging her bottom to edge of the seat. Gripping her thighs, he buried his face between her legs and Emma cried out as he ran his tongue over her soaked folds, then bit down on her clit. She couldn't stop herself from grabbing his hair and pulling while grinding her pussy against his mouth.

Just as he brought her to the brink, his mouth was gone, replaced with his cock, and he kissed her as he slammed into her. She held tight to one of the straps again, while he buried himself deeper and deeper, kneading her breasts, then rolling her nipples between his fingertips.

"Clayton!"

"Now, sweetheart," he panted, and she exploded.

Clayton wasn't far behind and she released her hold on the leather, looping her arms around his neck as they came down from their climax high.

"Wow," she breathed out.

He grinned, sliding out of her and righting his clothing. He pulled a handkerchief out of his pocket and cleaned her up before helping her with her blouse. The carriage began to slow down just as the couple finished redressing.

"Well, Mrs. Madden, what is your conclusion? Does the rocking of the carriage add to the pleasure?"

"I believe, Mr. Madden, that we will need to do a control test. We'll need to do the experiment both inside and outside the carriage to determine the validity of the data."

Clayton laughed. "Loving you is so easy."

"I hope you always feel that way," Emma said with a smirk.

He pulled her onto his lap and kissed her. "I will."

"I like that answer." She pushed herself off his lap. "Ugh, we need to stop touching, I think."

Clayton wrapped an arm around her waist and pulled her close. "Why is that?"

"Because, I can't keep my hands off you." She tipped her chin up to face him. "I never thought sex would be like this."

"What did you think it would be like?"

"I knew I would like it, but I had no idea I would crave it."

He chuckled. "I must be doing something right then. If you ever *don't* crave it, tell me and I'll take care of it."

"I promise." She smiled and kissed him one more time.

There was a knock at the carriage door and Jamie opened it, his hand covering his eyes. "Are you two decent?"

"We are now," Emma retorted.

Clayton jumped out and lifted Emma down. The driver took the coach and horses into the carriage house, which was located at the back of the property.

The townhouse was red brick, with a beautiful white columned portico on the outside. It looked to be about three stories high and both Emma and Sophie fell in love immediately.

"I missed all the detail before." Emma squeezed Clayton's arm. "This is exquisite."

He smiled down at her. "I hope you'll be very happy here."

Clayton surprised her when he picked her up and carried her over the threshold.

"You better be careful, honey. I might make you keep going all the way to the bedroom."

"Don't you worry, sweet, we'll have plenty of time for everything you desire."

"I'll hold you to that," she whispered and kissed his neck.

Emma heard Sophie gasp as they walked through the front door into the spacious foyer. It was much larger than one would have expected from the outside and it was spectacular.

"Wow," Sophie said in awe.

"I will never get you out of the foyer, will I?" Jamie chuckled as he wrapped his arms around his wife from behind and kissed her shoulder.

Sophie didn't answer.

"Is it the house or the history?" Emma asked her.

"Both," Sophie whispered.

"Would you like a tour of the house now, or would you rather wait until later?" Clayton asked.

"I'd really like to sleep, so if it's all right with you, can we do it later, please?" Sophie asked.

"Of course. Jenkins will show you to your room. Emma and I are on the opposite side of the house, so you will have an ample amount of privacy. Dinner is at six."

The butler led Jamie and Sophie to their wing of the house and Clayton took Emma's hand and moved towards theirs. Emma squeezed his hand. "Your butler's name isn't really Jenkins, is it?"

"No, it's Walter, but he does a very convincing English accent, so we nicknamed him Jenkins."

"Why does he need to do a very convincing English accent?"

Clayton leaned down and whispered. "Because he's not a butler."

Emma's eyes widened and she nodded. "Got it."

Clayton opened a door and stepped back to allow Emma to walk in first. She walked into an ivory and chocolate brown sitting room that was the perfect combination of masculine and feminine decorations. Not one frill anywhere. She turned and raised an eyebrow.

Clayton smiled and held his hand up. "Before you say anything, this is *our* bedroom."

"Seriously?"

He nodded. "Yes. I sent Gwendolyn a wire and she prepared everything."

"Gwendolyn?" Emma narrowed her eyes. "Gwendolyn redecorated your personal rooms?"

"It's quite the amusing story, actually."

Emma crossed her arms and looked at him in mock suspicion. "Do tell."

"She's a good friend of Mrs. Lincoln's—"

"Mary Todd Lincoln? *That* Mrs. Lincoln?" she interrupted.

Clayton chuckled. "Yes, that Mrs. Lincoln. When Mrs. Lincoln found out I was betrothed, she graciously offered to have Gwen redecorate a few rooms for me."

"I thought you said Gwen wasn't a friend."

"It's hard to describe. When I say friend... she's not someone I share things with—not like you. She's a bit like a little sister."

"Yeah, she really looks like a sister."

Clayton shrugged. "She and Christopher have been an incredible support to me, particularly with the situation with Richard."

Emma's stomach dropped slightly. "Beautiful and a saint. Great."

"Sweetheart, she doesn't even compare to you."

Emma rolled her eyes. "Oh, please."

"You'll get to know her better tonight."

"Why?"

"I invited Christopher and Gwen over for dinner." Clayton ran a finger down her cheek. "She's staying with Christopher for a few days."

"Where does she normally live?"

"With her parents in Maryland. Mary asked her to assist with a small dinner they are putting together, so she came to stay with

Chris in order to do that." Clayton cupped her cheek. "You are ten times as beautiful as Gwendolyn Butler will ever be." He erased her retort with a kiss that melted her.

"Let me show you the bedroom." Clayton led her through the door that connected the two rooms.

In the middle of the spacious room was a massive four-poster bed. She thought it might be bigger than a modern day king-sized bed. A lit fire bathed the walls in a romantic light, and the room was also in cream and chocolate hues, but the accents were in a turquoise. She had mentioned to him once that she loved this color scheme, but it was absolutely not typical Victorian décor.

Clayton opened the wardrobe doors. "I made sure that your things were put in here, nowhere else."

"Thank you."

"Do you like it?"

"I'm amazed that you remembered everything. It's perfect." She turned to him and stood on her tiptoes to kiss him. "Let me show you how much I like it."

Emma spent the next hour showing her gratitude and the couple fell asleep in each other's arms.

TWENTY
ONE

*E*MMA SIGHED AS a firm body cradled hers, and soft lips kissed her shoulder.

"It's time to wake up, sweetheart." Clayton ran his hand down her hip.

She slowly opened her eyes. "But I'm having the most delectable dream."

"Well then, by all means, keep dreaming." His hand slid between her legs and cupped her gently as his finger slid into her wetness. "Always so ready for me."

Emma mewed, dropping her head back and Clayton slipped into her from behind, cupping her breast with one hand, while he worked her clit with the other.

"Clay," she panted. "I...I..."

"Not yet, sweetness." He buried himself in her slowly again and gripped her hip when she tried to press harder against him. "Not so fast."

"Clayton," she growled.

"I want this to last."

She reached back and grabbed his thigh. "And I want you to fu—"

"Emma Justine Madden," he admonished, cutting off her curse as he applied more pressure to her clitoris.

"More," she begged.

"More?"

"God, yes," she hissed.

"On your knees."

Emma threw the covers back and tore off her nightgown before kneeling on the bed.

"I like your enthusiasm, sweetheart."

She waved her hand in a circle. "Get on with it, man."

Clayton laughed, but didn't make her wait, pushing his cock inside of her and sliding his hand between her legs.

"Clay…aaaah," she breathed out as he began to move. Gripping her hips, he slammed into her over and over, then, slowed his pace and fingered her clit, until she had to bury her face in the blankets to smother her scream.

Much to her frustration, but ultimate satisfaction, he built her up again before finally joining her in climax, and by the time they collapsed in a heap on the bed, Emma was wide-awake. "I had no idea."

Clayton wrapped an arm around her. "Neither did I."

"Oh, *please*. I'm sure you've done all of this before." She laid her head on his shoulder and kissed his chest.

"No, I have not done *all* of this before." He gave her bottom a gentle pinch. "But what I have done was never like that."

Emma slid her arm over his stomach and glanced up at him. "Really?"

"Really."

"I can't imagine how it wouldn't be. I mean, with a man like you."

"Emma, you're more than I could have ever expected. I have never and will never, love anyone as much as I love you. I have a feeling that's what makes this so…"

"Mind-blowing?" she added, smiling.

"Yes, that's a very good phrase."

223

"Ditto."

He raised an eyebrow. "Ditto?"

"It means, I feel the same way," she clarified. "I love you."

"Ditto." He climbed off the tall bed and pulled her with him. "Now, it's time for us to get ready for dinner. There is a bath set up in the sitting room for you."

Emma grabbed her robe and stepped into the sitting room. She could see the steam coming up off the water and the smell of orange essence wafted through the room. She stepped into the large copper tub and was surprised to feel Clayton grasp her hand.

"Careful." He smiled as he helped her in.

She sank into the scented water. "Mm, this is heaven."

"Heaven?"

She smiled up at him. "Well, as close to heaven as I can get without you between my legs." Clayton cleared his throat and Emma giggled. "You're blushing. Have I shocked you?"

He chuckled. "I'm not blushing."

"The bath is big enough for two, why don't you come and see for yourself?"

"I'm not sure orange is my scent."

She sat up and the water trickled between her breasts. "Are you sure?"

Clayton narrowed his eyes. "Slide forward."

Emma hummed as she did as he asked. "Boobies do the trick every time."

"I'm sorry?" He stepped in behind her and sat. The water level rose and slipped over the edge so he grabbed the towel closest to them, and laid it on the floor.

"Boobies. Breasts. Tatas. Men will do anything for a glimpse." Emma leaned back against his chest and ran the washcloth up and down his thigh.

His arms tightened around her waist. "Who have *you* shown your breasts to, Emma?"

She dropped her head back and smiled up at him. "No one, baby. Don't worry. It's something Sophie used to say about Jamie. If she wanted something—"

224

Clayton laid his hand over her mouth. "I do not want to know anything about your sister's personal conversations with her husband."

Emma laughed. "Oh, then I won't tell you it was Jamie who informed me that almost any man will do anything if a woman shows him her sweater yams. And if we let them touch them, well—"

"Emma!"

She shrugged. "After what you did to me in that bedroom less than an hour ago, you cannot act the prude."

"Have you ever heard the expression, you will be the death of me?"

Emma turned and knelt facing him. "Yep. And I'm flattered that you think I have that much power." She leaned over and kissed him.

Clayton cupped her cheeks and pulled her closer. In one fluid movement, he wrapped an arm around her waist and stood. She let out a quiet squeal. "How did you do that?" She wrapped her legs around his hips to keep from falling and Clayton stepped out of the tub.

"You're easy to carry." He pushed at her hips gently. "You can lower your legs now."

She shook her head. "No, I kind of like this position."

"I need to grab the towels and I don't want to drop you."

"You won't."

"Emma, be serious. If I let go of your waist, you'll slip."

She grinned. "Try me."

He frowned but did let go briefly. She didn't move. He glanced at her in suspicion and let go again, and she raised her hands above her head. "Look, mom, no hands."

He held her again. "How did you do that?"

"Probably a combination of dance and horses."

"I don't see how a waltz or quadrille would allow you the leg strength to do that."

She slid from his hips and he handed her a towel. "Oh, it wouldn't. The kind of dancing I'm referring to is something you have never seen. Would you like me to show you a couple of

225

moves?"

Curiosity filled his gaze. "Yes, please."

She slipped into a pair of the new underwear she'd had made—a lacy black pair of boy shorts—and was rewarded with Clayton's sharp intake of breath.

Clayton stood and pulled her close and then slid his hands down her hips. "I'm assuming these are from the future?"

"Well, *these* aren't from the future, but the design is. It would appear you approve."

Clayton laughed and kissed her again. "I very much approve, but perhaps I should get dressed in case we linger even longer."

"Probably a good idea. I'm glad I'm on the right track with my underwear. There will be more in our future. Besides, you wanted me to show you something."

"Yes, you're right." He released her and stepped away.

"Give me a minute to stretch."

Once limber enough, she stood in the middle of their bedroom and executed a perfect arabesque with her signature twist. Without flinching, she lifted her torso to grab hold of the ankle that was in the air, continually keeping the straight lines of her split.

Clayton stared with his mouth open.

Emma lowered her leg and bowed. "What do you think?"

"That was magnificent!"

"I have more moves so when we're alone, I'll let you put the iPod on again and I'll do a portion of one of my routines for you if you like."

"I would like." He smiled wickedly and pulled her close for another kiss. "Especially if you're going to do it in just your underwear."

"You're a bad, bad man, my love." She sighed. "Now, help me on with this ridiculous corset."

Clayton helped her dress and then led her down to the parlor for pre-dinner drinks. Jamie and Sophie hadn't arrived yet, so Clayton went to check on the dinner progress. Before he returned, the butler announced the arrival of Christopher and Gwendolyn Butler, and Emma wasn't quite sure what to do.

Should she find Clayton, or try to wing it?

The siblings entered the room and Emma was a little taken aback.

Gwendolyn was more beautiful than she remembered, and her brother looked like a masculine version of her, only much, much taller. He was gorgeous as well.

"Welcome to Washington, Mrs. Madden." Gwendolyn enfolded her into a warm hug. "I was so worried about you after you left. The only thing Andrew would tell me was that you were safe."

Emma smiled. "Yes, very safe. I'm sorry I worried you. Thank you so much for the renovations you did. They are magnificent."

"You're welcome. I had never thought to put those colors together before, but I love it. I may steal the idea for future use."

"You're welcome to."

Gwen turned to her brother. "Emma, this is my brother, Christopher."

Emma held out her hand, but rather than shaking it, he kissed her fingers. "It's lovely to meet you, Mrs. Madden."

"Please, call me Emma."

"I prefer Mrs. Madden, personally," Clayton said from the doorway.

"Clayton!" Gwen squealed and went over for a chaste hug. Christopher shook his hand and welcomed him home.

Clayton moved to Emma's side and handed her a glass of red wine that "Jenkins" brought into the room. He handed Gwen the other poured glass and turned to her brother. "Christopher, may I offer you a drink?"

"Whiskey if you have it."

Clayton nodded to the butler who left to fulfill the request.

"How was your trip? How's Richard?" Gwen sat in a chair near the fireplace.

"The trip was superb." He sent a meaningful look in Emma's direction as he pulled her down beside him on the large sofa against the wall. "Richard is much better, thank you for asking."

"And Andrew?"

"Gwendolyn," Christopher admonished.

Clayton smiled. "Andrew is doing well, Gwen."

Gwen sipped her wine. "Thank you."

"How have things been here?"

Christopher took the chair next to his sister. "Frantic with the plans for Gettysburg. Security has been our main focus."

"That makes sense. I have some ideas on that subject but will fill you in tomorrow. Tonight, I want to celebrate." Clayton grinned.

Jamie and Sophie rushed through the door and Sophie lifted her hands to check her perfectly coiffed hair. Clayton and Christopher both rose and the introductions were made.

"James, your reputation precedes you." Christopher waited for Sophie to sit and then took his seat again.

"Is that so?"

"Yes, we've heard about the successes you have been having with the cavalry at Harrisburg. There are in fact several units that would be interested in your leadership."

"Thank you. I'm excited to be here."

Gwen leaned forward and smiled. "Emma and Sophie, would the two of you like to join me on a tour tomorrow? With the men working, it will probably be very boring."

Emma nodded. "Yes, that would wonderful. Thank you."

"Yes, thank you." Sophie reiterated.

"Dinner is served," Walter informed them from the doorway.

"Shall we?" Clayton stood and led the small group to the dining room.

Dinner was surprisingly animated. Emma had always thought Sophie's Civil War sounded awfully boring. Everyone was so proper and no one ever said anything funny or uncivilized. She was proven wrong this evening. She couldn't help but adore the Butler siblings. They were warm and funny, not to mention intelligent. Christopher seemed a little too serious, but Gwen didn't seem to let it faze her. She was quite the wit. Emma could tell Sophie felt the same way and Emma had to admit, she was looking forward to their outing the next day.

When the evening came to a close, Clayton and Emma

walked the siblings to the door. Christopher assisted Gwen with her coat and scarf.

"I'll be by at ten to pick you both up, if that is agreeable." Gwen hugged Emma.

Emma nodded. "Yes, that's perfect."

With one last wave, Clayton closed the door and wrapped his arm around Emma's waist as they made their way back to the parlor. She looked up at him. "I'm not tired in the least."

He kissed her temple. "Neither am I."

"Let's get rid of the oldies, then."

"Sir?"

Clayton raised his head at the sound of Walter's voice. "Yes, Walter?"

"Mr. and Mrs. Ford said goodnight and wanted me to inform you they will see you for breakfast."

Emma leaned into Clayton. "I *do* love my sister."

"Thank you, Walter. We'll be turning in as well."

"Goodnight, sir, ma'am."

"Goodnight, Walter."

Emma gave him a little wave. "Good night, Walter."

When they got back to their room, Clayton helped Emma undress. She presented her back for help with her corset. "Okay, you win. Christopher and Gwen are very nice."

Clayton kissed her neck. "Yes, they are."

"What was all that business with Gwen asking about Andrew? Don't they have a relationship?"

"I believe it's very complicated." Clayton loosened her laces and chuckled.

"Why don't they make it uncomplicated? I mean if Andrew loves her, why doesn't he do something about it?"

"None of us know why he refuses to act on it." Clayton turned her to face him. "But I'd rather not talk about them right now."

Emma ran her hand down his face. "What would you like to talk about then?"

"I don't want to talk at all." He slid his arms around her waist and cupped her bottom.

Emma licked her lips. "Is there something else you'd like to do with your mouth?"

He leaned forward and ran his tongue over her bottom lip. "Yes...after."

"After what?"

He lifted her so she could wrap her legs around his waist and anchored her against a wall. "After I test just how strong you are."

She shivered, kissing him as he guided his cock inside of her.

"You all right?" he asked.

She nodded, weaving her fingers into his hair. No more words were necessary as Clayton took her against the wall, especially considering Emma came so hard and so fast, she could barely breathe. Clayton carried her to the bed, staying buried deep inside, settling her at the edge of the mattress and gripping her thighs. Emma lifted her hips slightly in an attempt to get closer.

"You want more, little minx?" he rasped, pushing in further.

She whimpered in answer, grabbing for his wrists and using them as leverage to pull him closer. Clayton settled his palms on each side of her waist and Emma locked her ankles around his waist. He slammed into her harder and harder, sliding a hand between them and fingering her clit as he moved.

"Clayton," she rasped. "Now, baby."

He gave her one more thrust, then she felt his cock pulse inside of her and she let herself go. He slid out of her, stretching out on the bed beside her, and wrapping her tightly in his arms. "I love you."

She grinned, stroking his cheek. "I love you, too."

He kissed her again and pulled the covers up around them.

"Will it always be like this?" she asked snuggling closer.

"Yes," he answered immediately, and she giggled.

"You're so very confident of that fact."

"We're perfect together, don't you think."

"So, so perfect," she agreed, and tried to bite back a yawn.

"Am I boring you, sweetheart?"

"More accurately, you wore me out."

His hand stroked her bottom. "Sleep, little minx."

He didn't have to tell her twice and she succumbed to slumber within minutes.

* * *

As promised, Gwen picked the girls up right on time the next morning.

"Good morning." Emma greeted her at the door, as Walter ushered Gwen in.

"Good morning, Emma, are you ready to go?"

"Shortly. Sophie is in the dining room, having a little bit of breakfast."

"I probably should have come later." Gwen removed her bonnet and handed it to Walter. "You had a long day yesterday and I didn't really think."

"No, it's fine. Truly. Sophie's pregnancy forces her to eat at strange times," Emma explained.

Gwen followed Emma into the dining room. Sophie smiled as she lowered her cup of coffee, looking a little less green. "Good morning."

"Good morning, Sophie, how are you feeling?" Gwen asked.

"I feel very well. Now."

"I will keep our day light today. I thought you might want to know where a few of the key shops are. We also have a very nice park."

Emma grinned. "I can't wait."

Sophie stood and laid her napkin on the table. "Shall we?"

The girls started to follow Gwen out to her little buggy.

"Oh, shoot!" Sophie said.

"What's wrong?" Emma asked.

"I need to visit Samson. He's in a strange place and won't know what's going on."

Gwen gave her a puzzled look.

"It's her horse," Emma supplied.

"Oh. Well, why don't we do that then? We have plenty of time."

"Thank you!" Sophie led the girls out to the carriage house.

231

They arrived to find Samson snorting and pounding his hoof and a stable boy starting to open his stall door. "Wait!" Sophie yelled, but it was too late.

The door was opened and Samson pushed the poor boy over as he bolted out of the stall. Sophie whistled and Samson turned and trotted up to her as though nothing had happened. She handed him a sugar cube and then made her way to the groom. "Young man, are you all right?"

He stood and brushed himself off. "Yes'm."

"Never open his stall door unless I'm here or there's an emergency, all right? He is rather like a spoiled child, a very large one, and you might get hurt. If he's pawing the ground like that, you have permission to find me. He only does it if he's getting ready to do some damage."

She turned back to Samson and stroked his nose, even though she was furious. "You, horse, need to start behaving. I will ride you later, I promise."

Samson continued to nuzzle her shoulder and Sophie spent a few minutes giving him some attention while the stable boy quickly cleaned out his stall.

"All right, Sammy. Back you go." Sophie walked to his stall and he followed her without a lead. She led him into the box and closed the door. "He should be fine now. I'm sorry, what's your name?"

"Jack, missus."

"Well, Jack, thank you for your diligent care. I'll come back later today and take him out for a ride. He shouldn't give you any more trouble, but if he does, please don't hesitate to find me, all right?"

"Yes ma'am."

Washington D.C. was an incredible city. Emma thought about what Sophie told her about the history and the reason it became the capital was due to the "Compromise of 1790." An agreement between Alexander Hamilton, James Madison, and Thomas Jefferson, which basically said that if the North would not raise objections to slavery, Washington, D.C. would be lo-

232

cated in two slave states, Maryland and Virginia. Many of Hamilton's colleagues fought for New York.

Emma started to appreciate the impact of where she was. Most of the time, history was a little lost on her. She got the appeal, but could never comprehend Sophie's absolute obsession with it. She was starting to see the intrigue, but admittedly, if it hadn't been for Clayton, she didn't know if she would have been able to accept the fact she was stuck in the past. She sighed when she thought of him. She missed him already, and it had only been a few hours since he'd awakened her to make love before he left for work.

Sophie squeezed her hand and Emma smiled. Gwen was the ultimate tour guide, showing them all of the sights of the beautiful city. She was a wealth of information and Clayton was right. She was friendly and easy to be around. Emma liked her immensely.

Before they knew it, it was lunchtime.

"I have a little surprise for you," Gwen said mysteriously.

She guided the buggy into the little park close to the townhouse, set the brake, and climbed down. Emma helped Sophie out and they followed Gwen, blindly, not knowing where they were going. They came around a corner of lush trees and Jamie, Clayton, and Christopher stood near a bench, seemingly deep in conversation.

Emma squealed quietly and regardless of how it might look in the nineteenth century, made a run for Clayton. He caught her as she threw herself into his arms. "Oh, I missed you so much."

He chuckled and buried his head in her neck. "Ditto, sweet."

Jamie pulled Sophie into his arms, a little more chastely, but must have whispered something dirty in her ear because she blushed and smacked his shoulder. He leaned down and kissed her despite the audience.

Clayton slid Emma's hand into the crook of his elbow. "Let's eat. We have a lot to do this afternoon."

TWENTY
TWO

ONCE LUNCH CONCLUDED, the girls climbed back into the buggy and started their trip back to the townhouse. As they traveled down a busy street, Emma saw something. Or someone. She grabbed Sophie's hand. "Is that Rose?" she whispered.

"Where?" Sophie whispered back and looked behind them.

The woman they were referring to looked sideways just as the girls turned.

"It *is*, Sophie! I think that's Rose!"

Sophie shook her head. "It couldn't be, Em. She was staying back with Richard, right?"

"Sophie, it was Rose. I'm sure of it."

"We'll talk to the guys later. Maybe Clayton knows something."

Emma nodded. "Okay."

Arriving at the townhouse, Gwen pulled up to the front of the house and set the brake.

"Would you like to stay for tea?" Emma asked as she stepped

234

from the buggy.

Gwen shook her head. "I would love to, but I'm meeting Mrs. Lincoln to help her plan a ball. I will see you in a day or so though."

Sophie gasped and Emma squeezed her hand. "We'll see you later, then. Thanks for the tour."

Gwen waved and took off toward the White House.

Emma raised an eyebrow at her sister's deer-in-the-headlight look. "Don't freak."

Sophie went white. "No!"

Emma nodded. "Um, yes. She's a close personal friend of Mary Todd Lincoln."

"Hold that thought. I'm going to be sick." Sophie ran for her room.

Emma removed her gloves and cloak and went to find Sophie.

She pushed open her sister's door. "Soph?" Sophie was leaning over the chamber pot losing her lunch. Literally.

"Are you okay?" Emma rushed to her side.

Sophie groaned. "The baby's killing me."

"Where are your pills?"

"They're in my reticule."

Emma retrieved the pills and grabbed Sophie a glass of water. "You look so pathetic right now."

"I know." Sophie took a deep breath and sat on the edge of the bed. "Give me a minute. I need to ride Samson before it gets dark."

"I'm not sure if you should ride right now."

"I have to."

Emma sat next to her. "Maybe you should wait for Jamie."

"It'll be fine, Em. You can go with me. We won't go far."

"You're probably right. I'm sure there's a nice horse in the carriage house." Emma stood. "I'll go change really quick."

The girls wore their newly made breeches under their skirts. They set out for the carriage house, excited about their ride.

Sophie whistled for Samson, who whinnied for her and stuck his head out of the stall in greeting. She asked Jack to saddle one of the other horses for Emma and then had Emma help with Samson.

Sophie sighed. "He's so calm with you, Em."

Emma tightened the girth. "He probably senses you and I are related."

"Well, I hope you can ride him when I get too big." Sophie poked her head over his back. "I'm not sure how long Jamie will let me once I start to show."

"He's beautiful. I'd love to ride him."

"Mrs. Madden, I have your mount."

"Thanks, Jack."

Emma mounted from the ground, but Sophie had to use the mounting block, so it took a little extra time to get going. The girls spent the next two hours exploring their new city. They even found a stretch of land where they could run, which was really what Samson needed.

They arrived back at the stable, elated and with very tired horses. Sophie had to slide off Samson butt first, but he stayed perfectly still, almost as though he knew she needed his support. "Good boy, Sammy."

As they walked inside, Emma decided that a bath was called for before dinner and organized one for Sophie as well.

* * *

Jamie paced the length of Clayton's office while Christopher and Clayton sifted through the mountain of paperwork they'd accumulated over the past three months.

"I have to tell Sophie what's going on."

Clayton shook his head. "You can't."

Christopher studied one particular message delivered that morning. "I agree," he said distractedly.

Jamie dragged his hands down his face. "She already knows something's going on. If she suspects I'm lying to her, I don't know what she'll do."

Christopher raised an eyebrow. "She's a woman, James. You have the power to dictate her actions."

Jamie snorted. "You don't know my wife."

236

Clayton signed the bottom of one of the pages he had been reading and leaned back in his chair. "Jamie, you can say nothing to Sophie *or* Emma. If they know, they'll be in the path of danger."

"I don't like this, Clayton." Jamie scowled. "Sophie will kill me when she finds out."

Clayton rose to his feet. "As long as she finds out *after* we've dealt with the threat."

* * *

Emma was dozing in the warm water when she felt soft lips on hers. "Fabio! I told you, we can't do this here, my husband might find out."

"Can this Fabio person do this to you?" Clayton chuckled and moved his hand under the water, sliding it between her legs. "Or this?" he asked, adding pressure to her clit.

Emma sighed as she reluctantly opened her eyes and smiled at him. "Hi."

"How was your day?"

"I have other things on my mind than how my day was, Mr. Madden. I suggest you get naked quickly." He laughed. Emma cocked her head in question. "Do you think this is a joke?"

"No ma'am. Yes ma'am." He pulled his shirt over his head. "I will take care of that immediately, ma'am."

Emma giggled. "I hope it's always this easy to make you obey."

He lifted her out of the tub and pulled her wet body closer for a kiss. She ran her hand down his bare chest. "I don't think I'll ever get sick of this view."

Clayton lowered her to the ground and handed her a towel. "I believe my view is far better."

Emma grinned. "You're soaked."

"Not for long." He kissed her nose. "You ordered me to remove my clothes, remember?"

"Get to it, then." He laughed as he made his way into their bedroom. Emma followed. "How was it being back at work?"

"Frantic. The President's trip to Gettysburg is only a couple

237

of weeks away."

"Are we going to go?"

"If you'd like to, I think that can be arranged."

"You don't know my sister." Emma secured her towel and sat on the bed. "She would absolutely die if she didn't."

Clayton washed his face and turned to her as he dragged a washcloth over his chin. "Really?"

"Yes, really. Sophie's a huge Civil War buff."

"How so?"

"For one, her library at home was filled with Lincoln biographies, Grant's memoirs, anything relating to the war."

Clayton lowered the washcloth. "Grant writes a memoir?"

Emma nodded. "Yes, apparently so. She used to do reenactments all over the country before she got sick. You should ask her about it. She remembers dates and places like no one else. If you ever need to know anything relating to the war, Clay, she's the one to ask. I know it's probably still strange for you, but seriously, she's an encyclopedia."

He removed his shoes and stood in front of her. "What's the significance of Gettysburg for her?"

"The President is going to give what ends up being one of the most well-documented and profound speeches ever given. When Sophie talks about the President, her whole face lights up. I think that if she was able to attend this particular speech, she would probably never have to see anything else."

"I'll make it happen, then. We wouldn't want to disappoint Sophie."

Emma giggled. "No, we wouldn't."

"More importantly, however, I would hate to disappoint you, so I believe we should take care of you." Clayton removed her towel and leaned down to kiss her.

"Mmm... more of that, please." Emma pushed his pants from his hips and spent the next hour welcoming her husband home.

* * *

Clayton and Emma joined the Fords in the dining room for a late dinner. Clayton held the chair for Emma and waited for her to take a seat. "Did you enjoy your tour?"

Emma laid her napkin on her lap. "Yes. The city's beautiful."

Clayton sat at the head of the table. "Was Gwen able to show you much?"

Sophie nodded. "A bit, but it was the ride later when we got to really explore."

"Ride?" Jamie broke in.

Sophie took a sip of water. "Yes, I took Samson out."

Jamie leaned forward and glared. "Excuse me?"

"Well, with Emma, of course."

Jamie laid his fork down slowly. "You took Samson out, with Emma of course?" His tone grew lethal.

Sophie rolled her eyes. "Jamie, it was a short ride."

"A short ride."

Emma glanced at Clayton and then back at Jamie. *Was that steam coming off his head?*

"Excuse us." Jamie took Sophie's arm and pulled her away from the table. He pushed her out into the hallway. "What the hell were you thinking to go riding alone in a strange city without me?"

"I wasn't alone, I was with Emma."

"Emma's in a strange city as well, Sophie!"

Emma squeezed her eyes shut at the sound of his anger.

"We were together, so we weren't alone," Sophie argued.

"Damn it, Sophie, don't you dare try to mince words with me!"

The door to the parlor slammed shut and then all they heard was muffled yelling.

"Emma." Clayton's voice was laced with warning.

She turned to look at him. "Yes, Clayton."

"Explain, please."

"What's to explain? We went for a short ride because Samson was freaking out. He needed to be ridden, and it's not like Sophie could have gone by herself. That would have been dangerous."

239

He took a deep breath. "Never again are you to ride anywhere without either me or Jamie. I would even be all right with Christopher, but no one else."

"What if none of you are available?" Emma crossed her arms and sat back with a huff. "You let us ride around alone with Gwen today."

"Then take Walter."

"What if he's not available?"

"Then you stay home."

Emma slapped her hands on the table. "You can't be serious!"

"Do I make myself clear, Emma?"

"Crystal!" she snapped and stood.

"Where are you going?"

"I'm leaving."

"Sit down, Emma. This conversation is not over." Clayton didn't raise his voice, but she felt his anger just the same.

"Yes, it is." She walked out of the room, but heard the scrape of a chair and his familiar footsteps behind her.

"Get back here."

She kept going. "No."

"Emma, we're not finished."

"You might not be, but I sure as hell am," she fired back and started up the stairs. She was almost to the top of the staircase when she was lifted into his arms and thrown over his shoulder like a sack of potatoes. She pounded his back and tried to yell, but couldn't catch her breath. "What are you doing, you Neanderthal? Put me down!"

He carried her down the hall, through their sitting room, and into their bedroom, where he threw her unceremoniously onto the bed.

"Why are you being such an ass?" Emma screamed.

"Women do not simply go for a ride alone in this century. Especially my wife."

"Why?" Emma hissed as she sat up. "Because I'm the so-called fairer sex?"

He paced the room. "You cannot comprehend the dangers

for you outside of this house, without a man to protect you."

"Oh, *please*! The melodrama. Sophie and I know how to take care of ourselves."

Clayton took a long deep breath and ran his fingers slowly through his hair. "What would you do, Emma, if something happened to one of you? Explain to me how you would take care of yourself?"

"Well, I would call—"

"You would what?"

"Um, I would find a police officer or a soldier."

"Really?" He crossed his arms. "And if there wasn't one around, what would you do?"

"I would—"

"What, Emma? What would you do?"

"Well, I would..." She didn't know.

He was right and she hated that. She realized she couldn't just whip out her cell phone or jump in a cab. She wouldn't be able to find a local hospital or lots of other things she could in the future.

The bluster went right out of her and she realized how stupid they'd been. They didn't know anyone here and they didn't know their way around. It could have been a dangerous situation and neither of them even thought about it.

"I'm sorry," she whispered. "You're right."

"Come here, sweetheart."

She stood and walked into his arms.

"If anything ever happened to you, I don't know what I would do. I love you and I want you safe. Do you understand?"

"Yes, I understand, but it wasn't like we thought about it and decided we didn't care. We used to go riding alone all the time at home."

He stroked her hair. "It's different here."

"I know." She laid her cheek against his chest. "At home, we had cell phones."

"What's a cell phone?"

"It's very complicated."

"Why don't you explain?"

She pulled away and looked up at him. "I think I should start at the beginning."

"Should we sit down?"

"Probably."

He sat on one of the chairs that faced the fireplace and pulled her onto his lap. "Please, continue."

"A telephone will be invented, I'm not sure when. Sophie probably does. Anyway, Alexander Graham Bell invents this device that will allow people to talk in real time. For instance, if you're at work, I could pick up the phone in this room, dial a number and we'd be able to speak – voice to voice. A cell phone utilizes cell towers and satellites and it allows you to take it anywhere in the world. You don't have to plug it into the wall."

"What do you mean by 'plug it into the wall'?"

"In the future there's electricity, so you don't have to light a candle to create light. You can just flip a switch on the wall, or plug a cord into the wall for a lamp to illuminate."

His eyes widened. "That's amazing."

"I know. Pretty cool, huh?"

"Yes, but still not a diversion enough to get you off the hook."

"Dang it!"

Clayton chuckled quietly. "Sweet, you need to remember who you're married to. I don't want to scare you unnecessarily, but at the same time, you need to be a little extra careful. These are dangerous times and I have enemies."

Emma sighed. "I'm sorry. I promise I'll be much more careful."

He gave her a squeeze. "That's all I ask."

"Oh! I almost forgot. I saw Rose today."

"What? Where?"

"Over by the park."

"Are you certain?"

She nodded. "I'm sure it was her."

"Did she see you?"

"No, we were in the buggy with Gwen, so pretty hidden."

Emma sighed. "Do you believe me now, that she's up to something?"

He frowned. "I wonder what her game is?"

Emma shrugged. "I don't know, but I'm hungry. Can we go back downstairs and finish dinner, please?"

"Yes, sweet."

They made their way downstairs and heard more yelling coming from the parlor.

"*Do I need to remind you of the stable incident, Sophie?*" Jamie yelled.

"*Oh, nice, throw that back in my face! You are such an ass!*"

"*You cannot just go off and do whatever the hell you want here. Think, Sophie. It's a different time, not to mention a place you're not familiar with.*"

"*Samson needed to be ridden, James. So, what exactly would you have had me do? Let him kick the stall out? He barreled poor Jack down trying to get free.*"

"*You aren't listening to me!*"

"*Perhaps because you're talking out of your ass!*"

"*I'm about ready to send Samson back.*"

"*You wouldn't!*" Sophie bellowed.

"*I would if it means your safety. I'm sick of you putting yourself and our baby in danger, and I won't sit by and watch you continue to do it. Pull anything like this again and that damn horse gets shipped back.*"

Clayton pulled Emma away from the parlor and back into the dining room. Emma grimaced as she took her seat. "I've never heard Jamie that mad before." She started to stand. "I wonder if I should go help."

Clayton grabbed her hand. "No. They need to work it out themselves."

Emma gave a little huff. They heard a door slam and then a few minutes later, Jamie walked in and sat at the table.

Clayton handed him a glass of whiskey. "Is everything all right?"

Jamie downed the drink. "It will be."

"Where's Sophie?" Emma asked.

243

"In our room."

"I'll make her a tray. She didn't eat much."

Jamie sighed. "Fine."

Emma prepared a plate for Sophie and then made her way to her bedroom and knocked on the door. No one answered, so she pushed the door open. "Sophie? I brought you a tray."

"I'm not hungry."

Emma set the tray on the nightstand. "You need to eat, Sophie. You'll get sick if you don't." Sophie sat up and wiped the tears from her face. Emma handed her a handkerchief. "If it's any consolation, Clayton was pretty angry too."

"Jamie's so smothering at the moment and it's driving me crazy."

"Um, hello... you're pregnant."

Sophie shook her head. "No, there's something else going on, but he refuses to talk to me about it."

"Are you sure it's not because you had a scare a little while ago?"

"No. It's more than that. And now he's threatening to send Sammy back." Sophie rubbed her temples. "He's been weird ever since they had that conversation with Topper. He's being such a jerk."

Emma sighed. "Did you ask Jamie what was going on?"

Sophie picked up a piece of bread and took a bite. "Of course I did. He won't tell me."

"Well, it's obvious they both know something we don't, so even if we hate it, maybe it would be better to be careful."

Sophie shook her head. "He's lying to me, Emma."

* * *

In a small row house on the outskirts of D.C., two men and one woman discussed their plans to take care of what they referred to as "The Problem."

"They arrived yesterday. They brought her sister and brother-in-law with them. That's a complication I was not expecting."

"Darlin', it's a small snafu. Nothin' we can't take care of.

244

James is with Clayton all day and the bitch's sister is pregnant. She won't be difficult to subdue."

"It has to happen before they leave for Gettysburg. If we can't get the information from her husband, we won't be able to take care of the problem. He needs a certain motivation."

"You were supposed to take care of the Wade boy. That should have been motivation enough."

"We didn't count on him being smart, Tony. That was your first mistake."

"I say we take care of them Monday, unless we can nab 'em this weekend. Lew, are you prepared? Don't kill them, understand? We'll just grab them and take them to the hideout."

"I understand. I'll take care of it."

TWENTY
THREE

*E*MMA VAGUELY REMEMBERED Clayton's kiss when he left for work the next morning. She climbed out of bed, wrapped her robe around her, and went in search of her sister. She found her in the dining room. Emma grabbed a piece of toast. "You're up."

Sophie sipped her coffee. "It *is* past nine o'clock."

Emma smirked. "Did you and Jamie work things out last night?"

"He thinks we did."

Emma poured herself a cup of coffee. "This is so unlike you. You don't hide stuff from Jamie. You never have."

Sophie sighed. "He's hiding something from me... payback."

"Sophie. Really? How do you even know he's hiding something?"

Sophie popped a grape into her mouth. "His sense of humor has disappeared."

Emma shrugged. "Yeah, he does seem a little less jovial.

246

Kind of like when we couldn't find you."

Sophie grimaced. "I guess I didn't get the pleasure of witnessing that."

Emma frowned. "It wasn't much fun."

"I just wish he'd tell me what's going on." Sophie dragged her lower lip between her teeth. "I don't like the rules being changed midstream, especially when no one tells me what the new ones are."

"How about we take our minds off this whole business." Emma rose to her feet. "Why don't we try another dance lesson?"

"Oh, yeah, 'cause that sounds fabulous."

"Come on, it'll help kill time. You'll want to know something, especially if we get invited to balls or soirees or whatever."

Sophie shook her head. "I don't feel like it, Em."

"What if we're somewhere and the President asks you to dance? A chance to dance with Abraham Lincoln, Sophie. What would you do?"

Sophie scowled. "You're absolute, pure evil."

"Yep. Come on." Emma grabbed her hand and dragged her into the parlor.

She spent the next two hours teaching Sophie some of the most popular dances and was thrilled when she began to pick them up. Emma made Sophie sing one of their favorite Metallica songs that just happened to be in the right time signature for a waltz. Emma thought it might help her pick up the timing and it appeared to be working. "You're getting it! I'm so proud of you."

"I can't believe it!" Sophie glanced at her feet. "That was really fun, Em. Thank you."

"You're welcome."

"Ladies." Clayton pushed the parlor door open.

"Clayton!" Emma threw herself in his arms.

"Good afternoon, sweet." He kissed her quickly.

"What are you doing here?"

"We were able to conclude our business early, so we thought

we'd join you for lunch and then go riding, what do you think?"

"Where's Jamie?" Sophie asked.

"He's checking on Samson. He'd like you to meet him out there if you don't mind."

Sophie left the room and Clayton pulled Emma down on the sofa next to him. She slid her arm around his waist as he pulled her close. "You look tired."

He forced a smile. "I'm fine."

"Did you sleep last night?"

Clayton took a deep breath. "A little."

Emma sat up. "What's going on, Clayton?"

"What do you mean?"

She stood and faced him with a frown. "Clayton Madden, I am not an idiot. Neither is my sister. We know something's going on, and I'd like you to tell me what it is."

He leaned on his knees and ran his hands through his hair. "I cannot discuss it."

"The horses are ready if you are," Jamie interrupted their conversation when he strolled into the room.

Emma raised an eyebrow. "I thought you wanted to eat."

Jamie shook his head. "Samson's freaking out, so we need to ride now. If you want to wait, I'll take Sophie alone."

Emma sighed. "No, it's fine. I'll change." She made her way to the stairs.

Clayton nodded toward Jamie. "We'll meet you outside in a few minutes."

Jamie nodded. "Okay."

Clayton jogged up the stairs and let himself into their sitting room. As soon as he closed the door, he pulled her into his arms.

Emma pushed away. "Don't. I'm mad at you."

"If I could tell you, I would."

"Don't you think it would be safer for me to know, so that I can be aware of my surroundings?"

"The less you know, sweetheart, the better." He leaned down and kissed her. "All you need to be aware of is me."

With a wicked grin, she slid her hand under the waistband of his trousers. "I'm already aware of you."

Clayton groaned. "I won't be able to concentrate now."

"All you have to worry about is staying on your horse."

Clayton chuckled and kissed her again. Emma removed her hoops and pulled her breeches on under her skirts. "Ready?"

Clayton and Emma joined Jamie and Sophie at the carriage house. Sophie was already on Samson and three other horses were tacked up and ready to go. Clayton assisted Emma onto her horse and then the men mounted and they took off for their ride.

"I thought I would take you to the capitol building and the White House," Clayton said.

"Sounds good," Jamie said.

Emma could tell that Sophie had to work double time to keep Samson from bolting. He pranced and sidestepped, anxious to run.

"Ten-Cow, are you okay?"

"Yes, he's just antsy today. He wants to run." Sophie bent down to pat his neck and croon to him.

Clayton nodded toward the north end. "There's an open strip ahead where we can let them go a bit."

Jamie frowned. "I don't know."

"Jamie, Samson needs to run. If you want to get on and ride him, feel free, but it needs to happen," Sophie snapped.

"Sophie."

"What? Your concern is starting to piss me off! I can ride better than any of you, and I'm on a horse that I have a bonded trust with. Nothing is going to happen."

"Fine, but a short run."

"Thank you, oh great and wise husband." She dug her heels in and let Samson fly.

"I hate it when she does that." Jamie took off after her.

"See ya," Emma said to Clayton, and followed.

"Emma!" Clayton hollered, but had no choice other than to pursue them.

They ended up running almost all the way to the White House. Sophie slowed Samson to a walk and patted his neck as she cooled him down. Jamie glared at her as he shook his head slowly.

"*Whatever*, Jamie. Look at him. He's totally calm now. And…" Sophie checked herself over, "…what's this? No injuries anywhere on my body? It's a miracle!"

"Sarcasm was never pretty on you, Sophie."

Despite the tension between the Fords, they spent another hour on a tour of the city. Emma was in love. It was much more modern than Harrisburg and even though it wasn't 2017, it suited her a little bit more than the wide-open spaces of Pennsylvania.

Clayton flanked Emma as they made their way back to the house. "Other than a small reception tomorrow night, we have no other commitments for the weekend."

"Does that mean we can explore the city more?"

Clayton nodded. "If you like."

She smiled over at him. "I really just want you all to myself for a few hours."

"Ditto," he whispered.

They arrived home just in time for dinner.

"I'm starved." Emma removed her gloves and cloak. "I say we eat now and change later."

Clayton handed his coat and hat to Walter. "I think that's a great idea."

Emma followed him into the dining room and took her seat. Sophie sat across from her, while Jamie and Clayton sat at each end.

Emma accepted a glass of wine from Clayton and took a sip. "Where is the dinner tomorrow night?"

"At Christopher's parents' home."

"In Maryland?"

"Yes." Clayton poured two glasses of whiskey. "Gwendolyn lives there with their parents and younger brother. It will be a small affair."

Emma raised an eyebrow. "How far is it?"

"Not far."

Sophie laid her napkin in her lap. "Will we have time to ride tomorrow?"

Clayton nodded. "You can probably ride Samson to their

home, if you like. It will take several hours, but we'll be able to stay overnight and come back at our leisure. The other option is to take the train to Camden Station and ride from there."

Jamie shook his head. "I'll take Samson out tomorrow and we'll leave him behind this time."

Sophie dropped her fork. "What? Why?"

"We'll discuss it later, Sophie."

"I'm tired." Sophie rose to her feet. "I'm going to bed." She stomped from the room.

Emma turned to Jamie. "Why are you being such a jerk? Just tell her already."

"Emma," Clayton broke in.

"Don't 'Emma' me. He's being an ass."

"Sweetheart," Clayton warned.

"No!" Emma turned back to Jamie. "Jamie, come on. She has more chance of being hit by a meteor than being hurt by Samson. You were never like this at home. We rode everywhere, without your permission. You know how independent she is, why are you trying to take that away from her?"

"Emma, this is none of your concern," Clayton said.

"Step off, Clayton. I'm not some quiet little Victorian bride raised to never speak her mind or stand up to you big strong men. Get used to it quickly or our marriage will be miserable."

"Emma."

"Forget it." She threw her napkin on the table and pushed her chair back with a scrape. "Feel free to sit here alone and beat your chests for each other. I'm going to bed."

Instead of going to her room, she went to Sophie's. She wasn't there. She went straight out to the carriage house and found her in Samson's stall. Emma leaned over the door. "I thought you might be here."

"I feel like I'm in jail, Em. He's driving me crazy." Sophie stroked Samson's nose.

"Clayton's not much better. He wants a quiet mousy wife who never makes waves. I'm sure they're in the dining room discussing the best way to 'handle' us."

Sophie dropped her forehead onto Samson's neck. "Maybe

251

we should have just stayed home." Samson nickered quietly. "I know, boy."

All of a sudden, they heard a yell and Emma stepped out of the carriage house to see Jamie in a frantic run towards her.

"Where's Sophie?" he snapped.

Emma pointed inside. "In there. What's wrong?"

He rushed into the carriage house and Sophie leaned her head outside of Samson's stall. Jamie grabbed her arm. "You said you were going to bed. I went to our room to bring you a tray and you weren't there. What the hell were you thinking?"

Sophie shrugged out of his grip. "I was thinking I'd like to visit my horse."

Samson snorted and started to paw the ground.

Jamie glared at her. "Get in the house."

Samson nickered loudly in protest. Jamie grabbed her arm again. Sophie tried to pull away, but Jamie wouldn't budge and before anyone could react, Samson stuck his head out of his stall and bit him. Hard.

Jamie let go several choice swear words as he rolled his shirt-sleeve up and they saw a large mark on his forearm.

"Samson!" Sophie tried to hide her shock as she stepped outside his stall. "Shh, Sammy, it's okay."

Emma jumped when Jamie hauled off and punched the wall. "Sophie Jane, get in the house, now. I'm not going to tell you again. Leave that damn horse alone and get up to our room!"

Without warning, Emma was scooped up into Clayton's arms. She hadn't even heard him approach. "What are you doing?"

Clayton sent her a warning scowl. "If I have to lock you upstairs, I will. You are going to learn to obey my word or suffer the consequences."

"Put me down!"

"You will mind me, Emma."

She tried to slap his shoulders. "Oh, my—!" Emma swore. "I am so not your chattel. Put me down!"

He continued through the back door of the house and stalked up the stairs and into their sitting room. "Emma, you can't just go off and do whatever you want to do. It's dangerous."

"How exactly is it dangerous, Clayton? We are on our own property, for Pete's sake."

"Listen. You cannot comprehend the level of danger right now."

"Then tell me! Help me understand."

He stroked her cheek. "I can't share that with you, you know that. It's confidential. Just trust me."

"Oh, okay," she snapped.

He sighed. "Emma."

"No! It's fine. I trust you, Clayton. There are big, bad men waiting around the corner to kill me and I should never go anywhere without you. Got it. What if I have to use the chamber pot at night? Should I wake you and let you know that I need to make water? I don't mind if you watch."

"Don't be ridiculous."

"What if I want a midnight snack? Will you escort me to the kitchen and butter my bread for me?"

"Sweetheart, don't overreact."

"Then don't be such a jerk! Talk to me." She waved her hands frantically in the air. "I can keep a secret and it's just us. Why do you insist on keeping everything so close to the vest? I'm your wife, not some terrorist waiting for confidential information."

He stood and seemingly debated his next move. "Let's go to bed."

"Fine." She turned her back on him and took off her clothes. He tried to pull her into his arms, but she deflected him. "Don't placate me. If you don't trust me enough to talk to me, there's nothing left to talk about."

"It has nothing to do with trust."

"It has everything to do with trust," she snapped. "Go away, Clayton. We'll talk later."

Clayton quietly left the bedroom and closed the door behind him. Emma flopped onto the bed, punched her pillow, and then punched it again. Her emotions went from angry to sad every few seconds and she knew she'd go mad if she was stuck in the house without anything to do. She heard her door open and grimaced.

"Emma?" Sophie whispered.

She sat up. "What are you doing here?"

"I'm going for a ride tomorrow morning, want to come with me?"

Emma snorted. "Sophie, I know you're mad, but don't be an idiot."

"I'm taking Samson out tomorrow. I'm going to prove to Jamie that it's perfectly safe, and he's worrying for nothing. If you want to come with, meet me in the carriage house at five."

Sophie stormed out of the bedroom, and Emma was left stunned. She'd never seen her sister mad enough to do something that stupid.

I must tell Clayton.

Best laid plans. Several hours passed and he hadn't returned to the room, so she went looking for him. She made her way through the sitting room and tried to open the door. It wouldn't budge. She glanced down and noticed the key was missing from the lock.

Oh, he did not lock me in!

She tried again and realized she'd been relegated to prisoner. She seethed as she made her way back to the bedroom and made a new plan.

TWENTY
FOUR

$\mathcal{E}$MMA'S EYES POPPED open at four-thirty, her internal clock obviously working overtime. Clayton wasn't in their bed, so she got up and got dressed. She walked quietly out of her bedroom and into their sitting room. Clayton was asleep in the chaise by the window.

How am I going to do this without waking him?

She sneaked past him and made it to the door. The key was back in it, she was relieved to see. She turned the knob slowly and opened the door.

Thank goodness for well-oiled doors and a husband who sleeps like the dead.

Emma stepped further into the hall. She waited a few seconds to see if Clayton came after her, but as soon as she realized she was safe she took off to the carriage house. She shivered as she slunk into the darkness of the stables. "Sophie?" she whispered.

"Over here," Sophie whispered back.

Emma made her way to Samson's stall. Sophie poked her

255

head out of the door. "Hi."

"Are you really going through with this?"

Sophie nodded. "Yes. I have to prove to Jamie that whatever he's hiding from me is not a real threat. We'll come back before they even wake up, and I'll be able to show him how ridiculous he's being."

"Well, I'm mad enough to spit right now, so I'm in even if it's for all the wrong reasons."

Sophie slid the bridle over Samson's head. "What happened?"

"At some point after you left me last night, my husband locked me in."

Sophie gasped. "He *didn't*!"

Emma sighed. "He did."

Sophie giggled. "Look who's met her match."

Emma narrowed her eyes and jabbed a finger toward her sister. "Don't start with me. Did you tack up the mare?"

"Yes. I had to get Jack to help me, but then sent him back to bed."

Emma grimaced. "I hope we won't regret this."

Sophie led Samson from his stall and Emma helped her mount. Once Emma was mounted, she followed her sister towards the White House. "It's so dark, Sophie."

"Emma, there are street lamps, we're good. What are you so jittery about?"

"I don't know." Emma gripped her reins a little tighter. "I just have a bad feeling."

"You're a rule follower. It goes against the grain to be sneaky."

Emma giggled nervously. "You're probably right. I hate the thought of lying to Clayton, but I'm still mad at him."

Sophie sent her a wicked smile. "You're not lying, you're just omitting."

The girls dug their heels in and the horses took off. They made it to the open area near the White House and pulled the horses to a walk.

"That was incredible!" Sophie whispered.

"Yes." A chill made its way up Emma's spine. "Maybe we should go back now. It's darker over here near the trees and it's creeping me out."

Sophie sighed. "Okay, Em, if you're uncomfortable, we'll go back."

They turned, but didn't get far.

"Good morning, ladies," came a voice out of the dark.

"Sophie?" Emma whispered nervously.

"Who's there?" Sophie pulled Samson to a standstill. "Show yourself."

A man moved out of the shadow and Emma gasped. "You were at the ball."

"Yes, ma'am. It's nice to see you again." Gregory Payne smiled. "Emma, isn't it?"

Another man came out of the shadows and Sophie's sharp intake of breath echoed in the quiet morning. Even Emma knew who she was looking at. Sitting on the horse across from her was Lewis Payne...one of the men who would be implicated in the assassination of Abraham Lincoln.

Emma gathered her reins and shifted her seat. "We should take our leave now."

"So fast?" Gregory crowded her horse. "Why are you always trying to run away from me?"

Emma dragged her lower lip between her teeth. "My husband is expecting us."

He chuckled evilly. "I have a feeling your husbands have no idea you're out here. Otherwise, what would be the point of riding this early in the morning? Did you decide to sneak out so that they wouldn't stop you?"

Samson sidestepped and snorted in agitation, and Emma's heart raced as she watched Sophie desperately try to calm him down. Before the girls could make a move, the men had jumped to the ground. Gregory pulled Emma off her horse and held a gun to her head as Lewis pulled Sophie off Samson.

Lewis snickered into the dark. "I'll kill her if you try anything."

257

The men slapped the horses' rumps and they took off, leaving the girls without any hope of escape. "What are you doing?" Emma squealed.

Gregory smacked her across the face, drawing blood. "Make another sound, Mrs. Madden, and I will hit you hard enough to shut you up. Permanently."

Sophie let out a quiet whistle and got her hair pulled for the effort.

"Shut yer mouth!" Lewis hissed.

They forced the girls' hands behind their backs and bound them with rope, and then led them to an alleyway, where a carriage waited for them. In the close distance, they heard hooves.

"What is that?" Gregory whipped around.

"That damn animal is following us," Lewis growled.

"Just leave him. We'll lose him and he'll make his way home. If he doesn't, we'll shoot him."

They threw the girls into the coach and climbed in after them. Gregory tapped the ceiling and the coach took off. They hadn't driven for very long when Sophie and Emma once again found themselves in an alleyway, being forced out of the carriage and into a side door of some type of row house.

The odors that hit them made Emma gag. She couldn't imagine what the smell was doing to her sister and raised an eyebrow in concern. "Did you take a pill?"

"No," Sophie grumbled.

The girls were dragged to a basement and tied to two chairs in a virtually empty room. A small round table sat in the corner with a lit candle on it, but there was no heat and no other furniture. There was a tiny window that looked like it was slightly ajar, but there would be no way anyone could fit through the opening, especially Sophie with her rounded belly.

The men left and closed the door behind them, chuckling to each other at their cleverness. The girls heard footsteps and the door opened again. In walked Rose. Emma gasped behind her gag.

"Surprised to see me, Emma?" Rose bent down to eye level and sneered. "Y'all thought I was just a simple-minded ninny, didn't you?" Rose grasped Emma's chin and turned her face up. "Did Gregory do this to you? It's too bad he marred your face." Emma thrust forward and swore... not that it mattered, it came out as a mumble. "Tsk, tsk, tsk." Rose removed Sophie's gag, but Sophie kept quiet. "You're apparently the smart sister. And just to show you that I have your comfort in mind, I have brought you a bowl. I know how sick you've been."

"What are you planning on doing with us?" Sophie asked.

Rose pulled Emma's gag from her mouth. "We aren't planning on doing anything with you, provided your husbands cooperate."

Emma hissed. "What exactly do you want?"

"Just information."

Emma frowned. "What kind of information?"

Rose gave a quiet cackle. "Nothing that concerns you, dear. Besides, Clayton will have no problem filling me in on everything. Especially when I arrive to comfort him with the disappearance of his wife." Rose laid her hands on her chest. "Where could she be, Clayton? Has she left you so soon? We must give those nasty men everything they need in order to get your beautiful Emma back safely. If there's anything I can do to help, please don't hesitate to call on me. I'm here for you."

Emma virtually jumped in her chair. "You stay away from him, you whore!"

"Emma," Sophie whispered.

"Yes, Emma, listen to your sister." Rose dragged a finger down her cheek. "I'd hate to do anything worse to that face."

Emma turned her face to bite Rose's finger... not fast enough.

"Now, ladies, I'm going to leave you, but don't you fear. Gregory and Lewis are right upstairs, you have no escape." She flounced out the door and they heard her disappearing footsteps.

"Emma, who was the man who grabbed us?"

"He's that soldier I danced with at Stephen's ball. The one who gave me the creeps."

Sophie hummed. "I wonder what he wants. And why he's

working with one of the men who gets hung for assassinating Lincoln."

"Isn't that guy's name Lewis?" Emma asked. "*The* Lewis Payne."

"Yes. Lewis Payne is what he goes by, but his real name was Powell."

"Seriously, Sophie?"

"What?"

Emma rolled her eyes. "You're pulling Scarlett at a time like this?"

"History makes me feel safe," Sophie whispered frantically. "If I know what's coming, maybe I can change it."

Emma frowned. "Do you think Rose is part of the assassination plot?"

"I don't know. She's not mentioned in any of the history books... neither is Gregory for that matter." Sophie narrowed her eyes. "How's your lip?"

"I'm fine. It hurts, but it'll mend." Emma fought with the ropes binding her hands. "What have we gotten ourselves into?"

Sophie shifted in her chair. "You mean, what have *I* gotten us into?"

"You didn't force me to go with you, Sophie."

Sophie squeezed her eyes shut. "Jamie's going to kill me."

"Yeah, I have a feeling Clayton will do the same."

Sophie whistled quietly toward the window.

"Shush!" Emma whispered. "What are you doing?"

Sophie raised her eyebrow at Emma and whistled again. The sound of heavy breathing wafted through the window.

Emma gasped. "No? Is that Samson?"

Sophie nodded. "He followed us. I just hope I haven't led him into the sight of the Payne's. If this room is tucked away from the alley, perhaps they won't see him."

"He isn't Black Beauty, Sophie, and this isn't some romantic television movie."

"He's a great horse, Emma. You underestimate him."

"Maybe he could bring in Lassie and Flipper as reinforcements. What's that, Samson? Sophie and Emma have been kidnapped by psycho confederates?" Emma whispered sarcastically. "No, wait. Sophie and Emma have fallen down the well."

Sophie rolled her eyes.

"Come on, Sophie, what's he going to do? Ride in with Shaggy and the gang in the Mystery Machine?"

"You're funny."

"Oh, I know, maybe he'll do it for a Scooby Snack?" Emma whispered frantically as she tried to pull her hands out of her bindings.

"Don't fight with them," Sophie admonished. "You'll burn your skin."

* * *

"Jamie!" Clayton yelled and pounded on the bedroom door.

"What's going on?" Jamie called from the other side of the door.

"Emma's gone."

Jamie opened the door. "What do you mean, she's gone, Clayton?"

"She's not in bed and not in the house. Where's Sophie?"

"I thought she'd gone downstairs for something to drink."

"Well, she's not there now."

"Shit!" Jamie grabbed his clothes and boots.

They ran for the carriage house. Finding Samson out of his stall, Clayton roused a confused stable boy from his slumber. "Jack, where are the girls?"

"They went for a ride, boss."

"What do you mean they went for a ride?"

Jack shrunk away from his angry tone. "They said you knew they was going. I's sorry, suh."

Hearing hooves, Clayton stepped outside. "It's one of the carriage horses. Where the hell is Samson? Jack, go and find Walter. I'll saddle two more horses and the three of us will go and look for them."

Jack ran for the house to find the so-called butler.

"This is all my fault." Jamie paced in obvious agitation. "I

261

should have told her what was going on."

Walter ran out of the house, partially dressed. "What happened?"

"The girls are gone." Clayton handed Walter a bridle. "One horse has come back, but we don't know where Samson is. I can only assume he's with Sophie."

Jamie jabbed a finger at Clayton. "This was about you and Christopher to begin with. Sophie should have never been involved. They should have stayed in Harrisburg where they're safe."

"I *had* to be here, Jamie. And had the women listened to us, they wouldn't be in danger right now." Clayton swore. "This isn't even about them."

"What do you mean, Clay? You said they were in danger."

"Christopher and I have been sifting through information about possible plots against the President. It would appear we got too close, so they're using Emma to get to me."

"Was it Payne?" Walter asked.

Jamie's head whipped up. "Excuse me?"

Clayton sighed. "We're somewhat certain about who took them and where they may have taken them. The tricky part will be getting them out safely. Their crew is generally pretty heavily armed." Walter took off to get reinforcements and Clayton and Jamie mounted their horses and grabbed pistols.

Jamie glared at Clayton. "Are you talking about Lewis Payne?"

"Yes." He narrowed his eyes. "How do you know that name?"

Jamie groaned. "We'll discuss that after you find my wife."

They took off toward the White House and headed west once they reached the strip where they would run the horses.

"Why didn't you tell me you had suspects?" Jamie accused.

"Confidential information, Jamie."

"Screw your confidential information, Clayton. You put my wife and my sister in danger. For that alone, I should kill you."

Walter met them halfway to their destination with an update. "They're not at Nineteenth."

"That means it has to be South B." Clayton shifted his weight in his saddle and then dug his heels into his horse. "Let's go."

They rode as fast as they could. Clayton pulled up less than a block from the house and dismounted. He ran toward the residence, Jamie in tow. Clayton gave a sign that he was going to move to the back of the house. There was only one alleyway for every three row houses—they would have to move quietly.

He noticed a couple of his men across the street from the entranceway and they signaled that they had the front exits covered. Clayton and Jamie moved to the back.

"I can't believe it," Jamie whispered and Clayton turned.

Samson stood next to the building, his head down as though he was trying to smell something. "Easy, boy," Jamie whispered as they approached the horse.

Clayton noticed a slit that could possibly pass for a small window and knelt down beside to look in. He saw the girls tied to chairs, but otherwise they appeared to be all right. "Emma?" he whispered.

Her head shot up toward the window and she gave him a very guilty smile. "Hi."

Sophie leaned her head back. "Is Jamie with you?"

"No, I'm at home sleeping like a baby." Jamie peeked through the window.

"Thank God."

Jamie removed his hat and lay flat on his stomach. "How many?"

Sophie shrugged. "I don't know for sure. Rose is involved and there are at least two others."

Clayton and Jamie moved quietly back down the alleyway. Clayton gave a silent signal to his men. They broke the front door down, while Clayton and Jamie went through the side.

They located the basement stairs in the back of the house, so while Payne's men were distracted, Clayton and Jamie slipped unnoticed down them.

Clayton let out a sigh of relief as they let themselves in quietly and closed it quickly behind them. Clayton put his finger to his lips when he saw his wife open her mouth. They still had to get out of here without getting shot. Jamie untied Sophie and she threw herself into his arms.

* * *

Clayton untied Emma and then noticed her lip. "Who hit you?"

"It was that man I danced with at the ball." Emma rubbed her wrists. "The one I said creeped me out, remember?"

"Gregory Payne?"

"Yes. Apparently, I was making too much noise."

He held her close and gave her a quick squeeze. "All right, sweet, we need to get you out of here. I have work to do."

Emma grasped his arm. "What are you going to do?"

"I'm going to deliver some justice, and then I'm going to destroy the son of a bitch."

"Or, we could just go," Emma pleaded. "You'll get hurt."

Jamie turned with a scowl. "You should have thought about that before you took off this morning. Now we're in a mess, and you two are the reason."

Emma's hackles rose, but Sophie put her hand on her arm. They heard Samson paw the ground outside and Sophie pulled her skirt from her hips so that she was left with just her breeches on. She motioned for Emma to do the same.

"If you help me get up on Samson, Emma can jump up behind me. You know he'll get us home safely."

Jamie nodded. They hugged the wall as they sneaked back up the stairs. It appeared that Clayton's men had Payne's men in hand, but Clayton wouldn't relax until the girls were on their way to safety. The group exited the building and Sophie whistled for Samson, who came running. "You are such a good boy," she whispered as she patted his neck. "I believe your Aunty Em owes you an apology... and a Scooby Snack."

Emma glared at her, but had to admit this was one pretty unusual horse. Jamie gave Sophie a leg up and then Clayton virtually threw Emma up behind her. She shot him a scowl. Sophie gathered the reins and maneuvered the horse down the alleyway. She dug her heels in and they took off toward home.

Emma gave her a gentle squeeze. "Sophie, remember what

Rose said?"

Sophie glanced behind her. "Which part?"

"The part about her comforting Clayton. We can't go home, she might be there. What if she brought backup, and we run into another trap?"

"Good point." Sophie slowed Samson down to a walk and continued to move away from the row houses. "Let me think."

Emma pointed in front of them. "Look, there's Walter."

"Yes." Sophie guided Samson to him.

"What are you doing here?" he asked. "Your husbands will not be pleased."

Emma filled Walter in on everything that had happened so far, and Rose's threats.

"Rose said she was going back to the house," Emma relayed.

Sophie nodded. "It's possible she could be there now. I'm not sure it would be the smartest place for us to go right now."

Walter agreed that they should stay with him, so Emma and Sophie slipped off Samson's back.

TWENTY
FIVE

CLAYTON AND JAMIE didn't return to their horses for over an hour. Jamie frowned when he saw Sophie. "Goddammit, Sophie, you were told to go home."

"There's something we need to tell you," Sophie said, and then filled them in.

Emma leaned against her husband. "I have an idea."

"I'm afraid to hear it," Clayton grumbled.

"Rose doesn't know we're safe."

"Yes!" Sophie pointed towards home. "She's probably going to show up at the house at some point as a surprise, pretending she knows nothing."

"We should trap her," Emma concluded.

Jamie frowned. "Are you crazy?"

Clayton shook his head. "Emma might have a point."

"Well, Sophie is not going to have any part in it."

Clayton wrapped an arm around Emma. "Neither of them are going to have any part of it."

"She won't know we're there," Emma said. "We'll hide up

in our room while you guys grab Rose. Otherwise, she might go underground and you'll never catch her."

"It might work, Jamie," Sophie whispered.

"Let's get you home and we'll sort it out there." Jamie lifted her back onto Samson.

Clayton pulled Emma up onto his horse, and they made their way home. They arrived to find Jack waiting for them. He looked petrified. Jamie helped Sophie down and then pushed her toward the stable boy.

Sophie lowered her head. "I'm sorry for lying to you, Jack. It will never happen again."

"Is awright, missus."

"And?" Jamie continued.

"And I'm never allowed to ride unless Jamie or Clayton is with me. You have permission to stop me."

Jack nodded and Jamie dragged Sophie into the house.

Clayton left Walter and Jack to deal with the horses, while he took Emma inside. She grimaced up at him. "Clayton, I know you're angry with me and I'll listen to whatever you have to say, but could we please eat something first? I should take a tray to Sophie too. We have to think about the baby."

"We'll give them some time alone and then *I* will take a tray to her," he said tightly.

* * *

Upstairs, Jamie led Sophie into their bedroom then closed and locked the door. He started to pace, but kept silent.

"Jamie," Sophie whispered.

He put his hand up, but continued to pace. "You could have been killed, Sophie. The baby could have been killed."

Tears slipped down her cheeks. "I'm sorry."

"Why didn't you listen to me? Do you think I talk simply to hear my own voice? Or is it that you think I'm talking out of my ass? YOU COULD HAVE BEEN KILLED!" he bellowed. "I lost you once, Sophie. I can't…"

He didn't really have the strength to say any more. He dropped down into one of their reading chairs, put his head in

267

his hands, and sobbed.

She knelt before him. "Jamie, I am so sorry. Please don't cry. You were right about everything and I have been an impossible shrew. Please, baby, say you forgive me. I'll never do anything like this again. I promise. I won't ever leave your sight for as long as I live, if you'll just forgive me. Please."

He took her face gently in his hands and kissed her. Within seconds, the kiss turned frantic. Jamie ripped the clothes from her body and pulled her over to the bed. He removed his own clothing and then proceeded to make love to her until his fears were vanquished. He had never been so frightened in his life. He would never let her leave him again. Never again.

* * *

Clayton heard the door lock before he reached the threshold of Jamie and Sophie's room, so he turned on his heel and went back downstairs. Emma gave him a confused look when he came back into the dining room, but Clayton shook his head and asked, "Have you eaten enough?"

"I guess."

Clayton turned and left the room. Emma assumed she was supposed to follow him, but he said nothing to her as they walked through their sitting room and into their bedroom. There was a bath set up in the middle of the room, but he still didn't say anything to her as he removed her clothing.

"Clay," she whispered.

"Don't speak," he warned. "Not right now."

She nodded and he helped her step into the tub before leaving her. She submerged her face into the warm water, forgetting about her lip and inadvertently inhaled when she gasped from the sting. She came out of the water with a sputter and tried to catch her breath. She suddenly realized how much worse it could have been and burst into tears. She wrapped her arms around her knees, laid her head to the side and cried.

"Emma." Clayton's soft voice made it even worse.

She jumped up and threw herself into his arms. "Clayton, I am so sorry. I should have listened to you. I should have trusted your judgment. You warned me, but I was mad at you and let it control my actions. I just went and did my own thing without any consideration to Sophie or the baby. I am such an idiot. Can you ever forgive me?"

She continued to sob as he pulled her the rest of the way from the tub.

"Shh, sweet." He ran his hand down her back.

"I am so sorry."

"I know, Emma," he said quietly.

"Please say you forgive me. I'll never ever do anything to make you angry ever again."

Clayton chuckled quietly. "I wish that were true, sweetheart, but I have a feeling this will not be the last time you make me angry. I do, however, sincerely hope it is the last time you put yourself in danger."

"I promise, I'll be a lot more careful. I'm so sorry."

"I forgive you." He stroked her cheek. "How's your lip?"

"It hurts."

"I brought you some ice." He handed her the compress. "I need to change and get downstairs to await Rose. I don't want you to leave this room, do you understand?"

Emma pulled her robe on and sat next to the fire. "I won't leave." He gave her a hard stare as he removed his shirt. "I promise," she reiterated.

"I have sent for Christopher."

Emma raised an eyebrow. "Why?"

"It will look as though I'm calling in the troops to find you. I'm hoping it will flush out anyone else she might be working with."

"Oh. That's a really good idea."

"I know, sweetness." Clayton smiled. "Which is why I did it."

She sat back. "You will be careful, won't you?"

"Yes, Emma. I'll be careful." He left the room, closing the door with a click.

Emma paced the room. Hearing a quiet knock on her door, she turned when Sophie walked in. Jamie followed closely.

269

"Hi." Emma gave her a quick hug.

Sophie smiled. "Hi."

"I know you know this, but don't leave this room until one of us comes and gets you." Jamie gently tugged one of Sophie's curls. "Got it?"

Sophie nodded. "Got it."

Emma grabbed his arm. "Tell Clayton that Rose said something about wanting information from him. I don't know what they're planning, but maybe you guys can keep her talking for a little while."

"I'll make sure Clayton gets the message. Remember girls. Stay here." Jamie kissed Sophie one more time.

"I love you," she whispered.

"I love you more," he said as he turned to leave the room. "Even if it's a choice today."

Sophie blew a kiss at him. Once he'd closed the door, she sat on the edge of the bed.

* * *

Downstairs, Christopher had arrived and he and Clayton stood by the fireplace in the parlor while Jamie paced. "I should have told her what was going on."

"They might have been in worse danger," Clayton said.

Christopher sipped his drink. "What would you have told her?"

"All of it."

"You'd tell your wife everything?" Christopher asked incredulously.

"I always tell Sophie everything. She knew Topper was involved and her motherly instinct kicked in. I should have let her know the truth." Jamie dragged his hands down his face. "The bottom line is that I've never been able to keep anything from her. She eventually figures it out. Emma and Sophie would be exceptional private detectives. Add Hannah into the mix and they're lethal. They always find out what they want to know and you don't see it coming."

Christopher raised an eyebrow. "Who's Hannah?"

Jamie nodded. "Emma's best friend."

Clayton frowned. "If this goes as planned, Rose will do everything to sabotage Emma's safety, and then we'll have proof that she's up to no good."

Walter made a quiet rap on the wall in warning and the men stopped talking. They heard the front door open, and Walter's low voice. Then he was in the doorway and Clayton pushed away from the fireplace.

"Mr. Madden, there is a Miss Rose Johnson to see you."

"Thank you, Jenkins, please show her in."

The men put on solemn expressions and Rose was shown into the parlor. Clayton reached his hand out to her. "Rose, what a lovely surprise. I did not expect you to visit."

She grasped his hand and smiled. "Is this a bad time?"

"Yes, as a matter of fact it is. You have found me in a difficult situation."

She laid her hand over her chest. "I do declare, Clayton, whatever has happened?"

"Sophie and Emma have been kidnapped."

"No!" Rose laid her hand on her throat. "That is just terrible news."

"Yes, we have been trying, unsuccessfully, to find them all morning. The horses they were riding came back to the house riderless, so we await ransom demands of some kind."

"And?"

Clayton frowned. "So far we've received nothing."

"That's just awful news, Clay." Rose removed her lace gloves and laid them on the table. "Is there anything I can do to assist?"

"Just having the support of a close friend is help enough, Rose."

Rose nodded. "I'm here for you in anything you need. I'll stay all day if you need me and would like me to."

"I'd like that very much." Clayton smiled and then turned her toward their audience. "Let me introduce you to Christopher Butler. You have already met James. Christopher, this is an old family friend, Miss Rose Johnson."

271

Christopher took Rose's hand and kissed it gallantly. "Nice to meet you, Miss Johnson."

"Please, call me Rose," she said as though she were royalty.

"Would you like some tea, Rose?" Clayton asked.

"Tea would be appreciated, thank you."

Clayton rang for tea and ushered Rose to the settee. Tea was delivered and Clayton continued to make small talk for close to thirty minutes.

Walter walked into the parlor holding a tray and Clayton turned to face him. "Jenkins?"

"Sorry to interrupt, Mr. Madden. A missive has arrived for you."

"Thank you, Jenkins." Clayton took the letter from the tray and opened it to read it. He ran his hand through his hair and let out a big sigh.

"Clayton? What is it?" Jamie asked.

"It's the ransom."

Rose gasped. "What does it say?"

"They have listed their demands."

"Oh, my." Rose waited for the men to look at it and then peeked a look for herself.

Clayton knew she noticed Gregory's handwriting. He didn't miss the little smile behind her hand, disguised as a gasp. Rose cleared her throat. "What do they want?"

"They want information about the trip to Gettysburg. The President's movements," Clayton answered.

Rose's eyes widened in surprise. "I had no idea the President was planning a trip."

"It's not public knowledge yet."

Christopher slapped the paper down on the table. "We can't just hand over that kind of information, Clayton."

Clayton frowned. "You're right."

"But what about Sophie and Emma?" Rose stood quickly and then sat back down. "You must give them the information to save their lives."

"Honestly, Rose, the state of the Union is more important than two individual lives," Clayton said.

Rose gasped. "Clayton, what a horrible thing to say."

"You bastard!" Jamie seethed. "You're talking about our wives."

Christopher shrugged. "It's a matter of national security."

"Yes, that's more important right now," Clayton said.

"But you need to think of these women's lives," Rose said. "And how guilty you'd feel if something happened to one of them."

Clayton could tell she was growing frantic. "I don't know." He paced in an effort to appear to contemplate his options.

"Clayton!" Rose said exasperated.

He nodded slowly. "You do have a valid argument, Rose."

"I do?" she asked slightly taken aback.

"Yes, I would feel guilty."

Rose smoothed her hands over her skirts. "Exactly."

"We could give them false information," Christopher suggested.

"Yes, they would never know," Jamie reiterated.

"No! You mustn't give them false information," Rose broke in.

Clayton knew the moment she realized that she might have tipped her hand by speaking too soon. He watched her recover quickly and take a deep breath. "You don't know how much these men already know."

"I think Christopher might be right. I don't know that we have any other option than to mislead them," Jamie said.

"But, Jamie do you really want to risk the life of your wife and child?" Rose asked. "And Clayton, you are a newlywed. Are you so quick to be done with your marriage?"

Clayton paced the room. "Let me think."

* * *

Emma laid her four of clubs over the five of clubs and glanced up at Sophie as she paced and bit her fingernails. Emma patted the table. "Sophie, come play. It might help take your mind off everything."

"I can't. I want to know what's going on."

Emma sighed. "Pacing isn't going to fill you in any faster."

Sophie scowled. "I can't believe you're so calm! You're usually worse than I am."

Emma shrugged. "I'm trying to relax and let Clayton work it out."

Sophie grunted but kept pacing. A quiet knock at the door had Emma out of her seat and up against the wall within seconds.

"Mrs. Madden, it's me," the housekeeper, Mrs. Price, whispered through the door.

Emma pulled the door open. "Is everything all right?"

She nodded and stepped inside with a tray laden with food. "Yes, everything's perfectly fine. I wondered if you might be hungry."

Emma smiled. "Starved."

TWENTY SIX

*A*S HE CONTINUED to pace, Clayton caught movement upstairs out of the corner of his eye. He tried to divert Rose's attention—unsuccessfully.

Rose leaned forward and glanced up the stairs. "Clayton? Who's that upstairs?"

Clayton was surprised when his housekeeper paused at the top of the stairs and called down, "Mr. Madden, I found a few things for the ladies in case they need them."

"Thank you, Mrs. Price, please bring them down."

The housekeeper brought the gowns downstairs and laid them on the back of one of the chairs in the parlor. "I didn't know if Mrs. Ford and Mrs. Madden would need clean dresses, so thought I would gather a few things in case."

"Mr. Ford, will this work for Mrs. Ford?" Mrs. Price asked.

Jamie walked over and appeared to inspect the dresses. "This was a dangerous move."

"I had to bring the ladies food," she whispered unapologetically. "I wasn't expecting Miss Johnson to see me."

275

"Well, that was quick thinking. This isn't going quite the way we expected." Then louder, he added. "These will be fine for Sophie. Thank you, Mrs. Price."

Using the distraction the housekeeper had created, Clayton sent Christopher on an errand. He organized a light meal, uncertain when they would get an opportunity to eat again, and as soon as they finished their repast, Christopher walked into the parlor with a guest.

Clayton heard Rose gasp as Christopher led Gregory Payne, in shackles, into the parlor. Walter and two of Clayton's men followed, armed with rifles and handguns. Mrs. Price came in to collect the discarded dishes, and Clayton smiled. "Mrs. Price, would you please bring the ladies downstairs?"

"Yes, sir," Mrs. Price said and left the room.

Rose's head whipped up. "Ladies? What ladies?"

"Surprised, Rose?" Emma asked as she walked into the room with Sophie.

"You're supposed to be dead," Rose snapped.

Emma shrugged. "Sucks for you."

Rose looked as though she was ready to bolt, but Christopher grabbed her and held her arms behind her back. Walter lifted one of the handguns and aimed it at Rose's head.

"Mr. Payne, we are prepared to offer you a deal. Tell us what your plan is and we'll spare her life," Clayton said.

"No," Gregory hissed.

Rose's head whipped up. "Gregory!"

"You had one responsibility, Rose, and you couldn't even do that right," Gregory seethed. "You're useless."

"You bastard! He'll hear about this."

Gregory hissed. "You stupid bitch, keep your mouth shut."

Christopher squeezed her arms. "Who, Rose?"

"Johnny Booth."

Clayton raised an eyebrow. "The actor?"

"He's going to kill the President," Rose shouted.

She's insane.

"Shut up!" Gregory bellowed.

"The actor is going to kill the President?" Clayton said patronizingly.

"Not just him."

"Rose, shut yer mouth!"

"Who else is involved?" Clayton asked.

"I don't know everyone involved, but I'll tell you what I do know."

"All right, Rose. Christopher, take Mr. Payne back to his holding cell and I'll follow with Rose."

Christopher left and Clayton put Rose in shackles to deliver her to interrogation. Rose struggled against the restraints. "Is this really necessary, Clayton?"

Clayton nodded. "I believe it is, Rose."

Emma squared her shoulders and closed the distance between herself and Rose. "One thing before you leave, please."

Clayton raised an eyebrow. "What's that?"

Emma formed a fist, and threw a very impressive right into Rose's face. Rose's bloody lip began to swell. "Next time, I won't be so nice." Emma stalked out of the room.

* * *

Gwen arrived for an impromptu visit, and Emma greeted her at the door just as the men were leaving.

"I don't know what has come over you, Gwennie," Christopher admonished. "It's unseemly to come and go as you please."

Gwen squared her shoulders. "Are you saying you want me to tell you where I am at all times, Chris? You're worse than Andrew!"

"It's unsafe."

Gwen let out a quiet snort. "I thought I'd visit my friend. How was I to know you were in the midst of an arrest? You don't tell me anything. I also had to pass the message on that the dinner party had been canceled. You were not in your office, so it was left to me."

"I don't have time to discuss this with you at the present time."

Gwen removed her outerwear and handed it to Emma. "Why

277

don't I stay with Sophie and Emma for a time, then? You can take care of whatever you need to take care of while sit here and anticipate your return... and subsequent lecture, later this evening."

"Gwendolyn."

Emma bit the inside of her cheek to keep from giggling. So much for the myth of subservient nineteenth-century women.

Christopher stared at Gwen for several seconds before turning and following Jamie and Clayton. Emma led Gwen into the dining room where lunch had been laid out. Sophie greeted Gwen and then handed Emma the icepack the housekeeper had prepared for her.

Emma filled Gwen in on their excitement as they filled their plates.

"Keep that ice on your hand, Em," Sophie directed.

Emma did her best to eat with her left hand. "As much as this hurts, I have to admit, it was so worth it!"

"I have never heard anything like that before." Gwen giggled. "It all sounds very exciting."

Sophie sighed. "Yes, it was. However, I think we're going to be kept on a tight leash going forward."

Emma nodded. "No doubt about that one."

"Mrs. Ford, ma'am?"

Sophie turned to see Jack frantically twist his hat in his hands. "Is it Samson?"

"Yes ma'am. He's started to kick out at the stall."

"I'll be there as soon as I can." Jack left, but she didn't move. "I don't know what to do."

Emma pointed her fork toward her. "Samson will do some real damage if you don't calm him down. He's probably still freaked about this morning."

"Yes, but I don't want Jamie to worry."

"We'll cover for you. You're only going to the carriage house. Besides, you might be able to get him calmed down before the guys even get back," Emma argued.

"All right." Sophie reluctantly left the room.

"Gwen, how long have you known Clayton?" Emma asked.

"Six years." She took a sip of her drink. "Although, not closely until he and Chris started working together."

Emma adjusted the ice on her hand. "How did you meet?"

"Chris invited him to dinner a few times before Lincoln was elected, and we kept him." Gwen smiled. "He became a good friend--actually, more like another brother and spent several holidays with us when he was unable to go home."

"I understand you have a relationship with Andrew Simmonds."

"I don't know that you can call it a relationship." Gwen blushed. "Although, I love him beyond reason."

"Then why are you apart?"

"I'm not entirely certain."

Emma helped herself to more food. "How did you meet?"

Gwen smiled. "I met him when I was fifteen. The saddle on my horse slipped and he saved me from a potentially serious fall."

"How romantic."

"Not really." Gwen blinked back tears. "After his injuries at Shiloh, he'll have nothing to do with me."

"His loss, then."

"Thank you," she whispered and concentrated on her meal.

Emma let the subject drop.

Gwen laid her napkin on the table. "Should we check on Sophie?"

Emma followed Gwen outside and heard Sophie swear. She wasn't having a particularly successful time getting Samson calmed down.

Emma rushed into the stall. "Are you okay?"

Sophie groaned. "Not really."

"Why is he so keyed up?"

"I don't know." Sophie rubbed her temples. "I have tried standing outside of his stall, but he keeps whinnying and pushing at my shoulder."

"Then let him out," Emma suggested.

Sophie sighed. "I'm afraid he'll bolt."

"He never has before."

"That's true." Sophie opened the stall door. "I don't know where you're going to go, Sammy. I can't ride you at the moment, and there's nowhere for you to run."

"Sophie?" The girls turned when they heard Jamie call for her.

"Over here," she called out.

The men walked into the carriage house and Sophie turned to Jamie with a guilty look on a face. "Sorry. I know I wasn't supposed to leave the house, but Jack was a little frantic and Samson kept kicking at the walls, so I thought I'd come and at least try and calm him, but it's not working. Can you take him out?"

Jamie shook his head. "No, sweetheart, but you can."

"Seriously?"

Jamie closed the distance between them and kissed her cheek. "Seriously. I've been an idiot. Will you forgive me? I should have told you everything that was going on. I promise I'll never keep anything from you again. How about we tack up one of the other horses and you and I go for ride?"

"Yes! I'm totally in." She threw herself into his arms.

They got the horses tacked up and started out for their ride.

"I'm going to take Gwen home." Christopher held his arm out for his sister. "I'll see you tomorrow, Clay."

Clayton nodded. "Thanks for everything."

Gwen raised an eyebrow. "Monday then, Emma?"

"Yes, Monday. I'm looking forward to it."

Clayton led Emma to his office at the back of the house. He sat down in his big leather chair and pulled her onto his lap. "Tell me what's happening on Monday."

"Gwen's taking me and Sophie shopping. If that's all right with you, of course."

He kissed her. "Yes, sweet, the danger is behind us."

Emma stroked his cheek. "How did it go?"

"Better than expected." Clayton kissed her palm. "Sam Powell has Rose over at the prison."

Emma snorted. "She's going to love that."

"Why do you say that?"

Emma gave a cheeky smile. "Because he's hot."

"Excuse me?"

"He's handsome."

Clayton frowned. "You think him handsome?"

She slid her hand inside his jacket. "Not as handsome as you. Although, he does have incredible eyes."

"Emma Madden, you should not have noticed his eyes."

Emma shook her head. "No? Oh, I meant to say, he's an ugly troll."

Clayton gave her a squeeze. "That's better."

Emma fiddled with one of the buttons on his vest. "What happened to Lewis Payne?"

"He managed to escape before we entered the house to get you, so we aren't certain where he is."

"What will you do?"

Clayton linked his fingers with hers. "We'll find him."

"What about Rose?"

"She's currently fuming in a cell." He put his hand on her knee and kissed her again.

"What will happen now? Will the President still take his trip?"

He moved his hand up her thigh and rested it on a hip. "Yes, we'll still go to Gettysburg." He started to unbutton her blouse as he kissed her again. He was pleasantly surprised to see she wasn't wearing a corset.

Emma's breath came in short bursts. "When will we leave?"

He slipped his hand inside her blouse. "We leave on the seventeenth." He slid his hand up her back and unlatched the hooks on her bra.

Emma arched her back. "Mmm and how long will we be gone?" She was having a difficult time concentrating on their conversation.

"We'll go for about three days."

"What about Thanksgiving?"

"We'll celebrate it in Harrisburg." Clayton kissed her neck. "Are we going to continue conversing, or do something else?"

Climbing off his lap, she removed her blouse and bra. She

281

slipped her skirt and hoops off and revealed a sexy pair of bikinis that matched her discarded ice blue bra. She climbed back onto his lap and straddled his hips.

"I think these might be my favorite." He ran his hands over her bottom.

"Oh, really?"

"Definitely." He kissed her as he ran his hands up her hips. She unbuttoned his shirt and slipped her hands inside to stroke his chest. "Baby, you have too many clothes on."

Clayton chuckled as she set her feet on the ground. He walked over to the door and locked it as he removed his shirt. After sliding her panties off, she pushed him back into his chair, kissing him as she lowered herself onto his rock-hard length. Clayton gripped her bottom and squeezed, shifting slightly to get a better angle. Emma grabbed the back of the chair and moved against him, her nipples hardening every time her breasts connected with his chest.

Clayton slipped his hand between her legs, running a finger along her clit. She licked her lips as he thumbed her clit while sliding two fingers inside of her.

"Feel good?"

"Feels amazing." He stood, walking her to his desk where he moved papers aside and settled her on top. Kneeling between her thighs, guiding her legs over his shoulders and lowering his mouth to her center.

Emma sighed, sliding her hands into his hair as he tortured her with his tongue. She dug her heels into his back, lifting her hips to get more of him, when he sat up, taking her with him and lowering her onto his cock. Emma let out a quiet breath as she looped her arms around his shoulders.

Clayton flattened one hand against her back and one against her bottom, carrying her back to the chair. "Ride me."

She nodded as she straddled him and rocked against him. Using his shoulders as a base, she raised her body and lowered herself slowly, leaning down to kiss him as she did. He cupped her breasts, pinching one nipple while he took the other in his mouth. Emma dropped her head and tried to focus on her breathing. "I can't wait," she whispered.

"Don't."

Her orgasm ripped through her and she fell against him, nestling her face in his neck as she tried to catch her breath. "Do you love me?"

"Of course I love you."

She bit her lip. "But you were so mad at me."

"You scared me, sweetheart, but that doesn't change how I feel about you. Now that I have you in my arms, however, I'm no longer angry...or scared." He lifted her and slid from between her legs. "Over the desk, sweet."

She didn't hesitate and bent over the mahogany as he slid into her slowly. She whimpered with need and he gripped her hips and surged into her a little faster.

"More," she demanded.

Clayton pulled out and slammed into her again, then faster and faster, building her climax the harder he thrust into her. She bit the inside of her cheek to keep from crying out.

"Now, sweet," he whispered, and she did.

He slid out of her and pulled her to the chair, settling her on his lap again. They stayed like this for a while, their breathing labored as they came down from their high when he whispered, "We're just getting started, Emma. Don't fall asleep."

Before Emma could get too comfortable, Clayton carried her to their bedroom. Their lovemaking ended in their bed well past dinner, so Clayton grabbed a robe and made his way to the kitchen for a tray. He arrived back in their bedroom to find Emma sound asleep, so he quietly set the tray down, undressed, and climbed into bed with her.

* * *

The next week was a bustle of activity as the group prepared for their trip back to Pennsylvania. Gwen and Emma spent more and more time together and were becoming close friends. Sophie spent every waking minute with Jamie, still trying to make up for her earlier actions.

283

Clayton and Christopher worked diligently to organize Lincoln's movements to Gettysburg. They had to change the itinerary slightly, due to the fact that they still hadn't been able to locate Payne and didn't know exactly how much he knew.

The Thursday before they were due to leave, the couples gathered in the parlor before dinner. Walter stepped into the room just as Clayton sat next to Emma. "Mrs. Hattie Jones and Mrs. Christine Martin to see you, sir."

Sophie jumped up as soon as she saw Christine and gave her a hug. "What are you doing here?"

Christine grimaced. "It's a very long story."

"Are you all right?"

"No," Christine whispered.

"Hattie?" Clayton gave her a chaste hug. "Did something happen with Richard?"

She shook her head. "No, Clayton. Christine needed an escort, so I volunteered."

"Would any of you mind if we stole Christine away for a few minutes?" Sophie asked.

Clayton shook his head. "Not at all. You may use my office for privacy."

Hattie settled herself into a chair. "Would you mind if I stayed here and caught up with Clayton?"

Sophie shook her head. "Not at all." She took Christine's hand, motioned to Emma, and the girls led her to Clayton's office. As soon as they closed the door, Christine burst into tears. Sophie pulled her into her embrace and stroked her back. "My dear sweet friend, what has happened?"

"He kissed me."

"Who kissed you?"

Christine sobbed. "Stephen kissed me."

"He did? That's wonderful! He's adored you for a while now. I was wondering when he would make his move."

"It's *not* wonderful." Christine threw her hands in the air.

Emma frowned. "It's not?"

"It most certainly is not!"

Emma glanced at Sophie. "I'm confused."

"He can't just go around kissing people. It's not right. And what about Peter? What would he say? He needs to have more respect."

Emma frowned. "Who's Peter?"

"Her first husband," Sophie said and then turned back to Christine. "Peter needs to have more respect?"

Christine huffed. "NO, Stephen!"

"Why does he need to have more respect?" Sophie asked.

"Peter?"

"Emma!" Sophie admonished.

Emma covered her mouth with her fingers. "*Sorry.*"

"He said that he's in love with me and he wants me to marry him."

Sophie grinned. "And what did you say?"

"I said I couldn't marry him and then I left him standing in Nona's parlor."

Emma raised an eyebrow. "Did he let you go?"

"In a manner of speaking," Christine said evasively.

Sophie gasped. "Christine! You didn't."

Christine shrugged. "I left him there and I came here. I didn't know where else to go."

"You ran away."

"If you want to call it that, then fine! I ran away. He shouldn't be asking people to marry him anyway. What kind of man does that?" Christine stomped her foot.

Sophie giggled. "A man who is in love with you." She grabbed her arm and led her to the window. "Christine, sit down."

Emma handed her a handkerchief.

Sophie took Christine's hand. "Tell me everything that's happened since we left. You two have been getting closer and closer over the past months, so what happened to make him act now?"

"Nothing in particular."

"Riiiight. So, what happened 'in general' then?" Sophie asked.

"I don't want to tell you," she whispered.

Sophie laughed. "Teeny, what did you do?"

Christine took a deep breath. "I had a little accident."

Emma frowned. "You had a little accident?"

Christine nodded. "Yes."

"What kind of accident?" Sophie asked.

Christine raised her chin. "It was nothing."

"Nothing enough for you to run away from a man who said he loved you," Sophie pointed out.

Christine sighed and picked at the embroidery on the handkerchief. "I rode a horse and Stephen objected."

"Heard that one before," Emma retorted.

"Emma," Sophie admonished. "Christine. Why did he object?"

"I was riding a horse unfamiliar to me."

"Why weren't you riding Ben?" Sophie asked.

Christine shrugged. "The doctors and nurses decided to get together for a group picnic and I wasn't expecting to ride."

"But you take Ben everywhere? Why not then?"

"I took the buggy this time, so chose one of the pull horses instead."

"And…" Sophie pressed.

Christine huffed. "And, I was thrown."

"You were?" Emma exclaimed. "What happened?"

"How, Teeny?" Sophie asked, ignoring Emma's question.

"Lila challenged me."

"Lila Sylvester?"

"Yes, exactly," Christine hissed.

"What do you mean, she challenged you?" Emma asked.

"Lila wanted to show off her riding skills to Stephen, so the trollop rode right past him and jumped one of the fences."

"All right. How is that a challenge, Christine, and how do you know she wanted to show off to Stephen?"

"After she jumped the fence, she rode up to him and asked him to lift her down. Then she kept her hands on his shoulders."

Emma rolled her eyes. "That's just awful."

"Yes, what a whore," Sophie quipped.

Christine hissed. "She was all over him—it was positively

unseemly. And people were going on and on about her magnificent riding."

"So?" Sophie challenged.

"Well, I guess I got a little bit angry, so I tried to do the same thing."

Sophie frowned. "You guess you got angry?"

"Yes."

"At the trollop?"

Christine nodded. "Yes."

Sophie squeezed her hand. "So, what was the problem?"

"The problem is that I'm not as good a rider as she is. The horse shied at the fence and threw me."

"Oh, I hate it when that happens," Emma murmured.

Sophie sent Emma a look of warning and then focused back on Christine. "How badly were you hurt?"

Christine shrugged. "I wasn't hurt. A few scrapes and bruises... but Stephen was livid."

Sophie met her gaze. "How do you know he was livid?"

"He growled at me, Sophie. He sounded like an angry dog." Christine burst into tears again. "He didn't stay for the rest of the picnic. He just took me straight home."

"You mean, you didn't get to pass "GO" and collect two hundred dollars?" Emma retorted.

"Emma," Sophie admonished again and then turned back to Christine. "So, is that when he kissed you and told you he wanted to marry you?"

"No, that was when he just kissed me."

"Then what?" Sophie probed.

"I didn't know what to think, so I went to the hospital the next day. Just as I do every day. He kept watching me and it made me very uncomfortable. Any time a patient did something Stephen didn't like, he was right there to move me out of the way. He kept overreacting! Remember Ryan Smith?"

"The young man with the amputated leg?"

Christine nodded. "Yes. He told me that he was in love with me and took my hand."

Sophie cocked her head. "*Okay*. And?"

287

"Well, Stephen waltzed right up and pulled his hand from mine and then pushed me away. It was frustrating."

"Why was it frustrating?' Emma asked.

"Because I couldn't do my job adequately." Christine went silent.

"You needed to hold his hand in order to do your job?" Emma took a deep breath. "I don't get how this whole Civil War hospital thingy works."

"Holy shit, Christine, you are driving me crazy! Spill for heaven's sake!" Sophie snapped.

Christine sighed in frustration, but finally continued the story. "Stephen showed up at Michael and Nona's that night because he knew I was having dinner there. He and Michael went off together for a few minutes and then he pulled me into the parlor for a private conversation."

"And that's when he proposed?"

"Yes and kissed me."

"He's kissed you twice?" Sophie asked.

"Three times, actually. But that's not the point!"

Emma giggled, but slapped her palm over her mouth at her sister's warning scowl.

"Did you like the kisses?" Sophie asked.

Christine lifted her fingers to her lips and stared into space.

"Teeny?" Sophie pressed.

"I loved the kisses."

"Then what's the problem?"

Christine blew her nose. "I have never felt this way before."

"Never?" Emma asked. "But you were married?"

"It's different."

"How is it different?"

Christine stood again and started to pace. "I can't eat, I can't sleep. It's not right."

Sophie grinned up at her. "Oh, honey, you're in love. It's perfectly right."

"But I was in love with Peter."

"No one's disputing that," Sophie assured her.

"But it didn't feel this way! I never felt sick over him and I never felt jealousy or insecurity when we were courting."

Emma grinned. "Is that how you feel with Stephen?"

"Yes! And I hate it. I can't go back," Christine cried and then looked at Emma. "Please, may I stay?"

"Of course you can, silly woman," Emma said.

"Thank you."

"So, tell me." Sophie patted the seat of Christine's chair. "Are you feeling guilty about your feelings for Stephen?"

"Because of Peter, you mean?"

"Yes."

Christine took her seat. "No, not really. It's been well over a year since he died, but he'd already been gone from our home a year before that, so I feel as though the grief is done. I can remember a sweet time in my life with him and little Ellie, but I don't feel the pain anymore. Just a precious memory."

"Then, why don't you let yourself love Stephen?"

"This can't possibly be love, Sophie. It's far too intense." Christine tapped her fingers on her knees. "It's better that I just distance myself from him and move on with my life."

"Ah, I see." Sophie rose to her feet. "Well, my friend, I'm famished and you must be too, so let's go and have some dinner. You'll get some sleep tonight and feel better in the morning."

Sophie linked arms with Christine and she and Emma led her down to the dining room. The girls walked into the room to find everyone seated, but the men stood and Jamie hugged Christine before he helped her sit.

Clayton raised his eyebrow in question at the look of Christine's red eyes and nose.

"I'll tell you later," Emma whispered. "We'll need a couple of extra rooms though."

Clayton nodded and informed Walter to have their housekeeper prepare the rooms.

289

TWENTY SEVEN

ON FRIDAY, EMMA decided to give Sophie another dance lesson. Gwen, Hattie, and Christine watched and tried to help, but without success. Emma spent the majority of the time dodging Sophie's feet.

Sophie pushed Emma away. "This is a stupid dance!"

Gwen smiled. "Sophie, you're doing fine."

"Yes. You can't learn it in one lesson, you just have to practice," Christine said.

Sophie waved her hand in the air. "I'll show you where you can shove—"

"Sophie!" Emma cut her off before she could finish the sentence.

Christine laughed. "Remember the ballroom incident when she nearly broke your toes, Emma?"

"Yes, the self-sabotaging session." Emma grinned. "You're doing it again, Sophie. You're over-thinking it."

"Can we please try a waltz?" Sophie whined.

"Would you like some cheese with that whine?" Emma

quipped.

Sophie stuck her tongue out at her.

"Sure we can," Emma said. "Christine, would you please play a waltz?"

"I'd be happy to." Christine sat down at the piano and began to play.

Sophie and Emma began to dance and Sophie did well, for about ten seconds, and then stepped on Emma's toes. "Ow!"

"Sorry, Em." Sophie threw her arms in the air. "This is lame. I'm never going to get it."

"You were getting it the other day, what's different now?"

"Probably the music," Sophie said.

"You need to forget about the tune, sis, and think about the timing. It's easy."

Sophie scowled. "It is not easy! It's stupid."

"Think of the song we practiced to," Emma suggested.

"That's easy for you to say. You're a freaking dancer, Emma. I'm not. I never was one, never will be one, and I suck at this."

Emma stepped closer and whispered, "Okay, but you're a singer, so hum "Nothing Else Matters" over whatever Christine is playing."

Christine laid her hands on her lap. "Perhaps we should take a break."

Sophie grimaced. "Or just quit. Quitting would be good."

Emma shook her head. "No, you're going to get this. We'll have Clayton help after dinner. It will be better dancing with someone who is an actual lead."

Sophie rubbed her stomach. "Well, right now, Peanut wants lunch, so can we start with lunch?"

"Fine. Let's start with lunch." Emma sighed. "First, though, I need to grab something from Clayton's office. I'll meet you in the dining room."

Emma made her way into the small room and pushed the curtain aside for light. She'd left a design for a new gown on his desk the night before, but it seemed to have disappeared. A quick shuffle of papers revealed something she'd not expected. A

291

modern-day driver's license.

"What the—?" A chill raced up her spine as she read the name and studied the picture.

"Em?" Sophie knocked on the door and stepped inside. "Are you going to eat with us?"

"Hm?"

"What's wrong?" Emma handed her the license. Sophie glanced at it and nodded. "Victor Cary's license."

Emma shook her head. "That's not Victor Cary."

Sophie dropped it back on the desk. "Of course it is."

"*No*, it's not."

Sophie snorted. "Em, it's right there in black and white."

Emma slapped her hand on top of the desk. "Sophie, that is *not* Victor Cary. I know who Victor Cary is, because he was all over the news. Standing next to his criminal of an uncle when they tried to steal the senate seat from Robin Wade!"

Sophie gasped. "Are you sure?"

"Positive."

"Oh, my—" Sophie sank into one of the chairs facing the desk and dropped her face into her hands. "No, no, no, no."

"What's going *on*?"

"He's the man who tried to kill me. The man that Andrew and Clayton interrogated, and the one who took some kind of suicide pill." Sophie stood and started to pace. "If that's not Victor Cary, then who was the man who tried to kill me?"

Emma grabbed her arm. "Sophie, stop."

"We need to talk to the guys."

"Sophie? Emma?" Christine pushed the door open. "Anything amiss?"

Emma slid the license into her pocket and shook her head. "Nope, we just got sidetracked." She squeezed Sophie's arm. "Let's eat."

Emma followed Sophie and Christine into the dining room and sat down with Hattie. Emma and Sophie handled stress differently. Sophie starved and Emma ate. Voraciously. She'd finished off two sandwiches and was on her third by the time Jamie and Clayton walked through the front door.

Emma heard their voices as the front door closed. She pushed her crumb-filled plate away and stood. "Excuse me for a moment, please."

"Me, too. Sorry." Sophie followed.

Clayton and Jamie were chuckling as they handed their coats and hats to Walter, but as soon as Jamie saw Sophie, he stalled. "What's wrong?"

"Emma?"

Emma grimaced at her husband's low voice. "We should go to your office."

Clayton nodded and led them to the back of the house. He waited for the threesome to cross the threshold and then closed the door. "What's amiss?"

Emma pulled the license from her pocket and handed it to him. "This."

Jamie snatched it from his hand. "Where the hell did you get this?" Clayton stepped to the window and Jamie advanced on him. "Clay?"

"Andrew."

"Goddammit," Jamie snapped.

Emma cleared her throat. "Okay, people, can we focus? The issue is not that he has it, or how he got it, but the fact that the information on it is incorrect—actually, more like a blatant lie."

Jamie's eyes widened. "What do you mean, incorrect?"

Emma pointed at the license. "That is not Victor Cary."

Sophie sat down with a groan. Jamie stood next to her. "Who is it, then?"

Emma shrugged. "He looks kind of familiar, but I can't quite place him. All I know for certain is that he is *not* Victor Cary. Not even close."

Clayton rolled his eyes. "Emma, the man is dead. It doesn't matter who he is."

Jamie dragged his hands down his face. "If what Emma's saying is true, Clayton, Topper wasn't delusional."

Emma frowned. "Delusional about what?"

Jamie groaned.

"Start talkin', Jamie," Sophie ordered. "What did Topper

293

say?"

"When the men were torturing him, he passed out—"

"Tortured?" Emma snapped. "You didn't tell me he was *tortured.*"

Clayton leaned against his desk. "I didn't think you needed to know that, Emma."

"You should have told me."

"I told him not to tell you everything." Jamie reached over and squeezed her shoulder. "I just didn't think you needed to hear all the specifics."

Emma crossed her arms. "Well, I'd prefer the big-brother act to stop going forward. Especially, when it comes to what is discussed between myself and *my* husband."

Jamie sighed. "Fair enough."

"Thank you." Emma gave a curt nod. "What happened after he passed out?"

"When he came to, he pretended to still be out cold and heard one of the men say the Wade family were a threat to the Cary family, and that Travis and Christopher Wade had to be killed. Since Travis had already been killed in battle, they were sent to take care of Topper."

Sophie gasped. "But why?"

"He said something about family allegiance and that if they weren't successful, the Cary family would lose."

Sophie started to pace. "Lose what?"

Emma squealed. "Oh, my... all that could be true."

Sophie stalled. "What do you mean?"

"In the future, the Cary family maneuvered Senator Wade out of office." Emma waved her hands in the air. "What if Topper had been killed? The name wouldn't continue. Michael and Nona don't have any children so Topper would be the last alive, right?"

Jamie nodded. "In theory, yes."

"So, if they got rid of the last of the line, so to speak, the Cary family could continue to take over politics."

Clayton raised an eyebrow. "How?"

"They travel back in time and get rid of their opposition."

294

"Emma." Clayton chuckled.

She wagged a finger at him. "Don't use that tone. It's all possible. Think about it. How did Topper learn a code used in a war eighty years in the future? Someone *from* the future would have had to teach it to him."

Jamie glanced at Clayton. "She's right, you know. As impossible as all of this seems, the fact is that it could have all happened exactly as she said."

Clayton shrugged. "It doesn't make a difference now."

Emma's head whipped up. "Why?"

"We've caught the men who tortured Topper, we have Rose in custody. It's done."

Sophie cocked her head and stared up at Jamie. "How do you know they are the men who tortured him?"

Jamie and Clayton shared a private glance, but stayed quiet.

Sophie rose to her feet. "Jamie? How do you know?"

"Topper confirmed it."

"You made him confront the men who tried to kill him?" she snapped.

Jamie cupped her face and forced her to look at him. "Ten-Cow, they didn't know he was there. He was hidden."

"But won't the men guess it's him ratting him out?"

Jamie shook his head. "They don't know that Topper's the reason they were caught."

Emma stood. "How could they *not* know?"

"These are bad men, Squirt," Jamie explained. "They have a lot of sins to account for."

"Do they know that?"

Clayton nodded. "Yes, sweetheart. They believe they have been brought up on war crimes, and since we're certain they have committed more than even we have named, they will more than likely be hanged."

"What about the man that followed Emma… the one with the scar?" Sophie asked. "He must have been the one who taught Topper the code. Can he just 'poof' his way back to the future?"

"He can't now," Jamie said.

Sophie raised an eyebrow. "How do you know that?"

Clayton sighed. "He's dead."

"What about this Victor Cary person?" Sophie asked.

Emma waved a hand dismissively. "He's in the future... or at least he was when I was. I'll know him if he ever shows up."

Sophie shuddered. "I still say we keep Topper close. Someone should be with him at all times."

Jamie wrapped an arm around her back. "We can do that, love. In fact, it's already in place."

A knock at the door brought Walter with a note. Clayton read it quickly and then threw it into the fire. "I need to meet with Chris for a few hours."

Emma slipped her hand into his arm. "Problem?"

He kissed her cheek. "Not at all. Just a logistical issue with the trip."

"Wait." Sophie groaned. "There's something you should know."

"What?"

"The President is sick, Clayton," Sophie whispered. "He has smallpox."

Clayton's head whipped up. "Excuse me?"

Sophie grimaced. "It's being kept quiet right now, but it'll be announced a week after the Gettysburg Address."

"No, that can't be right." Clayton shook his head. "Are you confusing the fact that Tad is sick?"

"No. Tad has something different. They think it's complications from typhoid, but many people come to believe he may have some form of cancer." Sophie waved her hand dismissively. "However, the President definitely has smallpox. It will take several weeks for him to get better."

"He's the picture of health," Clayton argued.

Sophie stared at him for several seconds. "Is he, Clay? Think about it."

Clayton paced the room and Emma frowned at her sister. Sophie gave her an apologetic shrug. "Have you ever had smallpox, Clayton?"

He paused. "No, I don't believe so."

Emma put her hand to her throat. "Oh, God, I didn't think

about this part of the past. What does that mean, Sophie? Will Clayton get it? What will that mean for him?"

Sophie grasped her sister's hand. "Don't borrow trouble, Em." She turned back to Clayton. "Clayton, I remember Richard saying you had dairy cows at one point in your life, is that correct?"

"Yes, for years, we had several and we would get milk for both of our families."

"Do you remember any childhood illnesses, specifically with spots?"

"Yes, as a matter of fact, Tim and I both got this itchy, feverish rash when we were boys. They called it cowpox or something like that."

Sophie's shoulder's sagged. "You should be fine."

"What?" Emma hissed. "That's it? 'You should be fine'?"

"Emma, a doctor in England has discovered that milkmaids who got cowpox seemed to be immune to smallpox. They have been making immunizations from cowpox in England for a little while now. America isn't far behind, it's just not widely used," Sophie said.

"What about the President?" Clayton frowned. "Is he in danger?"

Sophie glanced at Emma and Emma nodded her head. "You should tell him."

"He dies?" Clayton scowled.

"No, no, not now." Emma laid her hand on his knee.

"Not now? But, soon?"

"Clayton. The President will be assassinated in 1865," Sophie said.

Clayton whipped around. "You're speaking treason!"

Jamie stepped slightly in front of Sophie, but she pushed him away. "Clayton, I know this is really difficult, and if I could keep you in the dark and keep my conscience clear, I would. Lee surrenders to Grant on April 9, 1865. Lincoln will be assassinated on April 15, 1865."

"By whom?"

"John Wilkes Booth."

"The actor?" Clayton exclaimed. "That's what Rose said."

"It's true." Sophie sighed. "It's not single-handed, but he's the one who delivers the shot that kills him."

"He's shot?"

"Yes. He's shot while at a play at Ford's Theatre on April 14. He dies the next day."

Emma linked her hand with his. "I know this is a lot to take in, Clay. There is so much information about all of this and now might not be the right time to go into it. You and I can sit down some time over the next few weeks and I'll fill you in."

Clayton cleared his throat and absently kissed Emma's hand. "I must meet with Christopher. Excuse me."

Once he'd left the room, Sophie wrapped her arms around her sister. "He'll be fine, Em. Just give him time."

* * *

Clayton didn't return to the townhouse for several hours. When dinner came and went, Emma paced the parlor, worry growing rapidly by the minute.

"Em?"

She turned to the sound of her sister's voice and her stomach growled at the tray Sophie held. "I don't think that'll be enough food."

Sophie set the tray down on the sideboard and slid her arm around Emma's shoulders. "Jamie went to find him."

Tears slipped down Emma's cheeks as she nodded and piled a plate full of food.

"He probably just got caught up in the plans, Em. You know how guys are."

Emma pulled away from Sophie and shoved a piece of meat in her mouth, then resumed her pacing—and her nail biting. "Ouch!"

Sophie glanced at her. "What did you do?"

"I bit my nail too low." Emma shook her hand out. "Damn it! Where is he?"

Emma heard the front door slam and then heavy footsteps on the stairs. She hurried out into the foyer to see Jamie handing his hat to Walter. "Where is he?"

Jamie nodded toward the stairs.

Emma lifted her skirts and rushed up the stairs. She let herself into their room and quietly closed the door. Clayton sat at the edge of their bed and stared off into space.

"Are you all right, honey?"

He ran his hands through his hair. "I don't know."

Emma removed her clothing and pulled a nightgown on. She made her way to Clayton and silently began to unbutton his shirt. She slipped it from his shoulders and kissed his forehead. He wrapped his arms around her and laid his head on her chest. "I don't know what to do with this information."

"Shh. I know."

"How do I stop it? I can't let him die, Emma. I can't."

"I know." Emma stroked the back of his neck. "It took a lot for Sophie to tell you. She didn't know whether she should do anything to change history."

Clayton nodded.

Emma lifted his chin. "Let's go to bed."

* * *

Emma woke while it was still dark and reached for Clayton. He wasn't in bed. Sitting up, she rubbed her eyes and yawned. "Clay?"

"I'm here, sweet." He stood by the window, a blanket wrapped around his shoulders.

She climbed out of bed and shivered as she walked over to him. He held the blanket open and she slid into his arms. "Are you okay?"

"Just a lot to think about." He wrapped his arms around her. "You're freezing. You should climb back into bed."

"Only if you come with me."

He kissed her. "Let me start a fire and then I'll come back to bed."

She ran and jumped back under the covers. "If you hadn't ruined my warm nightgown, perhaps a fire wouldn't be necessary."

"If you'd sleep naked, perhaps I wouldn't have ruined your warm nightgown."

Emma giggled. "Hurry with that fire. I want you back in bed."

He finished lighting the kindling and added a log. "What will you do to me in bed, sweetheart?"

"Mmmm, come over here and find out."

By the time she was ready to sleep, the fire was somewhat unnecessary.

TWENTY
EIGHT

$\mathcal{E}$MMA SLEPT UNTIL well past nine. Finding Clayton gone from their bed and room, she made her way downstairs to look for him. She arrived at the dining room to find fresh coffee and breakfast still laid out. Pouring herself a cup of coffee, she turned when she heard the rustle of skirts.

"Hi," Sophie said from the doorway.

"Hi." Emma raised an eyebrow as she took her seat at the table. "Did you just wake up?"

"Who said I was awake?" Sophie grumbled as she poured herself a cup of coffee and sat down at the table.

Christine walked through the door. "Good morning."

Sophie raised an eyebrow. "You're up late."

Christine grinned. "I've been awake for several hours, my friend. Hattie and I went for a walk."

Emma buttered her toast. "I wonder where the guys are."

"I don't know, but it's too early for me to care." Sophie popped a grape into her mouth.

"About what, love?" Jamie made his way over to kiss her.

Sophie presented her cheek. "About where you were and why you left our bed so early."

Emma glanced back at the door. "Where's Clayton?"

"He's taking care of some last-minute travel details," Jamie said.

"What are you doing up so early, anyway?" Sophie wrinkled her nose. "You never get up unless you have to."

He stole a slice of orange from her plate. "Clayton woke me at eight. I nearly killed him for doing it, but he needed some information and since I happened to know the answers, I decided it would be safer for him if I took care of it, rather than waking you."

"Ah, good thinking."

Emma huffed. "So, when is my husband going to be back? Did he say?"

"I can't imagine he'll be long. He and Christopher are meeting again."

"Well, I'd like to go for a ride." Sophie pushed away from the table. "Anyone else?"

Emma took a last sip of coffee and rose to her feet. "I'll go for a ride with you, Soph."

"Great. How about you ride Samson? I'd like him to get used to you."

"I'll get the horses saddled while you girls change," Jamie offered.

Jamie was just finishing up with Samson when the girls arrived. Emma stood at his head and began to speak quietly to him. She let him smell her hand and stroked his muzzle. She mounted him from the ground and he stood perfectly still.

"Should I be jealous?" Sophie stroked his nose. "Don't go and fall in love with my sister, will you? You're still my horse."

The three of them took off toward the White House. This seemed to be their favorite morning jaunt and the horses knew exactly where to go. Their ride was cut short by the threat of snow, and they arrived back at the house an hour later. Emma guided Samson to the entrance of the carriage house and dismounted.

302

Jack took the reins from her. "Mrs. Madden, Mr. Madden is awaiting you in his office."

"Thank you, Jack." She glanced up at her sister. "I'll see you in a few minutes?" She didn't wait for Sophie's answer. Rushing through the back door and into Clayton's office, she found him sitting at his desk. "I don't like waking up to find you gone."

He stood and held his hand out to her. "Sorry, sweet. I got up early and didn't want to disturb you."

She removed her bonnet and gloves, dropped them on the desk, and took his hand. "Well, disturb me next time, please."

"Gladly." He kissed her. "Did you have a nice ride?"

"Yes, Samson is a magnificent horse. Are we all ready for Gettysburg?"

Clayton chuckled. "Yes, *we* are."

"Good. I'm starved." She strolled toward the door. "Up for a snack?"

Clayton followed with a grin. Emma removed her coat as they made their way to the parlor and dropped it on the bench by the front door before stepping into the warm room. Christine sat on the sofa reading a book.

"Where's Hattie?"

Christine glanced up. "Walter escorted her on a walk."

"Did he now?" Clayton raised an eyebrow.

"They like each other, Clay. Don't make it difficult for them, okay?" Emma whispered as she pulled him over to the window.

"Walter loves every woman he meets."

"Well, he likes her best."

"All right, sweetheart." He stroked his fingers gently down her cheek. "I'll check with Sarah about a light repast."

"Thank you."

Clayton left the room and Emma sat next to Christine. Sophie fluttered in a few minutes later. "I'm freezing!"

"Melodramatic much?" Emma giggled. "Come by the fire and get warm."

Emma heard the front door knocker and rose to her feet. "I'm assuming Walter won't be getting that." She made her way to the foyer and opened the door, her eyes widening in surprise.

303

"Dr. Paxton? What are you doing here?"

"I'm sorry to disturb you, Mrs. Madden. I was wondering if Christine Martin might be here." He removed his hat. "I know she and your sister are close. I hoped she might have come to see her."

Emma nodded. "She's here, Dr. Paxton. Come in."

"Thank you." He stepped inside and Emma led him into the parlor.

"Christine."

Christine jumped from the sofa and her book fell on the floor with a thud. "What are you doing here?"

Sophie rose to her feet. "We'll give you some privacy."

"Don't bother, Sophie. Stephen was just leaving." Christine crossed her arms and moved to the window.

Stephen closed the distance between them. "I'm not leaving, Christine."

"Yes, you are." She tried to escape, but he caught her arm. "I'm not leaving."

"What are you doing here?" Christine pulled out of his grasp. "How is it possible you were able to break away from the hospital? How long were you planning on staying? How did you find me?"

Stephen laughed quietly. "I'm here because I love you. Dr. Palmer allowed me a short leave. I will need to return tomorrow and I asked Michael where you went."

Christine hissed. "I can't believe he told you where I was!"

"He didn't, Nona did."

Christine fisted her hands at her side. "Traitorous sister!"

"Christine, I'm not going to let you run away from me." He took her arm again. "I'm not that easily put off."

"Why is that, Stephen? I can't marry you."

"You can't or won't, Christine?"

"What difference does it make?"

"It doesn't make a difference." He stroked her cheek. "Because you don't have a valid argument."

Christine tried again to pull away from him. "Stephen! This is ridiculous."

"Yes, I agree. It *is* ridiculous." He pulled her into his arms and kissed her.

Christine broke the kiss. "I can't do this, Stephen, it's too much."

Stephen shrugged. "Christine, I love you. We can take this slowly and I'll wait as long as you need. I just don't want you to deny what you feel. Can you do that?"

Christine glanced at Sophie and her face reddened. "We're not alone," she whispered.

"Look at me, Christine." Stephen tipped her chin toward him. "These are your closest friends, you don't need to be embarrassed." He chuckled. "Besides, I want witnesses."

Christine gave him a horrified expression. "Witnesses to what?"

"My proposal. I want you to finally agree to marry me. If I have witnesses, it will be harder for you to say no."

Sophie grinned. "Put the poor man out of his misery, Teeny."

Christine narrowed her eyes into a glare which elicited a laugh from Stephen. "Yes, *Teeny*. Put me out of my misery."

"I would love to." Christine huffed. "I'm just not certain my definition is the same as yours."

"Let me clarify. You marry me and we'll sort the rest out later."

Sophie rushed forward. "She accepts."

"Sophie!"

"Christine, if I have to force you into an arranged marriage, I will."

Stephen smiled and leaned down to kiss Christine's cheek. "Whatever works."

Christine's response was cut off by Jamie and Clayton entering the room carrying trays of sandwiches. Clayton raised an eyebrow in question. "Dr. Paxton?"

Stephen stepped forward, his hand out in greeting. "Mr. Madden. Sorry to drop in on you like this."

"Not at all." Clayton set his tray down and shook his hand. "Can I offer you a drink or something to eat?"

Stephen nodded. "That would be most appreciated."

305

"I'll make you a plate," Emma offered.

"Thank you."

Clayton indicated for him to sit next to the fire and handed him a glass of whiskey. "Where are you staying?"

"I haven't thought that far. I thought I would get a room over at the Willard."

Emma handed him a plate. "That seems like a waste of time and money. You should stay here. We have plenty of room."

"Yes, Stephen, you are welcome to stay," Clayton said.

"Thank you, that's very generous." Stephen smiled and glanced at Christine in question.

Christine sighed. "Yes, it's fine with me."

Stephen tipped his drink toward her. "I'm leaving tomorrow and I'm taking you with me."

Christine smirked. "We'll see."

Jamie cleared his throat. "Well, let's eat. I'm starving."

* * *

The next morning, the group met up for breakfast. Discussions naturally turned to their upcoming travel plans to Gettysburg.

"What time do we need to leave on Wednesday?" Sophie asked.

"We'll take the noon train." Clayton sipped his coffee. "Christopher is escorting the President later that day, but he'll try to meet up with us for dinner at the hotel."

Emma raised an eyebrow. "Won't Christopher be staying at the hotel?"

"No. The President is staying in a private home, so he'll stay to protect him, but he hopes to meet us for dinner."

"Is Gwen going to join us?"

"Not this time, sweet."

Emma frowned. "Why not?"

"Her parents have other plans for her over the next few weeks, so she'll be very busy," Clayton explained. "She and her parents, however, will travel with us at Thanksgiving."

Emma sighed. "She'll be disappointed she won't get to experience this."

306

"There will be other things for her to experience."

Sophie waved her fork dismissively. "Not quite like this, Clayton."

Stephen glanced at his pocket watch. "We should really think about getting to the train station."

"Stephen, we have nearly two hours." Christine dabbed her lip with her napkin. "Plenty of time to enjoy breakfast."

"You're already bossing me around." He grinned. "That's a good sign."

Christine rolled her eyes.

"Will you both make it for the speech?" Sophie asked.

"Yes, we'll be there. We'll join you for dinner on Thursday as well if you like," Stephen assured them.

Emma took a sip of orange juice. "How long does it take to get from Harrisburg to Gettysburg?"

"The train is a little over an hour."

"I didn't realize it was that close." Emma winked at Sophie. "Modern travel is a marvel."

Sophie smiled. "Yes, it is. Which means you must visit me often when we go home."

"I will. Don't worry."

Jamie and Clayton veered the conversation to horses and war. Before Emma knew it, almost an hour had passed.

Stephen rose from the table and stood behind Christine. "We really should get to the station."

Christine sighed. "Yes, I suppose you're right."

Clayton stood and ushered everyone to the foyer. "Jack's going to drive you."

"Thank you, Clayton." Stephen held Christine's coat open for her. "I appreciate the hospitality."

Christine slid her arms into the warmth and sighed. "Thank you for everything, Sophie."

Sophie hugged her. "I'll see you in a few days."

Christine slipped her gloves on with a nod. "Yes, you will."

Sophie grinned. "Safe journey, my friend. Be nice to Stephen."

Christine laughed. "I'm always nice to Stephen."

307

Jamie and Clayton bid them farewell and then made their way back to Clayton's office. Christine hugged Emma and then followed Stephen outside. Emma and Sophie stood in the street and watched the carriage roll away from them. Sophie sighed and followed Emma back inside. "I'm going to drag my husband out for a ride."

Emma grinned. "Good idea."

The girls entered Clayton's office and Sophie made her request. Once the couple left, Emma sat across from Clayton and settled her chin in her hand. "I think I'm going to take a nap."

He glanced up. "That's a good idea, sweet. I have to meet with Christopher again to finalize a few things."

"Oh," she said disappointedly.

"What's amiss?"

She stood and slid around to his side of the desk. "I thought perhaps we could nap together."

Clayton gathered various papers and set them in a pile. "I have no time for sleep, sweetheart," he said distractedly.

She swiveled his chair and leaned down to kiss him. "Are you sure?"

"Are you trying to sidetrack me, Mrs. Madden?"

She slipped her hand inside his shirt. "What do you think?"

He kissed her deeply and broke it with a groan. "I'll try and make the meeting quick."

"Don't try, baby. Do." She gave him one more kiss before he left.

* * *

Wednesday arrived with great anticipation. Emma could barely sit still on the train and when they finally pulled into the station, she jumped up almost as quickly as Sophie. Clayton grasped her arm and pulled her against him. "Emma, wait for me, sweet."

He led the group out onto the platform and the men left the ladies to collect the bags.

Sophie linked her arm with Emma's. "I'm so excited, I can barely breathe."

Emma giggled. "It might be the corset."

Sophie raised an eyebrow without comment. Clayton and Jamie returned with a porter, and after letting him know where they were staying, Clayton took Emma's hand and led everyone to a carriage.

"Would y'all like a tour?" Clayton asked as he assisted Emma inside.

Sophie nodded. "Yes, please."

Jamie took Sophie's hand and she climbed inside next to Emma. Once she was settled, the men sat across from them. Clayton gave instructions to the driver and they took off through town.

Emma squeezed her sister's hand. "Maybe your Civil War isn't so boring."

Sophie grinned. "I told you so."

Emma leaned her head out of the carriage and tried to take in as much as she could. Before she knew it, the driver had pulled up in front of the Gettysburg Hotel and set the brake. Emma frowned at Clayton. "That's it?"

Clayton chuckled and jumped down from the carriage. "The President won't arrive until late this evening, so we'll have time to explore after we check in."

Emma clapped her hands and let Clayton lift her down. "Yay."

Jamie climbed down and held out his hand for Sophie. She bent down and stepped through the door. "Tomorrow, I don't necessarily want to follow the parade route. I'd like to get to the town cemetery so that I can see everything."

"I thought he spoke at the new National Cemetery?" Emma's eyes widened. "Isn't that the whole point?"

Sophie nodded. "You'd think, but nope, it will be at the town cemetery."

Emma smirked. "Well, if anyone would know, you would."

Sophie smiled.

Once they checked in, Clayton led the group on an in-depth exploration of the city of Gettysburg, ending their tour at the battle site. Sophie stood in the middle of the field in between her sister and her husband, and squeezed their hands.

"A little different, isn't it?" Jamie observed.

Sophie nodded. "I can't believe it's only been four months since the battle. It's so surreal to me. It doesn't look much different than... you know."

They took a slight detour to visit the cemeteries and then made their way back to the hotel for dinner. The train with the President and Christopher on it still had not arrived, so they decided not to wait to eat.

They enjoyed a meal which began with oyster soup, followed by lamb chops with fresh vegetables and potatoes, and finished off with southern sweet bread.

Dessert was homemade bread pudding with fresh cream. They lingered over the sweetness and coffee before going back to their rooms. Just as they took their final sip of coffee, Christopher walked through the door of the restaurant. Followed closely by Gwen.

Emma gave a little squeal and jumped up to hug her. "What are you doing here? I thought your parents made you stay home?"

Gwen giggled. "I pouted and stomped my foot long enough for them to let me come."

"You did not!"

"No, you're right, I didn't. I simply explained that this was a once in a lifetime opportunity to hear the President speak, and I made Christopher back me up on the argument. He is occasionally good for something."

Christopher chuckled. "You're entirely too logical at times, Gwennie."

"Come and have some dessert," Emma said and they both sat at the table.

Christopher turned to Clayton, a look of concern on his face. "We have a small problem."

"What's that?" Clayton asked.

"The hotel is booked solid. No room for Gwen. I'm staying with the President and hadn't planned on staying here."

"We have a huge suite, she can stay with us," Emma offered.

"Yes, that's fine," Clayton said, although he didn't sound

310

like it was fine.

When Gwen and Christopher were done with their desserts, Emma pulled Clayton aside. "I'm sorry. I just jumped in."

"It's all right. I had other plans for us tonight that required us to take our clothing off. That won't be appropriate now."

Emma scrunched up her nose. "No, I don't suppose it would be appropriate. Bummer."

Clayton took her hand and kissed her palm. "We'll make up for it tomorrow night."

Emma heard Sophie gasp and turned to see the President walking through the door. Christopher rushed to greet him and Clayton followed. The three moved toward their small group.

Emma grabbed Sophie's hand. "Are you ready to meet the President, Sophie?"

"No." Sophie grimaced and leaned over to Jamie. "I think I'm going to pee."

Jamie chuckled quietly as he pulled her hand to his lips and kissed her palm. "You'll be fine. I promise."

"I hope so." Sophie took a deep breath.

Jamie smiled gently "You're overreacting, just a tad, don't you think?"

"Oh, really? How do you think you would feel if you got to meet Bono?"

He raised his eyebrows at her.

"Exactly. You'd have to pee too."

Clayton introduced the President to Jamie and then Emma. "May I present my wife, Emma? Emma, the President."

"It's an honor to meet you, Mr. President." Emma smiled and before Clayton could say anything, Emma pulled Sophie forward. "This is my sister, Sophie."

Sophie shook visibly as the President took her dainty hand in his very large one and bowed to her. His smile lit up the room and Emma could tell that Sophie was immediately smitten with him.

After several minutes of conversation, the President lifted Sophie's hand to his lips with a grin. "Pressing matters must take me from your presence, I'm afraid. It has been a pleasure meeting you, Mrs. Ford. I hope that when you are in town, you will join me and my family for dinner."

Sophie blushed. "I would be honored, Mr. President."

Christopher cleared his throat. "We must get back, sir."

The President patted Sophie's hand. "Yes. Of course."

Christopher escorted the President out of the dining room and Clayton grinned at his wife. Emma sat next to Sophie at the table. "Are you okay, Soph?"

"No, I want to throw up."

"Better aim for your reticule," Emma retorted.

Sophie let out a quiet snort in an effort not to laugh. Jamie held his hand out to her. "I think we should turn in. We have a long day tomorrow."

Sophie nodded and took his hand.

Jamie narrowed his eyes at Clayton. "Do not wake us before ten, unless it's an emergency. Got it?"

Clayton laughed. "Nine a.m., got it."

Jamie scowled.

"Come on, grumpy." Sophie squeezed his hand. "We'll give you an attitude adjustment."

Clayton turned to Emma and Gwen. "Shall we retire?"

At the girls' agreement, he led them up to their suite. Stepping into their sitting room, Clayton pointed to the bedroom. "I'll sleep on the sofa and you two can sleep in the bed."

"Are you certain, Clayton?" Gwen asked.

"Yes, of course."

She smiled. "Thank you."

Emma gave him an apologetic smile. "I'll grab you a pillow."

The girls stepped into the bedroom. Emma returned with a blanket and a pillow and dropped them onto the sofa. She wove her hands around Clayton's neck. He kissed her nose. "I'm going to miss you tonight."

"I'll make it up to you tomorrow, I promise."

He chuckled. "Yes, you will."

After his more thorough kiss, Emma went into the bedroom

and Gwen helped her off with her corset and vice versa. They climbed into bed and Gwen fell asleep immediately. Emma didn't have as much luck. She tossed and turned for over an hour before giving up and climbing out of the bed. She quietly opened the bedroom door and slid into the sitting room.

"Emma?" Clayton whispered.

"Hi."

He sat up. "Is everything all right?"

"I can't sleep."

Clayton held his hand out to her. "Come here."

She grasped his hand and he pulled her down on top of him. He drew the blanket over both of them and she settled her head on his shoulder.

"Better?"

"Much," she whispered and yawned as she snuggled against his warmth.

"Sweet, you need to stop wiggling," he said with a groan. "You're driving me to distraction."

"Oh, really?" Emma slid her hand down his chest.

"Emma."

"I wish we were naked."

Clayton chuckled. "Ditto, sweet. Now, lie still and try to sleep."

"Kiss me first." He did and she broke it with a sigh. "You're killing me."

"Who invited Gwen?" he whispered.

"Touché."

TWENTY
NINE

$\mathcal{E}$ MMA WOKE UP the next morning and raised her head slowly to find Clayton staring at her. "How long have you been awake?"

"About an hour," he said.

She ran a finger down his cheek. "Why didn't you wake me?"

"Because you needed to sleep."

"What time is it?"

Clayton glanced at the clock on the wall. "It's eight o'clock."

Emma rolled off him and tried her best not to elbow or kick him. The sofa just wasn't quite big enough for the both of them.

"You really can sleep anywhere can't you?" he joked.

"Apparently so. Of course, you are very comfortable to sleep on."

He smiled and kissed her. "I'm happy I could be your mattress for the night."

"I'm hungry, are you?"

"Yes. Why don't you wake Gwen and get dressed and we'll go downstairs. We won't wake Jamie and Sophie until later. Although, I'm a little tempted to do it now."

"That's because you're an evil man."

He chuckled. She went into the bedroom and woke Gwen. They dressed quickly and joined Clayton to walk down for breakfast. Christopher joined them just before they ordered and the small group enjoyed a simple meal. Emma was surprised to see Jamie and Sophie walk into the restaurant at nine.

"I was certain he said ten. Didn't he say ten, Emma?" Clayton joked.

"Oh was it ten? I thought he said eleven."

"Nice. Keep going, you're both very funny," Jamie said sarcastically.

"Join us for breakfast, won't you?" Clayton mocked.

"Yes, I believe I will. Thank you."

Jamie ate quickly and then it was time for the guys to work. He leaned down and kissed Sophie's cheek and whispered, "Don't get into any trouble, love. We'll meet you here in a few hours."

"Trouble? What kind of trouble could we possibly get into? Other than to spend your money."

Clayton kissed Emma's palm and raised an eyebrow. "Stick to a budget, sweetheart."

"Yes, dear."

Once the men were gone, the girls decided to have another cup of coffee before they did anything else. "What time was Christine planning on arriving?" Emma asked Sophie.

"She was expecting to be here by eleven. They said they'd meet us for lunch and then we'll all go to the cemetery."

"Shall we shop?" Gwen suggested.

"Yes," both the girls said in unison.

They set off for a few of the boutiques near the square and purchased more than might have seemed possible in their limited amount of time. The girls arrived back at the hotel just before eleven and found Stephen and Christine waiting in the lobby.

"How was your trip?" Sophie hugged Christine.

"It was perfect."

"How long have you been waiting?"

"Not long," Stephen said.

"Have you been shopping?" Christine asked.

"Yes, but we couldn't do anymore," Emma said. "Too hot."

"Yes, it's unbelievably warm." Christine fluttered her fan. "Today is a real Indian summer day, isn't it?"

"Perfect day for Lincoln's speech," Sophie said.

Jamie arrived a few minutes later and mapped out how the day would go. They sat down for lunch and waited for Clayton and Christopher to join them.

"Were they planning on arriving today?" Sophie quipped. "I'm starving."

Jamie squeezed Sophie's hand. "They'll be here any minute, but you should eat something now. I'll get you some bread."

Sophie nodded her head and Jamie went off to find her something to snack on.

"I wish I had a camera," Sophie whispered to Emma.

"I have mine, and I'm going to try and use it inconspicuously. I'm hoping no one will see it and freak out."

"Yes, we need Hannah right now with some of her spy gadgets."

"So true," Emma said a little sadly.

"You miss her, don't you?"

"Yeah I do. I miss dancing with her."

"You should dance some more, Em. Keep yourself limber and strong."

"I'll think about it."

Christopher and Clayton walked into the dining room at that moment and made their way to the table. Clayton leaned down to give Emma a quick kiss on the cheek.

"How is everything going?"

"Better than expected. We have scouted a little place at the cemetery that will be a perfect view. We'll make our way over

316

to it as soon as we're done eating."

"Sounds great."

Jamie returned with some warm bread for Sophie. They ordered their food and ate quickly, then the group left the hotel and made their way to the cemetery.

"I'm so excited." Sophie grabbed Jamie's hand.

"This is pretty incredible." Jamie raised her hand for a kiss.

Clayton led them over to the spot he'd reserved for them and Emma grinned at her sister. They had a perfect view.

"Will this work?" Clayton asked.

"It's better than we could have expected," Sophie said. "Thank you."

Clayton kissed Emma quickly and then he and Christopher went back to work. The area was getting crowded and both Emma and Sophie were once again thankful for the prime spot Clayton had found them.

"What happens now?" Emma whispered.

"Edward Everett will speak first."

"Is he any good?"

"Reports indicate that he's going to speak for a long time," Sophie whispered.

"I was afraid of that."

"He's not so bad, apparently. Just long winded." Sophie giggled.

At two-thirty, Clayton returned. He took his place next to Emma and then finally it was three o'clock and Emma grinned as Sophie's hero stood to speak. Emma reached over and took her hand. Tears fell slowly down Sophie's face and Emma smiled at her again. She then looked at Clayton and he put his arm around her waist.

She thought about this incredible life and didn't bother to question it anymore. She had her sister back and was spending her life with the man of her dreams.

"I'm glad I found you," Clayton whispered.

"Me too. I love you."

"I love you, too, sweet."

317

"Four score and seven years ago our fathers brought forth on this continent, a new nation, conceived in liberty and dedicated to the proposition that all men are created equal.

Now we are engaged in a great civil war, testing whether that nation, or any nation so conceived and so dedicated, can long endure. We are met on a great battlefield of that war. We have come to dedicate a portion of that field, as a final resting place for those who here gave their lives that that nation might live. It is altogether fitting and proper that we should do this.

But in a larger sense, we cannot dedicate - we cannot consecrate - we cannot hallow - this ground. The brave men, living and dead, who struggled here, have consecrated it, far above our poor power to add or detract. The world will little note, nor long remember, what we say here, but it can never forget what they did here. It is for us the living, rather, to be dedicated here to the unfinished work which they who fought here have thus far so nobly advanced. It is rather for us to be here dedicated to the great task remaining before us - that from these honored dead we take increased devotion to that cause for which they gave the last full measure of devotion - that we here highly resolve that these dead shall not have died in vain - that this nation, under God, shall have a new birth of freedom - and that government of the people, by the people, for the people, shall not perish from the earth."

318

ABOUT

PIPER

New York Times & USA Today Bestselling Author Piper Davenport writes from a place of passion and intrigue, combining elements of romance and suspense with strong modern-day heroes and heroines.

She currently resides in the Pacific Northwest with her author husband, Jack Davenport, and an obnoxious YorkiePoo named Pepper who may or may not be an international spy.

Like Piper's FB page and get to know her!
(www.facebook.com/piperdavenport)

Made in the USA
Monee, IL
25 January 2025

10036372R00184